Hyde School

8

Hurricane Season

Sonja Bentley Zant

2/08

authorHOUSE®

AuthorHouse™
1663 Liberty Drive, Suite 200
Bloomington, IN 47403
www.authorhouse.com
Phone: 1-800-839-8640

First published by AuthorHouse 9/24/2007

ISBN: 978-1-4343-3449-7 (sc)
ISBN: 978-1-4343-3450-3 (hc)

Library of Congress Control Number: 2007906241

Printed in the United States of America
Bloomington, Indiana

This book is printed on acid-free paper.

*To my mother, the late Diana Bentley: For being
such an amazing role model, mentor and confidant.
Thank you for giving me a strong foundation
to weather all of life's storms.*

*To my grandmother, Edna Ullrich: For sharing
your confidence, wisdom and love all the days of your life.
You are one of a kind!*

*And to Julie Seward: Whose tremendous worth
you simply cannot measure! I love you!*

Psalm 150:6

Chapter One

"Eloise Butts?"

It might just be my imagination, but it seems like every time someone says my name out loud and in public, people stop what they're doing and look to see who could possibly have *Eloise Butts* as a name. At first pass, I'm quite certain that most people are expecting to see a frumpy spinster with a very wide backside, and creaking with age and knobby arthritic knees. But no. It's me—Eloise Butts, age 33.

I can see the pretty young girl with the caramel colored skin crane her neck to see who responds to the unfriendly nurse holding the door open with her hip and impatiently tapping her clipboard. As I get up and collect my things, the pretty girl quickly averts her stare and turns the page in her *People* magazine. Her name is probably Tiffany or Ashley—or is it *Tiffani* or *Ashlee*?

I follow the nurse behind the heavy black door and enter a maze known as the Women's Health Center. I can't believe it's already time for my yearly gynecological checkup. I can't imagine any woman looking forward to this type of office visit, but for me, it's especially uncomfortable.

It's all blonde wood and slick granite surfaces behind that heavy door, and along the walls, there are black and white pictures of newborn babies and their proud parents framed in rich lacquered wood. Seeing these images evenly spaced throughout the corridor reminds me of the fact that this is an up-and-coming fertility clinic, and many of the women who enter this place come in filled with hope that someday they'll be mothers.

I've been coming to the Women's Health Center for about eight years or so, and each time it gets a little more difficult. Don't get me wrong—

there's nothing particularly different about this clinic, other than the fact that it's a teaching clinic. Oh, and, my doctor, Dr. Crosby, *is* a lesbian who raises Schnauzers as a side hobby.

To ease my tension during my checkups, I usually talk to Dr. Crosby about her dogs, which are featured on customized calendars that hang in every exam room. Believe it or not, these calendars come in handy for counting out the days since your last period, and I'm always amused by how much the ugly little dogs calm me down before my exam.

I'm a huge dog lover—I have an adorable Boxer named Sugar Ray who is quite literally my best friend—and to have something other than my female-under-yonder to discuss during these annual visits brings me tremendous relief. Dr. Crosby seems to like that I ask about her Schnauzers, and I can tell she's a proud owner who loves to brag. *Brag away*, I've learned to say! The longer we can keep the focus off of me during these awkward visits, the happier I am!

As the nurse leads me to an open sitting area, I am instructed to take off my shoes and step up on the scale. Carefully, the nurse slides the weights around, gently tapping them until they hover on the metal slider to reveal my precise weight.

"Let's see..." the nurse trails off as she enters the number on my chart. "You've gained a few pounds this year. Is somebody in a relationship?" she says in a patronizing tone as a wicked little smile spreads across her face.

What's that supposed to mean? Obviously I'm aware of the fact that I'm living in the land of anorexic women and freakishly thin super models, but is this nurse suggesting that you're only allowed to eat and live your life at a normal weight so long as you're in a relationship?

"No...I'm not in a relationship," I confess with a nervous chuckle. "I guess I've just been eating well."

I can feel my cheeks tingle with shame as I consider the fact that I've gained three pounds this year and now there is even documented proof! Maybe my clothing is just heavy. I *am* wearing a thick T-shirt and my long hipster skirt has a lot of fabric and some metallic beading on the waistband.

After the nurse takes my blood pressure and asks me some additional health-related questions, she takes me into Examination Room 5. Now I'm starting to feel really nervous. Even the smell in the room gives me the creeps. It has that antiseptic hand wash kind of smell, blended with the distinctive scent of plastic-coated paper from the new sheet crisply stretched over the examination table. And those stirrups! I guess the Women's Health Center thought it would be cute to put striped socks with pom poms over the metal footholds—as if *that* will make slipping your heels into them more pleasant!

"Hop up on the exam table, please," the nurse says as she pulls the Schnauzer calendar off the wall.

Obediently, I step up on the footstool next to the table and swing myself around, crunching my bottom onto the stiff paper. I can feel the paper bunching up under my thighs. Once I'm seated, the nurse hands me the calendar. I take it and can't help but smile at the homely little gray and white Schnauzer looking back at me with this ridiculous pink ribbon tied into a funny little knot on top of it's head.

"So, Eloise..." the nurse begins and then looks up at me with a furrowed brow. "Um...is that a family name?" she asks directly, like she's really curious about the origin of my name.

"Nope, just a regular name—Eloise Butts," I say like I am admitting to something I am blamed for all the time. "But my friends call me Elle," I quickly offer.

"Well, it certainly isn't a name you hear everyday for a woman *your* age," the nurse says with a light laugh, like she's the first person to ever say that thought out loud. "And I bet you're looking forward to getting rid of *Butts*!"

The truth is, I've always hated my name, but I'm completely surprised by how candid this nurse is being! Normally, I would reduce my embarrassment a bit by putting Elle down as my first name on the information sheet, but I worry a little bit that it might be important to have my *real* name on my medical forms—you know, for insurance purposes. But I guess the nurse is boldly confirming—right here, in the room where I am about to strip down naked and place myself in a very vulnerable position—that she really doesn't like my full name either.

If I've thought about it once, I've thought about it a thousand times. Why did my mom choose the name Eloise for her child, especially when she married a man with the last name Butts? It just isn't a pretty combination, and it never rolls off *anyone's* tongue in a way that sounds elegant or even interesting. It seems like it would be OK if you had a crummy first name if your last name wasn't so ridiculous. Or if you had a sexy first name—like Heather or Alexis—or a clever one—like Chloe or Madeline—Butts might not be so bad. OK, so Butts will always be bad, but at least a better first name would help! No matter how often I've analyzed the situation, the fact remains that when my mother married a Butts, and then chose to name me Eloise, the combination was destined to make my life significantly more difficult.

Every time I have asked my mother why she picked Eloise, she always gives me the same answer: "I just thought you looked like one."

What exactly does an Eloise look like? Well, for my mother, she looked like a petite baby girl with stick straight, extra thin, extra fine blonde hair. As a child, no matter how much my mother combed, pinned, curled or waxed my hair, it was nothing but a straw mat of wispy yellow strands sticking out in a hundred different directions. Not a gorgeous image, but certainly a cute and loveable one!

When my mother sits down and looks at childhood pictures with me, her face literally beams with pride as she tells me how many times she kissed my pudgy checks and how she loved to squeeze my doughy thighs. To her, the name Eloise is beautiful. Her recollections of me are some of my favorite stories. Whenever we get together and she starts to share, I always feel precious and adored. The truth is the only time I ever like my name is when my mother says it.

All through elementary and middle school, my peers called me Wheezy. It was a bit of a Jeffersonian throwback—*George* Jefferson, that is. Over time, I grew to accept it as an endearing name despite the fact that it wasn't much better than Eloise. My mother didn't care for this nickname at all. Not being much of a TV viewer, she asked me one day if the kids at school thought I had asthma or something. It took me awhile to explain to her that George Jefferson called his wife, *Louise,* Wheezy, and it was an affectionate name. But I think she simply refused to connect the dots on the subject, and when my friends would call the house and ask, "Is Wheezy there?" she almost always told them they had the wrong number. I'm not sure how she would have felt if she knew the *complete* name my peers gave me back then—*Wheezy Breezy Bottom.*

Eventually, Wheezy Breezy Bottom—the petite blonde girl with the long legs and freckle-speckled nose—grew into a tall, thin teenager that was both athletic and smart. I was more of a tomboy, and, while I never thought of myself as unattractive, my looks were usually the last thing on my mind. Oh sure, I had crushes on boys that made me spend an extra hour in the bathroom, primping and twisting my super straight hair into a full-blown Julia Roberts in *Pretty Woman*-style mane. But that was never my primary focus—especially since all my efforts to get "big hair" lasted about twenty minutes before the humidity of the South Florida air tamed my mane back into straight strings.

The name Wheezy followed me all through high school, by which time it finally lost some of the mean-spirited venom middle school boys seem to infuse into childhood nicknames. But by then, there were different variations on my last name. I was called Wheezy Ass, Wheezy Tooty Booty and several others I don't care to remember. But after Arnold Schwarzenegger starred in the first *Terminator* movie, I simply became known as *The Wheezinator.* I didn't mind it all that much by the time my senior year rolled around. It was just who I was back then. (And much to my mother's horror, "Eloise *The Wheezinator* Butts" appeared under my picture in my senior yearbook.)

In college, I blossomed a bit and managed to leave my awful nicknames behind. I finally became known as just Elle Butts. I was still not into the pursuit of being popular, but at least my name didn't seem to be holding me back from that option as much anymore. Straight hair was finally more fashionable and my friends were actually jealous of my effortlessly beautiful, long, silky locks. Sports and good grades were still my main focus—I ran cross-country in the fall and track in the spring and managed to maintain my place on the dean's list each semester. I think guys may have noticed me in college, but I just wasn't that interested in the transient nature of college dating, and I kept to myself most of the time.

There was, however, one guy I thought about the entire first semester of my freshman year. His name was Drew Macpherson. He was in my Macro Economics class, and he was beautiful to behold. But it was more than his looks that had my attention. It was his last name actually. I figured if Drew and I were to marry, I would be *Elle Macpherson*! In one simple wedding ceremony I could be transformed from a girl who got attention for having an ugly name into a girl who was noticed because I might be *the* Elle Macpherson—high fashion goddess and pin-up girl known the world over! OK, so it was a short-lived fantasy. I never actually spoke to Drew, and, once the semester ended, so did my dream of marrying him.

"Well, Eloise, can you tell me when you had your last period?" the nurse asks me while she starts setting up for the exam. She places a little blue towel on a tall platform-like table and then starts opening cabinets along the wall, pulling out some instruments I'm not sure I'm ready to acknowledge. So instead, I focus on the calendar, trying to remember the last time I had to buy tampons.

"It was about two weeks ago," I tell the nurse.

"OK, great," she says as she marks it down on my chart.

The nurse grabs the calendar from me and hangs it back up on the wall. I stare at it briefly, trying to channel happy dog energy into me. Dogs are so lucky—they manage to live in the moment and don't spend time worrying about much of anything. I wish I could do that right now. I dread what's coming up next, but I'm just going to have to brace myself and get through it—just like every other woman does.

After getting my instructions on how to put on the paper gown, the nurse leaves the room so I can undress. I carefully fold my clothes and place them on the chair next to the examination table and wrap the scratchy vest-like paper gown around my upper half—*with the front open*—as the nurse emphasized for me to do. Once I'm perched back up on the table, I gently tug and tuck the paper drape around my lower half underneath my thighs, mostly out of nervousness but certainly out of modesty, too. Then I settle in and listen for the tell tale signs that Dr. Crosby is getting ready to enter Examination Room 5.

Soon, there's a knock at the door, followed by, "Hello there, Eloise!" Dr. Crosby enters the room with my chart in her hands, never looking up to see my face. "It's always good to see you. How've you been?"

Dr. Crosby is a short little lady with cropped, blonde hair and is on the slightly plump side. But I've always thought she had a pretty face—kind of soft and round. She has big blue eyes, flawless skin and perfectly straight, long, white teeth.

"Hello!" I say in a shrill voice that barely sounds like mine. "I'm doing fine, I guess…" I offer as I do my best to swallow some of the rising tension in my throat. I'm sure Dr. Crosby is used to nervous women; I mean, who wants to go to the gynecologist anyway? Even women who are expecting a baby, thanks to all her efforts, can't enjoy this whole checkup process, can they?

Dr. Crosby continues to peruse my chart, flipping pages and looking up and down at all the details the nurse has collected about me. "I see you've gained a little weight this year—anything unusual going on with that?" Dr. Crosby asks without looking up.

"No…not that I can think of…" For crying out loud! I've gained three pounds! Is that so outrageous?

"So I see here that you are currently single and that you have marked that you *don't* use birth control. Is that correct?"

"Yes…it is…"

Dr. Crosby leans in slightly and looks me in the eye and says, "So Eloise, are we *still* a virgin? Or let me rephrase that to be more politically correct: Is *abstinence* still your birth control method of choice?"

Reluctantly I reply, "Yes, that's still the case."

"Isn't that something?" Dr. Crosby marvels as a little grin spreads across her face. "Every time I see your name on my patient roster, I wonder if you've managed to hold out for yet another year!" I can't tell if she is amused or impressed. Likely neither, but she seems to hold that little grin longer than I feel is necessary.

"Yeah, I guess I'm not your typical *South Beach* girl," I sort of mumble in response.

"Oh Eloise, that's an understatement if I've ever heard one!" she blurts out with a breathy laugh. "You have *no* idea!"

I'm taken aback—as I usually am during these female doctor visits—that my, shall we say, "wholesomeness," is almost laughable to her. After all these years as Dr. Crosby's patient, her predicted astonishment over my, shall we call it, "chasteness," always makes me cower. I can't see how my sex-life—or lack there of—can make such a huge impression on this very busy doctor. This is one of those things in life you don't really want to be remembered for—after all, it's supposed to be *private!*

Dr. Crosby continues, "But as I have said in years past, you really should consider the type of birth control you *will* use when the time comes. I know that you're going to say that this isn't an issue for you right now, but I really want to emphasize that you need to be smart about your sexual decisions. You wouldn't believe how many women I see each month who, *'get caught up in the heat of the moment,'* and, suddenly their whole lives are changed forever."

"I understand, Dr. Crosby. Thank you for your concern."

With this awkward exchange behind us, Dr. Crosby puts my chart down on the counter that runs the length of the room and prepares to get the exam underway.

"OK, let's have a look," she says as I feel myself cringe. I even notice that my breathing is starting to quicken.

Dr. Crosby crosses the room and washes her hands in the sink in the far corner. My nerves give a little flip, so I decide now would be the best time to get the conversation started about those wonderful dogs of hers.

"So how are your Schnauzers doing?"

"Oh, they're great!" she beams as she dries her hands on a paper towel. "I have a new one in the mix now—little Marty. I need to get some pictures of Marty in here, but I've only had her for about a month now. She's so adorable!"

I watch nervously as she begins to wedge her stubby hands into these purple examination gloves. The latex snaps and pops until both hands are finally shoved into place. The whole process is a bit unsettling. Her now purple hands remind me of the bratty girl in *Willy Wonka's Chocolate Factory* that chewed all that crazy gum and turned into a human blueberry—only in this case, I'm looking at the early stages of a human-to-grape transformation.

Dr. Crosby crosses over to me now, where I'm sitting nervously on the examination table. She begins feeling my neck for lymph nodes, I suppose, and her hands are cool and smell like latex and antibacterial soap. She pulls off the stethoscope from around her neck and sticks the earpieces firmly into her ears and then rubs the disc part on her lab coat in an attempt to warm it up.

"Deep breath, please..." she instructs as she places the still frosty stethoscope on my chest. I pull a hard breath in and let it out slowly. She moves the stethoscope around a few times on my chest and then moves it onto my back. "Again..." she says.

"Your heart and lungs sound great. Are you still running?"

"Yes—as often as I can," I answer as I try to keep my breathing steady. "Sugar Ray—my dog—loves to go for a least one or two jogs a day." A smile always seems to come to my face when I think of Sugar Ray.

"Oh, yes, I remember you mentioning you have a dog! A Boxer, right?"

I shake my head up and down, like the proud mother I am, as I push out another breath.

"I'm glad he's still doing well," she says like she genuinely means it.

The lovely banter ends all too soon as Dr. Crosby instructs me to lie back on the table so she can check for other lumps. I do as I'm told, all the while running my internal comfort monologue.

It's only a few more minutes. I can do this. She's just checking for lumps and bumps—no big deal... It'll be all over in no time...

"So are you still showing your dogs and stuff?" I manage to ask as I try to act calm and casual. But I can feel my torso stiffen as she works her way around my body. She's checking my breasts for lumps now, and I feel myself struggle to pull in a deeper breath.

"A little bit, but you know, I just haven't had as much time to work with my dogs these days. We're taking on some new interns here at the center and it's eating up so much of my time." Dr. Crosby expertly moves her hands under my armpits now, and I send up a secret prayer that my deodorant has one more burst of freshness to spare. "The paperwork we have to fill out on each intern takes hours to complete, and it is a real time commitment."

"I see…" I mumble like I'm actually following what she's saying. I just want her to finish up quickly, so I can put my clothes back on.

But I know it's coming now—the actual phase of the exam I presume all women dread the most. Dr. Crosby carefully closes my open vest-drape and then hooks her foot around the wheelbase of a stool in the center of the room, sliding it over in front of the exam table in one swift motion. She continues talking to me as she straps on this headlamp contraption that looks like something a miner would wear. Her hair bunches up under the head strap, and I wonder if she realizes how ridiculous she looks.

"We have about eight gynecology interns with us right now, and each one seems to require added attention. I try to involve them as much as I can so that they get the needed exposure to the actual practice of medicine before we turn them loose on their own. But as you can imagine, it takes up a lot of time. OK Eloise, put your feet in the stirrups please and slide your bottom up to the edge of the table…"

I reluctantly do as I'm told, but my knees seem to be hinged together as I do my best to postpone the inevitable. Dr. Crosby doesn't miss a beat as she gently, but firmly, pulls my legs apart at the knees and continues chatting.

"I have three interns with me today, following me from case to case. I try to include them on the more unusual cases—the occasional inverted uterus, any unusual palpations, some of my early IVF cases—that kind of thing." With the flick of a switch on her headgear, Dr. Crosby's headlamp pumps out a powerful beam of yellow light.

"Oh…" I manage to interject again as I feel myself shudder. I rotate my head to the side to avoid the glare from the headlamp.

Dr. Crosby is now poking around with her purple gloved fingers in my *personal area*, and I feel a wave nausea wash over me.

"Everything looks normal and healthy on the outside, Eloise. Now let's see what's going on internally, shall we?"

Is that a rhetorical question, or would she stop if I answered no? Too late. She's already standing up and punching around inside, then pressing her hands on my abdomen on the outside *and* the inside. *Oh I hate this...*

"Everything seems perfect, Eloise," Dr. Crosby assures me as she continues her palpations. "You could be the poster girl for abstinence! If more people could see your vagina..." she trails off with the look of a concerned doctor coming over her face. "The amount of disease we see in women anymore would really shock you. So, it's really incredible to examine someone like you. I can't recall seeing a patient with such a healthy vagina!"

Dr. Crosby looks up at me with a huge grin on her face—like a miner who just found the mother lode! My toes are cramped over the top of the stirrups, and I detect a light sweat beading up on my forehead.

Now Dr. Crosby is sitting on her stool again and grabbing that cold metal thing I remember from checkups in the past. She's starting to lube it up with some gooey jelly. She keeps twisting the adjuster knob on the apparatus, and the noise is rather disturbing. With one more lamp check on her headgear, she slides the metal gadget inside and starts to crank it open.

Oh gosh... I think as I hold my breath, hoping this phase of the exam passes quickly.

"We're almost done here Eloise. Just a few more seconds and we'll be all finished. I just need to get a cell sample from your cervix."

Dr. Crosby moves in like a Ninja, using some sort of thin tongue depressor-like stick with ridges on the end, to scrape some cells from inside my body. Seconds later, she expertly removes that metal crank thing, and I start to feel myself relax for the first time since I entered Examination Room 5. I can see the finish line now! I just can't wait to put on my clothes and get out of this place.

"Perfect!" Dr. Crosby announces as she switches off her headlamp with her knuckle. "Everything looks perfect!"

Then, as if she's speaking in another language, Dr. Crosby says, "Eloise, if you could just hang on for a minute or two longer, I would really like one of my interns to examine you. It's so rare to find such a healthy, disease-free cervix and vaginal area—especially at your age and living in this part of the country—and I really think it would be a great visual contrast."

What? A visual contrast?

Before I can even respond, Dr. Crosby is snapping off her gloves and lifting the receiver on the wall phone. She punches in a few buttons and I can hear a subtle *beep* echo outside Examination Room 5, followed by Dr. Crosby's voice:

"Heidi Miller, please come to Examination Room 5—Heidi Miller, Examination Room 5."

I can't believe this is happening! Dr. Crosby is about to put my *disease-free cervix and vaginal area* on display for an intern? Don't I have a say in all of this? Isn't there a thing called "patient consent" or something like that?

As if Dr. Crosby can read my mind, she volunteers, "Since this is a teaching clinic, you had to sign a waiver before we could even examine you today. I hope the girls up front explained that to you."

I have a vague recollection of this conversation, but I guess I thought it was so that Dr. Crosby could share my *file*—not my actual *vaginal area*—with her interns!

"I do hope you understand the important service you are providing the next generation of OBGYNs," Dr. Crosby says, clearly working the guilt trip angle on me. "We all rely on the openness of our patients when we're still learning."

Did she just say that I was providing a *service*? Is that what this is? *A service?*

There's no time for me to object, as a knock on the door signals that Heidi Miller is ready to enter the room. I watch as she carefully opens the door and peeks in.

"Did you page me, Dr. Crosby?"

"Yes I did, Dr. Miller. Come on in," Dr. Crosby says as she waves this tall, stunning blonde woman into the room. "Eloise Butts, I would like you to meet Dr. Miller—one of my most experienced interns. I just want her to do a quick examination on you."

"Hello, Eloise," Dr. Miller says as she walks toward me with her hand extended as a greeting. "It's great to meet you."

I'm still flat on my back on the examination table, but I've returned my knees to locked position, and I'm trying to act like it is my pleasure to meet her as well, but, honestly, I couldn't be less pleased! I manage to shake her hand and mumble a weak "Hello..."

Dr. Crosby starts to brief Dr. Miller on my patient history. "So Eloise has been a patient of mine for...eight years. Is that about right, Eloise?" Dr. Crosby asks over her shoulder in the general direction of my head.

I confirm with a little grunt and do my best not to make direct eye contact with the astoundingly beautiful Dr. Miller. I can see that she is about six inches taller than Dr. Crosby—which must put her at about 5' 10", or so, and has long, willowy limbs that make her look incredibly feminine next to Dr. Crosby. As she stares down at my file, she seems to be absorbing all the details being offered about my case. A long, blonde ponytail stretches down the length of her spine like a trickle of thick honey, and I wonder if she put herself through medical school working the fashion runways.

"Eloise is a *very special* patient," Dr. Crosby continues in what feels to me like a patronizing tone. "And I think you will see *exactly* why as soon as you begin your exam."

Dr. Miller has a curious look on her face, as I'm sure she is expecting some bizarre situation in my pelvis or some unusual or rare condition that is manifesting itself in my genitalia. I watch as she crosses over to the sink to wash her hands. Dr. Crosby gives me a little wink and a "thumbs up" like this is some sort of scheme we've planned together.

Carefully, Dr. Miller slides the stool into position and then lowers herself onto the cushioned seat. Dr. Crosby pulls off her miner's headlamp and gives it to Dr. Miller once she has a pair of purple gloves stretched over her long, elegant hands. Carefully, she adjusts the headgear and flips down this little magnifying attachment I hadn't noticed before.

Gee, she really wants a good look, I think. Then Dr. Miller flicks on the headlamp as I try to brace myself for another exam.

"Eloise?" Dr. Miller annunciates loudly, as if I'm hard of hearing. "I'm going to begin the examination now, so I'm going to have to ask you to *open your legs*." I wonder if Dr. Miller is expecting that she will discover that I'm actually retarded or something during her exam and that she needs to emphasize her words for my benefit.

I do as I'm asked, and I start to feel that old familiar dread sweep over me. Dr. Miller tentatively conducts her external exam as I pacify myself with the fact that, again, this will be over soon. Then a horrifying thought crosses my mind. Didn't Dr. Crosby say she had three interns with her today?

"Eloise, try to relax," Dr. Miller says firmly. "I'm not going to hurt you."

You try to relax! I think to myself. *This is my second exam today and I'm not really feeling too relaxed right now!*

I close my eyes and try to think of something other than the fact that some super-model stranger is checking out my *girly bits* for the second time today!

"The outer genitalia is incredible," Dr. Miller remarks to Dr. Crosby. "I can't say I have ever seen such a healthy vulva. So perfect and pink!" Dr. Crosby is standing over Dr. Miller's shoulder with her arms crossed over her chest, beaming in agreement with the remarks of her young protégé.

Now Dr. Miller, with her volume control still pushed to the maximum limits says, "I'm going to start the internal exam now, Eloise. Try to relax for me, OK?"

I take a deep breath and let it out slowly, hoping this process will wash away some of my stress. Dr. Miller is standing up now, moving her hands around to feel my abdomen. I see her brow slightly furrow, like she's perplexed. I think she's trying to figure out what's so *unusual* about me, since so far, I am totally normal.

"Wow, everything seems to be exactly normal," Dr. Miller marvels. "I don't feel anything out of the ordinary..." she trails off as she probes deeper. I shift slightly on the table as my eyes roll back into my head.

"The really *special* part is coming up," Dr. Crosby proudly assures. "Here's the speculum. Why don't you take a look."

Now Dr. Miller takes the speculum-thingy from Dr. Crosby and starts to re-lube the edges. The noise is just as unsettling the second time around. I try to tell myself to relax, but this is so uncomfortable! I sure hope she doesn't feel the need to gawk while she's down there. Carefully, Dr. Miller inserts the metal contraption and starts to crank it open. I feel myself slip into delirium as I get a blinding flash from Dr. Miller's headlamp.

"Oh my God!" Dr. Miller shouts. "The hymen is still intact! Did you have this surgically replaced, Eloise?" she asks dubiously as she continues to marvel at the sight between my legs.

"What?" I ask, unsure if I'm hearing her correctly. *Surgically replaced? What on Earth is she talking about?* Women have their hymen *surgically replaced?*

"No, Dr. Miller," Dr. Crosby quickly interjects. "This is the real deal!"

"I can't believe it!" Dr. Miller gasps. "I thought I felt it when I was palpating, but I figured she had hymen replacement surgery—but it looks way too perfect to be surgically manipulated!" Dr. Miller concludes with a look of complete awe on her face.

"Isn't that *amazing?*" Dr. Crosby retorts. "I knew this would blow your mind!"

"How old are you, Eloise?" Dr. Miller asks with astonishment as she peers up between my legs to see my face. The headlamp is beaming me directly in the eyes, like I'm under interrogation or something.

"I'm 33," I strain to reply. "And yes, I *am* a virgin! I know that's impossible and incredible and the most amazing thing anyone has ever seen or heard!" I start to feel myself unravel. "I know that I am providing a service and all, but are you almost done?" There's a slight crack in my voice, and I wonder if I'm going to be able to keep it together.

"Oh, yes! Yes, I'm done," Dr. Miller says, finally realizing that I am an actual person here. She quickly turns off the headlamp and then removes the metal speculum. I feel myself start to relax. Dr. Miller graciously pulls the drape around my waist up over my thighs.

Please let this be over now! I think as I do my best to regain my composure.

After placing the speculum on the exam tray, Dr. Miller smiles at Dr. Crosby as she pulls off her gloves followed by the headgear. "Wow! That's something else…"

Dr. Crosby nods her head in solemn agreement.

"Thank you *so much* for allowing me to examine you, Eloise." Dr. Miller is walking over to the side of the examination table, so she can look directly into my face. "It was a *real* treat."

A real treat? Did she just say this was a *real treat?*

"I have to tell you, we didn't ever get to see this sort of thing in medical school, and I've never seen anything like it here at the center either! It was really great of you to let me see this for myself!" As she's speaking, Dr. Miller reaches her hand out to shake mine and I don't know what to say.

"OK…" I manage as I give her a little wave instead of taking her hand in the shaking gesture.

Dr. Crosby gives me an appreciative smile as she says to Dr. Miller, "Let's go ahead and clear out and give Eloise some privacy."

As Dr. Miller starts to leave the room, I see her take one final look over her shoulder at *Eloise Butts—the 33-Year-Old Virgin.* I feel my face start to flush. This has to be an all time low—even for me.

Dr. Crosby walks across the room and places her hand on my forearm. "Thanks so much, Eloise. And by the way, everything looks great. You are by far the healthiest patient I've ever examined!"

"OK…" I say in response as I do my best to muster up a smile.

Just before she leaves the room, Dr. Crosby stops at the door and turns around to look at me one more time. "Eloise, I really do want you to think about what type of protection you want to use, and let me know if you need me to be involved in that process. OK? This abstinence thing is admirable, but pretty unrealistic, don't you agree?"

I'm so anxious for her to leave that I just blurt out, "Yeah, I'll let you know. Thanks…"

When I'm finally alone in Examination Room 5, I feel relief wash over me, and I scramble to get dressed as quickly as I can. I can't wait to get out of this place—thank God, I only have to do this checkup once a year. However, this year, I had it *twice* in one day! I make a mental note, as I pull on my hipster skirt and give it a good hard cinch; it's definitely time to find a new gynecologist.

I feel my blood pressure go down, and my anxiety starts to dwindle as I lace up my sandals. I start to feel much safer now that things are properly covered. As I look at myself in the mirror, I wonder how much all my clothes really weigh. Could the combined weight of my underwear, bra, T-shirt and skirt really account for the extra three pounds? It's entirely possible.

On my way to the reception area to check out, I can see some light spilling out into the hallway from an open door. As I approach, I start to hear voices and a few low murmurs that become clearer as I get closer. Then I hear someone say in disbelief, *"She's a virgin at 33?"*

Then I hear a male voice ask, *"Is she ugly or gross or something?"*

"No, she's not ugly," a vaguely familiar female voice interjects. *"And get this. Her name is* Eloise Butts!*"* the female voice adds, which is promptly followed by the sound of sputtering laughter and commentaries like, *"Tragic!"* and *"No way!"*

I feel my veins go icy as I realize I must be coming up on the intern's area, and they're talking about *me!* Oh my gosh! Dr. Miller must be telling everyone about my exam! I can't believe this! Isn't that totally unprofessional? Are they even allowed to do that?

I'm practically running down the hall at this point, but I manage to look over my shoulder just in time to catch a glimpse of a handsome young man peeking around the corner, trying to get a look at me.

Chapter Two

When I reach my car, I slide behind the wheel and sit for a few minutes, trying to decompress. Every year, being the only virgin patient at the Women's Health Center gets more and more traumatic. Today, I'm totally convinced that I am the only 33-year-old virgin in the entire greater Miami area. But when I think about the way Dr. Crosby and Dr. Miller were acting, I wonder if I'm the only 33-year-old virgin in the world!

I stick the key in the ignition and start my car. As I back out of the parking space, I start to feel much better. In just a few minutes, I'll be having lunch with Nora, one of my closest friends, and my doctor's appointment will be a distant memory.

The sun is out and the muggy summer heat starts to wrap around me like a silky damp scarf as I speed down Collins Avenue. The top is down on my convertible, and I already feel liberated from the morning's drama. I look at my watch and see that I'm a little early—which is perfect since I may actually find curbside parking for a change. As I pull my car around the corner onto Ocean, I spot a parking place less than a block away from the street-side café where I'm meeting Nora.

Maybe this day won't be so bad after all, I think to myself as I slide my car into the parking spot.

As I approach the café, I can see Nora looking over the menu while sipping on an iced tea in a tall, thin glass. She looks up and waves at me, almost relieved that I showed up. Nora is an advertising director at this big agency in town, and she claims that she's always on a tight schedule. When she invites you for lunch, she has one rule—don't be late! I secretly believe Nora's obsession with timeliness has more to do with the fact that she's too embarrassed to sit alone for any unreasonable length of time. I believe she has some deep-seated abandonment issues, and she gets downright panicked if she has to wait alone for more than five minutes. That's my theory, anyway, especially since this "tight schedule" never keeps us from having two-hour-long lunches!

Nora and I met our junior year of college, and, even though we instantly liked one another, we couldn't be more different. I remember my first impression of Nora was that she was too high-maintenance to be my friend. She always had her hair done up in the latest trend, and her clothes were much more planned than anything I was wearing. She was slightly boy crazy—in my opinion at least—and she was always dating multiple guys at the same time.

And there were other differences, too. Nora couldn't imagine joining the cross-country team, for example. She felt it was a lonely sport that didn't have enough of a fan-base to make all the training fulfilling. But it was the solitude of running my own race that made cross-country my favorite sport. Stepping across the finish line and relishing my own accomplishments made me feel more empowered than having a bunch of people cheering for me. The fact that she needed constant affirmation, when I really didn't, made us an unlikely but complimentary pair.

Even though we had our differences in how we approached life, we shared a knack for writing. This led us both to major in journalism (since majoring in English didn't seem to have as many lucrative job possibilities).

After taking one of the advertising electives in our major, Nora realized she wanted to work at a top agency where she would come up with campaigns that made her client's products household names. She spent the rest of her time in college coming up with slogans and catch phrases for everything—including funny code names to help me keep track of the guys she was dating. (Some of my favorites include: *Bulls Eye* for the guy who drove the '79 Dodge Dart; *Twirly Buns* for the guy who bought her a nasty vending machine snack on their first date; and of course, *Double Nickels*, for the slightly uptight guy who refused to drive over the speed limit. Ever.)

I ended up majoring in public relations, simply because out of all the majors offered in the journalism department, it was the one that seemed to have the most ambiguity. I really had no career visions for myself back in college that included any of the specifics Nora seemed to have mapped out for herself. All I knew was that I loved to write, and PR specialists had to be good writers.

I couldn't really picture myself as a professional at that stage of the game, and having Nora as a friend would sometimes make me worry that I was defective in some way. She always seemed so sure of what she wanted. The only thing I was sure of was the fact that I *didn't know* what I wanted to do with my life. Luckily, my parents kept reassuring me that my feelings were normal. So I decided to accept that as truth and stop worrying about it.

After graduation, Nora and I moved down to Miami's famous South Beach. Ironically, we both grew up in the same area of Miami—Coral Gables—but since I had gone to private school my whole life, we never met until college. Her family is wonderful—her mother is a public elementary school teacher, and her father is an attorney. She is an only child and the center of the universe as far as her parents are concerned. They spare no expense when it comes to their little Nora, and so when it was time to find a place to live in exclusive (and expensive) South Beach, we asked Bill and Silvia first.

Of course they were prepared to support Nora, but their idea of where we should live was not quite what we had in mind. Sadly, this difference in opinion climaxed in a decision to limit the amount we could spend on a place—I think in hopes of forcing us to move closer to home. But we were a determined pair, and despite our limited budget, we finally landed a very ratty little efficiency apartment in the heart of South Beach, which Nora promptly named *Purgatory—A short stop on our way to Heaven*. It wasn't much to look at, but the location was amazing.

My parents were equally unenthusiastic about our plans to move to South Beach. My mother is an emergency room nurse at Miami General Hospital, and my father is a doctor and professor of psychology at the University of Miami. Between what my mother sees in the ER and what my father discusses with his crazy patients and students, my parents have a tendency to project worse case scenarios (my mother) and overanalyze my every decision (my father). But eventually, they decided I was old enough to take care of myself, and they fronted me the money to move into this new part of my life.

Despite the fact that Nora and I were sure that living in *Purgatory* was the best idea, when we finally moved in, we had some serious concerns. The living conditions inside that apartment can only be described as ghastly! It was old and dingy with furry brown shag carpeting and an avocado-colored refrigerator that moaned and groaned in an effort to keep our food cool. The cupboard doors hung askew on rusty hinges that made the kitchen look like a crooked jagged mouth scowling back at us.

The walls in the main living area were coated with a beige layer of tar from the countless cigarettes smoked inside the place over the years. The pink, teal and black tiles that lined the walls in the bathroom were Art Deco-inspired with a thick coating of sludge and grime. The grout was actually black where the corners met, and we couldn't decide if the composition was dirt, mold or putrefied blood. The conditions were so bad that I was actually afraid to sit on the toilet seat in my own bathroom—even after some heavy-duty cleaning efforts on our part.

We loved our independence and having a place of our own in the heart of the hippest place to live, but it didn't take long for us to see that making money was essential to our immediate and future happiness—especially if we wanted to escape *Purgatory* and move on to the promise of *Heaven*. So we hit the pavement right away in search of perfect jobs with perfect pay. It was a mission we shared, fueled by the need for better housing.

But in truth, taking a year off to travel before settling into the daily grind of a *real job*, was something we each wanted to do—especially me! Postponing the process of figuring out what I wanted to do with my life was incredibly appealing, and, even though Nora knew what she wanted, I could tell she was getting pretty discouraged about the options that were available to her with no work experience to offer. So when I saw the ad in the *Miami Herald* for "charter flight attendants," we decided this job possibility was worth investigating.

The ad specified that a new, Miami-based charter airline company was looking for college graduates who wanted to travel and see the world while catering to wealthy clientele headed to resort destinations. How much more exotic could you get? So one hot, July afternoon, we put on our new interview suits and showed up in the lobby of the Fort Lauderdale *Hyatt Pier 66* for the open interview.

There were hundreds of hopeful flight attendants from all over South Florida loitering around the lobby when we arrived, and I remember thinking that I should just go home. There was no way I was going to be able to compete with all these people for a limited number of openings. But Nora convinced me to stay by promising that she would buy us drinks in the famous revolving bar on top of the hotel when it was all over. Not that I was a big drinker then (or now for that matter), I did want to see how it felt to sit in a revolving bar. So we stayed and put ourselves through the rigorous interview process. After all, we reasoned, we could use it as a practice interview.

After filling out our applications and waiting in three different lines, we joined all of the hopeful applicants in a fancy ballroom that was chilled to sub-artic temperatures. We sipped on weak coffee while we watched a continuous loop video introducing us to the world of *Windsong Resorts International*—or WRI, as it was called for short.

We learned that WRI is a huge resort company owned by an outrageous, Donald Trump-like billionaire named Wiley Bennett. Bennett apparently made his vast fortune the easy way—he inherited it. But to his credit, he managed to make his inheritance multiply tenfold over the past 20 years, placing him at the very top of the list of the world's wealthiest people.

The video went on to inform us that Bennett's father, Wiley Bennett, Sr., started buying up real estate all along the East Coast of Florida in the late 1940's. Later, the elder Bennett helped to develop much of this land into resort complexes, which quite literally turned South Florida into a tourist destination. To this day, Old Miami Beach and parts of Fort Lauderdale and Palm Beach are covered with the indelible fingerprints of the elder Mr. Bennett.

But the younger Bennett had even grander dreams than his father. When he took over the family business, he started to buy small, uninhabited Mediterranean, Caribbean, and Polynesian islands and several properties along the coasts of Turkey and Spain. He then converted these desolate islands and coastal strips into exclusive, high-end resorts.

The video showed images of lush, tropical islands with massive sandcastle-like structures erupting through the foliage and swimming pools with glamorous looking people lounging around. At that time, WRI owned 23 private resorts in all—most with four and five star ratings. These private resorts offered WRI's upper class clientele the most "innovative and discrete" travel experiences in the world. We were told that unnamed A-List stars were known to prefer the Windsong resorts when they wanted to unwind. With airport facilities built right into the resort, famous guests could fly in and out of these exclusive playgrounds in their private jets without the prying eye of the public watching their every move.

The video went on to explain that in recent months, Wiley Bennett decided to buy his own airline—*Windsong Air*. With a fleet of four wide-body jets—each seating about 300 passengers—Bennett could finally start offering the most complete travel packages in the industry. This also opened up a new market for WRI—upper middle class travelers. By creating all-inclusive packages that include airfare to these plush destinations, Bennett could offer the general public access to some of his older, less exclusive resorts. Additionally, plans were in the works for Bennett to develop contracts with other larger resorts to create new vacation packages.

We were told at this point that due to Federal Aviation Administration requirements, WRI could not legally operate an airline without securing a full staff of certified and trained flight attendants. The newly formed Miami-based *Windsong Air* was seeking the best and brightest people to join the team. Due to the charter nature of *Windsong Air's* business, a smaller staff could be maintained, meaning greater benefit to their employees. Flight attendant's chosen during this interview process were promised amazing perks, including housing in one of South Beach's most famous high-rise apartment buildings—*The Wiley*.

This magnificent 20-story complex was one of Wiley Bennett, Sr.'s first high-rise projects in the Miami area, and it is said to have great sentimental value—as well as market value—to the younger Bennett. The building is located right on the Atlantic Ocean with an amazing view of the beach on one side and the Miami skyline on the other. Using *The Wiley* to house *Windsong Air* employees was supposedly a creative way to leverage the property and provide employee accessibility for this latest WRI venture.

As Nora and I watched the video, both of our jaws dropped at how amazing this job could be. Travel to exotic destinations and a cool apartment at *The Wiley*? Could this actually be true? Once we learned all about *Windsong Air*, we both realized how badly we wanted to be flight attendants for Wiley Bennett. And looking around the room at all the other applicants, we realized we weren't alone.

But about five days after the grueling cattle-call style interview, a woman from the FAA called and left a message that both Nora and I had been selected by *Windsong Air* as potential flight attendant candidates. Then, following three more interviews with the FAA recruitment team and one more interview with the *Windsong Air* team, Nora and I were hired!

Of course our parents were skeptical, and convincing them that *Windsong Air* and living at *The Wiley* wasn't a scam was the final hurdle. Nora's father spent two days pouring over our contracts, examining the terms of our employment and our living arrangements before he would let us sign.

The contracts were solid, but both of our parents had their concerns about living at *The Wiley* and working for WRI. *"Too much Wiley Bennett in your lives"* is what we kept hearing. But by that time, Nora and I were packed and ready to leave *Purgatory* for good, and there was little our parents could say or do to stop us.

So within weeks of our first exposure to *Windsong Resorts International*, Nora and I were moving all of our things into *The Wiley* and getting ready to start our FAA training. It felt a little like our freshman year in college all over again—only the "dorm rooms" were posh, wildly furnished apartments with magnificent views. It was almost too good to be true, but neither of us wanted to say *that* out loud!

The actual flight attendant training lasted for three long and rigorous months. At the FAA facility, Nora and I—along with 48 other *Windsong Air* flight attendants—were taught how to handle hostage situations, terrorist attacks and emergency evacuations. (And here we thought learning how to serve coffee during turbulence was going to be the most challenging part of the job!)

Each day, we were tested on what we had learned the day before, and since Nora and I were fresh out of college and used to taking exams, we passed each test with flying colors. On graduation day from the FAA Flight Attendant Training Program, I received the program's highest honor—*platinum wings*. I had received a perfect score on every exam and showed the "highest promise" to be one of *Windsong Air's* finest employees.

By late December, Nora and I were working flight attendants, shuttling wealthy passengers to luxurious destinations in the Caribbean and off the coast of Spain. And living at *The Wiley* was incredible! We each had our own one bedroom apartment—mine on the 17th floor and Nora's on the 11th. I didn't think things could get any better! I was a nomad with a mindless job, and I got to see parts of the world I had never imagined. I was meeting other fight attendants who worked for *Windsong Air* and lived at *The Wiley*, which was rapidly expanding my social horizons. I was enjoying every minute of my new life, and I think my parents finally started to believe that working for Wiley Bennett was not a monstrous mistake.

But by the third month of working for Windsong Air, I noticed Nora was growing depressed. Sure, she liked living it up at *The Wiley*, and she loved our layovers in other countries. It's just that her personality was changing, and it started to become obvious to me that Nora wasn't going to last. I caught her circling ads in the *Miami Herald* for advertising jobs one Sunday afternoon, and I knew she was thinking about leaving. She always wanted to be in advertising—it was always her plan—and no matter how great it was to have this fancy lifestyle, she would always regret not trying her hand in advertising.

So after five months, Nora left *Windsong Air*, turned in her apartment key and moved back home with her parents. She was determined to hold out for her *real* dream job. Eventually, she landed a job at *Louis & Chavez*—

this very exclusive ad agency that specializes in Latin clients who want to brand their products in America. Nora got a job as a junior copywriter as a way to get her foot in the door. The fact that she spoke fluent Spanish was a huge bonus, and within the first nine months, she was promoted to senior copywriter. Then, exactly four years later, she was promoted to advertising director, which included a huge salary increase and an expense account. Nora was finally doing what she had always wanted to do—and she was great at it! I was so proud of her for going after her dream—and so amazed at how easily she worked her way up to the top.

Of course it was difficult for me when Nora first left, but I understood. The lifestyle of a charter flight attendant isn't for everyone. But it still seems to work for me. This summer, I will celebrate my 10-year anniversary at *Windsong Air*. I am only one of 15 original flight crewmembers still working for the company and living at *The Wiley*. This seniority gives me a certain status, which I love. I always get the best trips and can name my days off at the beginning of each month, which makes this job pretty easy.

If I'm being honest though, working for *Windsong Air* isn't exactly "my dream job," but the benefits are incredible and I haven't found anything else I would rather do. I have a great place to live—with a coveted oceanfront view—a convertible New Beetle and a great group of friends and co-workers that Nora and I named *The Sisters & Brothers of Fuselage*. And, even though in truth, Wiley Bennett does kind of "own" me, the trade offs are simply too good to pass up.

As the hostess walks me to the table, I notice that, as always, Nora is impeccably dressed. She has on a salmon-colored chiffon camisole and flowing beige silk pants with strappy leather sandals. Her thick, chestnut-colored hair is pulled back in a loose ponytail with light golden wisps of hair framing her face. She always looks so fresh—no matter how muggy and sticky it is outside. It's like she has some sort of invisible bubble that protects her from the elements.

"Hey you!" she says as she rises up out of her chair to hug me around the neck. "You're early!"

"Well, you know me…I hate to be late!" I say as I pour myself into one of the cushioned chairs.

26

"Listen, Elle, I hope you don't mind, but I invited my friend Brita from work to join us. Have you ever met Brita?" Nora asks as she sits back down and takes a quick look over my shoulder in anticipation of her friend's arrival.

I don't recall meeting this Brita person, but I can only imagine how exotic and amazing she'll be. All the women who work for *Louis & Chavez* are off the charts in the looks department.

"I don't think so. Does she work with you?"

"Not exactly—she's actually my boss's administrative assistant," Nora says with a bit of a conspiratorial giggle. "But she's really nice, and sometimes she'll cover for me if I'm out of the office for too long on *personal business*. She's a good one to keep in my graces—if you know what I mean!" Just then, Nora looks up, "Oh, there she is! Brita! Over here!"

As I turn to get my first look at Brita, I am pleasantly surprised to see an average height girl with curly, reddish hair sort of skipping toward us. Her face is beaming with a big, toothy grin and orange-colored freckles spanning the bridge of her nose. She is by no means unattractive—just not a classic beauty. But her bounciness makes her instantly likeable. What a relief! I'm not sure I could have handled a power lunch with one of Nora's other colleagues. After being around Dr. Miller, I need a break from the "super model in sheep's clothing" scenario.

Brita is wearing a short little pink plaid skirt that shows off her slender legs and trendy black platform sandals. Her white, silk tank top is coming untucked on the sides, and she has a messy kind of charm that makes me feel happy. She looks like she must be in her early twenties—and I can't help but wonder if she got her job through a favor her boss owed her father or something.

"Hi Nora!" Brita blurts out. "I was having trouble finding a place to park, so I hope I'm not late."

"Oh no, silly! You're fine!" Nora intones like she's the most laid back person around. "Brita, this is my best friend, Elle," Nora says as she pulls her handbag out of the chair next to hers and motions for Brita to sit there.

Brita and I exchange our hellos as she settles into her chair. We each take our oversized menu boards and study the selections carefully. My stomach lets out an embarrassingly loud gurgle, and Brita gives me a wink and a smile.

"I think I might try that salad special—the one with the shrimp. That sounds perfect for me," Nora announces to no one in particular.

"Oh, that does sound good," offers Brita. "I think I'm more in the mood for a cheeseburger though, but I don't see one on this menu..."

A girl after my own heart, I think as I tilt my menu and show Brita where the burgers are listed.

The waiter finally comes over, and we each place our orders. I'm secretly jealous when Brita orders her cheeseburger, medium rare with an order of fries. Remembering the three pounds I've gained this year, I can't seem to permit myself to order what I really want and instead order a house salad with *light* dressing, no cheese and a glass of mint iced tea. What a drag...

"So Elle, how was your doctor's appointment?" Nora asks once the waiter finally clears away our menus.

"Oh, please don't ask," I say in an exasperated voice.

"What kind of doctor's appointment did you have?" Brita asks innocently as she pulls the breadbasket over onto her plate. She starts digging through the basket in search of a piece of hot bread.

"The gynecologist," Nora answers for me with a crooked look of dread on her face.

"I absolutely hate going to the gynecologist!" Brita says emphatically.

"Who doesn't?" Nora says, grabbing the breadbasket from Brita and looking around the table to find the butter.

"Well, I think I have a reason to hate it more than most women," I say as I pass Nora the little white dish holding small pats of butter wrapped in gold foil.

"What do you mean? How could it be all that different for you than it is for me?" Brita asks me with the look of confusion spreading across her face.

"You wouldn't understand," I say, hoping that everyone will just leave it at that.

After a bit of a pause, Brita leans forward in her chair and says, "Try me."

I can't decide if I really want to get into this with Brita right now—I mean I don't even know the girl! And it seems like the subject of my virginity has had enough mileage for one day. But sometimes I feel better when I get things off my chest. Maybe a little female bonding is *exactly* what I need.

"OK, but you both have to promise not to freak out..." I tentatively begin.

Nora's face sort of shifts into a puzzled look as she sticks a tiny, perfectly buttered bite of bread into her mouth. Then her look changes to worried as she blurts out, "Oh God, Elle! Do you have a disease? Oh no! Are you pregnant?"

Brita stops buttering her bread and rests her knife on the edge of her bread plate. She has a sincerely worried look on her face, too, and she's leaning in closer to me now in anticipation of my words.

"No! Of course not... It's just the opposite actually."

I can see that Nora is slowly remembering why the gynecologist might be extra embarrassing for me, and, as she leans back in her chair, I think she's probably wondering how much I will reveal in front of this total stranger at the table.

"Well, you know how I haven't really...you know...had *sex*?" I say as I look directly at Nora, who is now looking back at me and mouthing the words, "I'm so sorry!"

"What!" Brita blurts out rather loudly.

Nora sits up abruptly and gives Brita a slap on the arm and a stern "shush." But I decide to press on. It's been that kind of day, so I might as well.

"Well, the truth is, Brita, I'm still a virgin," I gently admit, like I'm confessing that I'm actually another species visiting from a neighboring planet.

Brita's eyebrows spring up on her forehead and her eyes are suddenly wide. "Are you serious?" she asks in disbelief, and then adds, "I mean, wow! That's so...wow!" This is a reaction I am starting to know all too well today.

"I didn't know for sure if you were still, you know… *inactive*," enters Nora cautiously. "I mean it's kind of…" I can tell Nora is searching for the right word to not put me down, but to express her own disbelief. "Rare."

"Yes, I know! I've been hearing that all morning at the gynecologist. It's so *rare* in fact that my doctor insisted that an *intern* come in and see my pristine cervix and vaginal area for herself! And then, that very intern was in such a state of shock after she completed the exam that she went and shared her discovery with all of the other interns in the office!" I'm trying to keep my voice down, but reliving the whole thing all over again makes me realize how embarrassed I still feel.

"Oh, Elle! I'm so sorry—how awful…" Nora puts her hand on my forearm, and I can tell she is genuinely upset for me. Brita has the look of bewilderment on her face. I'm sure she doesn't even know what to say.

We all three sit in silence for a few minutes, nibbling on bread. I've decided to hold my bread intake to a one-piece minimum as I feel I need to be counting carbs and fat all of a sudden. I'm about to grab a pat of butter, but decide against it.

Just bread—no butter, I think. *That's better for me anyway.*

I look up to see Brita sitting quietly as if she is dumbfounded by my admission. Nora is quiet, too, but also seems to be working something out in her head, like maybe she's trying to figure out how to ask me a question. I let her fret, and wait patiently for her to find the words.

"So you're *still* a virgin…" she finally says, almost in a whisper after the waiter delivers our drinks and gives Nora a refill. "I mean, I knew you were back in college and the first few years at *Windsong Air*. But I just figured living at *The Wiley* all these years and traveling to all those resorts with the frisky passengers finally got to you and pulled you over to the other side. I mean…we're in our *thirties*, Elle!"

"Nope. Somehow, I've managed to contain myself," I say as I lean back in the chair and take a pull of iced tea through an ultra thin black straw. I hate that we're still talking about this. I guess I expect this sort of shock from a stranger, but I'm sad that I seem to need to defend myself to one of the few people in the world that I thought understood me without a lot of explanation.

After an awkward pause, Nora carefully asks, "Why do you think you're still a...you know...*virgin*?"

"Yeah, Elle. Help us understand why you haven't done it yet," Brita adds, looking at me with an expectant expression and a few breadcrumbs on her chin.

I'm baffled by the fact that Nora can't even comfortably say the word *virgin* and Brita—who just met me a few minutes ago—has a deep need to know why I haven't "done it" yet. Is it really that outrageous and unbelievable? I never thought so until today. It seems like people all around me—including one of my closet friends and an oddballish stranger—find it *unpalatable* and possibly even *wrong* to abstain.

Maybe I *am* from another planet after all, and I just never knew it until now. I mean, doesn't anyone else in my generation see sex as something to cherish? It's starting to become crystal clear to me that the answer to that question is no.

But I stop and think about Nora's question. *Why am I still a virgin?* That could take some time to answer. I guess it all really started when my grandmother—Edna Pearl Potter—challenged my sister and me to consider a few things at an early age.

(Just an aside—Edna Pearl is my mother's mother, and as you can see, this side of the family has a tendency to pick bad names. My dad's side of the family got *stuck* with a bad name, whereas my mom's side likes to *pick* the bad ones. Once I asked my grandma why her mother named her Edna Pearl and she told me her mother said she looked like one. Honestly, these women need help!)

Anyway, Edna Pearl—which is what she prefers to be called—has always been a mentor in my life. My sister, Abby, who is three years older than me, and I used to spend hours with my grandmother when we were growing up. She lived in Essex, England—where my mother and her two younger sisters grew up—and so when she and my grandfather would come over to America for a visit, they usually stayed for about eight weeks. Those eight-week stays with Edna Pearl are rich with memories and life lessons for me. She's always been funny and a bit eccentric, but very confident and accomplished, and everyone greatly respects her wisdom.

For nearly 40 years, Edna Pearl has run a women's shelter for battered women back in England. She founded the shelter in 1965 after her youngest sister, Agatha, ended up on her doorstep with a broken arm and a fractured skull—all the handiwork of her alcoholic husband. I don't think Edna Pearl was capable of standing by without doing something to help her sister. But once she got involved, it seemed to be a matter of helping her sister and every other woman that faced abuse.

At 80-years-old, Edna Pearl still has a way of cutting to the heart of a matter and protecting women from the mixed up men they marry. She teaches women how to be empowered, not defeated, and her message is always delivered with care and compassion. She's seen it all in her life, and she freely shares her wisdom with anyone who will listen—including my sister and me.

When we were preteens, Edna Pearl sat my sister and me down for a little chat. My sister was 13 and I was 10. Edna Pearl asked us if we had decided on our lifetime "non-negotiables." Obviously, being only 10, I didn't even know what the word meant, let alone what it meant in my life. So she explained it to us in a way that only Edna Pearl could.

"My darlings, non-negotiables are the things in life you simply won't tolerate or do without. They are the things that you decide in your heart you will guard and honor with all your power and strength. They are the things in life you won't allow to take you captive and the things you won't allow to pass you by. They are treasured decisions you make today and vow to keep forever."

I remember wondering at the time what sort of things I should make as my non-negotiables. Was vowing to always eat chocolate every single day a non-negotiable? Was making sure that I shared a daily belly laugh or two with my mom something Edna Pearl would accept as an entry on my list? I thought not. I got the impression that whatever non-negotiables I added to my list, they needed to be carefully considered. And even though I was unable to fully comprehend the weight of the word and the depth of those commitments to myself at the time, I pondered Edna Pearl's words for many years before deciding on my list.

When I was 15, my family traveled to England to attend my grandfather's funeral. It was a very sad time as I watched Edna Pearl bury her soul mate and one of the world's finest men. My grandfather was a wonderful man with the softest voice and most gentle spirit. He always made me feel special and I remember how much he loved my grandmother. His pale eyes were always happy—no matter what was happening in his life. Everyone adored him, and letting go of him was the first time I ever knew real grief.

I remember being amazed by how many people showed up to support my grandmother at the funeral. There were literally hundreds of men and women who all looked unfamiliar to me. But Edna Pearl clearly knew each one intimately. A special reception was held following the funeral at the *Essex Women's Shelter*—the very shelter my grandmother had founded 22 years earlier. People lined up and waited for hours to hug my grandmother and share their tears and heartache with her. My sister and I took turns sitting next to Edna Pearl as she connected with her fellow mourners. I wanted to know why these people needed to talk to Edna Pearl so badly. I wanted to understand what they were feeling, and why the death of my grandfather had impacted them so.

That day, I heard men and women pouring out their hearts to Edna Pearl. I heard the women tell her how they always prayed to have marriages like my grandmother's. They praised my grandfather for the way he always respected his wife, and how grateful they were that my grandfather was willing to share Edna Pearl with those in need. The men that came forward expressed what felt like a combination of grief and remorse for not being more like my grandfather toward their own wives. Then they cried tears of gratitude for the way Edna Pearl had helped to restore their lives and marriages. It was the most powerful display of emotions I had ever witnessed. It was beyond words for me at that time, and soaking it all in made me wonder about love and relationships.

When the crowd finally died down, it was time for my family to have some privacy. One of the women who worked with Edna Pearl at the shelter made us something to eat—English bangers and cranberry scones with Devonshire cream. None of us was very hungry, but I still remember how wonderful everything tasted. No one had much to say. We all just sat quietly in the great room of the shelter, soaking in the silence and the finality of death.

After a few days passed, I met my grandmother out in her garden. She was sitting on an old cement bench with her eyes pressed shut. I just remember sliding up beside her and resting my head in her lap. As she brushed my hair with her fingertips, she said, "Eloise, you know I love you very much, don't you?"

"Yes. And I love you, too," I told her.

She went on, "Whenever I see a woman come into the shelter with a bruised eye or a broken bone, I say a little prayer for you and Abby. I pray that you will never know the pain of abuse and that you will choose a man like your grandfather to love you and cherish you until you're old and gray."

We sat in silence for a while. I didn't know what to say. For the first time in my life, I realized that Edna Pearl wasn't just protecting other women with her shelter—she was protecting my sister and me with her prayers. I never thought we were in any kind of danger—we were still so young and had our whole lives ahead of us. But Edna Pearl seemed to have her gaze set on the canvas of my life, and she was trying to show me in her own way that the paintbrush that creates my future is partially in my hands.

"I know in my heart that no woman sets out to marry an abusive man," she started to explain. "I believe the women who end up in my shelter think they can *fix* a tortured soul and *love* a man into a place of wholeness. But Eloise, my darling, you simply can't be enough or do enough for someone who is broken. You have to hold out for what you want and need in a man. You have to respect yourself and not give your heart and soul away too easily."

There was a certain pleading in Edna Pearl's words that day, and I sensed that she was trying to express her own grief over the loss of a man who had loved her with complete, genuine love while she was grieving for the women who didn't choose as wisely. I could see that she wanted for me what she had in my grandfather and to never settle for anything less.

The next day, I took an old beat up sketchpad from the bottom of my book bag out to the garden and began to make my list of non-negotiables.

I dedicated the list in my grandfather's memory and vowed to do my best to hold my commitments in my heart forever. That day, in the garden on my grandmother's estate, I promised that I would save myself for the man that deserved my heart, my soul and my trust. I vowed to hold out for my soul mate. I vowed to remain a virgin until marriage.

I'm not going to lie—it's been very difficult to keep this promise to myself for all these years. I've had huge crushes on guys that I thought really cared about me. But as soon as my no-sex-before-marriage policy became an issue, they stopped calling. My heart has been broken more times than I care to count, and, after awhile, I stopped trying to date. In my experience, three weeks seems to be the maximum time a guy will invest in a relationship that's not going to lead to getting laid. Once a guy finds out that I'm not going to budge, I'm history.

Truthfully, when I wrote out my non-negotiables 18 years ago, I thought for sure that I would be married by the time I was in my twenties. It just seemed like a reasonable assumption at the time. But once I reached my mid-twenties, the fear of not finding my soul mate became very real. And now that I am in my thirties, I'm not even sure that I have a soul mate out there. Pretty much every guy I've met so far seems to be in such a hurry to get to know every part of me except my soul.

And despite the way I feel after my day today, I know that I can't just change things in my life because everyone around me thinks I'm crazy. I mean, since I've held on for so long, it's become who I am, and to give in now seems pointless. If I concede now, after all these years, it seems like it wasn't worth it to believe in the hope of a true match like Edna Pearl found in my grandfather. It's not like I'm doing this as a badge of honor or to prove anything to anyone else. It's just that now, I simply can't just "do it" with someone on a whim—I just can't. Plus, with all the diseases and the bed-hopping going on all around me, I realize that it's not safe—physically or emotionally—to experiment with something like sex. And, to be completely honest, no one has been worth even flirting with the risk.

After a long pause, I realize that Nora and Brita are still waiting for an answer. How can I make them understand the vows that I made to myself all those years ago? How do I communicate the fact that holding on to my promise means more to me than any guy I've met so far? But I know I need to let them off the hook.

"I guess I'm still a virgin because I want to be. It's really just as simple as that."

Brita nods her head in resigned understanding, and Nora gives me a thoughtful look.

"Well, that's fine then, isn't it!" says Nora with a reassuring smile.

"Yes, I guess it is!" I say, relieved to have pacified them both so easily.

Chapter Three

The main lobby of *The Wiley* looks a lot like the reception area of a fancy hotel. There's a long, wrap-around counter with a uniformed desk clerk in place to greet you, and a large, roaring fountain on the far side spewing chlorinated water about 15 feet into the air. Glass walls stretch upward for three stories creating an atrium affect and there are fern-like plants in shiny, metal urns hugging the edge of the fountain, making the lobby seem like a lush rainforest.

There's a doorman on duty at all times, and a team of facilities managers that basically monitor everything that happens at *The Wiley*. These WRI employees are known amongst the residents as *The Snoops*, and most of us try to stay out of their way as much as possible. After living at *The Wiley* for almost a decade, I've gotten used to the nosey staff camped out in the lobby, but admittedly, I often take the service elevator to avoid an unplanned run-in. Unfortunately, the residents' mailroom is located in the lobby, in a small room off the side of the reception area, making it impossible to avoid the scrutiny of a *Snoop* for more than a day or so.

On my way back from lunch with Nora, I realize that I simply can't avoid the lobby any longer—I really need to get my mail. A quick dash in and out is all it'll take. I manage to slip into the mailroom undetected, so I'm almost home free. I carefully slide my key into my mailbox and slowly open the door. It's been days since I checked my mail and I'm expecting it to be full, but instead, it's completely empty. Just as I start to close my mailbox, a knobby, bluish-colored hand pushes through the opening preventing me from shutting the door. I jump back slightly and let out a little yelp—it's not everyday a hand pops out at you from your mailbox!

"Elle Butts? Is that you?" I can hear the familiar gravelly voice of the mailroom supervisor, Verna Humphrey, hollering at me from the other side of the wall. Of all the *Snoops* in the building, Verna is by far the nosiest.

"Yes, Verna…it's me…" I say as I catch my breath and force my heart rate to return to normal.

Verna is a former chain-smoking New York City postal worker who's probably in her late sixties. About eight years ago, she came out of retirement to run the mailroom at *The Wiley*, turning it into a highly efficient hub of communication. She takes her work very seriously and keeps her arthritic finger on the pulse of everything going on in the building—including keeping tabs on what kind of mail you get and how many days it takes you to remember to pick it up.

"I was beginning to worry about you, Elle," Verna says condescendingly as we peer at each other through the square hole of my mailbox. "It's been four days since you last collected your mail, and I noticed that you weren't on any trips so far this week. Can I assume everything's OK?"

"Everything's fine, Verna," I reply flatly. "But thanks for your concern."

I see her motioning for me to meet her over by the mailroom counter, so I start to move in that direction. I can hear her rummaging around, collecting my mail with a few grunts and phlegm-filled sighs. I guess she needs to make sure I know that I've put her out with my lack of attention to the mail.

"I hate to alarm you, but there's a letter from the corporate office that I've been holding for at least four days now," Verna scolds as she meets me at the counter with an armful of envelopes and a few magazines. She plunks the pile of mail down on the counter with a dramatic flare, and I notice right away that the corporate letter is placed right on top. "You really shouldn't go so long without collecting your mail, Elle. The mail is still a vital form of communication—no matter how many people use that fancy computer-net for letter writing and paying bills," she says with a bitter tone.

"I know, Verna. I didn't mean to go this long without checking. I'll be more careful from now on," I say as I carefully lift the slender envelope with the embossed lettering in the return address out of the pile and study it for a moment.

Letters like this one from the corporate office make me nervous. A few years ago, several of my fellow flight attendants got letters in fancy envelopes just like this one, letting them know that they were being furloughed and that they would need to secure interim housing until further notice. It was supposed to be a temporary layoff—nothing permanent. But they never came back. The furlough lasted so long that they had to find new jobs and new places to live. It was awful. I feel slightly paralyzed as I stare at the envelope in my hands, wondering if it contains bad news about my future. I want to rip it open right now, but I can't seem to move.

"Back when I was with the USPS, people actually looked forward to getting their mail," Verna continues on as she digs through a gray postal bag. "Now, I have to *remind* you people to pick it up." A deep, phlegmy cough rises up from her lungs as she looks up at me with disdain.

"I'm really sorry, Verna. Thank you so much for keeping an eye on things for me. I really appreciate it," I say as I scoop my mail into a pile and shove the whole lot into my purse. "I'll see you again soon...I promise!"

I quickly make my way to the elevator alcove while my mind is racing about why the corporate office is sending *me* a letter. Have I done something wrong? Is there going to be another furlough? Am I going to have to move home with my parents? I'm sure it can't be good news—good news is given over the phone or through the company website. I don't want to open the letter until I'm inside my apartment, but I can feel the weight of it in my purse as the elevator slowly rises up to the 17th floor.

When I step off the elevator and enter the hallway, I start to fumble around for my keys. But with all that mail crammed into my bag, I can't seem to find them, so I squat down on the floor and start dumping out the contents of my purse. A tube of lipstick...gum...wallet...date book...cell phone...a trial sized stick of deodorant—*I didn't know I had this with me*—a pencil...a hair band... Aha! My keys!

As I'm cramming all my mail and personal items back into my purse, I can hear the sound of the locks moving on the door across the hall.

Oh perfect! I think. *It's Gabby.*

Gabriel Menendez is a tall Latin American beauty who lives in the apartment directly across the hall from mine. She's the epitome of the South Beach party girl and lives her life on the wild side—and not just by my standards. She has impossibly long brown legs that are always on display in her short skirts, and her wavy jet-black hair is so shiny that sometimes it looks like black metal. She has a gorgeous face—a perfect nose, big brown eyes and naturally dark red, pouty lips.

I actually like Gabby, even though we have absolutely nothing in common other than work. She's a good neighbor and is always nice to me when I see her in passing. But, truthfully, I hate getting cornered by her—believe me when I say that the nickname *Gabby* isn't just short for Gabriel! That girl can talk all day if you let her! And I'm really not in the mood to talk right now—I just want to get inside and open my letter.

"Hey Chica!" Gabby purrs from her doorway.

"Oh hey, Gabby," I reply over my shoulder as I hurriedly shove my belongings back into my purse and sling it over my shoulder. "I couldn't find my keys..." I offer in an effort to explain the situation and avoid any questions.

"OK... Well, I'm glad I bumped into because I have something really exciting to tell you!" Gabby is now leaning against the wall next to the door of my apartment, nibbling on the edge of her finger with a huge Cheshire grin on her face. She's wearing a stretchy white tube top, a black leather mini skirt and has a set of hot pink pedicure wedges crammed between her toes.

"I met someone, Elle!" she squeals like a giddy schoolgirl.

"What do you mean, Gabby?" I ask flatly as I move in and start to unlock the door to my apartment. I'm praying that Sugar Ray charges to door—Gabby's afraid of him, so I'm counting on my dog to help me cut our conversation short.

"I mean, I met someone *special* this time—someone different!" Gabby continues as she grabs my wrist, stopping me from opening the door. She's looking me in the eye and I can see that she's serious.

"Well, that's great, Gabby. That's really great."

"No, you don't understand. I think I may have met...*the one!*" Her face is all lit up like I've never seen it before. "He's a doctor, Elle! A doctor! And he's totally into me!"

"Wow! That's really wonderful, Gabby," I say, trying to sound interested. "What kind of doctor is he?" I ask in an effort to prove my interest.

"What do you mean *what kind?*" she replies in a slightly offended tone. "He's a *doctor*—you know...with a white coat and lots of money!"

"Well is he a medical doctor or a PhD?" I continue with this line of questioning, knowing full well that she won't know the answer.

"I don't know," Gabby snaps at me like I'm nuts. "What difference does it make? He's a *doctor,* and that's all that counts."

I can hear Sugar Ray whining at the door, which I hope will be enough to make Gabby scurry back into her apartment so we can end our little chat. But she's still standing right next to me with her fingers tightly wrapped around my wrist.

"I want you to meet him, Elle," she continues. "I need an opinion from someone I trust." Gabby says this with as much sincerity as I've ever seen her muster.

"Sure...I'll meet him, Gabby," I tell her as I try to figure out why Gabby trusts me. I mean, we aren't even that close.

"Oh thank you, Elle!!" Gabby releases my wrist so she can clap her hands together while she jumps up and down like a thirty-year-old Latin cheerleader. "The reservations are for tonight at 8:00 at *Grazie,* and you can bring someone if you want to," she rattles off as she makes her way back to her apartment.

"Tonight?"

"Well, yes, Elle. I wanted you to meet him as soon as possible, and I already made the reservations—*Grazie* is very difficult to get into these days, so I had to call in some favors..." She's standing in the doorway of her apartment now, looking at me with frustration, like I'm about to mess up her perfect evening.

"Gabby, I don't know, I mean, I'm happy to meet your new boyfriend, but I didn't realize you meant tonight..." I'm still trying to sort out how I let this happen.

"Come on, Elle! It's not like you already had big plans for tonight," she chides back at me. "I know you—you'll just stay home with your dog and read a book or something incredibly dull like that. You need to get out more and live a little."

I'm slightly hurt by Gabby's comments. I get out. I do stuff…all the time. Just because I don't go *clubbing* doesn't mean that I lead a dull life. It just means I'm comfortable with being alone, that's all…

"You could ask Scott LaMotte to tag along—I'm sure he's free tonight," she offers in a knowing and obvious effort to force my hand.

Scott LaMotte is basically my closest friend—even closer than Nora. We started working at *Windsong Air* at the same time, and over the years, we've become like family.

"How do you know Scott's free tonight, Gabby?" I ask in an aggravated tone, even though I'm pretty sure that I already know the answer to my question.

"Because I already *invited him.* And he accepted!" she retorts back proudly, like she's cornered me with a perfectly played checkmate.

"Gabby, you really shouldn't do stuff like that. What if I *did* have plans tonight? This little trap you've set could've backfired, you know," I say trying to sound a little threatening, while attempting to hold back my deep irritation.

"Oh please, Elle. It's a Thursday night—since when do *you* have plans on a Thursday night?"

"Still, Gabby—that was out of line." I can't believe this woman! Does she always get what she wants?

"Whatever…" she says dismissively as she studies the cuticle on one of her fingers. She obviously feels no remorse as she continues, "I told Scott to meet us down in the lobby at 7:30 and the three of us can ride together to the restaurant. Now remember, Elle, this place is hot right now, so wear something…sexy."

After a slight pause, she asks, "You *do* have something sexy, don't you?"

"No, Gabby. I thought I'd wear my bathrobe," I say sarcastically over my shoulder as I open the door to my apartment. Sugar Ray manages to poke his boxy head through the crack just enough to—I hope—frighten Gabby.

"See you at 7:30 then," she chirps as she quickly slams the door to her apartment.

I push open the door to my apartment all the way, and Sugar Ray starts to wiggle and dance, welcoming me home in his special little way. I stoop down and start rubbing him behind the ears and kissing him between the eyes. I love coming home to my dog—he's always so happy to see me! Once he's properly greeted, I stand up and hang my keys on the hook next to my door. I can't believe how easily people like Gabby manipulate me. I wish I *did* have plans of my own for tonight, so I could blow her off, but of course…I don't.

My apartment is cool and quiet, and even with the hard, Miami inspired interiors, it's always a welcome place to get my bearings. The floor plan for all of the apartments in *The Wiley* is pretty much the same. As you enter the apartment, a small, but open, kitchen with a brushed metal and glass island bar runs the length of the space. Stainless steel appliances and cabinetry fill the kitchen—making it look a little like a science lab to me. There are four hot pink velvet covered bar stools that line the outer edge of the bar, which in any other setting would scream tacky, but in here, they seem to work!

Straight ahead, all you can see is open sky and a vast expanse of water as the outer wall of the apartment is made up of 18 feet of tinted glass, overlooking the ocean. There's a sunken living room with a contoured cherry red and acid green sofa and two purple corkscrew-shaped chairs—perfectly positioned for taking in the view—and a small built-in desk situated in the corner. All along the lower section of the glass wall is a banquette-type window seat made of lightwood with stainless steel trim. Some of the sections of the window seat are closed-in boxes, and other sections have shelving for my books, stereo and knickknacks.

A sweeping metal staircase rounds up to a sleeping loft that hovers over the kitchen area. An oversized bed with a brushed metal headboard takes up the majority of the loft space, but there's enough room for two metal bedside cubes and a heavy-duty metal TV cabinet, which is angled to the side so as not to spoil the stunning ocean view. Funky electric blue wall sconces are mounted on both sides of the bed, and the floor is covered with industrial metal—which sort of reminds me of a playground slide platform.

A bathroom with a dressing area is located off the kitchen down a long hallway that runs the width of the apartment. Multiple closets line the hall leading up to a large bathroom with a huge bathtub and glassed-in shower. The bathroom has a cold, steely feeling with metal cabinets—similar to the ones in the kitchen—and two stainless steel floating sinks. The white tile floor extends into the bathroom from the kitchen and makes the whole area seem bright and rather sterile.

The contemporary interior design of the place is not exactly my favorite style, but everything is done so well that it's grown on me. I've done my best to personalize my place by including soft rugs and cozy linens. And while the furnishings are a bit on the extreme side—even for Miami—it just seems like what you'd expect to see inside *The Wiley*.

Home sweet home, I think, as I take in my apartment. This may be the last time I can call this place my home—if the letter from corporate contains what I think it does. There's no way I could ever afford to live in an apartment as cool as this one on my own. I can't believe how lucky I am to have lived here for so long. I settle in on my crazy looking sofa and pull the letter out of my purse.

I hold the envelope for a few minutes before opening it. It feels thick, like there are several sheets of paper folded up inside. I take a deep breath and force my finger under the sealed flap of the envelope and carefully rip it open. It is indeed multiple sheets of official looking pages, all stapled together in the corner. I unfold the packet of papers and run my finger along the backside to flatten out the creases.

The cover letter is on embossed *Windsong Air* letterhead, making it look very formal. The words CONFIDENTIAL CORRESPONDENCE are printed along the top of the page. Reading those words in bold black letters causes my heart to beat heavily inside my chest.

Dear Ms. Butts:

Windsong Resorts International is expanding by partnering with several Italian and French resorts to create travel packages that originate in Europe. The incorporation of Windsong Air into these packages is central to the success of this venture. As such, we are planning to send two crews of Windsong Air flight attendants over to Europe for a three-month stay, with an option to extend.

As one of Windsong Air's most senior flight attendants, we are contacting you to offer you the first right of refusal for this temporary base transfer. The first Windsong Air base will be in the Tuscan region of Italy. Flights will run on a regular schedule out of Florence three days a week. The rest of the days will be open days for both flight crews. We have negotiated travel reciprocity with other European air carriers as a benefit to those flight attendants who accept this base transfer. (A list of participating airlines will be included in your transfer confirmation package.)

Flight attendants will be paid based on the individual's current salary and in US dollars. Additionally, a per diem of $5.00 (US) per hour will be extended to flight attendants to cover out of pocket expenses incurred during regularly scheduled flights and layovers. Windsong Air will also cover meals and ground transportation during scheduled workdays. Flight attendants will be housed in partnering resorts for the entire three-month stay. At the end of the three-month period, flight attendants will have the option to request an extension, which will be granted based on crew performance evaluations.

Flight attendants will maintain their residence at The Wiley during the base transfer as long as the transfer does not exceed three months. Flight attendants who are granted an extension will need to make arrangements to vacate their apartment at The Wiley until returning to the Windsong Air Miami base.

I can't believe it! This is incredible news! It's almost like finding out I have a three-month, all-expense-paid vacation to Tuscany! Who wouldn't want to take the transfer? This is the most amazing news! I can't believe how silly I was to think this letter was ominous!

The rest of the information in the packet outlines the flight schedules and provides several forms that need to be completed and retuned to corporate in order to be eligible for the transfer. I feel dizzy with relief! It's an incredible opportunity. How could I pass it up?

As I skim over the letter for the second time, I catch something I missed on the first read-through. The actual transfer doesn't take place for roughly another month, but I only have until *tomorrow* to notify corporate about my decision to stay or to go! I waited so long to pick up my mail that my window of consideration is nearly over! I'm going to have to decide *right away!* I hate to admit it, but Verna was right—important things *do* still come by snail mail!

I'm really horrible at making decisions on the fly. I need time to think. And even though it's such an amazing opportunity, my mind immediately starts to race. *What about my life here in Miami? What about all my stuff? What about my parents?* As if on cue, Sugar Ray lets out a big sigh. His head is resting on the top of my foot, and he rolls his big brown eyes up to look at me. *What about Sugar Ray?* Aside from finding someone to take care of him, how am I going to survive for three months without my dog?

This is a lot to think about. I feel nauseous that I almost missed the chance to go and overwhelmed with making the decision on such short notice. I lean back against the sofa and try to calm down. I think the answer is obvious—I have to go! I should just pick up the phone and call the corporate office right now and tell them I'm in. But I can't... I need to think about it for a while.

I wonder who else got a letter. Maybe Scott got one, too! Suddenly, I feel excited to see him tonight—he'll help me sort out all of the details. Scott always knows what to do. Since we met, he's helped me with almost all of my major decisions—like which car to get and whether to buy or lease, how to invest my 401(k)—and most of my not-so-major decisions—

like what to order when we go out for dinner and what shoes look best with my uniform.

But what if Scott didn't get a letter? What if he doesn't even know about the base transfer? It might be upsetting to him if I got offered this amazing transfer and he didn't. We both started working for the company at the same time, and I am only senior to him because I'm alphabetically first. The letter said they are sending two flight attendant crews—which means 16 of us got a letter, and Scott is one of the original 15 still working for *Windsong Air*. So chances are, he got a letter, too. But I've seen him several times this week, and he didn't even *hint* to me that something was going on. Scott and I talk about *everything*—surely he would've told me about the base transfer if he knew.

I guess I'll just have to be careful how I ask him—maybe drop some clever little hints and wait to see if he takes the bait. Then I'll know if he's "safe" to talk to. One thing's for sure—I better not say anything in front of Gabby. That's the last thing I need—Gabby broadcasting this *confidential* news to the entire company. Luckily, she'll probably be so preoccupied with her "doctor man" that she'll never notice my intelligence gathering tactics with Scott.

Several hours later, I'm riding the elevator down to the lobby. I'm feeling a little nervous—perhaps even giddy inside—after thinking about Italy all afternoon. I can't wait to talk to Scott. If he's going, there's no question—I have to go! The two of us would have so much fun together, traveling around, experiencing Europe on our days off. And the truth is, I can't imagine going without him! Ever since the first time I met him, there's been an unexplainable bond between us.

Maybe our bond has something to do with our crappy names. Ever since elementary school, I've always bonded with people who've been stuck with equally bad—or sometimes worse—names than my own. In third grade, I met Harry Pitts, a little pale kid who had just moved to Miami from New Jersey. We instantly connected in the lunchroom on his first day of school when I introduced myself over a carton of milk.

Then there was Betsy Wettington—my best friend in eighth grade. Now you would think her given name was actually Elizabeth and that she could pick Liz or Beth as an optional nickname. But in fact, her given name was Betsy! Poor girl. The two of us weathered the abuse of pre-pubescent boys who tirelessly worked out new ways to embarrass, harass and ridicule us for our names. But as long as we had each other, we managed to laugh things off.

In high school, a heavy-set girl named Mildred Horshack transferred into my school. She attended public school all her life, so transferring into a small private school was quite a transition. On the outside, she had very little going for her—a plus-sized body and a pretty terrible name aren't two things that move you into the fast track of popularity when you're in high school. But Mildred was the most loyal and true friend to those of us who gave her a chance. She was smart and funny and generous beyond belief. And thanks to Mildred's brilliant tutoring skills, I passed math and chemistry my senior year!

So of course, on my first day of flight attendant training, when the roll was called, I immediately zeroed in on the guy who answered to the name *Scott LaMotte*. He was a very tall, slender guy with sandy blonde hair and a chiseled jaw. His face was bright and smiley and almost pretty in a way. During our first break, I introduced myself and we both just started laughing. From then on, we did everything together.

Scott grew up in New York City but ended up in Miami when he signed with the Ford Modeling Agency, and they decided he had a distinctive South Beach look. He worked as a fashion model in Miami for about five years until he couldn't stand it anymore. The money was amazing, and the lifestyle was outrageous, but for Scott, it wasn't what he wanted. He hated being the center of attention and worrying about his appearance all the time. So he left modeling for good about a year before *Windsong Air* hired him.

I'm sure that the people we work with think that Scott and I are dating because we spend so much time together, but nothing could be further from the truth. Honestly, when I first met Scott, I wondered if he was gay. So many of the amazingly gorgeous guys in and around South Beach are, so it was sort of my first assumption. Plus, flight attending doesn't exactly attract a surplus of straight men! And while I've never come right out and asked, after knowing him for almost 10 years, I'm pretty sure I'd know if he was gay. But on the other hand, I'm also pretty sure he isn't into women either. He never dates, never talks about women he likes, and never mentions anything about wanting to get married or have a family. It's really quite strange.

So, I've finally come to the conclusion that Scott is asexual—he is a neutral being with no desire for pairing off. He seems to rise above the need for intimate bonding and the pettiness of the current dating rituals of our society. All I know is that he's an incredible friend to me, and there is never any pressure to discuss sex or dating—which is perfect for me, since neither one of those topics is a favorite of mine! We enjoy discussing books, going to plays, talking about human nature, and making fun of the absurd. It's a pure friendship that I treasure, and I get the feeling, Scott does, too.

As the elevator doors open, I step out into the lobby and look for Scott. As I scan the room, I see him sitting on a chrome bench near the fountain. He's wearing a cream colored linen suit with a sapphire blue shirt and brown leather shoes with no socks. He literally looks like he just stepped off the runway. He looks easy and elegant, and, as I walk toward him, he gives me a huge smile.

"Wow, Elle! You look fantastic!" he says as he rises to his feet. "Like a *long cool woman in a black dress*," he sings, doing his best rendition of the song by the Hollies.

"Oh, don't be ridiculous! But thanks…" I say as my smile widens.

I do have to admit; I *am* looking pretty good tonight. I'm wearing a dress I bought on a layover in Madrid. It's a black halter dress that hits me just below the knee and is made out of a stretchy crocheted fabric that hugs my body in exactly the right places. I've paired it with some strappy black sandals that make me look long and sleek. My hair is down, but I've managed to create a sexy tussled look by using an entire can of styling product. I've added some simple silver drop earrings, a tiny red shell bracelet and a sheer scarlet wrap to complete the look.

"I staked out this bench so we would have the best view of Gabby making her lobby entrance," Scott explains smugly as he guides me over to the bench.

For Scott, "Gabby watching" is a true form of entertainment. She's so vain and obvious most of the time that she provides tremendous fodder for his jokes—which to me are always side-splittingly funny. The fact that Gabby invited him to this boyfriend preview dinner proves she's completely oblivious to Scott's sarcasm, which makes the situation all the more funny!

As we sit and wait for Gabby, I try to decide how to drop my first hint about Italy. I'm tempted to just come right out and ask, but maybe subtlety is the right approach at first.

"So, is *Grazie* an *Italian* restaurant?" I cautiously venture in.

"I think so," Scott says as he casually checks his watch.

"I love Italian food—especially from the *Tuscan region*," I slip in as casually as possible as I adjust the bodice of my dress.

"I think this is Northern Italian cooking, actually, but it all tastes the same to me," Scott replies with no indication of taking the bait. This might be a bit trickier than I thought. Maybe he didn't get a letter and doesn't have a clue about the transfer—in which case I better stick to hinting around versus coming right out and asking.

Just as I'm about to set another hook in my conversation, the elevator doors part and Gabby makes her grand entrance. And what an entrance it is! Everyone in the lobby suddenly stops to stare as Gabby struts out of the elevator wearing a cobalt blue, skintight mini-dress. She's wearing silver spiked heels that make her look 10-feet tall and her hair is wildly flowing down her back. She's like a tanned goddess emerging from the elevator, and even I can't help but stare with my jaw agape.

"Look Elle!" Scott says in a low tone. "South Beach Barbie is finally here," he declares as he gently pulls me to the standing position. He waves his hand in the air to get Gabby's attention, and she blasts us with a stunning smile.

I instantly feel like a wallflower as she makes her way toward us. The whole room seems to revolve around Gabby, and I'm overcome with the control she seems to hold with her presence. Her confidence is incredibly powerful, and, suddenly, I wish that I could change places with her so I could know what it feels like to be that bold, that sexy and that unabashed.

Gabby air kisses me on both cheeks and then presents her hand to Scott for a twirl-around. As Scott indulges her, I notice that the back of her dress is missing—or at least that's how it looks to me! With the exception of two tiny blue lines crisscrossing her back, and a little swatch of fabric covering up her lovely bottom, she looks naked!

"You look amazing as usual, Miss Gabriel," Scott says to her as she gives her thick black hair a quick toss with her fingers.

"I know," Gabby says with a coy little smile. "I wanted tonight to be amazing, so I had to start with a sexy, amazing dress!" I notice Gabby holding her gaze on Scott, waiting for him to reaffirm that she is perfect.

Graciously, Scott adds, "Well, I think you've certainly set the tone for the evening!"

As I watch this exchange between Scott and Gabby, I suddenly realize that Gabby *is* amazing on the outside—her body is perfect, her face is flawless and her choice of dress is indeed incredible. But everything about her requires an audience to give her validation. As it turns out, I'm just one of the many spectators in her life, carefully positioned to make her feel like the star of her own little drama. I'm here because Gabby needs me to be here to feel special, and for no other reason.

"So, Elle, you look really...nice," Gabby offers after giving me the once-over. And before I can even reply, she adds, "But do you think you can drive in those heels? I was hoping you would drive..."

"I think I can manage," I say as I realize that I was wrong—I'm also here because Gabby needs a driver!

Chapter Four

As we make our way to the parking garage, Scott grabs my hand and gives it a little squeeze.

"Are you alright?" he asks me in a low tone so Gabby can't hear.

"Yeah! I'm great," I say as I squeeze his hand back and give him a big smile. "I think I'm just a little hungry, that's all," I add just to make sure I'm covered.

The truth is, I really don't feel like going out tonight—especially with Gabby. And there's all this added pressure of meeting her new boyfriend. Plus, I'm dying to find out if Scott knows about Italy. It just feels like everything about tonight is so much work—trying to impress everyone, trying to fish around for answers to my questions about the base transfer— the whole thing. But we're on our way, so I guess I'd better make the best of it.

Gabby reaches my car first and leans against the fender while she digs around in her evening bag. "Elle, do you have a compact?" she asks as she continues searching in her tiny beaded bag.

"I think there's one in my glove compartment," I say as I hit the unlock button on my car key. My car gives out a little "*beep*" as the doors unlock.

Gabby quickly opens the car door and starts opening up the compartments in search of a mirror. Scott walks around to the driver's side of the car and opens the door for me. As I slide in behind the wheel, I realize how lucky I am to have him as my friend. He gives me a sly wink, which makes me smile.

"Elle, you have to put the top up on the car," Gabby demands while she checks her lipstick in the tiny mirror she found in my glove compartment. "I don't want my hair to be all blown out when we get there."

"No problem," Scott says as he releases the latch on the convertible and carefully lifts it up and over the top of the car. Gabby gets out of the way for Scott as he pulls down the latch on the passenger side of the car and I pull down on the driver's side. In unison, we lock the top into place, and then Scott slips into the back seat.

Gabby slides into the front seat and gives a quick glance at the clock in my car. "We have to leave *now!*" she snaps, and I catch a faint whiff of alcohol on her breath. "We're already late as it is, and I don't want Manny to think I'm standing him up or something!"

Manny?

I manage to catch Scott's eye in my rearview mirror, and I can see him pulling a face. I guess I never asked for his name, and now that I know it, I feel somewhat amused.

When we finally reach the restaurant, Gabby is a bundle of nerves. She's checked her makeup in every available mirror in the car—including the rearview mirror while I was driving. I've never seen her act so nervous.

As I pull the car up to the valet stand, I gently grab her hand and say, "Gabby, you look perfect!"

She seems to relax a bit and gives me a huge smile and says, "Thank you, Elle. I just hope you and Scott like him!"

Before I have a chance to reply, the valet opens Gabby's door, which I guess is her cue to turn on the charm. She carefully swings her long legs around to the side and reaches for the valet's hand. In a smooth, sultry motion, she rises up out of the car and practically purrs like a kitten as she makes her way to the covered entrance. The valet can't seem to take his eyes off of Gabby as she tosses her wavy black hair around her shoulders and stops to wait for Scott and me to join her.

Scott manages to pull himself out of the backseat just before the distracted valet slams the door on him—which makes us both laugh out loud. After I'm sure I have everything I need, I hand my keys to another highly distracted valet who seems entranced by the sight of Gabby primping outside the restaurant. After a few tries, he finally rips off my parking ticket like a zombie and mumbles, "Have a lovely dinner..."

Once we enter the restaurant, Gabby leads us into the bar area. It's packed with elegant looking people, sipping on martinis and casually swirling big glasses filled with red wine. The décor is elegant with cherry-wood paneling and amber lighting. Tiny low tables are clustered together in the bar area, and everyone looks so glamorous. Bare shoulders and sun-kissed skin are in abundance as I watch Gabby make a beeline for a handsome man, leaning up against the main bar. His face lights up as he sees Gabby gliding toward him, and Scott and I pull back a little to give them a chance to greet one another.

Manny wraps his arms around Gabby and gives her a long deep kiss hello. I notice that people in the bar can't help but stare as Gabby's dress slides up the back of her tight brown thighs even further with Manny's embrace. As we wait patiently to be introduced, Scott whispers, "I can't *wait* to meet South Beach Ken!"

Me neither, I think as I try to see what he looks like. He's clearly taller than Gabby with dark brown hair and very tanned arms. He has on an expensive-looking watch and...oh my gosh...I think I see a pinky ring on his left hand!

Without saying a word to Scott, he gently nudges me in the arm and says, "Very *manly* pinky ring..." We both let out a little snicker.

Once Gabby and Manny finally pull apart, Gabby turns toward us and takes Manny by the hand to make her introductions. Gabby's face is flushed as she says, "These are two of my closest friends, Elle and Scott. And this is my boyfriend, *Dr.* Manny Ruiz!"

Scott and Manny shake hands first, and then Manny gives me a quick peck hello on the cheek. Now that I have a proper look at him, I see that he is indeed quite handsome. He has olive-green eyes with a gold flint that are quite striking with his warm brown skin. His smile is bright white with perfectly straight teeth and full lips. He's wearing dark green Bermuda shorts with a creamy yellow silk shirt and brown man sandals. His legs are muscular and smooth which makes me think he must work out a lot. Not exactly what I was expecting, but, as I watch Gabby drape herself over his shoulder, I see what a beautiful couple they make.

"I think our table is ready," Manny offers once the introductions are complete. "Unless you would like me to hold it so we can have drinks in the bar?"

"I think the table's fine with us," Scott answers as I nod my head in agreement. I'm relieved because I wasn't lying earlier when I told Scott that I was hungry, and the thought of prolonging this night makes me cringe.

As the hostess leads us to our table, I struggle to keep my balance as we glide through the maze of tables on what feels like extra slick, extra polished hardwood flooring. But I do manage to take in the room—which is gorgeously decorated with more cherry-wood paneling and tables dressed in white linen with gold-colored tea lights flickering in the center of each. Waiters dressed in starched, white shirts and long, gold aprons float around effortlessly, spoiling their customers with delicious looking food and wine.

As we make our way down into the heart of the dining room, Gabby pulls me back a step and whispers, "What do you think?"

Her face is still rosy and flushed, and I can see a strange sincerity in her eyes. Even though I can smell the wine on her breath, it's clear to me that she really wants me to approve of her boyfriend. And, honestly, I'm still baffled by the fact that my opinion matters so much to *Gabby* of all people.

"He seems really great, Gabby!" I reply, trying to sound supportive. "I think getting to know him over dinner will be really…nice," I add before it becomes too obvious to the guys that we are talking.

"Yeah—I think you're going to *love* him," Gabby giggles before she pulls away and catches up with Manny. She gives me one last glance over her shoulder as she slides her arm under Manny's. I understand that she really wants me to like him, so I resolve to give it my best. I will enter the situation with an open mind and give Manny a real chance.

Once we're all seated, and the wine we've ordered has been served, Manny opens up the conversation with the first question of the night: "So, Scott, how long have you and Elle been dating?"

"Oh, they're just friends," Gabby quickly interjects. "Actually, they're more like siblings than friends in a way," she continues with a little laugh. She's swirling her wine around in a big Merlot glass, trying to look sexy, and pretty much pulling it off.

"That's true," I offer as Scott and I look at each other and smile.

"So you two don't date?" Manny confirms.

"Nope…" Scott replies as he brings his wine glass to his lips. He pauses and then adds, "But Elle *is* one hell of a catch!"

"Thank you, Scott…" I say, "That was really sweet!"

I notice that Gabby is already pouring herself a second glass of wine and acting a little put out that she's not currently the center of attention. So to remedy that, I venture in with my first question of the night.

"So, Manny, Gabby tells us that you are a doctor?" I say as I lift my wine glass and give Gabby a quick smile. Gabby smiles back with a hint of pride.

"Yes I am. I'm just finishing up my internship, and soon I'll be starting a practice of my own," Manny explains while Gabby playfully rubs his ear lobe. She takes a deep swig of her wine and then leans her body against Manny's and stares back at me with a very satisfied look.

"What kind of medicine do you practice?" Scott inquires as I take a big bold sip of my wine.

"I'm an OB-GYN, actually," Manny says rather quickly before he brings his wine glass to his lips.

Did he just say he is an OB-GYN? I think as I swallow hard to avoid choking on the wine.

"Oh, so you're a gynecologist!" Scott clarifies with a wry grin on his face as I struggle hard to keep my composure.

Gabby is dating a gynecologist? Not that there's anything wrong with gynecology, but it does seem like it would be uncomfortable to date someone who examines women all day—every day—for a living!

"That's correct," Manny replies as he swirls the wine in his glass distractedly. "But I prefer to use the term OB-GYN—*for obvious reasons*," he adds, giving Scott a smug look in response. Gabby starts to pull away from Manny as a growing look of disbelief starts to spread across her face.

"You mean you're not a baby doctor?" Gabby asks as she sits back in her seat with a disappointed and slightly pouty look on her face—like she thinks she may have been lied to.

"Well, sweetie, OB-GYN's do a lot of things, including female pelvic exams and baby deliveries," Manny explains in a gentle tone as he caresses Gabby's cheek with the back of his index finger. "I thought you knew that."

"I did…" Gabby trials off, clearly confused by this new information.

"Anyway, I only have a few more months to go with my internship, and then I have plans to open my own fertility clinic here in Miami," Manny continues proudly. "I hope to have about three other docs join me—I'm just working out the business side of things now."

"Wow, that sounds…very exciting," I add, just to be polite. The truth is, nothing having to do with gynecology sounds "exciting" or even nice after what I went through earlier today, and I would love it if we could avoid any further discussion about what Manny does for a living!

Manny exits the conversation briefly in order to reassure Gabby with a long, slow kiss, while Scott whispers to me, "*Manny…the gynecologist? With a pinky ring? Who knew South Beach Ken would be so…interesting?*"

I do my best to stifle a giggle. The whole image is rather ironic. Manny: the male female doctor! And unlike my own gender-confused gynecologist, Manny has decided to *declare* his masculinity, right down to his name! Scott and I quietly relish our private little joke, while the two lovebirds across the table canoodle each other, oblivious to the rest of the world.

As I study the menu, I can't decide what to order—everything sounds so fancy and heavy. I lean over to Scott, with my latest, carefully planned question. "If you *lived* in Italy, what would you order for dinner?" I look up at him with my eyebrows raised, hoping he will read between the lines.

"If I *lived* in Italy?" Scott asks me with a crinkled brow. "I guess maybe the Chicken Florentine…" he trails off as he continues studying his menu.

Aha! A bite! He knows! He said Chicken Florentine, *as in* Florence!

Or…did he just notice that the special for tonight is Chicken Florentine? Oh for crying out loud! I thought Scott said this place served

Northern Italian food! Now I'm even more confused, and I have no idea how to fish for answers. I guess I really don't know enough about Italy or the *Tuscan region* to be subtle anymore. If I'm going to be clever about this, I'm going to need a better strategy.

"Elle, are you alright?" Manny asks me as I stare off into space, trying to develop my next Italy query for Scott.

"Oh, I'm fine!" I say, a little surprised by Manny's interest in my well-being.

"I can't get over how familiar you look," Manny says to me as he leans forward in his chair. His face is all contorted as though he is straining to place my face.

I cock my head slightly and study his face, too, trying to find some trace of a familiar feature. He looks like any number of gorgeous men walking the streets of South Beach, but I don't recall ever meeting him before.

"Maybe you've seen me when you've picked Gabby up for a date at *The Wiley* or something," I offer to help jog his memory. "I live right across the hall from her."

"No...I don't think that's it..." Manny continues to stare at my face, making me feel rather uncomfortable to say the least.

Finally, Gabby jumps in and says, "Manny, you don't know Elle! She never goes out!" It's suddenly obvious to everyone that Gabby is drunk. "She and her big, mean doggie stay home all the time, just sitting on their *butts!* Get it? Butts!" Gabby starts laughing hysterically, looking to Scott to join her.

Manny gives Gabby a strange look and says, "No, I don't get it..."

"Her last name is *Butts!* She and her dog stay at home and *sit on their butts!*" she repeats with a slur, just to make sure he got it this time.

"You're name is *Elle Butts?*" Manny asks with the look of surprise spreading across his face. "As in *Eloise Butts?*"

Normally, this question would take me back to days of my youth when someone would be amused by my name, but as his face widens with surprise, I instantly put it all together. Gynecology intern. Good-looking face. Knows my *real name* although no one here has said it. Oh my gosh!

He's one of Dr. Crosby's interns—the one that was watching me run out of the office today!

A cold queasy sweat comes over my body as I say, "Yes…that's my name…"

"And my name's Scott LaMotte!" Scott enters the conversation with a defensive tone and bewildered look on his face. "So what?"

"Oh, it's just that I've heard your name before. You're a patient of Dr. Crosby's, right?" Manny asks me to be sure he's finally solved the mystery.

"Yep…" I confirm as I feel myself slip into a state of shock. I gulp down the last swish of wine in my glass and feel a red flush spread across my body. I can't believe this is happening! Will this day ever end?

"You were in for a checkup today, is that right?" Manny continues.

"Yes I was…" I say, while sending up a prayer that he doesn't ask any more questions, or—God forbid—blurt out any personal information about me in front of Scott and Gabby!

"I knew I knew you!" Manny says with an excited look on his face. "I think you met Dr. Miller today, too. She's one of the docs I'm going to be starting my practice with," Manny continues with a big smile and a knowing look on his face.

Well, there you go! That confirms it! Manny knows my secret! I can't believe this is happening. I want to crawl under the table or maybe make a mad dash for the door, but I know I can't do that. I look across the table at Gabby, hoping maybe she can help me transition the topic of conversation back to her. But as I meet her gaze, she seems to be giving me an evil look, which is both penetrating and slightly unnerving!

Manny puts his elbows up on the table and begins twisting his pinky ring around his finger while he takes me in. He opens his mouth slightly as he breaths in and out, and then ever so subtly licks his bottom lip. I feel all fidgety and totally aware that he is sizing me up, thinking about the fact that I've never had sex. I can tell that he's suddenly more interested in me than the sure-thing sitting next to him. I can see that Manny the predator has arrived, and I am his new prey. And like a defenseless animal, I feel panicked as I search for cover!

I give Scott a little nudge under the table and a pleading look. There's no way to explain to him exactly what's going on, but I pray he's able to pick up on the fact that I'm in danger. My heart is pounding inside my chest, as I realize that this can't end well.

"So, Manny," Scott asks in an attempt to change the subject. "How did you and the beautiful Gabriel meet?" Scott looks at Gabby when he asks the question, I'm sure in hopes of complimenting the tension out of the situation.

"We met at *Bash*," Gabby says flatly as she starts to get up out of her chair. Her eyes are watery and intense as she stares me down. "Elle, I need to use the ladies room. Why don't you join me?"

"OK," I reply, thankful for the opportunity to get away from Manny but slightly nervous about being alone with Gabby in her obvious state of anger.

As I rise up out of my chair, both Manny and Scott stand up. I give Scott a quick look of fear as I lift my purse off the back of my chair. I can feel both Manny and Scott watching us as we make our way to the bathroom. Gabby stumbles over her feet and grabs my shoulder in an effort to avoid falling. I instinctively put my arm around her to hold her up.

"Take your hands off of me, you boyfriend robber!" she hisses at me as she pushes me away.

"What?" I say in disbelief. She can't honestly think I was trying to *steal* her boyfriend! I can't think of anything more absurd!

"You know you were hitting on him. Just admit it, Elle!"

"Gabby, I was *not* hitting on your boyfriend! He just recognized me because I was at the doctor's office where he works today. That's it! Nothing more!" I plead with her as I start to open the door leading into the ladies room.

"Don't play innocent with me, Elle. I saw the way you were looking at Manny and don't think I didn't notice how you wanted to make sure he knew that you and Scott were *just friends*!"

"Gabby, you were the one who told him Scott and I were 'like siblings,' not me!" I snap back in disbelief as I huff through the doorway.

She really is drunk, I think as I walk over to the sink and begin washing my hands out of nervousness. Gabby leans in over the counter and begins checking her makeup. She hasn't said anything to me since we entered the ladies room, and I wonder if she's starting to realize that I have nothing to do with Manny's behavior.

I catch both of our reflections in the mirror. Gabby is stunning. Her long black hair is tussled about her face, and her dark red lips are smooth and luscious. From all appearances, she seems to be every guy's dream girl—gorgeous, dim-witted when she needs to be, cunning when she wants to be and sexually expressive—right down to her tiny blue dress.

And then there's me—the slender, pale blonde standing next to the goddess in the mirror. I feel positively transparent as I see myself standing next to Gabby. There is nothing exotic or alluring about me. And Gabby was right earlier when she said that I was dull. I *am* dull, and predictable. But that's one of the things I like the most about myself. I'm safe and I know who I am. I know that no matter what I look like, I will recognize myself in the mirror at the end of the day and be able to look myself in the eye with no regrets.

"Gabby?" I venture in gently, hoping to smooth things over. "Maybe Scott and I should just leave you and Manny to have a nice dinner alone. We haven't even ordered anything yet…"

"Stop!" Gabby interrupts me sharply. "I just want to know what's going on with you and Manny. I mean, he said he *knows you* already," Gabby says as her face crumbles. "Elle, you have to tell me the truth," she whispers to me as her eyes start to rim out with tears. "Did he ask you out today at the doctor's office?"

"No, Gabby! No! I didn't even meet him today," I assure her as I grab a tissue to dab her tears. "One of his fellow interns did my exam, that's all, and I guess he just remembered my name…" I can't bring myself to share more than that, and really, that's all she needs to know anyway.

"Really?" Gabby looks down at me as she wipes her nose.

"Really, Gabby! I promise!"

"Well, why was he looking at you like that? And why did he seem so interested in *you*?" Gabby questions as she grabs another tissue and starts blotting her cheeks.

"Honestly, Gabby, I don't know." But in truth, I think I do know. Her awful boyfriend saw me as a conquest and suddenly turned from her devoted knight in shining armor into a bloodthirsty game hunter, looking to mount my head on his wall. I feel disgusted at the thought, but it's not like I haven't had guys react to me this way before—albeit, not under these exact circumstances, of course!

"Listen, I'm gonna call Scott on his cell phone and tell him to make up some sort of excuse for us to leave. OK?" I offer.

Gabby takes a deep breath and considers my plan. "What will Scott say?" she asks.

"I don't know, but I'm sure he'll think of something," I say as I start digging in my purse for my cell phone.

"I don't want him to make a scene," Gabby says, suddenly sounding more like her self.

I ignore her as I dial Scott's number and cross my fingers that he doesn't say my name when he sees it pop up on his caller ID.

"Hello?" *Whew! So far so good...*

"Scott, I'm in the bathroom with Gabby. You have to come up with an excuse for us to leave!"

"Oh, you're kidding!" Scott says like he's shocked.

"No, I'm not kidding..." I say, and then realize he is starting the theatrics for Manny's benefit already.

"What time do I need to be at the airport?" Scott says, starting to play out the excuse.

"Scott, we have to go *right now!*" I demand, fully realizing how badly I want to avoid more contact with Manny.

"No worries," Scott says. "I'm on my way." Scott hangs up the phone. The stage has been set. Now all Gabby and I have to do is return to the table and act surprised that Scott got an urgent call from work.

"Gabby, Scott's going to tell us as we walk up to the table that work called, and he has to get to the airport to pick up a trip. OK?" I explain as I grab Gabby's shoulders.

"OK..." she trails off, like she's still working things out in her head. "But, Elle? Scott can't accept a trip! He's been drinking," Gabby says with a worried look on her face.

"Gabby! It's just *a story* so we can get out of here. It's just a story!" I say in exasperation.

"Oh! Of course!" she says as I can practically hear the penny drop. "OK, so you have to drive him because you drove us here—right?"

"Exactly. So act surprised when we get to the table. Can you do that, Gabby?" I'm worried that in the state she's in, she'll blow the whole thing.

"Yes, I can handle it, Elle. I just don't know what I'm going to say to Manny once we're alone..." she trails off.

"Gabby, honestly, I think you are misreading the whole situation. You've had a few glasses of wine, and because you're tipsy, things just seem...strange. Seriously, there's nothing to worry about here. Just join Manny back at the table and once Scott and I are gone, you can have a wonderfully romantic evening!" I feel as though I am pleading with Gabby, but it doesn't seem to be working.

"Well, I don't know if I can now that I've seen the way he was looking at *you*!" Gabby looks furious again. "I always thought you were the kind of person I could trust because you are so...plain...and boring... I mean men who like me could never be interested in someone like *you*. Right?"

"Of course not—they would *never* consider me over you, Gabby! Believe me—I'm still the same plain, boring person I've always been... And whatever you think you saw between Manny and me is all in your imagination. There's no way he could be interested in me over you—no way!" I don't have the time or the inclination to acknowledge how insulting this conversation should be to me because I'm so focused on getting out of the restaurant—and fast!

"OK..." Gabby finally concedes as she turns to give herself one last look in the mirror. She carefully drags her pinky finger underneath her eye and then pulls away from the mirror to make sure everything still looks perfect. "Of course he's not interested in *you*…" she says as she gives me a once-over in the mirror, too.

"Alright then. Let's just go to the table and take Scott's lead. OK?"

Gabby takes a deep breath and says, "Alright. I'm ready."

As we make our way back to the table, I can see that Scott is already standing. He's sliding his wallet into his coat pocket as we approach.

"Oh there you are!" Scott says in mock panic. "I'm so sorry, Gabby, but Elle and I are going to have to leave. I just got a call from work, and I need to have Elle drop me off at the airport." Scott is draping my evening wrap over my shoulders as he talks, and I am doing my best to have a surprised facial expression.

"Are you sure you can't just take a cab to the airport?" Manny asks as Scott starts to push me away from the table.

"No!" I say a little too forcefully. "I mean, I couldn't have Scott take a cab… I'm happy to drive him," I say as I link my arm under Scott's. "It was great to meet you, Manny, and I hope that our quick departure doesn't spoil your evening," I offer with an apologetic look on my face.

Before I can move, Manny is suddenly standing up and reaching for my hand. My body goes wire tight as he plants a kiss right in the center of my hand and says, "It was wonderful to meet you, Eloise Butts. I hope to see more of you someday…"

I look over at Gabby, who is staring in disbelief as her boyfriend holds my hand in his. I quickly pull my hand back and say, "Have a nice evening…"

Scott and I practically run out of the restaurant to the valet stand. As we wait for my car, we both keep looking over our shoulders. I don't know who I'm expecting to see—Manny or Gabby. But either one would be an unwelcome sight!

Neither one of us says a word until we are safely inside my car. Scott is driving, and I'm fidgeting with my seatbelt, trying to get it to lock into place. Once it finally clicks into position, I bring my hands to my face. I don't know if I'm going to laugh or cry.

"What just happened in there?" Scott begins with a tone of both amusement and disbelief.

"I don't even know…" I trail off as I try to sort everything out for myself. "I don't even know where to begin, Scott."

"Why don't you tell me everything over dinner—how does my apartment sound? We could order a pizza?"

"That sounds *perfect!*" I say as we speed away from the restaurant.

"And maybe we can even open up a bottle of *Tuscan wine?*" Scott says as a huge smile spreads across his face.

Chapter Five

Scott and I agree to meet in the lobby after we change our clothes. The plan is to take Sugar Ray for a nice walk on the beach while we wait for the pizza to be delivered. So I quickly change out of my dress and slide on an easy pair of jeans, a t-shirt and some old rubber flip-flops. I grab Sugar Ray's leash on the way out the door, and we quickly make our way to the service elevator. A little chill rushes up my spine as we pass the door to Gabby's apartment. I just hope they don't come back to her place tonight. I don't think I can handle another Manny encounter.

When the doors of the service elevator open into the parking garage, Scott is already waiting for us. He has on faded blue jeans and a gauzy cotton shirt. Sugar Ray starts to shake and dance around, obviously very happy to see his good buddy. Scott bends down and rubs my dog's head and gives him a few solid slaps on the side, which only gets Sugar Ray more excited. We slip down the back stairs that lead to the beach. When we reach the bottom, Scott takes my hand while Sugar Ray runs out into the water.

The surf is pounding, and the breeze is wet and tastes salty. I love being outside at night, feeling the balminess of the ocean against my skin and the crunchiness of the sand under my feet. It seems like out here, your problems find new perspective—suddenly, everything seems small in comparison to the vastness of the deep dark ocean churning away. We walk silently for a while, watching Sugar Ray jump the waves and kick up sand as he speeds down the shoreline. I feel safe right now, here with Scott and my thoughts. I don't really want to shift the mood, but I know I need to draw Scott in. After all, he helped me escape a bad scene; now the least I can do is offer him some sort of explanation.

"So…you're probably wondering what was going on back at the restaurant," I tentatively begin.

"The questions *have* started to stack up…" Scott replies gently as a warm smile spreads across his face.

"I don't even know how to explain it. This day has been so… embarrassing," I say as I release Scott's hand and start fiddling with Sugar Ray's leash.

"Elle, I think I kind of already know…" Scott confides as he leads us toward a set of empty beach chairs. I call for Sugar Ray and he comes racing over as Scott and I stretch out on a set of lounge chairs. Sugar Ray starts digging a hole in the sand next to my chair.

"Did Manny tell you something while we were in the ladies room?" I ask as I feel my face heat up with mortification.

"Well, he didn't exactly *tell* me anything, but I sort of put it all together based on the questions he was asking me about you." Scott is looking out to the ocean as he says this, as though he is as uncomfortable as I am right now.

"What did he ask you?" I inquire as a sinking feeling settles into the pit of my stomach.

"He just asked a bunch of questions about your dating experiences and if I had ever 'fooled around' with you—that kind of stuff…" Scott trails off like there is more, but he wants to spare me the details.

"And what did you say?" My heart is beating with a slow, hard thud inside my chest as I wait for Scott to answer me.

"I just told him that I respect you as my friend and that the two of us have always been just friends, and that even if you had shared private things about your past with me, it was not right to share those things with him. He was adamant on finding out more about your likes and dislikes when it comes to men, but I told him that we don't talk about that kind of thing." Scott is looking at me now as he continues, "He seemed to know something personal about you from your exam today, and that bit of information made you incredibly attractive to him."

"Yeah…I noticed," I say as I stare out into the ocean.

"Elle?" Scott's voice is calm and gentle. "You're still a virgin, aren't you?"

His words hang in the damp air for a beat, and I find that I'm actually relieved that he figured it out so I don't have to say it out loud again today.

"Yes…" I say in a voice that's barely above a whisper as I tip my head back against the rubbery slats of the lounge chair and shut my eyes.

Scott doesn't say anything. He just leans his head back against his chair, too, and lets out a little sigh. We sit there for what feels like hours, just listening to the surf and letting our thoughts wash in and out with the tide. A tiny beeping sound shakes me from the spell I'm in, and I watch Scott fumble around in his pocket.

"The pizza should be here by now, so we should probably head back," Scott says as he shuts off the alarm on his cell phone.

"Oh right," I say as I fully return to reality.

As we start making our way back to *The Wiley*, I feel somehow lighter, like maybe everything that's happened today isn't that important after all. So my secret's out. Who cares? For Scott and me, nothing's changed—we're still the same. And Manny is just a jerk—a jerk that likely won't be dating Gabby for much longer anyway. These revelations flood me with relief as I start to chase Sugar Ray down the beach. Scott follows me, and, suddenly, we are both laughing hysterically and pushing each other into the surf.

Ten minutes later, we are all toweled off and I'm sitting at the island bar in Scott's apartment, eating pizza. Sugar Ray is sitting at my feet with his head cocked to the side waiting for me to drop him a pizza crust while Scott is opening up a bottle of red wine.

"So Elle," Scott says as he struggles to pull the cork out of the wine bottle. "Does this sudden fascination with Tuscany have anything to do with a certain letter you got in the mail?" Scott is looking at me with a wry look.

"So you *did* get a letter!" I shout in relief. "I wasn't sure so I was trying to hint around all night, but you seemed to be ignoring me!" I playfully slap Scott's shoulder from across the counter in mock anger.

"Well, I wasn't sure if you knew either—I mean I got my letter days ago, but you never let on that you knew anything about it. I was afraid to say anything to you because I thought maybe they didn't offer it to you," Scott explains as he carefully pours us both some wine in big round glasses.

"I didn't pick up my mail this week until today," I sheepishly admit to him as I wipe the pizza grease off my fingers with a paper towel and reach for my wine. "And then I was afraid to open it! I thought it was going to be bad news! But then it was this incredible news that pretty much seems too good to be true!"

"It is pretty incredible, isn't it?" Scott says after he rolls a sip of wine in his mouth. "Did you call corporate yet to tell them you're going?"

"That's the thing. I was so late in opening the letter that I nearly missed the cut off date. And now with only one day to think it over, I feel sort of rushed. I haven't even told my parents yet or anything!" I can feel the panic rising in my voice as I consider the urgency of this decision.

"Elle—calm down!" Scott jumps in with a big smile on his face. "It's not a big deal. The cut off is tomorrow at noon—that's when the next set of letters will go out based on how many more people they need to recruit. So you still have plenty of time to think it over." Scott stops talking and holds his wine glass very still as he peers down into it. "Although I can't imagine what you have to consider!"

"I know...you're right. It's so obvious, but after I read the letter, I started to get all worried about what to do with Sugar Ray and how to prepare to leave my life here for three long months," I explain as I pull a pepperoni off my slice and stick it in my mouth.

"Elle, three months is *not* a long time, and I'm sure that nothing will happen to your life here in Miami while you are away. And you know Sugar Ray will be fine—you can just have Violet keep him. I'm sure she'll do it in a heart beat."

Violet Harper is my dog walker, and truth be known, I often worry that she actually spends more time with my dog in a week than I do! But Scott's right. I'm sure Violet will keep Sugar Ray—and the most depressing part is that he probably won't even miss me!

"I know…I guess I just needed to know that you were going, too," I say as I look up at him. "I'm not especially adventurous on my own, as you know…"

"Well, lucky for you, I'm adventurous enough for both of us, and I am definitely going! So now all you need to do is call corporate first thing in the morning, and in less than four weeks, the two of us will be off to Tuscany!" Scott raises his wine glass with a huge smile on his face.

So I raise my glass, too, and toast, "To Tuscany!"

For the rest of the night, Scott and I talk about what other crewmembers we think are going and what to bring. I feel slightly dizzy as we discuss all there is to do and to see while we are abroad—I can't believe I'm going to Italy! By 2:00 a.m., I realize just how tired I am, so Scott offers to ride down the service elevator with me, so I can let Sugar Ray out one more time before we go to bed.

After Sugar Ray finishes his business, I clip on his leash as Scott and I walk back toward the elevator. Just as we round the corner, Scott pulls me into an alcove that leads to the storage lockers with a sudden jerk. Adrenaline starts to course through my body as my brain tries to understand what's going on.

"It's Gabby!" Scott finally whispers in my ear. "She and Manny are sitting in his car in front of the entrance!"

"Oh no…" I moan. "Did she see us?" I ask as I pull on Sugar Ray's leash to keep him out of sight. He looks up at me with a confused look, but finally decides to sit down on top of my foot.

"I don't think so," Scott says as he carefully peers around the corner to get another look. "It looks like Gabby is upset—she's waving her hands while she talks and Manny looks like he's angry, too."

"Well, that may be good news for me—it doesn't sound like the makings of a sleep-over tonight! I've had this awful vision of seeing him in the hallway tomorrow morning or something," I confess in a hushed tone.

"OK…" Scott reports. "It looks like Gabby is getting out of the car…or maybe not…" he trails off. "Ouch! She just slapped Manny across the face!"

Amusement seems to spread across Scott's face as he continues peering around the corner to provide the play-by-play while Sugar Ray and I stay crammed up against the wall.

I can hear a loud thud that ricochets through the parking garage. Sugar Ray lets out a little growl, so I reach down and put my hand on his head to keep him from barking. "What just happened?" I whisper to Scott.

"Gabby just got out and slammed the door of Manny's car! And now Manny is saying something to Gabby—and if his hand gestures are any indication, he isn't telling her that he had a lovely evening!"

I let out a nervous laugh. "I know I sound crazy, but I do feel sorry for Gabby," I admit as I wait for Scott to tell me what happens next. "She was so excited about her *doctor*, but he turned out to be a huge *pervert!*" I practically spit the word as I consider how terribly Manny behaved at dinner.

"Step back!" Scott whispers with panic in his voice as his long arm swings around so he can shove me up against the wall. "The pervert is circling around!"

I pull hard on Sugar Ray's leash as we all three try to melt into the tiny alcove. Manny's car speeds by us with a deep rumble as Scott carefully peers around the wall to make sure he is leaving.

"Wow, he looks pissed!" Scott says after the car exits the garage.

"I wonder how Gabby is?" I say with apprehension in my voice. "When we were in the bathroom, she actually accused me of trying to steal her boyfriend!" I say, still in disbelief, as we make our way to the service elevator. "Knowing Gabby, she may hold me responsible for this mess!"

"I think you can count on that!" Scott says, which sort of surprises me. "In Gabby world, nothing is ever explained using reason."

"Do you think she's going to try to confront me tonight?" I ask with a nervous feeling sweeping over me.

"It wouldn't surprise me if she did..." Scott trails off. "Do you want to crash at my place?"

"Yeah...I think I do."

As golden sunlight streams into the room, I scramble to get my bearings. Once I fully wake up, I discover that I have a horrible pain in my neck from sleeping on the strange sofa in Scott's apartment. He wanted me to take his bed, but I couldn't do that. So Sugar Ray and I camped out in his living room with a soft blanket and purple suede throw pillow for my head. Not the best sleeping arrangement, but at least I didn't have to worry about Gabby pounding on my door.

I look around for Sugar Ray, but he's nowhere to be found. I call out for him in a raspy whisper, but he's gone. Scott must have taken him for a quick walk. I strain to see the time display on Scott's microwave—it's 7:17, but it feels much earlier. I feel like a bus or something sideswiped me and left my body bruised and stiff. I'm sure it's just a combination of a very bad day and a short night's sleep on a couch that's barely fit for sitting let alone sleeping! Just as I start to lift my body off the sofa, I can hear the doorknob rattle.

Seconds later, Sugar Ray is bounding through the door. "Man that dog is frisky in the morning!" Scott says in a breathy tone. "I was throwing a stick for him, and I think he would have been happy to fetch it for me all day!"

"That's my boy!" I say as I rub Sugar Ray all over. "Did you get much sleep last night?" I ask Scott as he makes his way into the kitchen area.

"Yeah—I slept great. How 'bout you?" he asks with a concerned look on his face.

"I'm fine. But I sure do have a lot to do today before noon!" I say as I start thinking of my initial action plan for the day. "But first things first! I need to get up to my apartment and feed this hungry boy!" I say to Sugar Ray as his tail wags in anticipation of food.

"Is there anything I can do to help you out today, Elle?" Scott offers as he starts making a pot of coffee.

"Nope! Not a thing. But I'll call you later, OK?"

"Sounds great. Oh, and let me know if you have a run-in with South Beach Barbie!" he adds as his face crinkles into a smile.

"Yeah, I'll be sure to do that," I say sarcastically as I gather up my things.

When the service elevator opens onto the 17th floor, everything seems so quiet. As we turn the corner and head down the hallway to my apartment, my heart starts to beat a little harder. I try to comfort myself with the fact that Gabby is probably still sleeping and won't be up for hours. But still, I can't shake this nagging feeling that I'm going to have an awkward encounter with her at some point today.

Once we're inside my apartment, I start to feel much better. I quickly measure out some food for Sugar Ray and dump it in his feeding bowl while I start to make a mental checklist for the rest of the day. First, I'll call my mom and see if we can have breakfast. She'll want to hear all about the transfer, and it'll be easier to fill in the details in person.

My dog walker should be here around 8:15 to take Sugar Ray to the park, so I'll find out if she can handle a three-month dog-sitting gig. Then, when I'm on my way to meet my mom, I'll call the corporate office and let them know that I'm on board for the base transfer. I still have about twenty minutes before Violet is scheduled to arrive, so I decide I better make my plans with my mom and get showered and changed for the rest of the day.

My mom is her typical sunshiny self when I reach her on the phone, and she agrees to meet me at our favorite French café on Miami Beach at 9:30. So with those plans confirmed, I hop in the shower while I try to mentally figure out what to wear for the day. I finally settle on a blue sundress with silver beaded flip-flops. To save time, I decide to pull my damp hair up into a twist and then add a squirt of ginger perfume behind each ear. As I fumble around with my watchband, I can hear the front door rattle and a familiar voice greeting Sugar Ray.

Once I make my way down the hallway into the kitchen area, I see Violet Harper hunched down in the squat position, kissing and hugging my dog as he slathers her in his own kisses of affection. I lean against the wall and watch the two of them as they communicate in their own special way. Suddenly, Violet turns and sees me and pops up to her feet.

"Hello, Elle!" she says nervously—like I've busted her doing something wrong. "I didn't realize you'd be home. I guess I should've knocked first..."

"Don't be silly, Violet! No harm done! It's good to see you!" I say as I give her a warm little hug.

Violet is quite a sight. From the front, she has a tight crew cut hairstyle that reveals an honest and loving face, while in the back, there's about 10 inches of flowing, sun-damaged hair with an orangish-yellow tint. The female mullet is not a hairstyle you typically see on the women walking the streets of South Beach, but it is part of what makes Violet so unique and, quite frankly, so loveable to me.

Violet is a single lady in her mid to late forties who openly admits that she prefers animals to people. Typically, Violet wears cut off jean shorts that hit just above the knee and dark-colored, baggy T-shirts that promote all of her favorite rock bands—Def Leopard, Guns N' Roses and AC/DC to name a few. To cap off this look, Violet usually wears a pair of old, thick high tops and a black fanny pack, which she uses to keep track of all of her dog walking supplies.

Violet started out walking Sugar Ray and three other dogs in my neighborhood after she lost her job as a county road construction worker. But now, she has 20 dogs in the area to tend to every day and is making more money than she ever has in her life. And, even as the demand for her service grows, she's just as easy going as ever, and she still makes me feel like my dog is the only one that matters.

The truth is, without Violet, I wouldn't be able to keep Sugar Ray—there's no way I could do it on my own. Even if I don't have an overnight layover somewhere, my day trips can be pretty long, and it would be cruel to keep a dog under those conditions. There are a few other flight attendants living at *The Wiley* that have little lap dogs, which they shove into oversized purses like they're Paris Hilton or something and then tote them along on their trips—which is *totally* against the rules, but so far, no one's ever been busted.

Sugar Ray is way too big to sneak on my trips—not that I would do it even if I could—and he requires a lot of maintenance, so Violet is indispensable to me. Small dogs and cats are allowed at *The Wiley*, but I had to get special permission from Wiley Bennett himself before I could even bring Sugar Ray into the building. Luckily, Mr. Bennett loves Boxers, too, and agreed to allow Sugar Ray to live with me—as long as I hired a full time dog sitter.

"I'm surprised to see you here," Violet admits as she hooks her thumbs in the front pockets of her jean shorts. Her short, stocky legs buckle at the knees as she holds her stance in the entryway of the apartment. "I had it in my notes that you were going to need me today."

"I *do* need you today!" I say brightly as I motion for Violet to follow me into the living room. "I originally had a trip but they canceled it earlier in the week, so I made some other plans, and I decided to keep Sugar Ray on your schedule."

"That's fine, " Violets says as she follows me over to the sofa.

"Actually, Violet, there's something I need to ask you," I start in once we are both seated—Violet on the sofa and me on one of the purple corkscrew chairs. So far, the longest I've ever left Sugar Ray in Violet's care was five days, so what I'm about to ask of her makes me kind of nervous. "I've been asked to take a three month base transfer to Italy, which means that I am going to need someone to keep Sugar Ray while I'm away." I try to study Violet's reaction, but her face is blank as usual.

"I see..." she trails off. "When do you have to go?" Violet looks up at me as she expertly works the zippers on her fanny pack in search of her trusty date book.

"We don't leave for another few weeks or so, but before I called and accepted the transfer, I wanted to make sure that you could handle the extended time with Sugar Ray."

"Sure... I think I can do it," Violet says as she flips ahead three weeks in her calendar. "As long as I can keep Ray here during the day—between his regular walks and such—while I tend to my other pals."

"Of course! You can have regular access to this place—whatever you need to make it work. The main thing is, as you know, Sugar Ray can't stay alone all night. It's fine with me if you want to take him back to your place or crash here—whatever works best for you."

"That'd be fine. I don't see why it couldn't work," Violet says with no emotion or change in her voice.

"I don't know what you will need to charge for this extra work, but why don't you think about it then let me know," I say as I realize this may cost me a small fortune, so I better get the quote up front.

"Alright," Violet says after a short pause. "I'll think about it and let ya know later on today."

"Oh thank you so much, Violet! I wasn't going to go if you couldn't keep him!" I gush as I feel a sense of relief and the reality of the situation flooding over me. *I'm going to Italy!! I'm going to live in Italy for three months!*

"No problem. You know I'm crazy about ole Ray," Violet says as she reaches down to pet my dog, who, incidentally is camped out by *her* feet.

"I think the feeling is mutual," I add as I look at the two of them.

Once Sugar Ray and Violet leave for the park, I flip through the packet of papers from the corporate office and fill out all the sheets that have to be turned in before the deadline. After I meet with my mom, I think I'll swing by the office and personally deliver everything, just to make sure I am officially going.

Excitement is pumping through my body as I zip around my apartment, tossing things into my purse. There's so much to do before I go! So much to plan! I glance at my watch and realize I need to meet my mom in less than 30 minutes, so I scurry out of my apartment and make my way to the main elevator. It isn't until I'm riding down in the elevator that I think of Gabby. I was so preoccupied with everything else that I didn't even worry about seeing her in the hallway.

I take a deep breath and I feel a smile warm across my face. I'm embarking on a new chapter in my life, and nothing can spoil the thrill of that for me today! Nothing!

Chapter Six

As I walk through the doorway of the café, I see my mother sitting in the corner reading a magazine with her reading glasses perched on her nose. I haven't seen my mom in a few weeks and a sudden rush of affection comes over me as I look at her.

She is still very attractive, even now in her sixties. She has soft, shoulder-length, brown hair with a few silvery highlights woven throughout and her skin is fresh and smooth—with the exception of a few papery laugh lines around her bright green eyes. She is in good shape with long, slender legs that lead up to a small waist and full chest. She's wearing brown, leather sandals and cream trousers with a chocolate-colored, linen blouse. On her wrists are several turquoise bracelets that are as familiar to me as my mother's pretty face.

"Mom?" I say in a low voice as I approach the table.

"Hello, Eloise!" she says as she rises up out of her chair and slides her reading glasses on top of her head. She carefully walks around the table and wraps her arms around me. She smells like Mom—like minty Crest toothpaste mixed with Cover Girl lipstick and baby powder. I breathe her in and realize how much I love having this woman as my mother.

"How are you, Sweetheart?" she says as she pulls away to get a "proper" look at me. Her face is beaming, as she looks me over with pride.

"I'm great, Mom—I have so much to tell you, but it's all great!" I say as the words quickly tumble out of my mouth.

"Well, have a seat and let's get you some tea," she says as she waves to our waiter over my shoulder.

My mother and I have been coming to this French café for nearly 20 years. It was a Saturday morning tradition for us to come here for a little one-on-one time when I was a teenager. Now it is the place we meet whenever we need to catch up. And over the years, nothing has changed—not even the waiters. Sure, everyone looks a little bit grayer, but their faces still have the same smug indifference, and the pastries are still out of this world. As our waiter approaches the table, my mother greets him with a happy smile.

"Jean-Claude, we'll take another pot of tea and bring us two chocolate croissants please," my mother says as she gives me a wink.

"*Oui Madame,*" Jean-Claude says with no change in his demeanor as he sulks off to fill our order.

"So, tell me everything!" my mother says as she closes her magazine and tucks it into her oversized leather purse. Then she leans forward in her chair with the look of great anticipation on her face.

I take a deep breath before I begin. "Well, something big is happening at work and I'm really excited about it!" I gush. "They are sending two crews over to *Italy* for three months, and they asked me if I wanted to go!"

I'm searching my mom's face for excitement, but her expression seems to fall and a look of confusion is there instead. "Italy? They are sending you to Italy? To work?"

"Yes!" I say enthusiastically as I struggle to get my mom to see the thrill of it all. "The company is expanding the business to include Europe so they're building new bases for the airline, and we're going to help them get it started. We'll be working out of Florence the entire time, but the company arranged for us to be able to travel *for free* on other airlines while we're over there so we can explore Europe on our days off! Isn't this fantastic news?" I say with a hopeful glimmer in my voice.

"My goodness, Eloise. That's a lot to take in all at once," she says as she adds a drop of milk to her tea. She begins stirring distractedly as she processes the information. "How long do you have to think it all over, Sweetheart?"

"Actually, Mom, I already accepted the offer," I say, omitting the part about how I did it over the phone this morning while I was driving over to meet her. "I just have to drop off the paperwork at the corporate office on my way home today, and it's all set." I can see my mother is struggling to process what I'm saying.

"Oh…I see. Well then…how lovely!" she says with forced happiness in her voice.

Jean-Claude returns to our table with my pot of tea and two fresh chocolate croissants. I carefully pour myself a cup of tea as a pit of worry settles in my stomach. I'm not sure what to think of my mom's reaction. I just figured she'd be happy for me, but, somehow, she seems to be saddened by the news.

"Mom, it's just for three months," I start in as my mother begins to pick at her croissant. "That's all it is, and I think we'll be helping to train the permanent crews they will be hiring in Europe. It's just a short transfer—and we're going to be able to keep our apartments at *The Wiley* during the transfer and everything…" I trail off before I add, "Mom, why do you seem so sad? This is a *good thing!*"

"Oh Eloise…I know it is. I'm sorry. It's just that I don't like the thought of you living so far from home," she says as she looks up at me for the first time since I shared the news. "I was so much younger than you are when I left my home in Essex to come to America, but I can remember how terrified my mother was to let me go. And I remember promising her that I was only going to stay for one year. *One year* was all I was going to stay! That was how long I told her I needed in order to *find myself*. And then…I met your father and one thing led to the next, and my one year stay turned into almost 38 years!"

"I understand, but Mom, I'll be back! My life is here in Miami—I won't stay in Italy. I won't!" I say emphatically as a dubious smile creeps across my mother's face. "I'm serious, Mom! Sugar Ray is here, you and dad—everyone I love is here! I'll be back! I promise!"

"Sweet Eloise!" my mom says as she takes my hands from across the table. "Whatever will be, will be, so let's just leave it at that—OK? No promises about things we can't possibly predict…"

"OK…" I say as my mind shifts, trying to fully understand her response. "I just think this might be an important thing for me to do right now, you know?"

"Why is that, Love?" my mother asks me after she takes a sip of her tea. Her eyes are soft and deep as she looks at me, waiting for my answer.

I pull off a piece of my flakey croissant as I consider my words. I want to tell her that I feel like I am in danger of never having more in my life than what I have right now if things don't change. And even though I do have a *good* life, I'm not sure it's enough anymore. I'm 33 years old and I've had the same job for 10 years, no significant relationship to speak of, and I don't seem to be going anywhere. I want her to understand that I know I want more for myself, even though I don't know exactly what that means. I'm ready to see and experience new things and embrace life. I want to redefine myself and reinvent who I am. But as I look back up at her face, I can see it in her eyes. She already knows how I feel, and that's what has her worried.

"I don't know… I guess I could just use a change of scenery…to help me gain some perspective for when I get back," I finally say with a weak smile.

"Right…" she trails off with a knowing look I can't quite read. "So when exactly does this *change of scenery* take place?" she asks me with a sincere grin.

"We leave in just over three weeks, and I have so much to do!" I say as I regain my excitement.

"What can I do to help?" my mom offers in a thick voice as she starts digging through her purse in an obvious effort to hide her watering eyes from me.

Suddenly, I can see myself in my mother's reaction for just a split second—but it's long enough for me to see that I'm restless and confused. I can see myself clearly for the first time, and it dawns on me that my hope is that this brief transfer will be enough to help me *find myself*. Those were her words to her mother 38 years ago—and now they are *my* words filled with *my* desires. The thought melts through me like butter on warm bread.

I need to venture out and let go of everything that makes me feel safe—even if it is only for a few short months.

"Just your being here for me helps," I say as I look at her with a smile from across the table.

It's been a little over three weeks since I agreed to the transfer, and there is only one day left until we actually leave. Between working my regular schedule of Miami based flights, I've been running around, getting ready to spend three months away from home. I've had dinner with my parents three times and spent every available weekend shopping with Nora. I've even flown up to Chicago to see my sister and her husband and two kids for a few days. To me, it feels like everyone is worried that I won't come home—which is just crazy. My loved ones seem to be kissing and hugging me a little more meaningfully than usual, and the whole thing is starting to frighten me. But the honest truth is that I have no plans to even put in for the extension. This is just a three-month deal—that's it!

The most difficult part for me is leaving Sugar Ray. He is the one constant in my life and spending time with him means the world to me. I've never felt the way I do about Sugar Ray for any other person or pet in my life. He is a part of me. Violet has been by to go over every detail of her "care plan" with me several times now, and I know everything will be fine—but I can't seem to stop hugging my dog and worrying that I forgot to do something crucial for him. It's totally irrational behavior on my part—I know—but I can't seem to stop myself from obsessing.

It's also been a little over three weeks since I've talked to Gabby. I thought for sure I would run into her in the hallway or in the laundry, but, so far, I haven't seen her. I've thought about calling her to see how things are going, but between being extra busy and a little afraid of what she might say, I haven't made contact. Scott thinks she's actually avoiding *me*—which could be true. No matter the reason, I still feel badly about how things ended that night at the restaurant, but I don't really know what to do or what I could say to smooth it over.

As I cram the last bit of clothing into my large *Windsong Air* regulation sized suitcase, I look around the room to make sure I didn't leave anything out. Packing one suitcase with three months worth of clothing is a pretty daunting task, but I think I've managed to pull it all together. Sugar Ray is used to seeing me pack my bags, but even he seems to know this trip is a big deal. He is leaning his body up against my satchel and looking at me with his suddenly sad brown eyes.

I crumple down on the floor next to him and take his boxy head in my hands. His stumpy tail wags slightly as I look him in the eye and promise him that I'll be back soon. I tell him that I love him so much and that Violet is going to just *fill in* for me—not replace me. I tell him that this is just an adventure I have to take, but that my heart will always be right here—with him in Miami. Even though I know he can't possibly understand a word I'm saying, there is this knowingness in his face that makes me hopeful that maybe he does. My heart aches at the thought of not having my dog with me every day. My face wells up as this thought takes a grip, and when a big fat tear rolls down my cheek, Sugar Ray kisses it off with the warm tip of his tongue.

When the doors of the elevator open into the lobby, a little rush of nerves flares up in my stomach. I sense that I might be running late, but it took me longer than usual to get ready this morning. I had to pick out just the right outfit for the plane ride over—I finally decided on a pair of dark denim jeans, a crisp, white T-shirt, a trendy, black linen jacket and a pair of black heels with an extra pointy toe that make my legs look over a mile long. Upon final inspection in the mirror, I think I managed to pull together the perfect travel-savvy look I was going for.

I thought we were supposed to meet in the lobby around 9:00 a.m. with all of our gear, but as I look around, I don't see anyone. Did I miss the van? It's only 9:10, but it's awfully quiet. Suddenly, I start to panic—they've left me! I'll have to catch a cab! I pull out my cell phone to dial the corporate office just as it rings in my hand. The caller ID tells me it's Scott, and a wave of relief washes over me.

"Hey! Where are you guys?" I ask in a bright and cheery voice.

"Where are *you*?" he shouts playfully. "We're all loaded up in the crew van, and you are the only one missing!"

"What! Oh my gosh! I'm so sorry!" I say as adrenaline pumps through my body. "Where's the van?" I shriek now that the panic has taken over.

"We're in the circle drive. Hurry up, Elle!" Scott blurts out as I begin to run across the tile floor of the lobby. My suitcase bumps and clatters along as I struggle to drag three-months-worth of clothing behind me while wearing my painful high-heeled shoes. I'm beginning to regret my travel-chic outfit already, and we haven't even left *The Wiley* yet!

As I reach the circle drive, I can see Scott rushing toward me with a huge smile. He's wearing a tan suit with a light blue shirt and leather shoes. *He sure does know how to dress*, I think, as he gives me a quick peck on the cheek, grabs my bag from me and pulls it toward to the back of the van.

"Get in the van and I'll put your suitcase up," he says over his shoulder.

When I hop into the van with my over-stuffed satchel hanging from my shoulder, I get my first look at our crew for the next three months. I'm delighted to see so many of my favorite people jammed into the crew van like a bunch of pickles in a jar. It's a tight squeeze with all of the luggage and carry-on bags, plus eight adults!

"Elle!" everyone seems to shout in unison.

"Hey you guys!" I say as my nervousness subsides, and a giddy excitement takes over. "I'm so sorry about being late," I offer, as I begin to wonder how long they've been waiting for me. "I had to wait for Violet to arrive—I couldn't leave Sugar Ray looking so sad…"

This is only partially true—I couldn't imagine leaving Sugar Ray on a sad note. But Violet was actually at my place for a good 20 minutes before I left and even suggested a change of shoes on my way out the door—which in retrospect, may have been a good idea.

"I totally understand, girl," Bobbi Henry says to me with a sympathetic smile. "I had to drop my cat off at my sister's house last night, and I cried like a baby!"

Bobbi Henry is one of my favorite flight attendants at *Windsong Air*. Nora and I first met her at the open interview all those years ago. Her husband had just left her for another woman, and she told us at the time that she was looking to "change her life." Ten years later, I can honestly say Bobbi has changed—she has bigger boobs, a new nose, platinum blonde hair extensions and a deep dark tan. But she's still the nicest, most giving person I know, and I am so happy to see her!

"Scoot over, Butts!" Scott shouts as he climbs into the van. He wraps his arms around me and lifts me up off the seat and onto his lap. "This van is loaded to the max—I just hope we don't get pulled over, Palo," Scott says playfully to our driver.

"Mi too, Mr. Scott," Palo replies as he climbs into the driver seat and starts to put on his seatbelt. "*Eberybody bedder hold on tight!*" he says with his funny little accent as he starts up the engine.

Everyone is in a great mood as we pull around the circle drive. I look out the window as we slope down the long entry road, and a sudden sense of nostalgia for this place comes over me. I know I'll be back in three months, but I can't help but feel sentimental as I study the familiar tree-lined driveway and the sidewalks cluttered with people in their bikinis and rollerblades. Scott gives me a quick squeeze and whispers in my ear, "It's just three months, Elle! Three little months."

"I know!" I say playfully back to him. But I can't stop myself from memorizing every detail of this place as it passes by me in the window. My favorite sidewalk café; the little store where I like to buy my newspapers and magazines; the public beach where all the posers hang out. It's all a regular part of my life here, and, even though in three months, it will still be here, I just want to remember it exactly how it is right now.

The van ride to the airport takes about 20 minutes, and by the time we arrive at the departures level, I feel slightly nauseous. But once we pile out and start dragging our bags out of the back of the van, I'm too distracted to feel anything. We've been instructed to meet at our regular departure gate for a brief meeting before we board the plane. Apparently we will be ferrying the plane over to Florence—so the only passengers will be *Windsong Air* crewmembers and WRI executives.

When Scott and I show up at the *Windsong Air* gate, it's already packed with familiar faces. The second fight attendant crew must have taken an earlier van, and as we walk up, everyone starts to clap for us—like maybe they've been waiting a long time for our arrival. I can feel my cheeks start to redden as I realize I may have been the reason we are off to a late start. This revelation makes the ache in my toes from my pointy high-heeled shoes feel even worse!

The gate area is filled with people I've worked with for 10 years, and I feel like I've just arrived at some sort of weird family reunion. The mood is festive as the rest of our vanload arrives, and we all start to mix with the other crewmembers, exchanging hellos and chattering like a bunch of silly kids. Everyone is laughing and hugging one another, and I get the feeling that this is going to be a fun three months!

After we've said our hellos, Scott and I both sit down on the floor near the front of the group. Several people from the corporate office are milling around by the boarding podium, and we can see Fozzy Rodriguez dragging a heavy cardboard box over to the boarding door. Fozzy's real name is Frederick, but he reminds everyone of Fozzy Bear from the *Muppets*. He's a big, swollen man with a round pockmarked face and has a silly, slaphappy personality, so the nickname suites him perfectly. He is in charge of the *Windsong Air* gate agents, but he works many of the flights himself, so over the years, we've gotten to know each other pretty well.

Fozzy eventually makes his way up to the podium and picks up the loudspeaker handset and brings it to his mouth. "Good morning! Can I have your attention in the gate area please," he says politely with a big grin on his face. The noise gradually dies down as everyone shifts around to focus on the big man talking up front. "Thank you," he says as he starts to pass the handset over to a woman with shoulder length black hair. She's dressed in a navy blue pantsuit with a crisp white shirt and about 20 pounds of makeup caked on her middle-aged face.

I vaguely recognize the woman as Michelle Maddox—one of the senior vice presidents or something like that of *Windsong Resorts International*. I've seen her face in the company news bulletin a few times, but this is the first time I've ever seen her in person. Despite all of the makeup, she's quite pretty—however, she strikes me as very cold and aloof. When she takes the handset from Fozzy, she gives her hair a self-important toss and begins to address the group.

"Good morning—I'm Michelle Maddox and I'm glad to be here with you today as we send you off to make WRI history!" Automatically, the group offers up a boisterous round of applause as Michelle takes a planned step back while she waits for the clapping to subside. "We are excited about the European expansion of *Windsong Air* and WRI, and we want to thank each of you for your willingness to participate in this new venture. It's going to be a very exciting time, and we are counting on all of you to help us make *Windsong Air Europe* a huge success. Now, without further delay, I would like to hand the mic back over to Frederick so that he can go over the specifics of today's flight and other details of your assignment. On behalf of Mr. Wiley Bennett and everyone at WRI, I would like to thank each and every one of you for your support."

As Michelle steps away from the podium, everyone gives her a polite round of applause. She steps back into a group of men wearing dark suits who all look like they'd rather be somewhere else. There are three men in all, and I only recognize one of them. He is a very portly gentleman named Gordon Goulette. He is the head of Human Resources for WRI and is often at training and service events that we have to attend. As Michelle blends into the pack, the suits all lean into each other, whispering things back and forth—they must be discussing very important corporate things, I'm sure.

"What do you think they're saying?" I whisper to Scott as I watch the suits conspire in the corner of the gate area.

"Well, for starters, they're trying to figure out where to have lunch once this petty little meeting is over," Scott begins in a hushed tone. "You see, Michelle doesn't eat dairy—*lactose intolerance*—and Gordy doesn't eat anything that isn't fried in lard, so with all these dietary restrictions, it makes picking a restaurant next to impossible," he explains with great authority.

"And how do you know all this," I say as I pull back and look at his serious face while he continues to study the suits in the corner.

"I'm paid to know this stuff, Elle," he turns and looks at me with a big grin.

"You're so weird," I reply with a smile.

Once Fozzy gets back on the mic, he seems a little nervous. Normally, he is at ease and even tosses in a few jokes here and there, but I bet he doesn't want to make any missteps in front of the corporate stiffs in the corner, so he begins his briefing rather cautiously.

"Good morning again everyone!" he begins with a cheerful look on his face.

Everyone replies in unison: "*Good Morning!*"

"We have a lot to go over in a short amount of time, so I'm just going to jump right in and get us on our way," Fozzy says, acting more formal than I've ever seen him. "As you board the plane today, I'm going to give you a packet with your crew assignments, your schedule for the next *three months* and your room arrangements for the entire stay." Fozzy holds up one of the very thick packets as he says, "As you can see, we just wanted to make sure you had something to read on the long flight to Florence today!" He gives a nervous a look over his shoulder to make sure the suits are OK with this little jibe.

I doubt the executives are even listening to a word Fozzy says. They're still huddled together, talking in low whispers. At the very least, they are doing an excellent job of looking important and indispensable—even if they are actually discussing their lunch plans.

I start to glaze over a bit as Fozzy continues to talk about boring base details, none of which surprise me. He covers show times and block hours—all things that are pretty much exactly the same as when we are working out of the Miami base—and how to submit our time sheets over the Internet. My stomach starts to grumble, and I wish I had eaten some breakfast. I sure hope they are going to feed us on the plane ride over—and not crap airline food either! I feel myself zone in and out while Fozzy rambles on. Finally, he sounds like he's about to wrap up, so I sit up a little straighter to stretch my back in anticipation of standing.

"One last thing before we go. I'd like to introduce you to our Florence-based crew of pilots and co-pilots," Fozzy says as he turns his attention toward a row of seats that line the outer rim of the boarding area. As I look in that direction, I see six well-dressed men rising up and striding toward the podium.

These are the pilots? I think as I watch these handsome men make their way through the crowded boarding area. I guess I didn't think about the pilots that would be going on this trip. The *Windsong Air* cockpit crews are all semi-retired pilots who sign up to work several trips per month, just to keep their instrument ratings up to date. Most of them are over weight, balding men in their late fifties and sixties who are totally unfriendly and just want to log some hours and then get home to their retirement hobbies.

Some of my friends who have left *Windsong Air* and started working for commercial airlines have very different stories of wild affairs that take place between flight attendants and their sometimes-married cockpit crews. Nothing that torrid ever happens at *Windsong Air*—in fact, I barely know any of our pilots by name! But as I study the Italian pilots assigned to the Florence base, I feel a shudder of interest ride up my spine.

As the pilots continue to make their way up to the podium area, Fozzy explains the arrangements for the front-end crews. "Because the base in Florence will eventually be permanent, we decided to integrate the pilots first, so these gentleman have been here in Miami for the past six weeks at the FAA training facilities and at our corporate offices to get checked out on our equipment and to learn *Windsong Air* protocols."

When all six men finally reach the front of the boarding area, I find that I'm awestruck by how attractive these men really are. Each of them is wearing a dark suit—some of the suits appear to be made of linen and some look like they might be silk—but the Italian tailoring is unmistakable. They all look well-groomed with fine leather shoes and belts—like they take a lot of pride in the way they dress. As a collective group in front of us, it's hard to see them as individuals—all I can see is just one big handsome presence.

"Wow," Scott says into my ear. "Some good looking guys are going to be carting us around Europe."

"Uh-huh…" I say as I stare up at them.

"You can get to know the pilots a little bit on your way over to Florence today," Fozzy continues. "Be sure to introduce yourselves, so they will know who you are and which crew you will be assigned to. We want to make sure this is an easy transition for our working pilots, and you people will be a big part of welcoming these guys to the *Windsong Air* family."

As I look over my shoulder, I can see that the pilots have had a similar affect on most of the female—and even some of the male—flight attendants in our group, and I feel very certain that these pilots will feel quite welcomed by the time we land in Florence. When I turn my attention back to the pilots all lined up in front of the podium, a sardonic smile spreads across my face as I consider this. They all seem so intriguing, so foreign, and a part of me is anxious just to find out their names and hear their accents when they talk.

"OK, then, before we start to board, I need you to listen up for a few more instructions," Fozzy announces, rattling me out of my reverie. "I need you to put your suitcases on the luggage carts to the right of the entryway, so that our baggage crew can take them through the scanners and get them on the plane. Then I need you to line up—single file—so I can distribute the packets as you board."

The pilots shuffle off to the side, as the rest of us start moving about the gate, grabbing for our bags while laughing and carrying on. Scott and I manage to be among the first to place our bags on the cart. Just as we make our way to the boarding door, my cell phone starts to ring. I can see by the caller ID that it's my mom.

"Hi, Mom!" I say enthusiastically. "We're just getting on the plane!"

"Oh, I'm so glad I caught you then!" she says pleasantly. "I won't keep you, but I just wanted to tell you how much we love you and how proud we are of you, Eloise." My mother's voice sounds weak and crackly like she is fighting back the tears.

"Thanks, Mom!" I say gently as I pull away from Scott and the rest of the crowd. "Are you OK?" I ask her in an effort to find out how I can reassure her that I'm going to be fine.

"I guess I just miss you already," she says after a bit of a pause with a voice that breaks off.

"I miss you already, too, Mom," I say as my heart wells up. "But I'll see you in just three short months! *And* while I'm in Europe, I think I'll pay Edna Pearl a visit! Wouldn't that be great?"

"Yes! That would be lovely!" she says as though the thought of her own mother seeing me takes away some of her sadness.

"Mom, I have to go now. But tell Dad I love him, and I will call you as soon as we get settled, OK?" I say as Scott starts motioning for me to get off the phone.

"Alright, Eloise," my mother sniffles into the phone. "And Sweetheart?

"Yes, Mom?"

"Have fun on your big adventure!" she says sincerely.

"I will, Mom! I will…"

Chapter Seven

Fozzy tells us as we board the plane that it's first-come, first-serve seating, so Scott and I literally run down the Jetway, so we can get the best seats possible. I feel like I'm in high school all over again, and we are on a class trip as Scott and I shove our way into the first class cabin and plunk our carry-on bags into two available seats. Since we are only ferrying the flight over to Florence, we were told that none of us has to work the flight—although we do have to secure the plane, make sure all of the safety procedures have been followed and serve the pilots and executives aboard the plane during the flight. It kind of sounds to me like we will be working the flight, but I quickly shrug it off because *we're going to Italy!!*

While Scott goes in search of pillows and blankets, I decide to make my way up to the first class galley to see what catering has delivered for us to eat. As I enter the galley, I see Miriam Ungaro going over the flight and service paperwork. Miriam is my boss. She is the head of the flight attendant department at *Windsong Air*, and even though she is a trained and certified flight attendant, I am surprised to see her on board, loading up the galley with food for the flight.

Miriam is probably in her mid to late forties and looks like she was once somewhat attractive—but I think it's safe to say that hard living has taken a toll. Her face is leathery and brown, and she has deep lines around her mouth that make her look harsh and unfriendly. Her black hair is kind of wiry and stiff, but she manages to straighten it with a flat iron so it at least looks smooth. She has a sort of egg-shaped torso and long, skinny legs with spider veins that look like a road map running up and down every inch. In my opinion, she often wears her skirts too short and her heels too high, but I think she believes this makes her look younger.

In the ten years that I have known Miriam, I've never been quite sure if she likes me or not. Her personality is very abrasive, and she tends to cut every conversation short—leaving out all pleasantries for the sake of time. But, since I'm in a good mood today, I decide to try to engage Miriam in a pleasant exchange and see what I can do to help.

"Hello, Miriam!" I say as she looks up from the catering clipboard with a sour look on her face.

She's wearing a tight, short, navy blue skirt and a snug-fitting, white spandex top that is horribly unflattering on her soft, fleshy torso. Her wrinkly, oversized breasts are protruding out of the scoop neck of her top, and she is wearing a choker with a strange-looking medallion dangling from the chain. Her legs are covered with sheer blue stockings that don't quite cover up the spider veins, and her heels are extra high today and look incredibly uncomfortable as she hunches down over the drink bins.

"Oh great! Elle, I'm so glad to see you," she says as the look of relief spreads over her miserable face. "Why don't you do this for me. It's been ages since I coordinated service for a flight, and I still have a few other things to go over with Fozzy."

Before I can even answer her, she shoves the clipboard into my stomach and rushes out of the galley. I'm a little startled by this change of plan, but no big deal. After all, I wanted to see what catering was delivering for us to eat, and now I'm in charge of it!

As I look down on the clipboard, I can see that there will only be a total of 38 passengers on board for this flight. The names of each of the passengers is neatly printed on the passenger manifest, and I can tell from the list that there will be four active pilots, 16 flight attendants, four gate agents and eight executive types on board. Toward the bottom of the page, there are six unfamiliar names listed off to the side. These must be the names of our Italian pilots! When I zero in on the names, I drift off a bit, wondering which one is which. I read: *Captain Alessandro Bandini; Captain Marco Maselli; Captain Nico Mirabella...*

Suddenly, I'm startled by a loud *bang* and a sprinkle of wetness on my foot—one of the caterers just tossed a bag of ice into the galley to break up the pieces. I was concentrating so hard that the noise nearly made me jump out of my skin!

"Didn't mean to startle ya there, Elle," Jimmy from the catering team says with a big surly grin. "You OK?" Jimmy is wearing his usual gray company-issued sleeveless jumpsuit and has a red bandana tied around his head. He is tall and slender and literally reminds me of a string bean.

"Yeah, I'm great!" I say as I give him a big grin in an effort to cover up my embarrassment. "Just checking out the list for this flight. What are you guys going to be feeding us today?" I say in anticipation of the food.

"They really rolled out the red carpet for you guys," Jimmy says as he takes a folded piece of paper out of his vest pocket. "I've got 38 first class mid-day meals with a choice of chicken salad or tuna curry; and 38 dinner meals with a choice of vegetable lasagna or steak; and ice cream sundaes for dessert. Then we've got 38 first class mid-flight snacks, 38 first class regular snacks and lots of bottled water and sodas... No beer, wine or liquor, though. They must've decided they wanted you sober before you land in Florence!" Jimmy concludes with a hearty laugh.

"Yeah...I guess they do," I concur as he hands me the catering checklist. I clip the list onto my clipboard and then hang the board up on the galley wall before I start to help Jimmy break up the bags of ice that go inside insulated service carts.

Jimmy starts unloading the evening meals into the ovens as I organize the drink bin with all the sodas and bottles of water. Before long, I shift into automatic mode as I set up the galley for the first class pre-flight service. I carefully place a starchy white linen napkin on a tray and line several rock glasses down the center. Just as I'm about to enter the first class cabin to see how many people I need to serve, Miriam pushes through the doorway with an angry huff.

"Elle!" Miriam snaps at me. "Are those *your* bags in seat 5A?" Her face is drawn in like she's been sucking on a lemon, and her eyes are squinted as she stares me down.

I look over her shoulder in the direction of seat 5A and reply, "Uh… yes. Those are my bags—and Scott has his bags in 5B."

"And *why* do you have *your* bags in the first class cabin?" Her mood seems to be going down hill by the minute, and I don't know exactly how to answer her.

"I'm so sorry, Miriam. Were those seats reserved?" I don't know what else to say. Fozzy told us *all* the seats were first-come, first-serve, but maybe he wasn't including first class.

"Why would we ever put *you* up in the first class cabin when we have *executives* on board? Think, Elle! Think!" She practically spits her words at me and then turns on her heel and storms out of the galley. Then I can hear her raspy voice shouting, "Scott LaMotte? Where's Scott LaMotte?"

"Wow, she's as charming as ever," comes a male voice from behind me. As I turn to look, I can see the captain emerging from the cockpit. I know I've flown with him before, but I just can't remember his name. He has salt and pepper hair and a very tanned face. I think he may be the pilot that has a deep-sea fishing company on the side which would explain the mahogany tan and his strong, sinewy forearms.

"She must be feeling a bit stressed out about coordinating everyone, I guess," I offer with a nervous laugh. That's not what I'm really thinking, but I figure it's never a good idea to trash your boss.

"Stress or no stress, that just seems like regular old ugly Miriam Ungaro to me," the captain says with a smile as he peers through the galley opening into the first class cabin. I follow his gaze and can see Miriam shoving my bags into Scott's stomach with an angry thrust. Scott seems mildly amused by her behavior and manages to remain unruffled by her actions.

"Can I get a couple of bottles of water from you?" the captain asks me as my attention returns to the galley.

"Oh sure!" I say. "Do you want ice or anything with that?" I ask as I dig out two bottles of water from the drink bin.

"No, just the bottles will be fine. By the way, I know I've flown with you before, but I'm terrible with names. I'm James Cramden—and you are?"

"Oh hi! I'm Elle Butts—nice to meet you…again," I say as I fumble my words and hand him the bottles of water.

Captain Cramden grabs the water from me with one hand and gives me a gentle smile. He looks like he's in his early sixties but he's still very handsome. He casually sticks one of the bottles under his arm and twists off the top of the other.

"Have you met any of the *European* pilots yet, Elle?" Captain Cramden asks before he brings the water bottle to his lips.

"Nope—not yet. We just had the general introductions earlier today in the boarding area. What about you?" I ask as I watch the water drain from the bottle into Captain Cramden's throat. He wipes his lips after the last drop of water pours out of the bottle.

"Yeah—they're a *dreamy bunch!*" he says with a wink.

"What do you mean by that?" I ask, very curious about his comment.

"Let's just say that these guys have had quite an affect on the female executives at *Windsong Air* over the past few weeks, and I think that might be one of the reasons Ms. Ungaro is so—how did you put it? '*Stressed out*'…"

Immediately, I understand the whole situation more clearly. *Miriam* wants first class reserved for our European cockpit crews and a few key *female* executives. That must be what she needed to talk to Fozzy about earlier.

"Mystery solved," I say to Captain Cramden with a smile.

"Listen, you've always seemed like a sweet kid to me. Don't you get yourself mixed up with one of these Euro-trash pilots, OK?" he says after he tosses his empty water bottle into the trash bin and transfers the water under his arm into his hand. "These guys will eat a sweet, little, naive girl like you for breakfast."

Captain Cramden is looking into the first class cabin again as he says this, so I follow his gaze. I can see Miriam Ungaro standing in the aisle, doing her best to look gorgeous and seductive as the Italian pilots make their way to their seats. But instead of looking sexy or alluring, Miriam looks like a middle-aged woman with a rusty face, gritty teeth and a saggy body. I almost feel sorry for her as I watch her trying to shift her posture around to show off her body and send an unspoken signal that she's available.

After a pause, I feel compelled to set the record straight with the Captain. "I'm not as naïve as you might think, Captain Cramden. But thanks for the warning," I say as I give him a wink.

"OK, Cutie…" Captain Cramden says in a patronizing tone as he ducks back through the cockpit door.

An irritating burn rises up my throat as I think about this exchange. Why did he say that to me? He doesn't even know me, and he's saying that I'm naïve? That's not right. I'm not so innocent and I can take care of myself! It's not like I'm still a baby. I'm 33 years old for crying out loud! I know how things work, and I can read male motives like a page out of a book.

Thank you for your concern, Captain, I think as I return to my work. *But you needn't worry about me!*

"Elle!" Miriam is standing in the galley doorway again, glaring at me. "Get out there and start the pre-flight service!" Her face is kind of flushed and filmy. "And be sure to offer the Italians some wine," she says in a harsh, but low, whisper. "They drink at all times of the day over in Italy, and we want to make sure they feel welcome."

"Miriam, catering said that they didn't have any wine or liquor on the catering order, so I don't have anything but water and sodas," I trail off, feeling kind of badly because I know that Jimmy is about to get blasted.

As expected, Miriam storms into the galley, rips the catering list off the hanging clipboard and studies the order. "Jimmy!" she practically screams.

Jimmy is tucked back in the back of the catering truck, counting out packages of coffee stirrers and paper napkins. When he hears Miriam screaming, he just looks over his shoulder and grunts, "What?"

"We need you to put together a beer and wine kit and one small first class liquor kit," Miriam seems to be trying to change her tone a bit in order to get her way. "Actually, you better give me three beer and wine kits, but skip the beer and just double up on all of the wine."

"I'm sorry Miriam, but I don't have the P.O. from the catering department for that. You'll have to call over there and get me some clearance," he says like this is a really sticky matter for him.

"Jimmy, *I* have the clearance for this!" she barks at him. "Just do it!" she demands. I'm standing over Miriam's shoulder pulling a face at Jimmy, and hoping that he will just do it so she'll leave the galley.

"Fine! But I need you to sign the catering receipt. I don't want me or Elle to get in trouble for this," he says as he rises up and grabs his catering clipboard off a nearby crate.

"Give it to me," Miriam snaps as she rips the receipt off of Jimmy's clipboard. She quickly scribbles her initials on the receipt and tosses it at Jimmy before she storms out of the galley.

"Man," Jimmy says with the look of disgust on his face. "How do you stand that woman?"

"I don't know, but thanks for helping out, Jimmy," I say as Jimmy starts pulling bottles of wine out of the storage cases inside the catering van.

"I did it for you, Elle," he says with a smile as he hands me a bin with four bottles of red wine and two bottles of white.

Once Jimmy has all of the alcohol loaded up and iced down in the galley, I sign the rest of the catering paperwork and shut the front galley door and pull down the heavy door latch. When I enter the first class cabin, I see all the seats are filled. I notice that in addition to Miriam and the six Italian pilots, Michelle Maddox and Gordon Goulette are both on board, along with the other two suits I don't recognize. I guess they weren't discussing their lunch plans after all.

"Elle, we're getting ready to push back," Captain Cramden says through the cockpit door as I make my way back into the galley. "We don't have time for the pre-flight service, so go ahead and prepare the first class cabin and galley for take off."

"Yes sir," I reply. Then I wonder if Miriam will be upset by this change of plans. I haven't had a chance to open the wine or even start serving any drinks. As I pull back the galley curtain and look into the first class cabin, I see Miriam seated next to one of the Italian pilots. She is leaning in as she talks, pressing her mushy chest up against the pilot's shoulder. The strangest thing of all is that the pilot doesn't seem to mind!

Back in coach, everyone is spread out all over the place. All you can see are a few heads here and there and feet sticking out into the aisles as people stretch out for the long flight to Florence. Scott set up two rows of seats with pillows, blankets and fashion magazines for us in the mid cabin, and I can hardly wait to sit down and take my painful, pointy shoes off.

After take off, I dig around my satchel in search of the information packet Fozzy gave us. I want to find out which crew I'm on and where we'll be staying. Fozzy wasn't kidding about the size of the packet. There must be a hundred pages all held together with an industrial sized staple. I carefully flip through the pages in search of the crew lists.

Finally, I find the page that lists the crews. I quickly scan the list, looking for my name. It appears that I am on Crew 2—the evening flight crew. As I read over the crew scheduling information, I find out that both crews will only work on Friday, Saturday and Sunday, but Crew 1 will handle the morning flights while Crew 2 will handle all the evening flights. On Fridays, the flights will be from Florence to Munich and back; on Saturdays, from Florence to Madrid and back; and on Sundays, from Florence to Paris and back.

As I scan the list of names under Crew 2, I see that we have a great group. After flying with these people for so many years, we've all learned to get along and really enjoy each other—for the most part.

Besides me, there's Marta DeSoto, the thirty-something-year-old woman from Cuba. Marta is a small woman with short, dark hair, coal black eyes and chocolate brown skin. She is pretty in her own way, but sometimes she can seem aloof and arrogant. Marta is one of only a few married flight attendants at *Windsong Air*—and to make things more complicated, she's married to one of the WRI executives, which tends to make some people nervous. I get along with her fine, but, I have to admit, I am surprised to see her name on the list—three months seems like a long time to be away from your husband.

The next name on the list is Bobbi Henry. I'm glad to have her on my crew—she is a hard worker and sort of looks after me in a way. She's only about ten years older than me, but there's just something very comforting about the way Bobbi talks to me. I've watched her morph from a plain-Jane housewife into a striking blonde bombshell over the years, but no matter how she changes her appearance, she still has the same good heart.

Sebastian Jones is by far the most flamboyant flight attendant at *Windsong Air*, and rumor has it that when he was younger, Sebastian was a high-level corporate accountant by day and drag queen by night. Now in his early 40's, Sebastian's looks have started to fade a bit, but he still does the Miami club scene religiously and tells the most outlandish tales of lewd and lascivious behavior. Clearly Sebastian and I are not that close, but I do find him entertaining in small doses, and I'm certain things won't be dull with him around.

Suzanne Keller is the only flight attendant on this trip that is not a part of the original *Windsong Air* crew. Suzanne—not *Sue, Suze,* or *Suzie,* but always *Suzanne*—started working at *Windsong Air* shortly after Nora left. She is 29-years-old and very tall and thin with straight blonde hair that she wears in a severe bob with bangs. I really like Suzanne, but sometimes I wonder if she struggles with an eating disorder—all she ever talks about is food, yet she looks as if she never eats any!

Enrique Suarez is widely known among the group as the Latin Loser. The poor guy seems to be in love with being in love, yet he tends to pick the most horrible women to date. He's not bad looking—he is average height with a muscular build, dark brown hair and hazel eyes—and he is incredibly kind and interested in others. But the entire time that I've known Enrique, I can't think of a single time when he's been in a happy relationship or when he hasn't been nursing a broken heart.

Then there is Isabelle Watts—or Izzy as we call her. Izzy is my age and looks like an all-American girl. She grew up in St. Louis, Missouri but spent four years at the University of Miami where she studied biology and was a starter on the women's volleyball team. When she graduated, she didn't want to go back home to the Midwest, so she stayed put in Miami until she landed a job with *Windsong Air*. With thick, long, blonde hair, an athletic figure and a voracious appetite for partying, Izzy is like the American version of Gabby—so needless to say, I don't spend much time with her other than at work!

Of course Scott is on my crew as well which makes me very happy. This whole adventure just wouldn't be the same without him. As I look up from reading, I spot Scott leaning against the bulkhead wall of the mid-cabin galley talking to Bobbi Henry. He's holding two meal trays in his hands as Bobbi loads them both up with silverware and tinfoil-covered meals. My stomach starts to rumble in anticipation of the food, and I hope that Scott remembered that I don't like tuna.

Before I close up my information packet, I scan down the crew list to find out the names of our pilots. There are four names listed: Captain Marco Maselli; First Officer Andre Umbarto; Captain Antonio Cordova; First Officer Luca Renaldo. After committing each name to memory, I close my eyes and practice saying each one—in my head, of course—with my best *Italian* accent. *Marco Maselli. Andre Umbarto. Antonio Cordova. Luca Renaldo.* Even their names are more romantic!

When I come to, Scott is standing over me with two trays of food and a silly grin on his face.

"What are you doing?" he asks me with a little laugh.

"Nothing," I reply as a pink flush washes over my cheeks. "What'd you get me to eat?" I ask enthusiastically in an effort to shift my awkwardness.

"Well, I know how much you *love* tuna…" he says, his eyes wide with anticipation of my reaction. Just before I blurt out how much I hate tuna, Scott places my tray down in front of my face and says, "So I got you chicken salad!"

I gratefully grab the tray from him and flip down my tray table. As I lift the tinfoil covering off the plate, the chicken salad looks completely edible. *Windsong Air* actually serves pretty decent meals. I guess since WRI promises a luxurious vacation experience for their clients, it wouldn't do to have a disgusting meal at the start of your trip! I carefully unwrap the rest of the food on my tray, a small mixed green salad, two slices of Swiss cheese, a chunk of fresh French bread and a gourmet cookie for dessert.

Scott appears to be as hungry as I am as I see him hastily unwrapping and eating everything on his tuna curry platter. The two of us are silent as we stuff our faces with food, only coming up briefly for air. Just as I am breaking off the first piece of my cookie, Scott ends the silence.

"So, did you see that we're on Crew 2?"

"I did!" I confirm pleasantly. "It looks like we have a great group of people to work with for the next three months!"

"I agree," Scott says just before sticking his last piece of cookie into his mouth. "And, according to Bobbi Henry, we have the '*hottest captain*' on our crew." Scott chomps down on his cookie with a wry look in his eye as he awaits my reaction to this Bobbi Henry tid bit.

"Well, that just makes things even better, don't you think?" I say as I return Scott's look. I can't help but wonder which captain is the hottie! Is it *Capitano Marco Maselli* or *Capitano Antonio Cordova*?

"Oh, for me, it makes all the difference," Scott blandly replies as he gathers all of his tinfoil covers and balls them up on the tray.

I can't quite tell for sure, but there is a slight hostility in Scott's tone— almost like he doesn't want to like our new pilots. But it's probably just me thinking something silly. After all, Scott likes everyone.

As I begin to clear up my mess, I can see Bobbi Henry making her way down the aisle. Her cheeks are slightly flushed, and she has a huge grin on her face. She slides into the row of seats in front of mine and then climbs into the aisle seat, perches up on her knees and hangs her torso over the back of the seat so she can talk to me.

"Listen, Elle," she begins in a bit of a conspiratorial whisper. "Miriam has been calling for you to come up and finish the first class service, but I was hoping that you wouldn't mind if I just finished things up in the front galley myself." Her eyes are bright and happy, and I suddenly realize that she is wearing a different shirt than she was wearing on the crew bus earlier today. This new shirt has a deep V-neck, and Bobbi has her breasts shoved together with a push-up bra that makes it very difficult not to notice her.

"Of course you can finish up, but is Miriam going to be upset at *me* for not doing it?" I ask as I consider how misunderstandings and Miriam are a bad combination.

"Oh don't worry. I'll come up with something that makes you look good, Elle! She'll think you are doing something very important back here—I promise!" Bobbi pushes herself out of the seat after blowing me a kiss and mouthing the words, *"Thank you"*. Scott and I both lean into the aisle and watch Bobbi as she shimmies down the narrow aisle in her ultra tight pencil skirt, clingy top and spiked heels.

"Work it, girl!" Scott hollers after her.

Bobbi looks over her shoulder briefly and gives us a wink and a smile and then disappears behind the first class curtain.

"Wow," Scott remarks, "Bobbi isn't wasting any time with these pilots!"

"No, I guess not, " I agree as I ponder the scene on the other side of the curtains.

Chapter Eight

A few hours later, I've read one fashion magazine from cover to cover and am flipping through my second when I see one of the Italian pilots walking up the aisle. I can't help but wonder if this is the "hottie" that Bobbi Henry was referring to. He certainly qualifies as one in my book, but what do I know?

Most everyone around me is listening to music on their headsets or sleeping—including Scott who is passed out in the row of seats directly behind me. As I watch the pilot saunter his way into the mid-cabin, I suddenly feel very aware that he is on his way back to talk to me! But first, he ducks into the mid-cabin galley and grabs a large bottle of water and a glass and then continues to walk in my direction.

I feel my heart start to race a little as I watch him glide toward me. He is very tall and sleek and has a commanding presence. He has thick golden brown hair that has a graceful wave to it and kind of comes down over his left eye. I can see that his shoulders are strong and round under his gauzy white linen shirt. His torso tapers down into a flat stomach with a thin waistline. His trousers are perfectly tailored but have a loose, easy fit.

Suddenly, I'm aware that I've been so obvious with my eyes as I check out this strange, beautiful man walking toward me, and I start to feel my cheeks redden with embarrassment. The pilot must have noticed, too, as a confident smile starts to spread across his face, and he says, "You like?"

"I'm sorry?" I say in response. *Did he just ask me if 'I like*? What does that mean?

"You like for me to come and talk to you?" he clarifies in a gloriously rich voice, thick with his Italian accent.

"Oh…sure!" I say with slight hesitation as I'm still recovering from my extreme embarrassment.

He settles into the aisle seat in the center section of the cabin and shifts his body so he is facing me from across the aisle. His face is perfect. His eyes are caramel-colored with light specs of gold, and both lids are rimmed with dark, thick eyelashes. His nose is small and narrow, and his cheekbones perfectly frame his face. He has full lips that curl up slightly on both sides and two rows of straight, white teeth. There is a slight indentation on his chin—a sexy cleft that makes me want to take my pinky finger and push in on it like a button.

"Would you like to share some water with me?" he asks after what feels like an awkward amount of time. The question feels so intimate that I feel nervous about how to answer.

"Oh, no thank you," I reply as I awkwardly shift around in my seat, trying to keep myself from staring. "I have my own drink…" I trail off as I lift up my empty plastic cup sitting on the tray table next to me. "Well, maybe a splash would be nice," I sheepishly add after realizing that my throat is as dry as sandpaper.

"A *splash?*" he asks me with a wrinkled brow.

"Oh, sorry! Um…just a little bit, thank you," I say as I use my fingers to show him how much to fill up my glass.

Carefully, he wraps his long fingers around the bottle cap and slowly untwists it, all the while never taking his eyes off of me. I feel myself quiver slightly as I have never been so captivated by a total stranger before. When he reaches out to take the glass from my hand, a cold sweat rushes over my skin.

What's wrong with me? I think as he pours the cold water into my plastic cup. I can't recall a man ever having such an affect on me—I mean he's just pouring me some water for goodness sake!

When he hands back the plastic cup, I take a quick sip and then place it on the tray table next to me. I am horribly aware of how badly I'm trembling, and I certainly don't want *him* to notice!

"What is your name?" the pilot asks me as he pours some water into his own glass. Once it is full, he twists the cap back on the bottle and looks up at me, awaiting my answer.

"My name?" I repeat back, as though I didn't understand him. I feel myself go all wobbly as I try to regain enough composure to remember my own name. I look up at his handsome face as he gives me an encouraging nod in an effort to get me to answer the question.

"Oh…yes…" I stammer. "My name is Elle…" I look up at him for approval and then add, "And what's your name?"

"My name is Marco. Captain Marco Maselli," he says as he holds my gaze with his eyes. "I think that you are on my crew," he offers with a smile—a big gorgeous, steamy smile.

"Yes, I think you're right," I add happily as I wonder how in the world he knew that. Did he memorize the names of everyone on his crew…or just mine?

"*Elle*…" he says in a dreamy voice. "The name is so lovely," he continues. "It is the word for '*she*' in French, no?" he asks me with a quizzical look on his face.

"Well, actually, I'm not sure about that, but it's really just a nickname for me…" I trail off once I realize that he doesn't know what I'm saying, and neither do I.

"A *nickname?*" His face is so fresh and clear as he begs the question with his eyes.

"Oh, that just means that my real name isn't *Elle*—it's *Eloise* actually, but people call me *Elle* for short." I can't believe that I just told him my real name is Eloise! My only hope is that I can keep my composure long enough not to go into any discussion about my *last* name!

"Ah, *Eloise-ah!* Yes, I know this name!" he says excitedly as my name rolls off his tongue like a song.

I watch him as he closes his eyes and seemingly savors my name in his mouth. When he opens his eyes again, I can't be sure, but I think he sees me looking back at him with hooded eyes and my mouth slightly agape, nearly drooling in my seat. I catch myself in this state and quickly shift around in my seat, turning my attention directly in front of me.

"So Eloise-ah," Marco intones, clearly determined to keep a conversation alive between us. "Will this be your first time to Florence?" His face is so perfect as he gently stares at me in anticipation of my answer.

"No. I mean yes… Actually, yes," I stammer as I try to figure out how to make my mouth and mind work in unison. "I've been to Rome—as a young girl—but never to Florence." I feel awkward and gawky as I speak, completely aware of my every gesture and movement. My American accent sounds so flat and boring. I feel so ill at ease and sweaty, but I can't seem to do anything about it.

"Well then, I shall have to show you around Florence *myself*," Marco says with a seductive smile as he brings his glass to his lips. I watch him intently as his lips part, and he tips his glass to meet them.

Instinctively, I grab my plastic cup and quickly bring it to my lips. I tilt the cup and knock all of the water back, like I'm doing a Tequila shot or something.

"You are very thirsty, I see," Marco comments with a sheepish grin on his face. "Do you want more?" he offers as he slowly and deliberately wraps his fingers around the neck of the water bottle that he has squeezed directly between his legs.

"Oh, no!" I blurt out, feeling incredibly self-conscious. "I'm fine, thank you!" I can feel my chest rising and falling in an obvious way, and I will myself to settle down and get a grip over my emotions.

"So Eloise-ah, you must promise to allow me to show you my city," Marco continues with a smile as I struggle to stay on course with the conversation.

"OK…that sounds really nice…" I reply as my emotional spasm subsides, and I slip under his spell.

"There are so many things to show you, so many places to take you, so you can see my proud city," he says as his accent punctuates every word in a way that makes me weak.

"That sounds really nice," I lamely repeat like a moron with a limited vocabulary. But it's the only thing I can come up with at the moment!

There is movement near the galley that diverts both of our attention. It's Miriam Ungaro untangling herself from the cabin curtain. She looks a little haggard—her hair is flattened on one side and her face looks slack with sleep. Her short skirt is sort of twisted off center, and her tight stretchy top looks like some of the spandex is as tired as she is as it shows large puckers where her body bulges normally protrude.

"*Permesso,*" Marco says to me as he sees Miriam making her way toward us. He rises up out of his seat and stands as she maneuvers down the aisle. She looks like she is forcing her face into a pleasant smile, but it is such an unnatural look for her that it's almost painful to witness.

"Ah, *Signore Miriam,*" Marco says to Miriam when she slides up next to him in the aisle. "Did you sleep well?" he asks with genuine concern.

"I did, Marco—I did," Miriam replies in her raspy voice. "How long have you been *wandering about?*" she asks with a slight hint of irritation in her voice.

"Not so long," Marco smoothly replies. "I was just talking to *Eloise-ah* for a bit—she is one of the members of my flight crew, so I wanted to say my hellos," he continues as he looks at me and gives me a sexy wink. I'm pretty sure Miriam doesn't notice Marco's gesture, but she tucks her arm firmly under his and gives me a nasty glare.

"Well, now that I'm up, why don't you come up to the *first class* cabin and keep me company?" Miriam says in a sappy, sweet voice as she starts gently tugging Marco down the aisle in the direction of the first class cabin.

"Very good," Marco replies obediently. But before he goes, he says, "Eloise-ah, it was my pleasure to meet you, and I am looking forward to spending more time with you in Florence."

Upon hearing this, Miriam shoots me a vicious look. Unsure what to do, I simply stare up at the two of them with their arms linked in the aisle. Miriam tightens her grip on Marco's arm and literally begins pulling him down the aisle. But just before Marco disappears behind the first class curtain, he turns to look over his shoulder and gives me a lustful smile.

"Wow," comes a voice from behind me. "Now that's what you call smooth."

I crane my neck into the aisle and look around my seat. Scott is all stretched out in the row behind me with his head propped up against the fuselage wall with at least six pillows padding him in. When he sees my face, he smiles and gives me a little wave.

"So when exactly did you tune in?" I ask him coarsely, knowing he was likely listening in the entire time.

"Well, let's just say long enough to see and hear you in action!" Scott says with a hoarse giggle.

"What do you mean by that?" I shoot back defensively. Did I really sound as lame as I think I did? Oh gosh, I hope not!

"Well, I'm sure *Capitano Amore* knows you think it will be '*really nice*' touring the city with him," Scott blurts out with a loud guffaw.

"Whatever," I say as I turn back around in my seat. I feel all ruffled inside, and there is a wash of embarrassment coming over me. I don't understand what's going on. Wasn't Marco Maselli sort of asking me out? Or is that just Italian men? Do they come on to *all* women?

I start flipping through the magazine on my lap, trying to sort out this surreal exchange. I can hear Scott moving around in the seats behind me. Once he's untangled his long legs from the pile of blankets and pillows, he manages to slide into the seat Marco was just occupying.

"Are you mad at me now, Elle?" he asks as he leans in to get a better look at my face. His face is playful and sweet, but I do feel a little irritated with him at the moment.

"No," I reply acidly as I peal back a perfume sample flap inside my magazine and pull the page up to my nose. It is a sticky sweet smelling fragrance that makes me want to vomit. Or maybe it's just everything going on around me that is making me feel uneasy.

"What's the matter, then?" Scott asks. "Talk to me, Elle—talk to me!" Scott seems genuinely concerned, but I don't even know what to say to him.

I can't really decide the precise thing that is bothering me. I guess I just feel silly. Silly that I was falling for the whole seduction scene Marco Maselli was laying on me—and even more silly now that I know that Scott heard the whole thing! I can't believe how easily Marco swept me under his spell—the same spell he cast on *Miriam Ungaro* of all people! All he had to do was say a few words in his fancy accent, and, all of a sudden, I'm a puddle on the floor. I hate to say it, but I think that Captain Cramden was right about me after all—I *am* too naïve for these Italian men.

I carefully close my magazine and look Scott squarely in the face and say, "There's nothing wrong with me that a little food can't fix!"

"I'll lead the way!" Scott replies with the enthusiasm of someone ready for anything.

After discovering that all of the food in the mid-cabin galley is pretty much gone, Scott and I decide to see what's left up in the first class galley. So with Scott leading the way, we slip through the curtains and enter the first class cabin. I've resolved in my mind that I won't even try to make eye contact with Marco Maselli. I won't give him the satisfaction! Plus, Miriam Ungaro is under the distinct impression that Captain Maselli is her new "boy toy," and, frankly, that's just fine with me!

I stare straight ahead, nearly boring a hole in the back of Scott's neck as we make a beeline for the front galley. I do my best to seem easy and breezy as we practically glide down the aisle, but I'm in such a hurry to get inside the galley that I kick the back of Scott's heel twice, causing him to react in pain.

"*Jeese*, Elle!" Scott says in a harsh whisper. "Watch where you're going!"

"I'm sorry," I say in a panic as I push on his back in an effort to maintain our forward momentum.

We sort of tumble our way into the galley, and once we're safely behind the curtain, I start to calm down. There are at least six people hanging out in the galley, sipping on wine and eating cheese wedges from the first class snack containers.

"Hey you two," Bobbi Henry says as she stands up to grab a bottle of red wine. "Are you here to join our little party?"

"But of course!" Scott replies as he snatches a plastic cup off the counter and thrusts it out for Bobbi to fill.

Bobbi smiles to herself and graciously pours Scott some wine before refilling her own glass. I look around the first class galley and see that everyone is drinking wine and clustered into small groups around each of the jump seats. It's cozy and relaxed—not like a normal flight at all. I'm not sure that even on a ferry flight, flight attendants should be drinking. But no one else seems to really care, so I shrug it off.

"Elle, do you want some wine?" Bobbi asks me.

"Oh…no thank you," I say after a moment of consideration. "But do you have any more bottled water up here?"

"Sure thing, Sweetie," Bobbi replies as she grabs a bottle of water from an ice bucket on one of the beverage carts and hands it to me.

On the other side of the galley, I recognize Nina Harrison sharing the jump seat with one of the Italian pilots. Nina is a few years older than me, but to me, she seems much older. Scott says it's because she is more worldly than I am, but I think it's simply because she has more self-confidence than any other woman I know.

Nina has a great personality and is unusually beautiful, too. She has dark brown hair with natural golden highlights. Her skin is flawless with a brown, tawny tone that sets off her deep green eyes, and she has peach-colored lips that are almost always curled into a smile. In addition to all of these great features, Nina is pencil thin and about 5' 10" tall. I guess it would be easy to be self-confident if you looked like Nina. The Italian pilot sitting next to her is resting his hand on one of Nina's long legs, and she appears to be transfixed by his every word.

"It figures that Nina would reel in the hottie," Bobbi says as she leans against the counter in the galley and pops a small cube of Swiss cheese into her mouth. "She picked him out first thing, and the poor guy never had a chance…" she tapers off as we watch Nina throw her head back in laughter.

"Well, I, for one, don't feel too sorry for any of these pilots," I add, a little shocked at my own cynicism. I find myself leaning in slightly to try to get a better look at the pilot—so I can see if he is better looking than Marco—but Nina's shoulder is blocking my view.

"*Rrrear!*" Bobbi screeches as she cranes her neck to look at me. "Aren't we a little vicious today!" she says in a teasing tone.

I can feel my cheeks redden ever so slightly as both Bobbi and Scott look at me. I feel the need to say more, but I really don't know what else to say. My introduction to Marco Maselli left me feeling confused and embarrassed, and I don't want to add any more emotions to the mix.

"Let's just say that these *Italian Stallions* get what they deserve," Scott finally adds while peeking through the galley curtains.

Bobbi and I follow his gaze out into the first class cabin and see Marco feeding Miriam a grape. Miriam is all wrapped up in a blanket and Marco is sitting close to her while she swoons over his every move. I feel slightly grossed out by the sight of Miriam and Marco together—and not just because of my earlier exchange.

Scott draws the curtains closed, and the three of us pull various faces of disgust over what we just saw and then start laughing.

"At least Captain Cordova over there may actually *enjoy* being trapped by Nina, but that poor sucker must be dying!" Bobbi blurts out with a peel of laughter.

It actually feels good to laugh about it. I feel my body start to ease up and relax as Scott and I settle in on one of the only open jump seats. Scott grabs a handful of grapes and attempts to feed one to me the way Marco fed Miriam—which makes me laugh with a loud snort. Bobbi sees the exchange and starts laughing, too.

"I heard Miriam's been all over that one ever since the pilots arrived in Miami for their training," Bobbi offers after she regains her composure.

I feel sort of relieved to hear that it was Miriam that was doing all the pursuing and not Marco, but still, the whole thing is really strange. I decide not to think about it anymore as Scott and Bobbi settle into a conversation about our arrival.

We stay up in the galley with Bobbi and the others for the rest of our flight, discussing all of the information we've each gathered on our own about our new hometown. Everyone is in such a happy mood that any dark feelings I was having earlier seem to have melted away.

When Captain Cramden announces that we are making our initial decent, it is about 3:30 a.m. local time. We should be on the ground in twenty minutes. Scott and I help Bobbi straighten and secure the galley for landing while the others disappear into other parts of the plane. Once everything is in tiptop shape, Scott and I make our way back to our seats in the mid-cabin.

As Scott and I pass through first class, everyone seems to be awake now, and most of the women are primping and preening in anticipation of our arrival. Michelle Maddox is brushing her hair while one of the Italian pilots seated across the aisle is tucking his shirt into his trousers.

I try not to look for Marco, but I can't seem to control my eyes from looking in the general direction of where he and Miriam are seated. I catch a glimpse of Miriam holding up a tiny mirror while applying a new coat of thick red lipstick to her craggy lips. But there is no Marco.

A zing of adrenaline shoots through my body as I realize that Marco isn't where I thought he would be. I try to shake it off, but my thighs feel heavy at the prospect of another encounter. I try to squeeze that thought out of my mind as Scott and I head toward our seats.

Suzanne Keller and Marta DeSoto are cleaning up the mid-cabin galley. Things are looking pretty messy, so I stop to offer some help. As I step into the galley and start picking up empty bottles and used napkins, Suzanne just looks at me with a big smile.

"You should just go to your seat, Miss Elle," Marta says with a knowing smile. "I think someone has an admirer!" Marta and Suzanne both start laughing.

"What?" I say as confusion mixed with curiosity enters my mind.

"Just go look!" Suzanne says as she practically rips the empty water bottle out of my hand and nudges me out of her way.

Casually, so as not to seem too excited, I glide out of the galley and head toward my seat. Scott is shoving folded blankets and pillows into the overhead compartments as I approach our area. He has a look on his face that I can't quite place. It is a cross between annoyed and amused.

When I reach my row, I look down at the open tray table. A small Smirnoff Vodka bottle rests right in the center with a paper rose made out of a red cocktail napkin and a coffee stirrer for the stem. Next to the bottle is another red cocktail napkin with a note. I reach down and pick it up.

It's written in dark black ink that bled a bit on the napkin, so the lettering is thick and hard to read. But the heart shaped squiggle is unmistakable, and the initials "MM" are still readable.

Chapter Nine

As the Italian gate agent greeting our flight nudges the Jetway up to meet the mid cabin door, I feel a heaviness in my limbs. I pull in a deep breath to try to regain some energy, but the recycled air in the cabin smells thick and stale, and I instantly regret drawing so much of it into my lungs.

All around me, everyone is bustling. People are slamming the overhead compartments and gathering their gear while laughing and shouting out their plans for when they get off the plane. The mid-cabin is a wash of activity, but I find I can't seem to join in. I carefully open the side compartment of my satchel. Tucked away under the canvas flap is the paper napkin rose. A tingle settles in my stomach. As I wait patiently for Fozzy to open the door that separates me from my Italian adventure, I wonder what Marco Maselli is up to. Did he give *Miriam* a rose, too? The thought makes me blanch.

Scott is up in the first class galley pilfering bottles of leftover water for our rooms. He hasn't said anything to me about my rose other than, "*Capitano Amore* has hidden talents, I see!" He's just teasing me—which is a normal part of our relationship—but I feel so defensive when he does it. Maybe I'm just tired and irritable. I bet I'll feel better after a decent nap. I know I should let it go and enjoy the fact that I'm finally here.

I'm in Italy! I remind myself, willing the reality of this fact to enliven me.

The deplaning process takes no time at all and soon, we're entering the terminal of the *Vespucci* airport for the very first time. I study the detailing in the architecture of this nearly empty airport facility and do my best to translate various signs located throughout the terminal. The Italian gate agent who met our flight is leading our group down a narrow corridor. The sign above the entry reads *Dogana*. I can tell by the weary-looking official standing under the sign, sipping something hot and steamy out of a Styrofoam cup, that this must be the customs area. The official waves us in and points out where to go—relying on his empty hand to communicate everything to us while doing his best to avoid spilling his morning drink.

We all filter our way into the open area and queue up into three different lines. As I dig through my satchel to find my passport and *Windsong Air* credentials, my hand brushes past the paper napkin rose. Scott sidles up next to me and elbows me.

"You want some gum?" he offers as he pops a tiny square of peppermint Dentine into his mouth and mashes down on it, flexing his jaw muscles in a very manly way.

"Oh yeah," I say, grabbing the gum out of the palm of his hand. "I needed this!"

"I wasn't gonna say anything, but…" he trails off. "Plus, you want to make sure you have fresh breath in case *Capitano Amore* comes around looking for you!"

"Scott, why do you keep teasing me about him?" I demand a little more harshly than I intended to.

"Oh come on, Elle!" he laughs. "I'm just having fun!" His face looks only partially sincere as he gives me one of his winning smiles. "I just think it's kind of funny that you and *Miriam* seem to attract the same kind of man, that's all!" he snickers.

"Listen, Scott," I say in a low whisper. "I don't think this is as funny as you do for some reason, so can we just drop it?"

Scott seems to suddenly realize that I really can't find the humor in the situation and shifts his demeanor to be in alignment with mine.

"I'm sorry, Elle. I didn't realize you were so *sensitive*…"

"Well, I just feel uncomfortable about it, so if you could just let it go, I would appreciate it, OK?"

"Fine," Scott says as he pans the room with his eyes. He has a faint smile on his face like the situation still amuses him.

"Fine," I reiterate irritably.

Fozzy is tapping on a podium handset to see if it works. The loud crackle of the overhead speakers jolts everyone into attention before Fozzy begins to speak.

"Sorry about that folks," Fozzy says with a weary grin. He looks exhausted. His round face looks even more swollen than usual, and his eyes are puffy and red. "If I could have your attention for just a minute, I'd like to fill you in on a few things while we are clearing customs."

Fozzy holds up a sheet of crumpled paper with some notes to help him stay on track. The Italian gate agent is standing beside him as he begins his instructions. She is a petite woman who looks like she may be in her mid to late twenties. She is very pretty with glossy, long, black hair that is pulled back into a tight ponytail. Her skin is golden brown and her features are fresh and bright—a striking contrast to Fozzy's disheveled and worn out look.

"Once you've cleared customs," Fozzy continues, "please wait in the holding area for everyone to finish. Don't worry about your checked luggage—it's already on the way over to the resort," Fozzy assures us as he ramps up for his next announcement.

"Maria here," Fozzy gestures in an effort to introduce the gate agent to the group, "is going to then take us to our vans. You will need to pay attention to where the vans pick us up as this will be our regular pick up and drop off location here at the airport once we start flying. We have three vans waiting to take us to the resort, so just get on one—they're all going to the same place. You already have your room assignments in your packet, so if you haven't looked that up yet, you may want to do it before you get on the van."

"Do you know what room you have?" I ask Scott in an effort to try to smooth over our recent awkward exchange.

"I'm in *Villa Quindici*—which I looked up in my Italian to English dictionary, and it turns out, I'm in Villa 15. And if I remember correctly, you are in *Villa Venti*—or 20," Scott replies with added flare on the Italian words.

"*Sì!*" I say enthusiastically to play along. "This Italian thing is no problem!" At that, we both laugh. I'm relieved that the tension of our previous conversation has passed, and we are back in synch.

Fozzy bangs the loudspeaker again as he fumbles around to give us another announcement. "One more thing, folks. Crew 1, your first show time is in exactly two days, so use this time to rest up and be ready for your *5:00 a.m.* arrival back here at the airport. Crew 2, we'll see you all here at 5:00 *p.m.* on the same day. Now be smart and enjoy your first days in Italy!"

A weary but happy clap fills the customs area as Fozzy leaves the podium. He tucks his notes into the front pocket of his heavily starched khaki pants and leans down to talk to Maria.

"Do you want to get a bite to eat with the others, or do you want to go sleep?" Scott asks as he shoves his carryon bag with his foot, nudging it along the ground as the line moves up a spot.

"I think I might just crash," I say as I work to stifle a yawn.

"I can't decide what to do," Scott says after looking at his watch. "It's probably gonna be about 5:30 when we finally get checked into the resort, and if I go to sleep then, I'll be all out of whack for the rest of the day." It appears that Scott is putting a lot of thought into his decision, and, now, I'm starting to question my own.

"I see your point," I offer while wondering in the back of my mind how long I'll last if I join the gang.

"Why don't we move our gear into our villas and then try to find a café near the resort that serves an early breakfast," Scott begins to plot. "Then maybe we can push through the morning with a swim in the pool and lounge around in the sun for the afternoon."

"You know, that actually sounds pretty good," I say after considering his suggestion. "But I'm going to need a real nap at some point ya know. I'll be cranky if I don't get some sleep!"

"Oh girl!" Scott moans. "Don't I know!"

Once we are on the van, I lean my head against the window and fight off sleep. The sky is navy blue with the first hints of dawn, and my eyelids are so heavy I can barely stay awake. My feet feel swollen and sore. The flight over didn't do anything to make my choice of shoes more comfortable, and I can't wait to get to my villa so I can kick them off for good. The rest of the people on the van are carrying on and laughing loudly as we make our way through the sleepy streets of Florence. It's still too early to see any regular daily activity, so I guess my first look at my new home city in action will be delayed a bit longer.

I'm really looking forward to seeing the resort that will be our home for the next three months. Fozzy included some detailed notes on the resort, which is called *Il Girasole*—The Sunflower. According to the notes, Wiley Bennett purchased the resort last year with the intention of turning it into a very exclusive five-star health retreat. His renovation plans have been placed on hold so that *WRI* can use the property to house the Miami-based flight attendants while establishing *Windsong Air's* first European base.

There are 35 individual villas on the property—each with one bedroom and a private bath with attached veranda, a full kitchen and a small living room. Additionally, there are six larger suites that have multiple bedrooms and bathrooms and are said to be quite luxurious even before the remodel. Fozzy listed some of the amenities—such as a huge salt-water swimming pool, three whirlpools, a day spa with both a sauna and a steam room and small gym facility.

As our van pulls into a circular drive, I get my first glimpse of *Il Girasole*. In the predawn light, I can see a set of ornate iron gates attached to aging brick walls covered in ivy. When I finally extract myself from the crew van, I can smell the lush fragrance of lavender in the dew-filled air. In the driveway to the left of the iron gates is a huge pile of luggage. I feel my body groan at the thought of finding my bag as I survey the huge pile of identical *Windsong Air* issued suitcases stacked up, waiting for retrieval.

"Oh man," Scott says as soon as he sees the bags. "Do you think we should start digging?"

"Maybe we should get our keys first," I suggest as a group of people start pushing their way over to the mountain of luggage. "It might be easier to find once some of the bags are cleared away."

"OK," Scott says as though he couldn't care less.

Behind the iron gates—which incidentally are made up of iron sunflowers intricately welded in place for a grand entrance—there is a large, open courtyard with a series of terracotta pathways stretching out in all directions. Small, dim lights line each of the pathways as they disappear into the shadowy darkness. To the left is a small building with large windows along the front. A sign shaped like an arrow with the word *Ufficio* painted on it is pointing to the building.

As if on instinct, our small mob of people pushes toward the *Ufficio*, waiting for instructions on how to find our villas. A tiny, elderly man is waiting on the steps of the building as we approach. He is probably about 5' 5" tall—if that—and is wearing baggy linen trousers and a white cotton sweater. Brown leather sandals wrap around his small feet as he stands in anticipation of our arrival. His face is very kind, and it crinkles up with a grin as we assemble ourselves at the base of the steps. With his hands, he motions for us to move into a tight group, so we can all hear his instructions.

In very broken English, he begins: "*Buongiorno!* Welcome to *Il Girasole!* My name is-ah Bruno and I am-ah your new friend-ah and *proprietario.* You must-ah be very sleepy, so here are the…keys to your *villas,*" he says as he gestures to a large board with key hooks and painted numbers propped up against the wall behind him. "We have the little…ah…*segno*…by the… *sentiero* to show you the way," he says pointing to another arrow-shaped sign next to one of the narrow, dimly lit pathways.

Bruno smiles brightly at the group before he steps aside and motions for us to climb up the steps to get our keys. In surprisingly smooth fashion, our group forms a line leading to the keyboard. Scott is up ahead of me and reaches the board first. He quickly motions to me that he'll get my key, so I back away from the line and start looking for the "*segno*" that will point us to Villas 15 and 20.

When Scott joins me on the sidewalk at the base of the stairs, his face is full of excitement as if he has just caught his second wind. "Let's find the villas first and then go back for the bags," he suggests.

I'm too tired to really care, so I say, "Perfect!" Unlike Scott, my second wind hasn't arrived yet, and I feel weary and faded. It's all I can do to fake the enthusiasm required to match Scott's mood.

When we find the pathway to the row of villas numbered *Dieci— Venti* (which Scott translates as *10—20*), I step down carefully on the cobbled path. The surface is uneven and hard, and the garden luminaries do very little to show the way. In the early dawn light, I can see that each of the villas is neatly tucked into the landscaping with ivy climbing up the outer walls. It smells fresh and flowery as we make our way down the stretch leading to our villas. Even in this light, you can tell that the villas have that old world charm that is distinctively Italian.

"Here's my place," Scott points out as we see the words *Villa Quindici* spelled out in small lettered tiles next to the front door. "I'll come back. Let's find your place." Scott leads as we make our way down three cobbled steps and cross a tiny bridge leading to *Villa Venti*.

Two narrow steps lead up to a small entry porch in front of my villa. There are flowery bushes that close the porch in on both sides giving it kind of a natural railing. A tiny bistro table and chair are set up to the right of the doorway, and a potted sunflower surrounded by leafy greens in a shiny, painted urn rests quietly on the table.

"I want to check out my pad before I get my gear," Scott says once I've climbed the two steps to my porch. "Why don't you go in and splash some water on your face, and I'll get your bag when I get mine," Scott offers as he starts walking toward his villa.

"No, Scott," I reply after him. "You don't have to do that—I'll go get my bag…"

"No!" Scott replies emphatically. "I insist! You need to get your second wind, so we can go get something to eat. Now, take off those stupid shoes and go freshen up! I'll be right back with your bag."

Leaving me with no room to protest, I call out a quick, "You're the best, Scott!"

He waves me off and disappears down the path. I dig into my jacket pocket and pull out my key. The thick wooden door has an ancient-looking handle with a keyhole just below it. I slide my key into the lock and twist it open. I can hear a loud pop as the lock releases. I give the long handle a gentle push, and the door to *Villa Venti* glides open, revealing my new home.

It's very dark inside, so I start patting the walls in search of a light switch. After sliding my hand down all the plaster covered walls near the entry door, my eyes finally start to adjust to the dim interior, and I can make out a slender lamp on a table to the left of the door. I reach up under the shade in search of the switch. The light snaps on with a warm yellow glow, and I get my first look at my lovely new living room.

To the far left is a small, open fireplace with a rustic, wooden mantelpiece suspended up above. A tall, slender, metal bucket is resting on the mantel, and it is filled with what appears to be dried sunflowers and lavender buds. Nestled in the corner next to the fireplace is an overstuffed, beige-colored armchair with a snow-white blanket draped over the armrest. A beige love seat and an extra-large, overstuffed pale blue armchair hover around a large wooden coffee table in the center of the living room, which completes the simple seating area.

The table with the lamp I just turned on is sitting next to the inviting blue chair, so I toss my satchel and carryon luggage into the welcoming seat and kick off my shoes, so I can explore the rest of the place in comfort. The cool terracotta tile feels amazing on my sore, fat feet as I examine the room and prepare for my tour.

I can see a small kitchen situated to my left and a closed wooden door directly ahead, and a set of double wooden doors ahead and to my right. I open the double doors to my right first and slide my hand along the wall inside the room in search of a light switch. This time, there's a switch, and, when I flip it, the most beautiful bedroom appears!

There's a large four-poster bed to the right of the doorway, and it is covered in fluffy, white linen with pale yellow throw pillows. There's a wooden bedside table on both sides of the bed and a tall shelving unit in the far corner with a TV and four drawers underneath. There is a beautiful window seat directly in front of me with a purple seat cushion and lemon yellow and mint green pillows lined up along the edges. I can't believe how beautiful this room is! There is a small closet on my left and a simple wooden chair holding a pile of neatly folded plush white towels.

The kitchen is pretty basic. There's a long countertop bar that separates the kitchen from the living room, and there are two heavy, iron barstools pushed up under the lip of the bar. The countertop seems to be made of a solid piece of wood that has been sealed with a thick polymer, and underneath it, there are three cabinet doors that open into the kitchen. Directly on the other side of the bar are a small refrigerator, a narrow stove and a microwave oven hanging up above the stove. A wooden wine rack with several bottles of wine is positioned on top of the refrigerator, reminding me that I am indeed in Tuscany!

The last door must lead to the bathroom, I reason, as I carefully push open the thick wooden door. The early dawn light illuminates this room with a mystic glow from a skylight above and two French doors to my left. The room is long and slender. Other than the French doors, the walls of the bathroom are covered with floor to ceiling terracotta tile. A small mirror hangs on the tiled wall to my right, hovering directly over a sink enclosed in a rustic wooden vanity. A small, white toilet is nestled between the vanity and the shower.

There is a long sheer shower curtain that is gathered and pressed against the tile wall and hangs from a taught wire suspended between the bathroom walls on either side. The sunflower-shaped showerhead and knobs extend from the tiled wall, and a silver drain is notably placed in the floor below.

It is such a simple room, but the skylight and clear glass doors make it feel like you are outside. The French doors open out onto a large veranda that is closed in along the backside by a tall ivy-covered fence. There is a double-sized chaise lounge set off to one side and two cushioned armchairs and a low round table on the other. The veranda can only be described as enchanting, and I can already picture myself relaxing on the chaise lounge in a plush bathrobe after a long hot shower.

I flip up the light switch on the bathroom wall, and two mounted sconces illuminate the room with golden yellow light. There is a small gray wicker basket placed on the far edge of the vanity that has all sorts of soaps, lotions and shampoos in it. I grab one of the soaps and hold it up to my nose. I take a deep breath in and smell the combination of honey and lavender.

I turn the tap on and let the water run as I open up the soap. After washing my hands with the rich, fragrant suds, I splash some water on my face before I look at myself in the mirror. I look tired. My eyes are red, and my hair is a mess. I grab one of the fluffy white hand towels piled up in a second larger wicker basket underneath the vanity and dry my face. It feels so good to stimulate my tired skin against the clean white towel.

After hanging the hand towel on an iron bar suspended above the toilet, I drag my fingers through my long hair in an effort to make myself a little more presentable. I'm looking forward to getting my bag soon so I can brush my teeth and maybe change my clothes before we head out in search of food. I turn off the light and walk out into the main room of the villa.

The early morning light is streaming through a large window that stretches across the front of the villa and abutting the front door. Pushed to each side of the window is a set of wooden slat-shutters. Everything about this place is perfect! It's soft and welcoming, and I instantly feel as if this is my home. I walk over to the love seat and flop myself over the backrest and land on my back. I let my legs stick straight up in the air, hoping that gravity will pull some of the blood out of my thunderous feet and give me some relief. It feels amazing to be lying down, and I wonder when I can expect my so-called second wind.

As I stare up at the ceiling and study the sky blue painted plaster, I can hear footsteps out on my porch. Too tired to get up and open the door, I simply shout out, "Door's open, Scott! Come on in!"

Slowly, the door opens with a faint creek, and an unfamiliar voice says, "*Eloise-ah?*"

I raise my head up off the love seat, so I can see over the blue armchair that is blocking my view of the door. I instantly feel my limbs go icy as I see Marco Maselli standing in the doorway.

I struggle to turn my body right side up, but between the heaviness of my feet and the shot of adrenaline coursing through my body, it takes me a couple tries to get situated. When I finally manage to sit like a normal person on the little sofa, I don't know what to say.

"*Buongiorno!*" Marco says brightly.

"Oh...*buongiorno*..." I say with a nervous giggle.

"May I come in?" he asks me as he pushes the door open a little bit wider.

"Yes! Sure. Please do," I say, probably a little too eagerly. I suddenly feel very alert and aware—as if along with Marco came my second wind.

"I hope I am not bothering you," Marco says as he enters the villa and places his hands on the back of the overstuffed blue chair. "I just wanted to make sure that I found you before you fall to sleep or some such thing..." he trails off with a hopeful look in his eyes.

"Oh, I'm just waiting for my friend Scott to bring me my suitcase, and then we're going to go and get some breakfast," I explain in a nervous sounding voice.

"Ah, I see," he says with a little smile. "Well, you must promise me that, very soon, you will allow *me* to show you around and take you to breakfast at dawn."

The look he gives me makes me feel like I'm falling under his spell again. My tongue feels dry, and I don't know what to say in return, so I just nod my head up and down and smile back.

The clatter of luggage wheels on terracotta startles us both back into reality. I can hear Scott banging his way up the steps to the porch while shouting, "I have your *valigia signorina Elle!*"

I rise to my feet with a nervous smile as Marco pulls open the door for Scott. Scott looks up and sees Marco. His smile fades a bit, and then he looks to me. "Gee, I hope I'm not interrupting anything here," he says with a forced politeness.

"Not at all," I say giving Scott a genuine smile. "Captain Maselli was just saying hello, and now he is leaving," I say directly to Marco in hopes that he will simply leave.

"*Buongiorno*, Scott," Marco says as he stretches his hand out to properly greet my confused friend standing on the porch. "Welcome to Florence!"

Scott shakes Marco's hand and replies, "*Buongiorno*, Captain Maselli."

This awkward exchange is taking way too long, so I step in front of Marco and grab my bag from Scott. "Give me ten minutes to change clothes, and I'll meet you back at your villa."

I manage to make it very clear to Marco that I don't want any help with my bags, so he steps outside onto the porch to give me room as I lug my large suitcase into the villa.

"Thanks for stopping by, Captain Maselli. I'll see you later, I guess," I offer in a final effort to get him to leave.

As I close the door, I briefly peer out through the peephole at Scott and Marco, who are both standing on my porch looking awkwardly at one another. I listen in closely and hope that Scott doesn't feel the need to say anything to Marco on my behalf. I can't really hear anything through the thick wooden door, so, just in case, I dash over to the window and peek out to see if they are talking to one another.

I can see them both standing on the pathway leading up to my villa now. They are talking, but I can't hear what they're saying. I lean in close to the window hoping their words will carry. As I try to get my ear as close to the window as possible, my shoulder bumps one of the slat shutters against the wall! The sound is surprisingly loud, and I do my best to quickly duck out of sight.

I stay hunched down for a few more seconds until I can hear the hum of Scott's voice just a few feet away. I carefully rise up and peer out the corner of the window. Marco appears to be laughing politely, and Scott seems a bit more serious. After they exchange a few more words, Scott turns and walks toward his villa. Marco walks off in the other direction.

My mind is a flutter with what they could have said to one another. Were they talking about me? Was Scott asking him questions about Miriam? I consider the exchange while I drag my suitcase into my amazing bedroom and start unpacking a few of my things. I pull out my *Windsong Air* uniform and hang it up in the closet before I start to dig for some clothes to wear to breakfast.

I pull out a stretchy teal tank top, a ruffled white skirt and some spongy white flip-flops with teal beading. It feels so good to change into this summery outfit. My jeans were beginning to feel stale and my T-shirt has lost all of its crispness. I wad up my dirty clothes in a corner of the closet and then slide the closet door shut.

As I carry my toiletry bag into the bathroom, I wonder why Captain Maselli seems to upset Scott so much. Is it because he's flirting with me? Or is it because he seems to be flirting with me *and* Miriam? Is Scott just protecting my honor? Maybe. There isn't a better explanation so far, but, whatever it is, Scott obviously doesn't like Marco.

I apply a thin line of toothpaste to my toothbrush and run it under the water. As I brush my teeth, I multi-task with my free hand and unload some of my toiletries into the wooden drawers of the vanity and place several of my personal items in the cabinet behind the mirror. After running a hairbrush through my gnarled hair, I pull the stringy mass back into a lose ponytail. I feel so much better now, and, suddenly, I realize how hungry I am!

I grab my satchel off the chair and dig around to find my purse hidden deep inside. When I find it, I stick my villa key inside one of the inner pockets and then dash back into my room to get my jean jacket. I think I'm ready to go as I zip around the villa shutting off lights and making sure I have my money and passport in my purse.

When I open the door to the villa, I notice that my potted sunflower plant has been moved from the little bistro table to the center of the porch. After closer inspection, I can see that there is a note nestled in the leaves of the plant that has my name on it. I reach down to pick up the note.

Just then, I hear Scott holler out, "Come on, Elle! I'm starving!"

I quickly shove the note into my purse and place the potted sunflower back up on the bistro table. I turn to lock the door to my villa and shout, "Be right there," over my shoulder as I sense Scott waiting for me on the little bridge up ahead.

Chapter Ten

In the light of the morning, I finally get a proper look at the villas that make up *Il Girasole*. Each villa has a deep-orange terracotta rooftop, but the facades differ slightly. Some villas have porches like mine, while others have no porch, but have huge sunflower beds surrounding the front of the villa instead. There are little cobbled pathways that zigzag in all different directions connecting the resort together in some chaotic way that requires an aerial-view map to actually follow.

When I catch up to Scott on the bridge, he seems to be in a big hurry. He's wearing light khaki walking shorts and a dark brown camp shirt with pockets all over it. He looks very Euro-chic in his funky man sandals and dark sunglasses. A sudden excitement grips me that we are about to see the city for the first time as Scott grabs my hand and we make our way down the cobbled pathway that leads to the front gate.

"Why are we in such a hurry?" I finally manage to ask Scott as we race past the *ufficio*. My feet are feeling much better in my comfy flip-flops, but they still ache a little as I do my best to keep up with Scott.

"I don't feel like being social, OK? I just want to find a place to eat. Trying to plan anything with this group is like herding cats," Scott explains with exasperation over his shoulder.

He's right about the herding cats thing. Every time we try to do something on a layover with our crew, Scott and I end up waiting on everyone—sometimes for hours! So even though I'm sure Scott's telling me the truth about why we're in such a hurry, there's still a small part of me that wonders if Scott is rushing to avoid something—or maybe *someone*.

After we make our way through the iron sunflower gate, we take a sharp right and start heading down the cobblestone sidewalk. "Bruno said that there are lots of cafés along this street," Scott explains as he brings our pace from a sprint to a stroll.

"Sounds great!" I say with some of my newfound enthusiasm. "I'm getting pretty hungry!"

"Me too," Scott adds as we continue to walk, but no longer hand-and-hand.

Motorbikes and tiny cars whiz past us on the rutty cobbled street, making their way into what appears to be a little open market area. Up ahead, I can see several wooden carts with assorted fruits and vegetables, and I smell the heavenly aroma of fresh-baked breads. Everything has such a warm glow—all the orange rooftops on the buildings that stretch as far as the eye can see make me think the morning sun has set the city ablaze with heat and excitement.

After walking for about five more minutes, we take a quick right and find ourselves in a charming courtyard. In the center of the courtyard is a small fountain, and all around there are street vendors and tiny cafés. I am delighted by all the colors and the smells—metal buckets filled with vibrantly hued flowers and wooden carts overflowing with fresh fruits greet my senses and liven up the morning. I soak in the sounds of vendors shouting out their hellos in a rolling language to their regulars as they pass by with thick loaves of bread in their arms. It's just how I imagined it would be—only better! The fresh morning air invigorates me as I take in my surroundings.

"Is this place all right with you?" Scott asks as we approach a café with tiny iron tables smattered throughout the courtyard.

"Yeah! This looks great!" I reply, excited about sitting down and doing some people watching.

There are already people taking up some of the tables, so Scott and I wander to the outer edge and pick a table directly in the early morning sun. A plump woman in a dingy apron nods her head at us as we sit down. A few minutes later, the woman approaches our table with a pad and pen, ready to take our order.

"*Buongiorno*," Scott begins tentatively.

The woman nods and simply replies, "*Si?*"

"Oh, um..." Scott stammers around briefly before regaining his composure. "*Due cappuccino, per favore.*" The woman nods her head in recognition and scurries off to fill our order.

"Impressive!" I say to Scott as a smile widens across my face. "And very smooth I might add!"

"I try," Scott says with mock pride. "What do you want to eat?" he asks me, as he looks me dead in the eye.

"What do Italian people eat for breakfast? Eggs? Bacon?" I ask with no idea as to the answer. When I went to Rome with my parents as a kid, we stayed in a hotel that strictly catered to Americans, so we pretty much ate whatever we wanted to eat—which my father considered to be a real shame. He went on and on about how we missed out on the true Italian culture. Well, not this time—I'm fully embracing the expression, "When in Rome" (even though I'm actually in Florence this time!)

"Breakfast is not that big of a deal here in Italy," Scott explains with authority. "But it's the only time of day a *real* Italian drinks cappuccino, so that's why I chose that first off. But they mostly eat pastry in the morning— like a croissant or something like that."

"OK, I can handle that. Just order me whatever you get yourself," I say as I sit back in my chair and watch the people milling around the courtyard. There's a woman selecting fruit from one of the carts, and she looks so beautiful in the glowing light that I find myself transfixed by her every move. Her simple cotton dress clings to her curves, and she looks so fresh and happy.

Our waitress returns with our cappuccinos and carefully places them on our table. She looks to Scott once again, and he mumbles something to her in Italian. She taps her pen on her pad and nods her head, and then she dashes off again to fill our order.

"You seem to do all right with the Italian people," I say before I take a sip of my foamy coffee drink.

"When I was with Ford, we did a lot of fashion shows in Milan, so I have some experience with Italian people and with ordering my food at least," Scott explains as he brings his cup to his lips. His stylish sunglasses are big and wide, and he looks so at ease sitting next to me.

"Man, this tastes so good—and I don't even *like* coffee that much!" I marvel as I take another slurp of my cappuccino. The hot, frothy mixture goes down easily and wakes me up from the inside out.

"I know," Scott adds. "The Italians have a way of making everything taste good."

We both sit silently for a bit, taking in our surroundings and allowing the caffeine from our drinks to take its full affect. The pretty woman I was watching earlier has picked out her fruits and said her goodbyes, so I pan the courtyard in search of someone else to watch. After our waitress delivers our breakfast—which turns out to be a chocolate-filled croissant called a *cornetto al cioccolato*—Scott finally breaks the silence with a question.

"So, how's your villa?"

"Amazing!" I reply emphatically. "It's so perfect—I actually like it better than *The Wiley!*" I admit with a sheepish grin.

"Yeah, mine's really nice, too," Scott replies. "Did you check out your veranda?"

"Yes! I am so looking forward to spending some time out there with a good book!"

Scott just smiles at my reply. He seems tired now, like maybe the traveling and all of the getting situated is catching up with him.

"Are you losing your second wind, Scott?" I ask as I wipe my lips. The buttery *cornetto* tastes so good that I fear I may be making a pig of myself.

"I'm a little tired, I guess," he says as he pulls off a piece of his pastry and looks around the courtyard with heavy eyes.

"What's on your mind, then. You seem kind of funny..." I trail off, feeling a little worried about what he might say.

"Elle," he says in a direct tone before taking another sip of his cappuccino. He places the tiny cup back on the saucer and then looks down at his lap as he begins to speak again. "I'm a little worried about you and this Marco Maselli."

"Why?" I ask, trying not to sound defensive, but fighting hard to keep my irritation at bay.

"There's something about him that's bothering me."

"Can you be more specific?" I question him, wanting to know what's really on his mind.

"Well," he begins tentatively. "For starters, he seems to be leading Miriam on while making advances toward you."

"Well, you heard Bobbi say that Miriam is the one who is doing all the pursuing there, so maybe Marco is just being polite," I say, in an attempt to defend Marco for some reason that I can't explain.

"Yes, but *who* was feeding *whom* grapes on the plane?" Scott says, as the painfully embarrassing scene flashes into my head.

"I know…" I concede after a moment of reflection. "I do have to admit that I'm kind of confused by everything. He keeps coming around and seeming so interested in getting to know me and all, and I don't know what to think…"

"When you closed the door to your villa and left Marco and me on the porch, he asked me if you were seeing anyone," Scott confides in a low tone.

"What did you say?" I ask as a buzz of nerves rises up my spine.

"I asked him the same question," Scott says as he tucks his napkin underneath his saucer and looks up at me. I can see irritation in his eyes.

"And…what did he say?" I ask Scott, trying hard not to sound pathetic.

"He gave me a little laugh and said that he is 'not attached' to anyone. So I said to him that maybe he ought to consider the fact that *your boss* seems to be attached to *him*."

"Then what did he say?" I'm nearly falling off the edge of my seat at this point in anticipation of his reply.

"He just smiled and walked away," Scott says matter-of-factly. "But that smile really pissed me off, Elle. It was so smug and so selfish. I'm no big fan of Miriam Ungaro, but I don't want to see her get hurt. And you—you're my best friend. I can't stand by and let you get caught up in some sick Italian man's game…"

I let Scott's words soak in as I consider the situation. I hate the thought of being mixed up in a silly love triangle with Marco and Miriam, too, but I have this feeling that it's not exactly like Scott thinks. I mean, maybe Marco was waiting to get back to Italy to let Miriam down, and now that he's in his hometown, he can finally do it.

"Elle, don't you have anything to say about all of this?" Scott finally asks me after a long pause.

"I don't really know what *to* say," I offer up, wondering what it is that Scott wants to hear.

"Well, you can do whatever you want to do with what I've told you," Scott says calmly but with a trace of defeat in his voice. "But just know that you've been warned."

"Understood," I say in response as I give Scott a sincere smile.

"I'm gonna pay for this. I exchanged some cash for Euros at the resort," Scott says as he scoots his chair back and then rises up to walk inside the café.

As soon as he disappears into the doorway of the café, I grab my purse and start digging around inside to find the note from my porch. It's a simple folded sheet of paper with my name scrawled in thick black ink—just like the ink used on the napkin note on the plane. I glance up once more at the café entrance to make sure Scott isn't coming. When I see the coast is clear, I unfold the paper and begin to read.

Eloise-
I have some things to explain. I will come find you tomorrow.
MM

I quickly fold the note back up and tuck it inside my purse. *He has some things to explain*, I repeat in my mind as I see Scott walking up to the table. I don't think I'll mention the note to Scott until I find out what Marco has to say. Scott may be right about Marco, but, then again, he may just not understand the circumstances.

"Are you ready?" Scott asks with a fresh smile on his face.

"Yep! Where to now?" I ask as I hop up out of my chair. The caffeine mixed with adrenaline from reading the note has my engines rattling, and I feel slightly shaky as I push my heavy chair back under the table.

"Maybe we could just go for a walk and then head back to the resort?" Scott offers up as he takes my arm.

"*Questro andra benissimo!*" I say showing off my one and only Italian phrase—that will be perfect!

After about two hours of strolling around the city and shopping, Scott and I both decide we're ready to head back to the resort. I've exchanged some of my money for Euros and bought a few things for my villa— including some fresh fruit, bread, Italian whole grain crackers, some tiny chocolates and water. Scott bought a selection of cheeses and Italian salami, and the two of us are feeling quite intercontinental by the time we get back to *Il Girasole*.

The plan is to unpack our purchases and then change into our swimsuits and meet out by the pool. Scott gives me some general directions on how to find the pool from my villa, and I agree to change quickly so we can enjoy the intense rays sooner than later.

Twenty minutes later, I make my way up to the pool. I can hear the sounds of people laughing and splashing in the water, so I'm sure I'm moving in the right direction as I navigate down one of the many tree-lined cobbled pathways. I finally reach a wooden gate connected to an aging ivy-covered wall with a small sign that says *Il Girasole Piscina*.

When I open the gate, I'm pleasantly surprised to see a gorgeous pool area with sunbathing decks stretching out in every direction. A large square pool with terracotta tiles rimming the outer edge is beckoning in the middle of the walled-in area. There are at least ten familiar faces bobbing up and down in the water as I walk up onto the first sundeck. I have my beach bag slung over my shoulder while I scan the area in search of Scott. I finally spot him, moving two lounge chairs around on the upper sundeck, positioning them perfectly for the late morning sun.

As I walk along the edge of the lower deck, I see Nina Harrison and Captain Cordova passed out in a double chaise lounge. They appear to be holding hands as they sleep side-by-side. It's the first time I've gotten a good look at his face, and I have to agree with Bobbi—Captain Cordova *is* hot! Out in the pool, I can see Suzanne floating on an inflatable mat shaped like a sunflower. She gives me a weary wave as I cross to the sundeck where Scott is setting up our places.

"Isn't this place gorgeous?" I marvel to Scott as I make my way up the steps to the upper deck.

"Yeah—it's very *Wiley Bennett*!" he says with a wink and a smile.

I unfurl my extra wide beach towel on the lounge chair and spread it out. The air is filled with the sugary aroma of buttercups and sweet blossoms from the flowering bushes lining the outer wall of the pool area. I take a deep breath in and give my arms and back a good stretch. Scott is wearing a pair of Hawaiian-print swimming trunks and is applying a healthy coat of sunscreen to his nose.

"Are you going for a swim?" he asks me as I motion for him to toss me his tube of sunscreen. He casually tosses me the tube and continues working the white goop into his skin.

"No," I say as I squeeze a big blob of screen into my palm. "I think I'm going to relax for a bit first. How 'bout you?"

"I'm gonna soak for a minute and then come back and crash," he says as he starts making his way toward the pool.

By the time he returns, I'm buttered up and stretched out on my lounge chair soaking in the Tuscan rays. Scott flicks water from his wet head on to my stomach, and I wince at the sting of the chill. But before long, the sun, the sweetly scented air and the whispering breezes have lulled me into a deep, restful sleep.

I'm not sure what wakes me up—it could be the sound of someone taking a plunge into the salty pool or maybe the thud of footsteps on the sundeck, but when I come to, I'm hot and sweaty. I look at my watch and see that it's almost noon and estimate I've been asleep for nearly two hours. When I roll up into the seated position, I can see that Scott is fast asleep on his side—which may make for an interesting suntan!

From the upper sundeck, I can see people sitting along the sides of the pool, splashing water onto their sun-kissed legs and chatting in hushed voices. Everyone seems to be in a state of slow motion. The realities of the long flight from Miami to Florence are catching up to people at different rates, but there's an undeniable laziness in the air, and I am completely spellbound by it.

I look around the different sundecks, making mental notes of who all is resting by the pool. I spot Sebastian Jones sprawled out on one of the lounger chairs wearing a hot pink Speedo and a thick layer of neon yellow nose coat. Peter Jameson—one of Sebastian's closest friends and a member of the other flight crew—is also passed out on a lounge chair. Peter has a beach towel covering his entire body, and the only thing exposed is his unmistakable shiny, balding head.

I see Marta DeSoto seated at a pool-side table, working on a Sudoku puzzle—this highly popular, maddeningly addictive number game that seems to occupy all of her free time on layovers. She's wearing a modest, one-piece, navy blue bathing suit. She looks very serene pouring over her puzzle in the bright Tuscan sun.

As I work my way around the pool, watching my co-workers relax and unwind, I'm startled at the sight of Miriam Ungaro. She's stretched out on a lounge chair underneath a large yellow umbrella. She appears to be painting her fingernails. She has on a red, two-piece, tank-top style suit—which seems surprisingly modest for the typically unaware Miriam, and she has her hair pulled up into a messy bun on top of her head. My heart rate seems to quicken at the sight of her. When I pan the area near her chair, I notice that Marco isn't by her side, and a feeling of relief washes over me.

I slide my sunglasses down over my eyes and fix my gaze on Miriam. What could Marco possibly see in her? As I watch her dig around in her tiny bag for a nail file, I do my best to see her in a new way. If I had to find something physically redeemable about Miriam, I guess I could concede that she *does* have lovely fingernails. She always paints them a bold color, and they are perfectly shaped into rounded points.

And, if I'm being extra generous, I guess in a certain light, Miriam *does* have pretty cinnamon colored eyes. I mean, I know she wears those colored contact lenses, but on her, the orangey contrast the lenses create in her eyes can be kind of pretty. And who knows? Maybe she has a nice personality—when she isn't your boss, that is. Maybe when you get to know her in a different setting, she has a funny sense of humor or a quick wit.

Miriam pulls out a bottle of dark-colored fingernail polish from her kit and starts pounding the bottle against the heel of her hand. The sour look on her face is both familiar and startlingly ugly. After she opens the bottle and begins to stroke the first glossy line of pigment onto her left thumbnail, I feel a sense of rivalry stirring inside of me. I want to win this battle over Marco—and I want her to know I've won. I'm rather surprised by my feelings, but as I bake away in the hot sun, I feel my competitive nature take over. Through the dark plastic of my Jackie O style sunglasses, I stare Miriam down. She has no idea who she's dealing with now.

As I wander around the grounds of *Il Girasole*, I'm pleasantly surprised to find the day spa Fozzy mentioned in his notes. It looks like a small villa with an oversized porch and large windows along the front. There are outdoor massage tables lined up under billowy tents along the side of the villa, and I can see strong women kneading the weary bodies of the people draped over their tables. I carefully make my way into the spa so as not to disturb the dreamy atmosphere with my clomping feet. There is the distinctive odor of fingernail polish mixed with hot wax and heat-singed hair as I enter through the open doorway.

A plain looking woman dressed in a black smock greets me with a gentle smile and hands me a list of services without speaking a word. I scan the list and see that manicures are listed among the available services. The woman gives me an encouraging look as I consider my options. There's a small acetate display board with different acrylic nail selections splayed out in a circular pattern. I tilt the board toward the lady and then point out one of the selections for her to see.

In broken English, the woman asks, "You like?"

I flash to the memory of my first conversation with Marco Maselli on the airplane when he asked me that same question. "Yes, I like," I respond with confidence. If Marco likes long fancy nails, then I'll give him long fancy nails.

About an hour later, I emerge from the *Il Girasole* spa with long, shiny, fire engine red fingernails. The process was much more involved—and much more painful, I might add—then I expected. There was quite a bit of grinding of my nail beds with a power tool, and there was considerable time involved in the shaping process. But the end result was exactly what I had in mind.

I casually walk back to the pool while admiring my new nails. As I look down at my hands, I can hardly believe they belong to me! I've always kept my nails short and sporty, but this new look makes my hands seem older, more refined. Miriam—my so-called rival—has nothing on me now! My nails are even more gorgeous than hers!

When I reach out to work the latch on the pool gate, I'm careful not to jam my new fingernails into the handle. I carefully slide my left hand under the handle, ever so mindful of the tacky paint on my nails, and use the heel of my right hand to push down on the latch release. So far so good; however, protecting my nails is going to take more consideration than I'm used to. But it's all a part of my new strategy, and I'll just have to find a way to make it work.

I tiptoe over to my lounge chair, mindful of my every step on the sundeck. Scott is still asleep, only now he's curled up on his other side. The good news is, this will probably even out his tan a bit! I quietly turn my lounge chair—using only the palms of my hands—to maximize my angle in the sun. Using my foot, I flip the backrest down flat so I can lie on my stomach and continue evening out my own tan. The backrest flops down noisily, and I notice Scott stir.

My new nails look spectacular in the bright sun, but they do make it more difficult to use my fingers. My button-up beach cover is a bit trickier to un-do with these red extensions attached. I work my fingers at different angles, finally discovering that if I wedge the fleshier side portion of my thumb up against the button and the pad of my forefinger, the button can be coaxed through the hole with only minor effort.

With only the top three buttons undone, I shimmy my way out of my cover up and let it fall to the deck. I think the polish is still too tacky to handle the terrycloth fabric without damaging the luster, so I leave the cover up on the floor in a crumpled pile. Once I'm positioned on the lounge chair—bottom up—I place my lovely new hands out in front of me.

"What did you do to your nails?" a tired voice says from over my shoulder.

I look up to see Scott peering down at my new nails with an astonished look on his face. "I had them done over at the spa," I say with a hint of pride in my tone.

"Why?" Scott asks as amusement and wonderment wash over him.

"I don't know…" I trail off, not knowing how I should answer the question. "Just seemed like fun, I guess…"

"OK," Scott concedes. "I'm hungry—are you?" he asks me.

"I am," I say pleasantly. "Do you want to go eat some of the stuff I have in my villa?" I offer as I roll over onto my back.

"That sounds fine," Scott says as he rubs his eyes. He's clearly still groggy from his nap. "Do you want to go now?"

"Sure—but I'm gonna leave my stuff, so I can come back after I eat," I explain as I rise up off of my lounge chair and make no attempt to gather my belongings. I wonder how long it actually takes for this polish to harden?

"Whatever," Scott replies. "I think I've had enough sun for one day." He's surveying the skin on his arms as he says this, noticing some places where his sunscreen application may have missed the mark.

As we make our way down to the lower levels of the sundeck, I see Miriam Ungaro, sipping on a cold drink and reading a magazine. She's wearing a big red straw hat that seems to be blocking her view of us as we make our way to the pool gate. But I manage to sneak a quick look at her nails before we leave. They are painted a dark plum color. I look back at my own new nails as I follow closely behind Scott and decide that my color choice is much better. Much better indeed!

Chapter Eleven

Who knew fingernails could be so much trouble? I'm beginning to really doubt my decision to get my new nails—no matter how good they look. So far today, I've nearly sliced my thumb off in a salami cutting accident, stabbed myself in the cheek—which could have just as easily been my eye—and practically dislocated a finger knuckle while unpacking my suitcase. These things are far more dangerous than I ever expected! Plus, my nailbeds ache from the attachment process. All that drilling and scraping must have done some major nerve damage to my tender fingertips. But they do look good. Even Scott commented twice at dinner about how pretty my hands look with these new nails.

When I got home from dinner, I took a nice hot shower, put on my favorite nightshirt and wrapped myself up in a thick terrycloth bathrobe. Tying the waist sash was a bit of a struggle with the extra long extensions jutting from the tips of my fingers, but I'm learning to adjust. Now, as I'm about to climb into my big, fluffy bed, the task of removing the throw pillows is before me. The old Elle—with the sporty nails—would carefully remove each pillow, and place them one-by-one on a chair or somewhere out of the way. But the new Elle with the long red nails isn't like that. *Red Hot Elle*—as I like to think of myself now—pushes things out of the way and lets them flop on the floor with no regard to order at all.

As I climb into the downy bedding and lean back against the thick white pillows, I feel so regal—and maybe even a tad rebellious! Careful not to mash my throbbing fingernails, I gently grip the edges of the blanket using only the pads of my fingers and tug the covers up to my chin. I pull in a deep breath and still myself in the silence of my new room. I'm so tired—and a little sunburned, too. But all in all, my first day in Italy was pretty great.

I reach over and flick the light switch on the wall, and my room goes dark. Lying there in purpled darkness, I can't help but think about the note from Marco. He said he would *"find me"* tomorrow. Will it be in the morning when I wake up? He did say he wanted to take me to breakfast at dawn some time. Perhaps I should rethink my pajamas, just in case. I'd hate for Marco to see me wearing my very worn, very large T-shirt from high school that says, *"The Wheezinator"* on the front and *"She'll be back"* on the back. Somehow, I don't think it will send the right message.

But you never know—he may be the kind of person who sleeps in on his days off. So then maybe he'll show up around lunchtime. That's a pretty casual time of day—it's safe. But then again, Marco seems like a romantic kind of guy, and I can imagine him showing up around sunset with plans to take me to his favorite restaurant. He may want to pour his heart out to me over candlelight at a charming, dimly lit hideaway that only the locals know about.

My body is so heavy and tired, but my mind is racing with thoughts of Marco and what it is he wants to explain to me. My imagination could really get the best of me here. I'm sure it's probably nothing, but, then again, it might be something incredible! Maybe he wants to tell me that I had a love-at-first-sight affect on him, and he doesn't know what to do other than to tell me of his feelings. I actually feel flush at the thought of this scenario. No one has ever been so bold or so smitten with *me* before. But I decide it's better to stifle such thoughts. In my experience, those are the kinds of thoughts that can only lead to disappointment.

After tossing and turning for nearly an hour, I decide to give up on sleep and read a book or something. I sit on the edge of my bed, debating about turning on the light. It feels so good to be in the dark, but it's pretty much impossible to read with no light. Maybe a candle would be nice.

As I crawl out of bed, I recall the gift basket Mr. Wiley sent to each of us to thank us for our willingness to launch the Florence base. (Seriously, *we* should be sending *him* the gift basket!) I think I may have noticed a candle among the mix of items, so I pull on my bathrobe—carefully, to avoid hurting my tender fingers—and pad my way out to the kitchen. The little hood light over the stovetop is glowing in the dim room, giving me just enough light to inspect the contents of the basket.

The actual basket is so elegant. It's made of pieces of gold and blue fabric twisted into a gorgeous braided bowl and filled with all sorts of beautiful things. There is some handmade Tuscan soap, a small bottle of lotion, a box of real Italian chocolates, a book of postcards displaying brilliant scenes of the Tuscan region and, of course, a small candle inside a dainty metal tin. I manage to twist off the lid of the tin and smell the candle. It's lilac-scented and smells heavenly.

Next, I'll need to find a match. I think I saw some matches over by the fireplace, so I pick up the candle and carry it over to the seating area. Up on the mantle, there's a small box of matches. I can see in the dim light that the box has a picture of a sunflower glued to it. I carefully wedge the box open and fish out a single match using just the tips of my nails like a pair of tweezers. I reposition the match a bit in my right hand, making sure it's secure between the fleshy part of my thumb and the pad of my forefinger—which has become my new go-to position for most of my holding and un-doing needs. With my left hand, I tilt the matchbox up to expose the flint strip along the side.

In one fluid motion, I strike the match across the strip and a flame sizzles to life. I pick up the candle and tilt the wick toward the flame. The wick doesn't seem to want to take the flame, so I tilt the candle a bit more as the flame eats its way down the matchstick toward my thumb and forefinger. I continue to hold the wick in the thick of the flame, but it just won't light. I'm feeling a little nervous as the flame continues to approach my fingers. I jerk slightly, as I can feel the heat growing more intense on the flesh of my fingers. Just then, the flame seems to ignite. I can hear the fizz of the flame transfer, but suddenly, I realize, it's not the wick that's on fire! It's my thumbnail!

I drop the candle, and it lands with a clang on the wooden coffee table. I start blowing and manage to get the match to go out, but the bigger problem is my flaming thumbnail! So I blow directly on my thumbnail, but the flame just seems to be getting started! Instinctively, I start shaking my hand, hoping that I can create enough wind to extinguish the flame. But no such luck—the flame is transfixed to my nail and isn't going out!

In a panic, I run to the kitchen sink and turn on the tap. I stick my thumb under the flowing water and, to my relief, it goes out. I let my thumb remain under the water for a bit, just to make sure the flame is sufficiently drenched. I turn off the tap and grab a small dishtowel from a neat pile stacked near the sink. I gingerly wrap my thumb up in the towel and hold it in my other hand. I'm almost afraid to look. I can't tell if I've burned any flesh—I have no authentic nerve impulses in any of my fingertips, so I can't really rely on my neural responses for assurance.

I lean into the dim glow from the hood light over the stove and carefully unwrap my thumb. To my horror, all I can see is a charcoal black thumbnail surrounded by bright, pink, swollen flesh. I pull my thumb up to my face for closer inspection, and I can smell the intense chemical aroma of incinerated nail polish and acrylic. I carefully run the pad of my finger on my other hand over the black nail. A little soot mark rubs off, and there is no lovely red beneath it. The runaway flame charred off all the polish and left only a thick, chalky fake nail glued to my thumb. No more *Red Hot Elle*. All that's left is an ugly, black nail.

I don't know if I'm going to laugh or cry. The whole experience of lighting my thumb on fire was horrifying! I can't believe this doesn't happen more often. Who knew fake nails were flammable? Maybe I'm just not cut out for this high-maintenance manicure. I've spent the better portion of my day thinking about my nails, and, frankly, that's just not me.

As I make my way into the bathroom, I decide that if fancy fingernails are that important to Marco, he better stick with Miriam. I flick on the bathroom light and dig around in the vanity drawers until I find my nail clippers and some cotton balls. I find a sample-sized bottle of fingernail polish remover in my *Il Girasole Terme* (spa) bag and then flip the toilet lid down. I seem to remember something about how nail polish remover and acrylic nails don't mix, so maybe if I soak my fingers in it, the nails will just fall off.

As I sit on the lid of the toilet, soaking my fingertips in the toxic smelling liquid and then clipping off the long spotty red nails and dumping the remains in the wastebasket, a sense of knowing comes over me. I can't compete against Miriam by being someone I'm not. And how do I even know there's a competition? I wonder what came over me in the first place that made me so sure that a fancy manicure of all things was the key to landing a man like Marco.

Nearly an hour later, I've managed to pick off all the red acrylic nail bits. The removal process seems almost as agonizing as getting the nails put on in the first place, but the tips of my fingers are so raw and numb by this time that I can't really be sure. With all the acrylic removed, my natural nails look scuffed and ragged. But, at least, they look more normal. After I sweep the last bits of red nail into the wastebasket, I wash my hands with the honey lavender soap. It feels nice to have my old fingers back—even if they are throbbing and swollen. My neck is stiff from looking down at my nails with such intensity. I'm definitely ready for sleep now.

When I enter my bedroom, I stop to pick up the throw pillows off the floor and place them neatly on the window seat. Then I carefully remove my bathrobe and place it on the end of my bed. I look down at my favorite nightshirt and smile. *Yes indeed,* I think. *The Wheezinator is back!*

As I climb into my bed, I say goodbye to *Red Hot Elle* for good. Then I pull the covers up and drift off into a deep sleep.

The room is dim with early morning light when I wake up, and I struggle to remember where I am. When I roll over in my unfamiliar bed, a feeling of panic washes over me as I search the room for Sugar Ray. Slowly, the details start to come back to me, and I remember that I am in my villa in Florence and Sugar Ray is about a million miles away from me. I close my eyes and try to picture him, frolicking in the tide while Violet Harper waits for him on the shore.

Sadness squeezes my heart as I realize how difficult it's going to be to go through all my days without my dog. I so miss kissing his head and rubbing his tummy after he eats. The one good thing is that I *will* see him again—just not for a long time. I stretch my legs in an effort to wake up. I feel weary from traveling and from my long night of picking acrylic off of my fingernails. As I look at my puffy red fingertips, I wonder what Sugar Ray would have thought of those long red nails? The thought of his reaction makes me smile.

Scott and I never really made any plans for the day, so I think maybe I'll just do my own thing. A nice long run followed by a steamy shower sounds like the perfect way to start this day. So after I make my bed, I pull on a pair of white cotton running shorts and a purple jog top. I gather my messy hair back into a tight ponytail and dig through my dresser drawer for a pair of running socks.

After I lace up my running shoes with my still throbbing fingers, I duck into the bathroom to wash my face and brush my teeth. I feel springy this morning, and I know this run is exactly what I need. It isn't until I'm rinsing out my mouth in the sink that I remember Marco. A flutter of nerves dances in my stomach as I recall his promise to "find me" today.

I do my best to push the thought of Marco out of my mind. I can't spend my day waiting on him. I've done that in the past for guys. After they've dropped a vague hint or promise into a conversation, I've felt compelled to spend my entire day waiting for them to deliver. What a waste of a perfectly good day! And besides, I'm not even sure I like Marco that much in the first place, and I am way too old to play those silly games. Nope. I'm going to start my day as if Marco never existed.

I grab a long-sleeved T-shirt from one of my drawers and tie it around my waist, and then I shove some money into the hidden pocket inside the liner of my shorts. This way, I can stop for breakfast somewhere in the city. When I open my front door, the clean morning air greets my nose, and I breath in the freshness. The air is cool, and the colors of the surrounding grounds are just starting to awaken for the day. I lock up my villa and then hide the key under the seat cushion of the bistro chair on my porch. I take a moment to stretch my legs on the steps, making sure that I am limber enough to begin my first run in the city of Florence.

As I reach my arm up and over my head to stretch my left side, my eye catches the potted plant sitting silently on the bistro table. I take an extra second to examine the thick leaves of the plant, making sure there isn't a note hidden somewhere in the leafy folds. To my surprise, I'm disappointed to discover that there's no note. I do my best to shake off this response as I stretch my right side.

So there's no note. Big deal. I'm not even sure I like this guy anyway. And why would he leave another note? Whatever…

I slowly jog over the tiny bridge in front of my villa and make my way up the pathway that runs in front of Scott's. There are no signs of activity in *Villa Quindici*, so I keep on jogging toward the front gates of *Il Girasole*. It's still quite early in the morning, and it seems like I'm the only one up—besides the birds, of course! They are happily chirping away up above in the trees that populate the grounds of the resort. The gate opens with a rusty creak as I slip outside and enter the busy streets of Florence.

Off in the distance, I can hear the sound of cathedral bells ringing. I count to seven as each gong bellows with vibrato over the weary city, begging the residents and visitors alike to get up and start enjoying the day. It's a beautiful morning as I run up a rolling street lined with small gated properties and ancient-looking structures. It seems like everything in this city has been here forever. As I bounce along the cobbled sidewalk, trying to find my perfect pace, I think of how many other people over the centuries have trampled these streets.

I make my way down a side street in an effort to avoid some of the heavier traffic that is starting to pick up along the main drag. Tightly packed structures line the side street and reflect an orangish glow from the terracotta rooftops and the first heat of the morning sun. As I round the corner, I realize that I must be close to the train station, so I make a sharp left and jog down another side street that is lined with more ancient-looking buildings. I pass a few dapper gentlemen walking along the street. They greet me with a smile and a subtle nod as I continue exploring their world.

The smell of watery earth fills my nostrils as I make my way down the street. Up ahead, I can see that my street t-bones into a much busier street that is a main thoroughfare for zippy sports cars and fancy motor scooters carrying well-dressed people. All the heavier traffic seems to be moving to my left, so I cross the busy street and slip up onto the cobbled sidewalk and continue my jog in the same direction. The street runs along side the embankment of a deep and moving river, and based on what little I know about my new city, I'm pretty sure this must be the *Arno*. I look across the water and notice a beautiful church with a domed top nestled in among aged structures that seem to want to tell me a story.

Up ahead, I can see a bridge hovering over the river that is stacked with what appear to be shops of some sort. As I near the bridge, I realize this must be the famed *Ponte Vecchio*. I've heard about this bridge many times, and even my mother told me this was the place to shop for fine Italian jewelry. But as I approach the bridge, I can see that it is unlike any bridge I've ever seen!

I ease my jog down to a walk as I start to cross the sturdy bridge, hovering over the slow moving water down below. What I see before me is really quite surreal! There are shop windows to my right and to my left that are jammed with gleaming gold jewelry! I stop myself in mid-step as though I'm a lucky Leprechaun that just found a pot of gold at the end of the rainbow. Every arched doorway and portico seems to welcome you into a golden cave filled with exquisite pieces of wearable fine art.

As I peer into the window of one of the shops, I can see a small man, hunched over a table in the back. He is gently braiding and twisting pieces of gold together, and then tapping the braid with a rubber mallet as he works his way down the length of the chain. He looks up briefly and sees me staring. He gives me a proud smile and then continues on with his work.

The shops are still closed, but there are lots of people bustling through the bridge, weaving in and out of each other's way as they scurry off in every direction. I take my time looking into every shop window, down one side of the bridge and then up the other. It is a literal feast for the eyes, and I can't wait to bring Scott back so we can do some shopping. I follow the bustling crowd into an open courtyard area surrounded by important looking buildings with a fountain and various sculptures placed near the largest of the buildings.

This must be the *Palazzo Vecchio*. I am overwhelmed by the size of this place and how old everything seems. As I near the end of the courtyard area, I literally stop in my tracks and lean my head back and look up at the enormous bell tower hovering directly above me. I feel so small and insignificant as I blend in with all the people milling about the courtyard below this majestic spire.

I follow the flow of people moving around the courtyard and take a sharp right. The smell of fresh-baked bread guides me the rest of the way as I stumble upon a street café mixed in with a bustling straw market of sorts. Vendors are setting up their narrow stalls with their leather goods and souvenirs. I watch as a portly older man dressed in saggy cotton pants and a ratty sweater hangs gorgeous handbags on hooks that line the outer doorframe of his stall. I make another mental note to return to this place with Scott, too!

In the middle of the sidewalk, another vendor is setting up his offerings on the ground on a dingy looking blanket. He appears to be an Asian man—sort of short and compact. As I approach, he hisses, "You want some Gucci scarf?" He cautiously pulls out a fancy silk scarf with the Gucci emblem smattered all over it and holds it up for my inspection. He has a tattered and well-worn satchel full of these so-called Gucci scarves hanging over his shoulder.

"No, thank you," I reply nervously as I sidestep his makeshift display.

I stop at a fresh fruit stand and buy a peach and a bottle of water. The shopkeeper is a kind, elderly woman who speaks English, which is a relief since my Italian is pretty horrible. I continue my leisurely stroll around the market area as I eat one of the most delicious peaches I've ever had! As I wipe my chin with the sleeve of the T-shirt tied around my waist, I take in all of the beautiful things I can buy when I return with Scott. I see a gorgeous belt I know my dad would love, and some amazing sandals that look like they might last forever! The sound of cathedral bells seems to be ringing in every direction of the city, alerting everyone of a new hour in yet another splendid Tuscan day.

Suddenly, I sense some commotion over by the fruit stand. As I turn, I see the little Asian man that tried to sell me a knock-off Gucci scarf grabbing the corners of his blanket and gathering up his display in one swift motion. He shoves the blanket in his shabby shoulder bag and takes off running. Then he scurries off down a side street. Seconds later, a man dressed in a light blue uniform and a peaked cap races out of no where and follows the Asian vendor down the side street.

Everyone seems to stop and watch the scene unfold, but once the vendor and, what I assume, is a police officer vanish from sight, everyone continues on with what they were doing, as if nothing ever happened. The whole exchange leaves me a bit unnerved. What if I had wanted to buy that scarf? Could I have gotten in trouble? A tingle of nerves settles in my thighs as I realize that maybe I shouldn't be wandering around alone in the city. I do my best to shake it off and move on, but I think maybe I ought to start thinking about getting back to the resort.

I walk a few more feet and come upon a little bakery near the market that is selling pastries that simply look too good to pass up. So I point and grunt to the gentleman behind the pastry case until he pulls out this long, sticky, chocolate looking creation. He wraps the delicate pastry in parchment paper and hands it to me. My mouth begins to water the second the confection is in my hands! After taking one bite—followed by a deep, carnal-like moan of satisfaction—I hand the gentleman some wadded up Euros from my secret pocket.

The man waves me off and gives me a sultry grin. Then he says, "No money from such-ah *beautiful* lady."

I give him a big smile as my face starts to flush with embarrassment, and I do my best to gesture my appreciation. I sure hope that my thankful body language—in combination with my spontaneous moaning—is appropriate and isn't sending the wrong signals. My mother warned me that Italians use a lot of gestures in communication, so you better be sure about what you are doing with your hands! But the gentleman behind the counter seems to understand and gives me a friendly farewell wave as I move along from his shop.

My stomach is full and rather bloated after my fruit, water and chocolate fest, and the thought of jogging back to *Il Girasole* is rather troubling. So I pull out the remainder of my money and try to figure out if I have enough for a cab. I find a taxi stand near the main entrance to the *Palazzo Vecchio*.

When the tiny Fiat pulls up to the stand, I carefully slip into the back seat and say, "*Il Girasole?*"

"OK," says the driver in clear English. "Are you an American?" he asks me after he pulls the tiny car away from the curb.

"Yes, I am!" I reply, filled with surprise to hear my Italian taxi driver speaking such plain English. "Are you?"

"Sort of," he offers over his shoulder as he darts in and out of the crazy traffic that seems to me moving along rather swiftly. "I've lived here most of my life, but my parents sent me to university in the United States. They wanted me to be a doctor, but instead, I'm a taxi driver," he says as he snaps quick looks at me in his rearview mirror.

I can see that he has kind eyes. I don't really know what to say, so I try to come up with something clever. "Well, you and I have a lot in common then," I begin.

"Oh, we do? Your parent's wanted you to be a doctor, too?" he asks with a twinkle in his eye.

"Not that I know of, but they *did* send me to *university* in the United States, and I also ended up in the transportation industry," I say with a smile.

"Oh yeah?" he responds as he shifts around in his seat so he can see more of me in his rearview mirror. "Are you a taxi driver, too?"

"No, but I'm a flight attendant," I say with a smile.

"I see," the driver says with a hearty laugh. "You are right! We do have much in common!"

He accelerates down a side street, and I feel my stomach do a little flip as we narrowly miss a young man making a sharp turn on his scooter. Neither the taxi driver nor the scooter driver seems to notice the close call, but I have my fingers firmly wrapped around the door handle as I say a little prayer for our safety. In retrospect, I actually think jogging home on a full stomach would have been less nauseating!

The taxi driver makes a series of quick turns and, suddenly, we are pulling into the front of the resort. A flood of happiness pulses through my body once the tiny car comes to an abrupt stop at the front gate. I hand the driver the last of my crumpled bills, and he waves me off—just like the man at the bakery.

"You keep it," he says to me as he turns to look over his shoulder. He smiles at me with a big toothy grin.

"Oh no," I stammer in protest. "I *must* pay you!"

"No, it's my pleasure!" he insists. "Professional courtesy!" he says with a wink.

"Well, gosh… Thank you so much!" I say, not knowing the proper thing to do. I've never been offered so much free stuff in one day!

"Anytime," he says as I climb out of the taxi.

"*Arrivederci!*" I call out to him as I shut the door of the taxi.

"*Ciao!*" he says in reply after giving me a happy wave. He pops the clutch on his car and races down the street.

Grateful to be out of the deathtrap on wheels, I take a deep breath and settle my nerves. I slip through the front gate and start making my way back to my villa. A quiet hush remains over the resort as I glide over the cobbled pathway that leads to my villa. As I pass Scott's villa, there's still no sign of activity, and I feel glad that I didn't wait for him to get my day started.

When I reach my villa, I slip my hand under the seat cushion of the bistro chair to snag my door key. As I lean over to pull the key out, I check the potted plant one more time for a note from Marco. Again, there's no note, and I feel ridiculous for expecting to find one. I wish this whole crush of mine would vanish. I wish I could take it all back, start from scratch and control my feelings better. But the truth is, even though I barely know this Marco Maselli, the first buds of a very big crush have started to bloom, and I can't help the tingles that race through my body at the thought of him.

I stick the large key into the lock and twist it until I hear a loud pop. The thick wooden door opens easily, but I can hear the sound of something sliding along the floor underneath the door. I peer around the door and look down at the terracotta tiles. I see a small white envelope pinched between the door and the floor, and my heart starts to pound with a thick thud inside my chest, and my palms instantly feel sweaty.

I bend down and pick up the envelope and examine it carefully. My name is printed on the front in block letters—ELOISE. The envelope isn't sealed—the flap is just tucked inside—so I carefully slip my finger under the flap and remove a small white gift card-sized note. My hands are trembling as I begin to read.

Eloise—Please be with me tonight in my city. I left a gift for you on the veranda. I will be here at 6:00.
MM

My legs feel weak from the note, but, suddenly, I find that I am running through my villa while my mind races at the thought of what Marco left for me. Before I can even unlock the French doors in the bathroom that lead out to the veranda, I spot the beautifully wrapped package silently waiting for me on the double chaise lounge. I fling the doors open and step out onto the veranda. I can't help but stop and stare at the package in disbelief as I try to understand why this virtual stranger felt compelled to leave me a gift.

It's a medium-sized, square box wrapped in gorgeous purple and gold swirled paper and all tied together with a white silk ribbon. I'm almost afraid to pick it up because this is one of the most romantic moments of my life so far, and I really don't want it to end. But curiosity builds inside my chest and I can't wait any longer. So I sit down on the lounge chair and lift the gift into my lap. Upon closer inspection, I can see the detailing in the wrapping paper—I think it must be handmade. I slip off the ribbon and then gingerly remove the wrapping, so that I can save it.

I lift up the lid of the box and find folds of buttery yellow tissue paper inside. I gently remove the tissue, one layer at a time. Hidden within the folds is a garment. At first, I can't tell what it is, but as I lift it out of the box, my jaw drops. It's the most beautiful dress I've ever seen! It's a slip dress made of milky chocolate silk with a bronze sheen finish. Over top of the slip is a gauze-like overlay that hangs down below the hemline of the slip and looks like it hits somewhere about mid-calf. The overlay is hand-embroidered around the waistline and along the bottom in mint green silk thread. The ornate pattern is striking in light green against the bronzed brown fabrics, and it is the most feminine creation I've ever seen.

The mint green stitching is continued around the neckline of the dress and in several pleats that run down the front and back, giving the overlay the ability to sketch out the subtle curves of a woman's figure. As I examine the dress and all of the amazing detail work, I can't help but notice the small label stitched inside the collar. The label is made of a piece of white silk that has *FM—Florence, Italy* embroidered in black thread.

I'm literally stunned by this gift. The dress must have cost a fortune, and Marco hardly knows me! A homemade paper rose in a vodka bottle is one thing, but a handcrafted Italian dress is entirely different. Needless to say, I'm overwhelmed by the gesture and completely unsure what to do next. So, I do what I normally do when I'm nervous—I begin to tidy up. I collect the sheets of tissue paper and fold them up and slip them back into the box. Then I carefully fold up the wrapping paper and stack it on top of the box. I carry the dress and all the wrappings inside my villa and lay it all out on my bed.

I grab a spare hanger from my closet and slip the delicate dress onto the wooden arms and then remove my bathrobe from a hook on the wall and toss the robe on my bed. I slip the hanger onto the wall hook and step back so I can look at the dress. It is simple, yet elegant, and I can't believe it belongs to me! But the longer I look at the stunning dress, the more the pit of worry grows in my stomach. Should I be accepting such a gift from Marco? What exactly does he expect in return? What does it mean when a handsome Italian man offers a young woman he hardly knows such an expensive gift?

I do my best to shake these thoughts and concerns from my mind, and, instead, I try to picture myself in the dress. It's exactly my size, and the color will suit me perfectly. My skin is already turning golden brown from my time around the pool yesterday, and I'm sure the dress will compliment my sun-kissed complexion. And let's be clear about this. If Marco didn't want to give me such an extravagant gift, he wouldn't have done it. Maybe this is a common gesture in Italy—like the free pastry and cab ride this morning. Maybe this is the way Italians share their culture with newcomers.

And regarding Marco's expectations—how could he have any? We haven't even had but one or two strange conversations, so certainly his expectations of me are as vague as my expectations are of him. Surely there are no *real* strings attached.

I grab my bathrobe off the edge of the bed and make my way into the bathroom and turn on the shower. As the steam starts to gather in the bathroom, I breathe in the thick moisture and try to find my center. After my shower, I wrap my hair up in a thick white towel and then use the palm of my hand to wipe the steam from the mirror. I take a good long look at myself and wonder what I've gotten myself into. A tingle rushes down my spine as I officially acknowledge that Marco Maselli may very well be the man that changes my life forever.

Chapter Twelve

After lunch, I decide to try to call my mom and dad. With the six-hour time difference, I should be catching my early-rising parents just as my mom is pouring my dad's first mug of coffee. I use the calling card my mom slipped into my wallet a few weeks back and punch in all the numbers while listening for the various bongs and beeps indicating that my call is being connected.

"Hello?" My mom's voice is perky, but sounds worried.

"Hi Mom! It's just me," I say, glad to hear her voice.

"Oh, darling! I'm so happy you called!" she blusters into the receiver. I can hear a chair scraping across the floor as she settles in for our first intercontinental chat. "How are you, Love? Is everything wonderful?"

"I'm fantastic! And yes! Everything *is* wonderful! You wouldn't believe how incredible my villa is, and I'm totally blown away by Florence," I blather on without even taking a breath.

For the next fifteen minutes, I tell my mother about every detail of my experience so far—minus the mention of Marco, the paper flower on the plane, the potential love triangle with Miriam Ungaro and, of course, the dress. There's no need to share those details at this point. My mom listens quietly, only interjecting her comments and reactions at the most appropriate times. After a bit, she puts my dad on, and we discuss the weather—one of his favorite topics. He's sort of a meteorology buff on the side and an avid hurricane tracker, so you can usually count on a lengthy exchange about the weather—*especially* when it's hurricane season.

"Did you check out the list of names for this year's hurricane season, Sweetheart?" my dad asks, like this is something everyone does.

"No, I sure didn't, Dad," I reply distractedly as I stare at the dress hanging on the hook in my bedroom.

"Well, oddly enough, for the year 2006, our sixth named storm will be *Florence!*" my dad blurts out, obviously amused by the irony in the situation.

"Oh really?" I say, making a mental note of the coincidence. "That's pretty wild."

"Well, we certainly hope that we don't have a *Hurricane Florence* this year, but I thought it was quite interesting, given your current situation and all," he adds.

"I agree—it *is* interesting," I respond, even though to me, it's really *not* all that interesting. I am so used to my father's full-scale obsession with this topic that the whole conversation is really nothing new to me.

"One more thing while we are on the topic of storms. Does Mr. Wiley have you covered here in Miami for hurricane season, Elle?" he asks just before we wind up our little chat.

"I don't know," I say as I begin to officially tire of the topic of hurricanes. "I guess so—I mean I know we have evacuation drills every year at *The Wiley,* and we usually get briefings on stuff like that…"

"That sounds smart," my dad intones with authority. "By all accounts, things have been lining up for a very active hurricane season this year—in fact it looks like we have a tropical depression heading our way as we speak—and I was just wondering about all your belongings at your apartment. I'm sure they must have a plan—especially since *The Wiley* is located in the direct line of impact for a storm surge—but you know how I feel about all that. You always need to know what to do."

A smile widens across my face as I listen to my dad. He is like a full-grown boy scout—he's always prepared! "I'm sure everything will be fine," I say confidently.

"Well, we're here if you need us, too," my dad offers before we say our goodbyes.

My mom comes back on the line one more time to send her love and to give me Edna Pearl's home number in Essex so I can plan a visit. I can tell she isn't ready to hang up, but there's a constant beeping sound that keeps transmitting over the line to let me know my calling card is nearly out of juice. So, with a final *I love you* and promises of another call very soon, I sign off with my mom and rest the receiver in the cradle.

I lean back on my bed and think of Sugar Ray. I wish I could call him, too, so I could tell him how much I love and miss him. I told Violet I would call her every Monday, and it's only Thursday. Monday seems like an eternity away. I wish Sugar Ray were with me right now. I reach over and grab my English to Italian dictionary on the bedside table. I look up the word for sugar—*zucchero*—and then try to figure out how to pronounce *Ray* in Italian. Gosh I miss my dog—*Zucchero Ray-oh*.

About an hour later, I decide to make my way out to the pool to even out my tan a bit—I need to get a little more sun on my back so it matches my front. I grab a book and a bottle of water and stick them both in my beach bag and then head for the pool. I haven't seen or heard from Scott all day, and I wonder if he's still sleeping. I debate about going over and knocking on his door, but if he needs the sleep, I better let him have it.

The truth is, I know that I'm going to have to tell Scott about my dinner plans with Marco tonight, and I don't know what to say, so I think I might actually be trying to avoid him. He really seems to dislike Marco, and I don't know why. But knowing Scott the way I do, if I let him in on all the details, he's going to ask me too many questions about the dress and the notes I've gotten, and I'm going to end up feeling frustrated and bad inside. Scott seems to have a very bleak impression of Marco, and, right now, bleak is not what I need.

As I open the gate to the pool area, I can see that it's packed with familiar faces. Not feeling terribly social, I do my best to duck behind a row of lounge chairs near the gate and make my way up the outer edge of the sundeck toward an area with a bunch of open chairs. I flip one of the lounge chairs down flat and pull my beach towel out of my bag and spread it out on the chair. I'm bent down, digging through my beach bag in search of sunscreen, when I feel a shadow cross my back. I look up and see Scott's handsome, happy face beaming back at me.

"Where have *you* been all day?" he asks me brightly.

"I went for a run early this morning—before you got up—and then I've been settling into my villa, making myself a little lunch and talking to my parents on the phone…you know, stuff like that…" I trail off, suddenly realizing how fast I'm talking and how I sound sort of defensive or like I'm trying to cover something up.

"OK…" Scott says with an amused smile. He has this ability to see right through me, but he also has the grace to let things slide.

"What about *you?*" I toss this question back to Scott in hopes of buying enough time to get my nerves settled. Plus, I need to try to keep the topic off of me and my dinner plans for as long as possible, so I can figure out what to say.

"I slept in until about 10:00 and then made myself a little brunch," he says while pulling a lounge chair over next to mine. He looks up at the sky to gauge the angle of the sun and nudges his chair a few times until he's satisfied. I look at his rippled back muscles as he lowers himself onto his chair. His skin is caramel-colored and flawless. "Then I came down to the pool to continue working on my tan," he says followed by a big smile.

"Sounds like you had a pretty good morning," I say, finally feeling myself return to normal Elle. As I shift myself onto the lounge chair, I remember that it's just Scott. I love Scott. He's my best friend. I shouldn't have to worry about him being upset! I dab some sunscreen on my face and then hand the bottle to Scott. I motion for him to slather the sunscreen on my back. He obliges as I continue chattering.

"I ran down to the *Ponte Vecchio* this morning, and I can't even begin to tell you how amazing the shopping is down there!"

"Oh yeah?" Scott says as he works sunscreen into my shoulders. "Did you buy anything?"

"No—unless you count a scrumptious peach, a bottle of water and the most decadent pastry I've ever eaten in my life!" I say with a smile as Scott hands back my sunscreen bottle. I omit the part about how the man at the bakery gave me my pastry for free— that's just a little something I'm going to keep to myself!

"But I'm telling you, Scott," I continue on, "there are so many places to buy gold on that bridge, and each window had something different. I was completely blown away. Oh, and the market area had the most incredible leather stuff—belts, purses, shoes, posters... We have to go back there!" I say emphatically as my excitement over shopping becomes abundantly clear.

"That sounds like a plan," Scott says casually as he wipes off the excess sunscreen on his hands onto his swim trunks and leans back into his lounge chair. "How 'bout we go there tonight and walk around, get some dinner?" he suggests before he closes his eyes and concentrates on his sunning.

I feel a load of dread drop into my stomach as I realize that I totally set myself up for this. Now I'm going to have to give Scott some sort of explanation or excuse, and I haven't thought one up yet! I stare at the side of Scott's face. His nostrils flare slightly as he breathes in and out. I guess I should just tell him the truth—or some edited version of the truth, that is. It's just Scott—he'll understand.

"Scott," I say in a soft voice.

"Hmm?" he hums in return.

"I kind of have to tell you something..." I trail off as I begin choosing my words in my mind.

"What's up?" Scott says as he turns his head so he can see my face. His blue-green eyes are so sparkling against his caramelized skin, and I look into them hoping my words won't disappoint him too much.

"Well, Marco Maselli offered to take me on a bit of a tour of the city tonight," I say as I blanch in anticipation of Scott's reaction.

"Oh, really?" Scott replies softy and then turns his head toward the sun again and closes his eyes.

"Yes... So I told him that I would go with him..." I feel the apology in my tone, and I can't seem to shake off the feeling that I'm doing something wrong here.

"OK," Scott says matter-of-factly.

Scott's response, while it lacked the drama I was dreading, was too abrupt. Doesn't he have any questions? Isn't he going to object? Did he hear what I said? I don't really want to share *all* the details about my evening plans, but, somehow, I feel as though he should at least care a little bit more than he seems to! Certainly he should have more to say to me than, *OK!*

I wait a beat or two and then softly ask, "Are you upset with me, Scott?"

"Why would I be upset?" he asks plainly without opening his eyes or even tilting his head in my direction.

"I guess I thought you would be unhappy because I'm meeting up with Marco, that's all…" I trail off, feeling very cautious about how much to say.

"Elle," Scott says as he turns his head to look me in the eye. "You know that I have some concerns about this guy, but what can I do about it? You seem to need to find out for yourself what kind of person he is, and what kind of friend would I be if I made you feel badly about your need for exploring a relationship?" He says all of this with no tension in his voice, and his face seems so clear and lovely.

"Well…what will *you* do tonight?" I ask, feeling somewhat relieved, but also a touch let down that Scott isn't putting up any resistance at all to my date with Marco.

"I don't know…" he says as he turns his head and closes his eyes again. "Maybe I'll take Miriam Ungaro out tonight since it sounds like *she'll* be free!" Scott starts laughing and then looks over at me.

"Don't you dare!" I screech followed by a peal of laughter. I can't help but laugh as the tension in my body finally releases, and I allow myself to relax.

"By the way," Scott says after our laughing fit subsides. "What happened to your *fancy fingernails?*"

I can feel my face start to redden. I look down at my hands and see how bumpy and uneven my nail beds look. Most of the swelling has gone down in my fingertips, but, in general, my hands look pretty bad. "I kind of had an accident involving my thumbnail… and a candle…and a match…" I finally admit, feeling rather foolish about the whole thing.

"Wow," Scott says as he looks at me with amusement in his eyes. "Do you want to talk about it?" he offers, obviously trying to withhold his laughter.

"Not really," I say while letting a little snicker slip out.

"Oh, Elle," Scott says as he reaches over to muss my hair. "You certainly are entertaining!"

I feel a warm affection for Scott come over me. He is truly one of the only people in my life that seems to get me. And even though I'm embarrassed about the traumatic and fiery death of *Red Hot Elle*, I know that Scott would still love me even if he knew all of the details.

About fifteen minutes later, I can hear Scott snoring softly. I watch his chest rise and fall as he slumbers in the lounge chair next to mine. I know I should be happier that Scott doesn't seem to care that I'm going on a date with Marco, but, for some reason, I'm disappointed in his reaction. Maybe I was just so prepared for the opposite response that I never considered the idea that he might be OK with it.

And truthfully, I also feel rather conflicted about the gorgeous dress hanging in my bedroom. I feel almost guilty when I picture myself in it—even though it really will look amazing on me! But I can't seem to shake this undeniable knot of worry tightening in my stomach that perhaps the dress does indeed have some expectations attached. And I know that if I didn't feel this way, I would totally tell Scott about the dress and even try it on for him. Normally, I tell Scott about everything in my life—no matter what! But this dress and all of the little notes from Marco are too...personal, I guess. In all the years that I've known Scott, I've never felt so private about my feelings, and this need for secrecy is very new to me.

As strange as it seems, after only two brief exchanges, I think I'm falling for Marco Maselli. The way he says my name, the way he pursues me, the way he is such a man while I still feel like such a girl. The whole experience of the past couple of days has made me want to throw caution to the wind. It's made me want to be more courageous and adventurous with my life. I want to feel uninhibited the way other people do. I want to know what it's like to be the center of attention and not worry that I don't deserve it or that it might make me spiral out of control. I want this adventure, and maybe if I tell Scott all the facts, he might bring me back to my senses and talk me out of letting go for the first time in my life.

When Scott rolls over onto his stomach, he rattles me out of my silent reverie. He smiles at me, closes his eyes, and falls back to sleep. I decide to give my own mind a rest and allow myself to slip off into a dream. In the dream, I'm wearing my new dress and standing in center of the *Ponte Vecchio*. Handsome men are coming out of every shop and presenting me with their most beautiful golden creations while other women encircle me and look on with jealousy.

With only two hours to go until Marco picks me up, I decide to gather my things and head back to my villa. I want to take my time getting ready—which is unusual for me, since I normally don't have anything special to wear and typically have no place special to go! But tonight, I want to be perfect.

I take my time in the shower—shaving my legs and indulging every inch of my skin with a sudsy mixture of lavender soap and vanilla body wash. I wrap myself up in my bathrobe and sit out on the veranda and apply lotion to my sun-drenched skin. I work the cream into my legs and arms, massaging my muscles and invigorating my senses. I lean back on the lounge chair for a few minutes and watch the shadows lengthen across the tile work of the veranda. The air is light and balmy as I close my eyes and try to memorize this feeling. It is a feeling of contentment, excitement and anticipation all wrapped into one.

I take my time blowing out my hair. I've decided to wear my hair down and straight. It is the only style that I can predict lasting through the night. I've noticed that every time I try to get too fancy with my hair, I end up being concerned about how I look, so if I stick with my mainstay style, I'm sure I'll feel more confident. Plus, I think long straight hair will compliment the dress better, and after all, tonight is all about the dress! Once my hair is dry, I run my flat iron down it in sections, smoothing out any fly away pieces and adding a golden shine.

I complete my routine with a light dusting of translucent power over my face and neck and then add a touch of peachy blusher on my cheeks. With a quick swipe of mascara on my eyelashes, I'm fully dolled up for the evening. I dab a little vanilla cologne behind each ear and on my wrists. I dig through my jewelry kit in search of my Mother of Pearl earrings—my dad gave them to me for Christmas one year, and I think they will look perfectly elegant with my dress. A quick time check reveals that I still have 45 minutes until Marco arrives, so I decide to make myself a quick snack. I don't want to be too hungry, just in case we don't eat right away.

So I cut up some salami that Scott left in my fridge and pull out a few crackers. Then I pour myself a tall glass of cold water. I'm just about to carry my snack out to the veranda when I hear a knock at the front door. I freeze in my tracks. It can't be Marco—it's still too early! I set my plate down on the counter and tiptoe over to the door. I peer through the peephole and see Scott standing there. Relief washes over me as I unlock and open the door.

"Hey you!" Scott says in a friendly voice. He's wearing loose jeans and a crisp, black linen shirt. His skin smells sweet as he gives me a quick peck on the cheek. He looks very handsome with his sun-browned skin and freshly washed hair.

"Hi!" I say brightly. I'm happy to see him, but part of me wants him to go away. For some reason that I can't explain, I don't want him to see me all fixed up. I feel embarrassed by the fact that he is seeing me with more than my usual amount of makeup, and I try not to look directly into his face. Luckily I'm still in my bathrobe, so only my hair and makeup give me away.

"Are you getting ready for your big date?" Scott asks as I show him into my villa.

"It's not really a date," I say, hoping to downplay the whole thing. "Marco is just showing me around, that's all." A queasy feeling settles in my stomach as I realize that I'm basically lying to Scott. I can't tell him that Marco asked me to "*be with him*" tonight! It just sounds too fishy, and Scott will definitely misinterpret the whole situation.

"Do you have any idea where he's taking you," Scott asks as he walks over to the counter and snags one of my crackers. He's leaning down on the counter on one elbow as he pops the cracker into his mouth. He looks up at me in anticipation of my answer.

"Not really sure," I say as I join him in the kitchen. I slide around to the other side of the counter and pull up a barstool. Then I take a piece of salami and stack it on a cracker and crunch down. "He just wanted to show me around the city," I say with my mouth full of cracker, doing my best to sound casual about the whole thing.

Once I swallow, I ask, "So what are you going to do tonight?"

"I'm actually going to go to a Tuscan wine tasting with Sebastian and Peter this evening," Scott says in a swishy gay-sounding voice. "It should be excellent!" he adds with a big smile.

"That *does* sound fun," I offer up, all the while thinking, *Poor Scott.*

"Well, it's no date with *Capitano Amore,* but it will have to do," he finally says.

I give Scott a half smile as a guilty feeling settles over me. I wish I didn't feel so conflicted here, but I do. I wish I could make myself feel better about everything, but I don't know how. Then I think of the perfect thing to change the subject.

"Do you want to go see Edna Pearl with me next week on our days off?" I ask with excitement in my voice.

"Sure—that would be great," Scott quickly replies rather nonchalantly as he pops another cracker into his mouth. "I haven't seen your grandmother in ages," he says after taking a swallow of my water to wash down the cracker.

"My mom gave me her number today, so I'll try to give her a call tomorrow and get things lined up." I'm not completely satisfied with this exchange, but at least we're talking about something other than the here and now.

"Perfect," Scott says as he starts to walk over toward the door. "So, let's catch up tomorrow some time, OK?" Scott says as he reaches for the door handle. He seems like he's in a hurry to leave all of a sudden—like his popover satisfied his curiosity, and now he's ready to go.

"Sounds like a plan," I say, relieved that he is leaving, but sort of worried about the abruptness of it all. "Maybe we can hit the *Ponte Vecchio* tomorrow?" I feel like I'm throwing him a bone or something to make myself feel less guilty about tonight.

"We can do that in the morning," Scott says casually as he opens the door and steps out onto the porch. "But remember, we're here to work, and tomorrow evening is our first show time."

"That's right," I say as the reality sinks in that we are not here just to have fun. "I almost forgot about that part." I give Scott a sincere smile, and he winks back at me as he steps off of the porch. Then I add, "Have fun with the *girls* tonight, OK?"

"And you behave with *Capitano Amore!*" he says over his shoulder.

I just smile at Scott as I close the door. I feel so strange about everything, but I don't have time to think about it. Scott's impromptu visit cost me some valuable time, and now I have less than 30 minutes left to get ready. I shove another piece of salami and a cracker into my mouth and head for my bedroom.

I dig though my drawers in search of my most dainty bra and panties—not because I think Marco will be seeing me in them tonight, but because I'm sure the silk slip will show off every bump and lump if I'm not mindful of my foundations. I'm not even sure if I can wear a bra with this dress—the slip straps are so thin, and I may have to forgo the bra all together.

After working out the details, I slip the dress over my bra-less body and carefully adjust the layers of fabric against my skin. There are at least a million tiny hidden snaps that run up the side of the dress, which pull in the silk fabric lightly against my body, allowing the slip dress to hug every curve. The silk feels sexy against my skin, and, when I step back to look at myself in the mirror, I can't believe how incredible this dress makes me look.

The slip portion of the dress is close fitting, while the gauzy overlay hovers over the dress and kisses my curves with a subtle and beautiful drape. The contrast of the brown and mint green is stunning, and I can't believe how much this dress transforms me. I pair the dress with some strappy, brown leather sandals that are high—but not too high—so I can at least walk. Then I add a cottony brown wrap that magically matches the dress better than I expected.

I dig around in my closet until I find the tiny Mother of Pearl evening bag that matches my earrings. The whole look is complete, and as I stare at myself in the mirror, I can hardly believe that it's me! I make my final preparations in the bathroom with only minutes to spare. I toss my hair back over my shoulders and make sure the slip dress is covering my chest, and then I dig out a tube of bronzed lip liner and some lip-gloss from my makeup bag. I brush my teeth extra well—I don't want to have salami breath!—and dust off some stray cracker crumbs from around my mouth. Then I line the outer contour of my lips and fill them in with a light coating of bronze tinted lip-gloss. Once my lips are plumped and slathered, I slip the liner and the gloss into my evening bag.

As I rush around the villa, tidying up and turning on lights, I remember to grab some money and some breath mints—just in case—and stick them both in my evening bag. A rush of nerves takes over my body as I look at the clock on the microwave and see that it's now 5:55! I don't know exactly what to do with my remaining five minutes, so I decide to go into my room and take one more look at myself in the full-length mirror. I drape my wrap over my arm and clutch my evening bag in my hand. I feel stunning. I take a deep breath and try to stay in the moment.

On my dresser, there's a framed picture of Sugar Ray. I walk over and pick it up and stare into his adorable face. He's sprawled out on the ground with his legs sticking out on both sides, and his chin is pressed down against the pavement. His eyes are fixed off in the distance, and he looks sort of sad. I wish I could kiss the little space that lies in-between his eyes and just above the bridge of his nose. That is home to me. Just as I finally start to relax with my Sugar Ray in my hands and in my heart, I hear a knock at the front door. I breathe in slowly and then let out a long push of air. I place the picture frame back on my dresser. With one more check in the mirror, I glide out into the living room to answer the door.

Chapter Thirteen

I take a quick peek through the peephole, and I can see Marco standing there. He looks so confidant, so self-assured. He's holding something in his hand, but the peephole won't allow me to see that far down, so I'll have to wait until I actually open the door to find out what it is. I pull in a deep breath and twist the latch. Using the broad wooden panel as a bit of a buffer, I peer around the door and get my first full-length look at Marco.

He is wearing a black tailored suit with a frosty green open-collared dress shirt. His hair is much more golden then I remembered, and his eyes are bright and seem to sparkle along with his smile. He's holding a single daisy in his hand. He is even more handsome than I remembered. His chiseled jaw line looks so manly, and his shoulders look square and strong. I feel my knees go a little weak when he says in his rich voice, "*Buonasera, Eloise-ah.*"

"Hi," I whisper in reply as I remain in a bit of a trance. My throat suddenly feels dry, and I sense that all the moisture has been reassigned to the palms of my hands.

"May I come in?" Marco asks after a long pause with me standing behind the door, unsure of what to do next.

"Oh, yes! Please come in," I say as I snap to and struggle to find my composure. This man seems to have this dumbing affect on me, and I tend to stammer and sputter a lot when he's around—which is not good!

As Marco makes his way into my villa, he takes a step toward me. I'm still half hiding behind the door, but Marco gently pulls the door away from me and kisses me on both cheeks. He smells amazing—like citrus, sandalwood soap and mint. I close my eyes as he quickly presses his lips to my face, and I feel the adrenaline coursing through my veins. Marco turns to shut the door and then refocuses his attention on me.

I self-consciously take a step back and sort of bump my backside against the wall as I watch Marco take me in. His eyes travel up and down my body. I stick my left foot out a bit and angle it just a little in hopes of displaying the dress properly. I've seen models do this pose on that show *Project Runway*, but as soon as I do it, I feel completely self-aware and rather embarrassed. I can only assume he is inspecting the fit of the dress, but I am filled with nerves as I wonder if I managed to catch all those snaps running up the side.

"*Perfezione!*" he finally says with pride. "You look perfect," he translates for me, as he looks me in the eye. "I knew this dress was going to be a perfect match for your natural beauty."

He reaches out and takes my hand and walks me over to the seating area. I'm quite literally frozen by the whole exchange—completely unsure of what to do—so I'm grateful that he seems to be taking over. Marco sits down on the little sofa, and so do I. We are seated facing each other with our knees nearly touching. His face is so fresh and expressive as he smiles at me.

"This daisy is for you," he says as he offers me the delicate flower in his hand. "In Italian, it is called a *margherita*. It is my mother's favorite wildflower because it is so simple, yet so elegant—just like Florence."

I take the flower from Marco and twist it between my fingers. The flower twirls around as I nervously fidget in my seat. "*Margherita*," I say, doing my best to imitate the word with my dry, throaty voice. "It's beautiful…" I add, just to be polite.

"Are you nervous?" Marco asks me at the end of another awkward pause. His face is gentle and encouraging as I consider his question.

"You know, Marco, I really am," I finally admit, as I seem to start to return to my senses. I'm actually a little surprised by my response, but also relieved that I was able to be so truthful. After hiding things from Scott all day—and possibly myself—it feels good to actually give an honest answer.

"Don't be nervous, Eloise-ah. You have nothing to fear," he says with his sultry voice and that thick, rolling accent.

"I know..." I begin, not knowing for sure what I'll be saying next. "But this dress...it is so beautiful, and no one has ever given me something like this—especially someone who barely knows me! And... actually...I'm confused...about you and Miriam..." I end up admitting very unexpectedly.

Marco smiles at my openness and then takes my empty hand in his. I quickly wrap my fingers around his hand in an effort to hide my hacked up fingernails. He seems to smile faintly and then presses his lips to the center of my hand.

"This dress is a part of our tour of the city," he explains as he turns his attention to my face. "And, as for Miriam, she is just a friend who needed to be reminded of her...womanhood," he concludes unapologetically, as if this should make total sense to me.

"I see..." I offer back, more confused than before. "So you aren't in any sort of *relationship* with Miriam?" I add to try to get some additional clarity.

"Not that I know of..." he plainly replies with a smile.

"And the dress. It's a part of our tour?" I am having such a difficult time unwinding the Miriam thing, so I decide to give the dress another go.

"*Si!*" he quips back with a glorious smile. "Tonight, I will show you the greatest things about my city—the city of Florence!"

"OK," I simply reply, not sure what he means, but so smitten with his excitement. I guess I'll have to let the Miriam thing go for now. But we will need to revisit it later, that's for sure!

"So, how does this tour begin?" I ask, wondering how in the world a dress fits into a tour of a city. A slight rush of apprehension washes against the back of my mind as I wonder if Marco is planning on taking a "tour" of the person in the dress while she is in the city. That actually sounds like something Scott might wonder, so I immediately banish the concern and focus on Marco.

"My car is waiting for us," Marco begins as he gently takes the flower from my hand and then pulls me to my feet. "Are you hungry?" he asks.

"Yes, I am," I say with a smile.

"Then let me take you to *cena!*" He places the lovely daisy on the coffee table and begins to lead me around the tiny sofa and toward the door.

"*Cena?*" I ask.

"Dinner!" Marco obliges with a big smile.

I feel as though I may actually be floating outside of myself—which is really strange for me because I don't get like this! But I manage to grab my wrap and my evening bag, and even concentrate long enough to lock the door to my villa behind me. As we walk over the cobbled walkways, Marco is careful not to hold my hand, but gently places his palm in the small of my back as we walk down the narrow, wobbly path that leads to the front gate. I feel a tingle of nerves rushing around my body as I wonder if Marco is checking out my backside. I strain to remember if I examined my backside view in the mirror or not. I'm pretty sure I did, and if I remember correctly, the dress looked gorgeous from all angles.

Miraculously, we manage to slip through the grounds without bumping into anyone—which is a huge relief to me. I'm not sure if I want everyone to know that I am going out on a date—in a stunning dress, no less—with one of our pilots. When we reach the sunflower gate, I see a fancy sports car parked at an angle in the circular driveway. In the early setting sun, I can see that it is candy apple red, and, if I'm not mistaken, it's also a Ferrari! Marco gently pushes the gate open from behind me, and we step out into the driveway. He continues to guide me toward the passenger door of this amazing car and reaches down to lift the handle.

"This is your car?" I ask, stunned that he could afford such a car on a pilot's salary.

I know for a fact that *Windsong Air* doesn't have to pay their American pilots that much since they are all doing the job to keep their instrument ratings in the first place. But now I'm thinking that the Italian pilots must make much more.

"It is," he says with pride as I slide into the bucket seat.

Once I've managed to gather the folds of my dress and my legs into the car, Marco gives me a smile and then gently closes the door. I watch him as he walks around the front of the car. He looks so elegant and masculine, and there is a part of me that can't believe this is happening to me.

Marco slides into the driver's seat and looks directly into my eyes. "Have you ever been in a Ferrari before, Eloise-ah?"

"No, I haven't," I admit, feeling like this is the part of the dream sequence that is all about what guys think women want. Yeah, it's a sexy car, but whatever. It's a car. I'm not that into automobiles, and while it is pretty cool to be driven around in a red-hot Ferrari, when you live in Miami, it's hard to be impressed solely by what a guy drives.

"Well, this car once belonged to my father, and he gave it to me and my brother, Andre. It was in pretty poor condition when he gave it to us, but together, Andre and I have restored this gorgeous piece of our Italian heritage back to its original condition. So, for me, it has great meaning and much pride."

As Marco says this, I instantly feel like a jerk for my thoughts. He is a proud man who loves his country and his heritage. And here I am just judging him all over the place and trying to make him into a typical American guy. He bought me a gorgeous dress and has planned a very special evening—something most American men I know aren't in the habit of doing for me—and here I am thinking such terrible thoughts.

In an effort to excuse myself, I reach over and place my hand on top of Marco's hand—which is casually resting on the gearshift. Then I say, "Listen, before we go, I just want to thank you."

"The tour hasn't even started yet, Eloise-ah!" Marco replies with a smile and a light laugh.

"Thank you for the dress, thank you for the flower on the plane, thank you for the little notes, and, most of all, thank you for the promise of a night I know I will never forget…" I trail off, worried that I've said too much, but too overcome to really care.

"Eloise-ah," Marco whispers. "*Prego.*"

With that, Marco twists the key in the ignition, and the car jolts to life with a deep, low rumble. I can feel the vibration from the engine in my seat, and I look over at Marco who is still staring at me.

"Are you ready?" he asks me as a sense of adventure fills his face.

"I'm ready!" I reply, unsure of just about everything but the fact that I'm ready to let go and live a little!

But, as the tiny red car lunges out into traffic, my body automatically tightens in fear. I haven't put on my seatbelt or anything, and I feel very vulnerable as Marco takes a sharp turn and catapults us down what feels like a very steep hill. I grip the door handle so tightly that my fingers instantly go numb! I say a silent prayer that we make it to our destination—wherever that may be—safely.

Marco zips around another corner, and I feel my grip on the door handle loosen momentarily. As my body shifts in the seat, my bottom rubs against the supple black Italian leather, emitting a sound that is horrifyingly similar to gas! Out of the corner of my eye, I see Marco turn his head to look at me, but all I can do is stay frozen in my seat.

Oh no! I think as my mind searches for a way to let Marco know that it was the *seat,* not *me* that made that noise.

"Nice seats!" I say over the roar of the engines.

"*Si!*" Marco says with a smile.

Marco slams the car into a higher gear, and I have the sensation of being on a runway, getting ready to lift off. I tighten my grip on the door handle even more, and I do my best to use the strength in my thighs to press my bottom firmly into the cup of the seat. Marco takes his eyes off the road for an instant, and I can feel him notice my clinched jaw and stiff body, which feels slammed against the seat.

"You don't like the speed?" he questions, as he shifts into a lower gear. The car rears back a bit, like he's pulled back on the reins of a charging stallion that's ready to run.

"Oh, I'm fine," I unconvincingly assure him as I make eye contact with him without turning my head. "I'm just not used to the way people drive in your city," I weakly offer, feeling badly about spoiling all his fun.

"Can you trust me, Eloise-ah?" he asks me in a kind and sincere voice.

I turn my head slightly to get a better look at his face and can see genuine care. *Can I trust you?* I ask myself as I quickly memorize the gorgeous lines around his eyes. Right now, I'm not even sure I trust myself.

I take a moment to consider my answer and then say, "I'll try."

Marco looks back at me with a wink and a wide grin. "You are safe with me, Eloise-ah. I promise. Just sit back and enjoy the speed!"

And with that, he shifts the car into another gear, which unleashes the beast under the hood, and we rocket down a tiny side road. I take a deep breath and decide to trust Marco with all my heart, pushing all my fears aside and allowing the exhilaration of the speed to overcome me. I will myself to let go and to allow this experience to unfold, as it should.

In a matter of minutes, I am smiling from ear to ear, feeling my body sink into the turns and bottom out as we race over the tiny undulations in the road. I watch from the window as the city starts to fade away. Soon, we are racing past open fields carpeted in deep greens with purpled mossy highlights. In the setting sun, the countryside looks lush and is flecked with golden light and fantastic hues of yellow, brown and green. The sky is painted in pink and orange, and, just below the skyline, I can see the rugged hills surrounding the countryside.

Marco pulls the car over to the side of the road and brings the engine to an idle. I catch my breath as I peer out my window and drink in the stunning landscape that surrounds me.

"Do you see the vineyard up on that hill?" Marco asks me as he leans across me and points up toward the hill. I follow his gaze and manage to see a tall house seated among a patchwork of color. Perfectly straight lines stripe the countryside below the house and deep greens and dark yellows fill in the lines with color and vivid symmetry.

"I see it," I finally say once I've managed to focus in on the details.

"That vineyard belongs to my family," Marco begins, never taking his eyes off of the hillside as he studies it with pride. "My maternal great grandfather planted his first grapes on this land, and it has been a way of life for my mother's family ever since…" Marco trails off as I turn my gaze back to the hillside.

"It's beautiful," is all I can manage as I stare at the glorious view.

"Yes, it is," Marco replies, after he shifts his gaze back to me. He leans back into his own seat and gives me a seductive smile. "I will take you there sometime to meet my family and to taste our wines."

"I'd like that," I say sincerely as I fight off this wave of lust that seems to have broadsided me without warning.

I've never known such a powerful desire for anyone in my life, and my reaction scares me—even more than racing down hills in Marco's fancy car! I will myself to let this lust thing pass. I know that I need to keep a clear head.

"But, for tonight, we will spend our time in the city," Marco says as he gives the engine a rev and shoves the car into gear. "Tonight, I want to show you Florence!" he says over the roar of the engine.

And with that, we peal away from the side of the road and speed back toward the city. I watch as Marco's family vineyard melts away into the hillside, and I begin to make a mental list of questions to ask Marco about his life. As the car speeds up, my body rides each of the curves without hesitation, and I realize that for one of the first times in my life, I've fully let go! My hands are resting peacefully in my lap, and the stinging breeze whipping across my face entrances me. There is nothing but joy and anticipation pumping through my veins—and it feels great!

We float along, racing past other cars and slipping through the gaps, making our way back into the city—a city that is aglow in the final moments of the red hot, setting sun.

None of the passing structures seem familiar to me as Marco expertly maneuvers his car through the tiny streets of Florence, but the pungent, earthy smell of the Arno River is unmistakable as we make a sharp left onto a busy thoroughfare. Marco weaves in and out of traffic—aggressively honking his horn as other drivers honk back in reply. I do my best to stay calm and focus on my new carefree approach to life, but, every so often, I find that my fingers have managed to wrap their way around the door handle without my actual permission.

"Is that the Arno River?" I ask Marco as we pull up along the walled embankment.

"Yes, it is!" Marco says, surprised, I think, that I knew that.

I look out the window at the quiet, smooth river. In the setting sun, it's aglow with a rich yellow sheen that makes it look like molten gold, gently oozing its way toward the famed gold shops of the *Ponte Vecchio*.

"I went for a run this morning and ended up at the *Ponte Vecchio*," I mention as we continue zipping through traffic as if the other cars are standing still. "It's an amazing place," I add in a slightly shrill voice as Marco makes a power move on a slow-moving Mini Cooper.

"Then you already have an idea of where we are going," Marco replies with a sidelong look. "Only *you* will be going where regular tourists cannot go!" he says with a hint of mystery in his voice.

After Marco makes a quick left turn, large, very old-looking buildings on all sides suddenly dwarf us. Marco pulls around a few stone-like structures in the middle of the road and zips around chained off sections that appear to be only meant for foot traffic.

"So, do you get to drive wherever you want to in this city if you're in a Ferrari?" I ask, hoping that Marco's sense of humor is equal to his sense of adventure.

"I have special permission," he assures me with a smile. "But the car does help!" he adds as we dodge another road obstacle and slip down an alleyway.

Marco brings the car to a halt on the backside of a very tall, ancient-looking building. It looks pretty non-descript from this view, but I feel certain that it is important. He shuts off the engine and grabs a small cell phone from under the seat. He flips it open, dials a number and then holds the phone to his ear. I can hear the faint ringing on the other end. Then I can hear a woman's voice answer with an enthusiastic *"Marco!"*

Marco responds to the caller on the other end with a smile and launches into a rapid conversation—his Italian is so lovely, but I can't pick up a single word! After a minute of discussion, Marco says, *"Ciao,"* and then snaps the phone shut.

He redirects his attention to me and then asks, "Are you ready to go inside?"

"Sure!" I say with great anticipation.

"Wait here," he says as he slips out of the car and walks around to my side.

He opens the car door and reaches for my hand. As I take his hand, I realize how low this car actually is, and it takes me a few muscle thrusts to get my body up and out of the bucket seat. I feel like an old grandma as I spread my legs apart to give myself more leverage and heave one last time in an effort to extract myself from the car.

Suddenly my face feels hot with embarrassment as Marco says, "Are you alright?"

"Oh yes!" I quickly respond. "I think my dress was just caught up in the seat…" I stammer as a light sweat washes over my body, and I wonder if the dress thing was even believable.

Marco smiles at me sheepishly, and I wish I could have a total do over. *What a buffoon I am! I can't even get out of a car gracefully!!* The whole exchange, plus the exhilarating car ride and that embarrassing *sound* my seat made, have all left me feeling a bit wobbly.

Marco closes the door of the car just as a tiny almost hidden door of the building swings open. An attractive woman wearing a dark, two-piece dress suit steps out and greets us with a smile. Her long legs are hard to miss, and I feel a little self-conscious as she makes her way over to Marco. She has golden blonde hair that is tightly twisted into a perfectly styled chignon. Her face is stunning—her olive skin is fresh and flawless, and her lips are painted with a flush of pink. Her teeth are long and straight, and there is something so disarming about her smile.

"Marco!" she says with a deep, sultry voice.

"Francesca!" he replies as he reaches out for her. He embraces her with a kiss on both cheeks and then takes his hand and holds her face in it for a moment. He smiles at her longingly and seems to drink in her presence with his eyes.

Suddenly, I feel invisible. This whole exchange between Marco and this mystery woman feels incredibly intimate.

Who is she? I think, as I watch and listen intently to the two of them jabbering in Italian. *Is this some kind of Italian thing—to have two women to fawn over at the same time? Or is this woman another* Miriam *who also needs Marco to remind her of her 'womanhood'?*

At the thought of Miriam, irritation rises up inside my stomach and hits a bottleneck in my throat. I'm still not completely satisfied with Marco's response to that situation, but, right now, I'm not sure what to think about anything at all.

My thoughts are rushing into my head faster than I can sort them out, but I'm so confused as Marco continues to chat with this Francesca woman without even so much as introducing me. Then, as if Marco is finally reminded of my presence, he turns his attention toward me.

"Francesca, this is my *Eloise-ah*," he says as he takes my arm and gently pulls me closer to him. His fingers are warm and soft and as soon as he touches me, electricity starts zigzagging through my body.

Did he just call me his *Eloise?* I think, as my mind starts to turn to putty. He did! He called me *his Eloise!* Suddenly, all is forgiven, and Miriam is a distant memory. I notice as the outside of my arm is pressed up against the side of his body, I'm overcome with the magical powers of Marco Maselli.

"Ah, Eloise! It is lovely to meet you," Francesca replies with a sincere smile and gracious tone. Her English is perfect—so when she says my name, it sounds ugly and flat. I wish I could ask her to call me Elle, but the moment has passed. "Marco has a very special evening planned for you that happens to require a lot of help to pull off!" she says as she gives Marco a teasing, playful look.

"And *Marco* has done other people favors before, too!" he chides with a smile as he and Francesca square off in their private little game.

"Ah…you win," Francesca concedes with a huge smile for Marco.

"*Eloise-ah*," Marco says as he angles his body between his mystery woman and me. "Francesca is my cousin, and she has helped me arrange something very special for you this evening."

His cousin! I think as relief spills through my body.

"It is so nice to meet you!" I reaffirm as I take her tiny, well-groomed hand in mine, hoping that my relief isn't too obvious. Again, I feel foolish for misjudging Marco. First the car, and now this—I need to be more confident in this man. He must be genuine—the real deal. I have to let go of my doubts even though I still have some questions about Miriam

"So, Eloise? Are you ready to start your *All-Things-Florentine* evening?" Francesca asks me with a glorious smile.

"Yes!" I reply lightly as my imagination starts to race.

"Then follow me," Francesca says as she turns back toward the door.

Marco wraps his arm around me and gently guides me in the direction of the doorway. I can smell his aftershave—that citrus blast from earlier this evening—and I can feel my senses dance as I work to memorize every second of being *Marco's Eloise*. His hand is firm, but steady, as he wraps his fingers around the top of my shoulder. It's such an intimate gesture—one that makes me feel safe and lovely.

As we approach the door, Francesca pulls out a small white credit card of sorts and flashes it in front of a tiny red light that appears next to the door. The door unlatches with a click, and Marco reaches around me to hold the door open for Francesca and me to enter the building.

The doorway leads to a musty, dark hallway of sorts. A bare bulb hangs from the low ceiling above, and it almost feels eerie and cold, like we are entering a dungeon or a place haunted with sinister memories. Marco continues to guide me from behind as we make our way through the narrow hallway, down a few steps and out into an open portico. I feel a flush of relief wash over me when we exit the tiny hallway.

"Eloise?" Francesca begins. "Has Marco told you anything about where you are?" Her eyes are fixed on me as she asks me this question, and I feel nervous about my reply.

"Not really," I say as I look over to Marco for support. He offers none, but gives me a quiet smile instead. "But I think we might be near the *Ponte Vecchio*?" I tentatively add.

"You are correct!" Francesca replies, clearly pleased at my guess. "Marco has arranged for you to have your dinner in a place that is very rarely open to visitors—especially after hours. It's called the *Corridoio Vasariano*."

The three of us start walking through the portico and out into an open courtyard. I feel nervous butterflies swirling around in my stomach, and I am very aware of myself at this moment. I want to remember every detail, every second of this evening. I turn to look at Marco, and he gives me a dreamy smile as he walks quietly behind me.

The huge clock tower above starts ringing, reverberating throughout the courtyard and sending birds flying in every direction. We all amble silently as the clock rings out. I count out seven gongs, which brings me back full circle to my first venture into the city of Florence exactly 12 hours ago. Once the courtyard is still again, Francesca continues leading the way while she launches into what feels like a script she's memorized and said a thousand times.

"The *Corridoio Vasariano* was built by Vasari in 1565 to link the *Uffizi* and the *Palazzo Vecchio*—which is where we just entered—with the Medici family's new home—the *Palazzo Pitti*—which is across the river. This covered walkway enabled Duke Cosimo de' Medici to commute between these buildings without having to enter the elements."

As I listen to Francesca go on about the walkway and the Medici family and some of their extravagant tastes and little known eccentricities, I can't help but feel like I am on a school field trip and there might be a test afterward. I do my best to absorb all the details, but I'm so distracted by Marco.

When we climb up to the covered walkway, Francesca continues to provide little details about the architecture and the various techniques that were used to build the bridge and the eventual passageway.

"You no doubt noticed all of the amazing gold shops below," Francesca continues with a proud smile on her face. I nod my head with wide eyes as I recall what I saw this morning.

"Well, prior to the building of this secret passage way, the shops were filled with butchers—hog butchers to be exact. But once the Duke was using this passageway, he evicted all of the butchers and replaced them with goldsmiths. This was the beginning of a great Florentine tradition of jewelry making," Francesca says brightly.

Francesca continues on with more details about all the gold, but I'm starting to get nervous that our date is going to be one long lecture. I feel myself wishing she would wrap things up, so I could be alone with Marco. I can't concentrate with that amazing cologne wafting all around me.

Once we're finally inside the actual passageway, Francesca points out all of the various portraits and paintings that adorn the walls in perfectly staggered rhythm. It smells old and musty, like this place has been here forever. Francesca begins sharing pertinent details about some of the more important paintings, but, by this time, I'm no longer listening to her at all. The only thing I can think about is the tiny table set up in the middle of the long, open passageway.

The table has a white linen cloth stretched over it and two iron chairs, each set at an angle, like they are open and waiting for us to be seated. As we approach the table, I can see red rose petals sprinkled about the surface and two place settings of white china with a tiny gold pattern etched around the edge. There are two wineglasses next to each plate and perfectly positioned silver on either side. On one of the plates is a small box wrapped in swirled paper—similar to the paper I saved earlier when I opened up the dress box. An identical silk ribbon is tied around the box, and I can see a gift tag attached with my name on it.

I eventually notice that Francesca has stopped talking, and I realize that both she and Marco are watching me. I step aside and look at both of them and smile.

"This is amazing!" I say to Marco, slightly overcome by all the effort he is putting into our first date.

"*Florence* is amazing," Marco says in reply as he carefully guides me to my chair.

Francesca walks around so she is facing me once I am seated at the table. She looks into my eyes and gives me a warm smile. Her eyes are the color of green olives, and her sincerity sparkles as she speaks.

"Eloise," she begins. "You must be a very special girl! We don't open up this historic landmark after hours for just anyone." She gives Marco a wink as he slides into the seat across the table from me.

"Thank you, Francesca," I say in an effort to let her know how impressed I am and that I understand how special this evening is. "I will never forget this as long as I live," I promise her.

She and Marco exchange words in Italian, and I strain to figure out what they are saying. Francesca walks over to Marco, they kiss, each other on each cheek and then she approaches me.

With her hand extended, she says, "Enjoy your evening, Eloise. It has been my pleasure to bring you to this place."

I shake her hand to thank her again, and she turns and walks back toward the entrance where we came in. Now Marco and I are sitting alone in a museum-like secret passageway that extends over a bridge that houses countless pieces of gold and spans a lazy, ancient river. As the final shards of evening light pass through the barred windows along the center of the passageway, I feel the need to pinch myself because this can't actually be happening to me!

Chapter Fourteen

Now that Marco and I are alone, I start to feel pings of anxiety and jitters coursing through my body. *Why am I so nervous?* I wonder as I try to get comfortable.

"Remember to breathe," Marco says to me from across the table. His face is soft and placid as he sends a smile my way. I smile back at him after I take a deep breath.

"Thank you," I say once my composure has returned. "This is just so special. No one has ever gone to so much trouble over me."

"It's my pleasure," Marco says with a dreamy smile. "Now, do a favor for me and open up the gift on your plate."

Ah, yes—the gift on my plate. There it is, patiently waiting for my undivided attention. *When does this generosity end?* I think as I look up at Marco and then back down at the gift. It looks so delicate in the swirled purple paper. As I reach down to pick it up, Marco begins to speak.

"The paper is handmade," he offers. "It is a Florentine tradition. I have sisters who own a shop where this paper is made. The design of the wrapping is the marbled technique they use, and no two sheets are alike. Everything they sell in their shop is made using the Florentine traditions of fine paper-making." I can sense Marco's pride, and I'm touched.

I carefully slide my finger under the seam. Now that I know his sisters made this, I would really hate to rip it! After working and gently tugging the paper, I finally remove it—undamaged. Inside is a medium-sized, square gift box. I wedge my still tender fingers into the box and pull off the lid. I am taken aback by the contents.

"Marco!" I gasp, shocked by the glimmering gift resting inside the box on a bed of mint green tissue paper. "This is too much!" I look up at him in disbelief and see that he is on his feet, making his way over to my side of the table.

"No, Eloise-ah—it is just a gift to share my love of this fine city," he says with a smile in his voice.

Marco reaches his arms around me and removes the gold necklace from the box. The chain is so thin that it almost looks like a thread of spun gold. In the center of the chain is a tiny golden oblong bead. It is so dainty and understated that I can hardly believe how perfectly balanced it looks hanging on the thin chain.

"This is a Florentine *amuleto*—it is meant to bring luck and love into in your life," Marco explains as he carefully pulls the chain around my neck and fastens it in the back. "It is a gesture of the deepest friendship—from me to you—handcrafted in one of the shops directly below us by my Uncle Giuseppe."

Once the chain is clasped, Marco carefully lifts my hair up and over the chain. The act is so intimate, so personal that my heart starts to pound inside my ears, and I feel a flush of heat rising up over my shoulders. I reach up to touch the tiny bead, partly in an effort to calm my nerves and partly to feel the dainty creation as it encircles my neck.

I'm completely speechless. The necklace is gorgeous, and the meaning is so precious. I don't even know how to properly thank Marco. I'm simply too blown away. I look across the table where Marco is now seated again and give him a pained expression. How do you possibly say thank you to someone who keeps giving you things you don't deserve?

"Eloise-ah, please allow me this pleasure," he pleads calmly in response to my unspoken dilemma. Then he reaches for my hand. So I slowly creep my mangled fingers across the table. He takes my fingers into the palm of his hand with a gentle embrace. His palm is soft and warm, and I feel connected to Marco in a way that fills my heart with desire.

"Marco, thank you," I say in a weak voice that is overcome with emotion. "This is the most incredible gesture…" I stammer.

"It is my pleasure. Now did you finish looking inside the box?" he asks me with one raised eyebrow.

With a sigh, I peer down inside the box that is now resting on my lap. I carefully pull my fingers from Marco's embrace so that I can dig deeper into the tissue paper filled box. Wrapped in the folds of mint green is something hard and square. I remove the tissue and see divine little note cards and envelopes nestled inside. As I flip through the small stack, I can see that it is the same handmade paper, only on a card stock. Each card is a different color with a slightly different pattern, but all equally stunning, and the envelopes are white, but lined with patterns that correspond with the cards.

"My sisters wanted you to have more than wrapping paper as a keepsake of this fine tradition," Marco explains with a smile. "They are very proud, too, and this is a token of their desire for you to experience Florence at her finest!"

"Marco, I just don't know what to say…" I admit after I tuck the cards back inside the box and give him a long look. "I am so in love with this city!" I finally blurt out with a rush of laughter. Marco joins in as he sits back in his seat and beams with pride over my reaction.

Then, as if on cue, a tall, thin man dressed in black pants and a chef's jacket enters the room from the other side. He is handsome in a strange and surprising kind of way. He has a large nose, wide mouth and pointed chin, but when you put them all together with his warm, brown skin and his thick, black hair, he is notably attractive.

As he approaches the table, I notice that he is carrying a bottle of red wine in one hand and a bottle of white in the other. Marco gives him a big smile as he sidles up next to the table with his offerings in hand.

"Eloise-ah," Marco says. "This is my cousin Vicenzo—Francesca's little brother."

"*Buonasera, Eloise-ah,*" Vicenzo says as he nods his head in my direction. His smile is sincere and lovely, and I find his brown eyes to be very serene.

"*Buonasera,*" I repeat back to our lovely waiter. "How many family members are involved in this evening's festivities?" I can't help but ask now that the tension has started seeping out of my body.

Marco takes a moment to calculate, and then says, "Ahhh…maybe twenty…"

"Twenty!" I gasp.

Marco just smiles at me. "Do you prefer red or white wine to start the evening?" he asks as Vicenzo holds both bottles out for my inspection.

"Red please," I say, surprised at my ability to actually admit that I want to drink red instead of white. Usually, I am so concerned about trying to pick what I think everyone else wants that I seldom give my real opinion— except with Scott, of course. He always knows what I want! But I'm a bit baffled by my behavior this evening with Marco. I seem to vacillate between being an idiot and being extra blunt.

"Red it is," Marco replies with a smile and says something to Vicenzo in Italian. Vicenzo nods his head and begins uncorking the bottle of red wine. I watch as his hands expertly work the cork from the bottle. Then he pours Marco the first taste. After Marco inspects the color, he swirls it around and breathes in a deep pull of the aroma from inside of the glass. After a quick taste and a roll on the tongue, the wine passes the test, and Vicenzo pours me a glass.

"Is this wine from your family's vineyard?" I ask as Vicenzo wipes the lip of the bottle with a white napkin and then begins filling Marco's glass.

"No, this is another wine I selected for tonight—I wanted to save my family's wine for our next date," Marco replies with a seductive smile.

Our next date? I think as his words travel down my spine with a tingle of excitement. *You mean we'll be going on another date? He already knows he wants to date me again?* My stomach is all a flutter with butterflies like I'm in junior high all over again, and Brad Cooper—*my biggest crush ever*—just passed me a love note in the middle of English class! I feel silly to have this wash of emotions flooding my entire body, but I can't remember a time when anyone has made it so clear that he want to be with me.

After Vicenzo fills Marco's glass, he slips away from the table and disappears into a shadowy alcove. Marco leans in on the table and raises his glass for a toast.

"To discovering Florence," he says as I raise my glass. "She is the grand lover who teaches us to live in the moment—always." And with that, Marco taps my wine glass. The sound rings in my ears like a dainty bell. I do my best to let the vibration warble through my body as I soak up the romance of this moment—this *Florentine* moment.

After I take my first sip, I look up and see Marco staring at me. Normally this would make me fidget and falter, but for some reason—maybe it's the wine or maybe it's a spell that Marco has managed to cast on me—I stay in the crosshairs of his stare without even a hint of shame or embarrassment.

Vicenzo returns to our table three times in all, carrying plates filled with incredible things (and I don't necessarily mean *incredible* in a good way!). Marco finally explained that Vicenzo's family owns one of the most authentic and expensive restaurants (or *ristorantes)* in the city. Since it is usually mobbed every night of the week—with locals and tourists alike—Marco decided to hire his cousin to create a traditional Florentine meal especially for me. Then, he paid him a little extra to come serve it to us in this special location so we could be alone. Francesca owed him a favor, and so she used her connections as one of the top art historians working for the *Uffizi* to secure this romantic setting—which totally set the scene for the evening.

The first course was a gorgeous antipasto plate. Roasted red peppers and a wide assortment of cheeses, meats, melon and olives, all expertly displayed, created a feast for the eyes, but a troublesome feast for my mouth. The meats were extra salty and sort of chewy, and the cheeses were very strong. I did my best to listen to Marco as he described the hidden flavors each item on the plate could unlock in the wine, but in the end, it just tasted like salty meat and funky cheese followed by some very dry red wine. I have to say that I was a really good sport about it, though. Even though I don't care for green olives, I ate each one as if I was eating candy. (I'm still not a big fan of green olives, but they weren't as bad as I thought!)

The second course was a dish that Marco called *trippa alla fiorentina.* I'm told it is a very popular dish among Florentine natives, and Vicenzo served it with great pride. I wasn't quite sure what to say when Marco interpreted the name of the dish as fried *tripe* with olive oil and onions! Oh gosh! That was a little daunting for me—the bland eater that I am! But surprisingly, once I shut down the idea that I was eating fried stomach lining from a cow, it actually tasted OK. It was light and very thinly sliced, and I ate every bite with a smile—a nervous, *I hope I don't barf all over this historic place,* kind of smile!

I think I may have wolfed down the third course which was a bowl full of thick ropes of homemade spaghetti tossed in olive oil and garlic. It was delicious and normal, and I figured if I forced the pasta into my system, it would mix in with the tripe and prevent it from haunting me for the rest of the night.

The final course was my favorite! It was the dessert course which Marco called *dolci.* Vicenzo carried out two crystal serving cups full of lemon *gelato.* The zesty dessert was the perfect ending to the meal, and I was so thankful it was something I wasn't afraid to eat.

All through dinner, Marco told me fascinating details about his fine city. He went on and on like a history teacher, but I never got bored. And while I'm sure I could never pass a test on the information he shared, I was riveted by his rich voice, rolling over all the details he shared, lulling me into a bit of a trance at times.

Now that the meal is over, Vicenzo starts clearing away our dessert cups and all the silver, leaving us with only our glasses and the last swish of wine in the tall dark bottle. Marco pours me a splash and pours the rest for himself. I finally see a break in the conversation to transition the topic of conversation from Florence to Marco.

"So, Marco," I begin tentatively as he holds my hands from across the table. "How many brothers and sisters do you have?"

"I have four sisters and four brothers—all but one still living and working here in Florence," he replies. He releases one of my hands briefly to take a sip of wine and then continues clarifying the answer to my question. "I am the youngest, believe it or not!" he says with a wink.

"Wow! That's a big family!" I say, as I try to figure out exactly how old Marco is. I'm guessing he's in his 40's, but as I look at his handsome face, I can see that time has been especially careful with him.

"My father is in banking along with my oldest brother, Andre," he continues without acknowledging my comment.

"That's the brother that helped you restore your car!" I offer to prove that I've been paying attention.

"Yes!" Marco says, clearly impressed with my recollection. "And, of course, my mother is in the wine making trade with her side of the family. Then there are my three oldest sisters who own the paper shop. They are each married to bankers, as well, and they all live here in the city. Then there are my three middle brothers. Two of them work at the vineyard with my mother, and the other one is in *fashion*," he says with a particular hint of pride. "Then there is my sister, Gia," Marco says as his voice takes a noticeable dip. He finishes the last swig of his wine and stares into the bowl of the glass as he continues. "Gia died when we were young..."

Somberness envelops both of us as his words trail off, and I see how painful it is for Marco to think of his sister Gia.

"You two must have been close," I offer in an effort to break the silence.

"She was very important to my life..." he trails off. I watch as Marco squeezes the wine cork in his hand as he remembers his sister.

"I'm so sorry, Marco," I offer in what feels like a weak effort to show my concern.

"Well, we live on..." Marco replies after a lengthy pause. He looks up at me with a pained smile.

Outside, I can hear bells ringing, shattering the awkward moment and reminding us both that time does indeed move on. I count out eight gongs this time, and when the final bell vibrates through the passageway, Marco seems revived.

"Are you ready to continue our date?" he asks with raised eyebrows.

"You mean there's more?" I ask with surprise. "How much more can there be?"

"Oh, Eloise-ah, you have no idea!" he says as he stands up and walks around to my side of the table. He pulls my seat out, gathers up my wrap, my gift box and wrappings, and my pearly evening bag.

"Follow me," he whispers into my ear, sending a fizz of shivers up my spine and causing gooseflesh to flare up on my arms and legs.

As we walk toward the stairwell opening, Francesca miraculously appears and greets us with a huge smile.

"Did you enjoy your dinner, Eloise?" she asks with genuine interest.

"It was really special," I reply as graciously as I can. "Thank you again for making this evening so incredible," I add as Marco guides me into the stairwell entrance.

"No problem," Francesca replies as she turns and walks back into the stairwell.

With Francesca in the lead, the three of us make our way back down the stairs and out into the open courtyard. Marco catches up to Francesca and begins whispering in her ear. This time, no tinge of jealousy courses through my body, but I can't help control my anticipation. It seems that Marco has one surprise after another planned for me, and I can hardly wait to find out what's next!

As Marco pulls away from Francesca, he asks, "Eloise-ah? Do you need your wrap?"

I briefly turn my attention to my exposed arms and legs. The night air is fresh and cool, but it feels as though the breeze is wrapped in silk as it coils around my body and hugs me with a sensual grip. "No, I'm fine," I say as Marco makes his way toward me.

"We are going to walk for a bit, so I wanted to make sure you are comfortable," he explains as he moves in next to me. I notice that he has given Francesca the gift box and wrappings, and she is carrying them as she walks away from us. "Francesca will take care of the rest of your things," Marco explains as he continues to guide me toward a well-lit area surrounded by shops and cafés. A feeling of endearment washes over me as I notice that Marco is still carrying my evening bag and my wrap in his hand.

We make our way across a busy street, and Marco has his arm wrapped around me as he guides me up and over the curb and onto the sidewalk. We continue walking—arm in arm now—passing the open cafés and small shops. I am starting to feel less nervous and more confident around Marco. We are making easy small talk as we pass by other couples on the street—most of whom look to be tourists in their goofy sandals and novelty T-shirts with images of the famous *Duomo* and *Michelangelo's David* printed on the front.

"So Marco," I tentatively begin. "There is still something I want to ask you."

"What is it?" he says as he leans around to see my face. We are slowly walking past an open-air shop that sells gelato by the tub.

"I guess I just don't fully understand your *friendship* with Miriam," I boldly forge ahead. I feel as though I have to get this out in the open or else everything about this magical evening is going to be called into question.

"Ah…I know that you must be confused by that, and that is why I wanted to explain it to you," Marco responds evenly as we continue to saunter along.

"Well, it's just that on the airplane, she seemed rather possessive, and I thought you were kind of *with* her and stuff, and then when you were sort of inviting me to spend time with you, it just all seemed rather confusing. And while I am not really close friends with Miriam or anything, she *is* my boss, and I feel uncomfortable around her now because I think she thinks that you are her…*special friend*…" I trail off once I realize how much I am jabbering.

I catch Marco's face out of the corner of my eye, and he seems to be mildly amused. I start to feel a flush of embarrassment creeping across my face, but the truth is I just need to have some answers!

"Let us go and sit, OK?" Marco suggests as he casually guides us toward a stone bench just outside a small private courtyard.

He stops short of the bench and then hands me my evening bag while he opens up my wrap like a large blanket. He unfurls the folds of brown fabric and perfectly drapes the cloth over the bench. He then motions for me to sit down on the covered bench. I take my cue and sit and look up at Marco, who is standing directly in front of me.

"Eloise-ah," he begins as he looks up to the sky, like he is in search of the perfect words. "American women are very different from the women of Italy. I have spent much time in America, and one thing I know is that women in your country are unsure of their value—of their worth. They are so busy trying to keep up with the men that they forget they are women—full of power and allure, the kind men cannot even fathom."

As Marco starts this dramatic clarification, I feel drawn to his words. I so badly want him to have the perfect explanation that completely justifies wrapping himself up in a blanket with my hideously ugly boss and feeding her grapes in a very overtly sexual way right after hitting on me in the back of the plane. But so far, his words are severely lacking, and I can feel a sense of total disappointment washing over me as he continues on with his little monologue.

"Women like Miriam have become hardened to their own womanhood, and all it takes is the smallest bit of attention and affirmation to bring a woman like this back to her natural senses..." Marco has his gaze fixed on me as he says this. "While I was training with *Windsong Air* in Miami, Miriam was in great need of attention, so I gave it to her—not because I needed her attention in return, but because it is what she needed from me."

It's all I can do to keep from rolling my eyes and saying, "*Oh brother,*" as Marco continues on with this explanation. What he's said so far is almost laughable! It seems to me that Marco must see himself as some kind of humanitarian who is reaching out to bitter, middle-aged American women with open arms to affirm them back into a healthy self-esteem. Maybe he thinks he's the Italian version of Dr. Phil or something, but all I can think is, *What a load of crap*!

He continues, "I think deep down, Miriam knew that I was only respecting her value as a woman, and she enjoyed this time of adoration and appreciation. But never during my times with Miriam did I ever lead her to believe that I wanted more from her than to be a man in her world that could see her true worth. I simply reminded her—as I do with many women in my life—that she is endowed with great power and beauty, and I respect that."

As Marco continues to blather on, I feel bile rising up inside of me. I can't believe I pretended to enjoy *tripe* for this guy!! *And* green olives! Does he actually think I am so naive that I can believe that he *pretended* to like Miriam to make her feel better about herself and for no other reason? Does he honestly think that someone like Miriam could simply get an ego boost from someone like him and then move on?

My pulse is racing as I sit listening to this drivel—this first class, *Italian Stallion* drivel! Marco seems to be completely unaware of how his words are affecting me as he launches into another segue that is presumably supposed to help me better understand.

"Miriam knows that I am her friend—her adoring friend, I should say—but that my personal feelings for her go no deeper," he explains with conviction as he locks eyes with me. "She knows that she is a free woman to pursue her life as she chooses with no attachments to me and no expectations of me, other than friendship."

"Are you *sure* that Miriam understands all this the way you think she does?" I can't help but ask.

"Eloise-ah, she knows," Marco says firmly as he moves in toward the bench and then sits down next to me. His hip is touching the length of my thigh. He keeps both of his hands on his knees as he cocks his head to look at me.

"So…then…are you just showing me *my womanhood,* too?" I ask with a slightly acid tone. I'm not even worried that I'm offending him by asking this question because I need to know how far his *humanitarian* efforts go. I need to know if I am indeed just another American charity case.

"No, I am not," Marco says calmly. "Eloise-ah, you make me want to be…*egoista.*" He looks into my eyes without even a hint of reservation.

"What? What does that word mean?" I ask, desperate for clarity.

"Selfish. You make me want to be selfish," he clarifies, his eyes intense and unwavering.

Selfish? "What does that mean—selfish?" I question.

"It means that the first time I saw you in the airport in Miami, sitting with your legs crossed in the front of the group, I wanted to know you for myself," Marco responds. "You, with your golden hair, your fresh face, and your long legs—you are an all-American beauty and I can't help myself."

A flush of adrenaline seeps into my thighs upon hearing this. It's the *love-at-first-sight* scenario I wouldn't even allow myself to consider the night Red Hot Elle died; and now, it sounds as if it might be the truth! But the problem is, I'm not even sure how to react in this situation because I never properly prepared myself for such a response! My palms are damp with sweat, and my mouth is dry again, but I think I need to hear more.

"Keep going," I prompt as Marco shifts his body to face mine more directly. Our knees are now touching as I shift a bit, and Marco squares up his shoulders with mine.

"I wanted to know you for myself—and for no other reason," he clarifies as I slip into a bit of a trance. "I wanted to know what it was like to hear your voice in my ear, to smell your hair, to touch the skin on the back of your arms...to taste your neck..." Marco trails off and holds me in his gaze.

I feel a huge lump growing in my throat and find that I am literally frozen in the moment. I don't know if he is going to kiss me—in which case I wish had popped in a breath mint before I sat down on the bench—or if he's just going to keep saying these amazing things. I decide to delay any physical contact and hear more.

"Keep going," I say again in a breathy tone, wanting to milk this moment for a bit longer.

Marco smiles at me and takes my hand in his. "I am a man who sees what he wants and then goes after it. And what I want right now is *you*, Eloise-ah!" he says with his face full of color and emotion.

This latest declaration sends my heart rate into a rapid flutter The world around me starts to slant and spin, and there's nothing I can do to stop it!

"You, are unlike Miriam in every way," he continues. "You are naturally beautiful, yet you seem as if you don't know it. I see that you are aware of the worth of your heart but unaware of your stunning beauty. I want to drink you in like a fine wine and share things with you from my heart. I want to spend hours with you in my city, showing you every part of my home *and* my heart. You make me want to be selfish, Eloise-ah. *So very selfish…*"

I'm speechless—yet again—and I don't know what to do or say in response. Nervously, I reach up and begin twisting my earring around in my ear—an old habit of mine that for some reason helps me think. I give Marco a bashful, self-conscious smile. I'm not sure I'm ready for him to kiss me—breath issues aside. No one has ever said things like this to me before, and a little voice inside my head is still questioning all this selfishness stuff.

Marco finally breaks the awkward silence by saying, "I know I have said too much." He pulls his hand away and stands up. His back is turned to me, and his hands are on his hips. I watch his back heave as he pulls in a deep breath.

A rush of panic sweeps over my body, and I feel desperate to fix the moment. "You didn't say too much, Marco," I nervously assure him. "You just said a lot…that's all…"

Marco slowly turns to face me. He takes a step toward me and reaches out his hands for mine. When I take his hands, he wraps his fingers around mine and guides me up so I'm standing right in front of him. Then he frees one of his hands from my grip and slides it under my hair, settling his cool fingers into the nape of my neck. I tilt my head up to meet his gaze. His eyes are clear and intense, and my knees go weak as I feel him pulling me in.

"*Eloise-ah,*" Marco says with a noticeably thicker accent. His breath is sweet and fruity, and his lips look soft and dewy. He lowers his head to mine and gently knocks up against my forehead. "*Oh, Eloise-ah…*"

Marco pulls up sharply, and I watch as he throws his head back and takes a deep breath. Then he tilts his head back down, tenderly kisses my forehead and says, "Let's keep going—I still have a lot to show you!"

Marco slides past me—brushing up against the side of my body and sending an explosion of tingles throughout my system—and grabs my wrap off of the bench. Then he takes my hand in his, and he locks his fingers around mine.

"Shall we go see my brother, Franco?" Marco asks me excitedly as we begin making our way back to the main sidewalk.

"Yes," I reply in a thick voice, as I'm still stunned from the exchange that just took place—stunned and maybe a bit woozy.

Chapter Fifteen

Under normal circumstances, the journey to our next destination would be painfully long. My strappy sandals weren't made for walking on these uneven sidewalks, but because I'm holding on to Marco Maselli's arm at the moment, I feel as though I may be floating. I drift past beautiful old buildings, tethered only to Marco's arm and the sound of his voice as he offers up interesting details about his city.

I'm blissfully fixated on Marco's every word until we make a sharp right onto a street called *Via de Tornabuoni*. Suddenly, my feet hit the ground, and I am fully present to the realities of my surroundings.

"This is the most famous shopping district in Florence," Marco explains as I slow our steps down to a snails pace. "This is where all of the most celebrated Italian fashion design houses have their Florence showrooms."

I am stunned by the eye candy popping out at me from every direction—or perhaps spellbound is a better word! Each window display is more amazing than the next, and I feel slightly dizzy! I can barely contain myself as Marco guides us past each window, only giving me a second or two to drool over the beautiful clothing before we move on.

"Up ahead is Prada," Marco casually remarks as my attention lingers on a pair of amazing leather sandals in one of the windows. They are made of some kind of treated leather that shines spectacularly under the lights. "My brother Franco is meeting us there," I hear him say as we make our way down a few small steps.

Most of the shops appear to be in the process of closing, which means we really can't go inside, so window shopping is going to have to do. Every so often, I close my eyes and embed visions of brightly colored clothing, handbags and shoes into my memory so that I can remember which shops I want to hit with Scott before we leave this amazing city!

Marco guides us down a narrow alleyway and stops when we reach a small glass door which he says is the side entrance to the *House of Prada*. When I crane my neck, I can just see the front display window. There are dozens of gorgeous handbags and matching shoes resting on metal pedestals with hot white spotlights beaming down on them. One bag in particular catches my eye. It looks to be a medium-sized, dark black shoulder bag with silver stitching along the sides. From where I'm standing, the bag looks very clean and elegant, and I briefly imagine myself walking down the street with it slung over my shoulder.

Marco lightly taps on the thin door, which rattles me from my daydream. As I come back around, a wash of excitement comes over me as I anxiously await my introduction to his brother, Franco.

I can see a young woman wearing a black halter-top standing behind the shop counter. When she looks up, she instantly recognizes Marco. A big smile spreads across her face as she moves from behind the counter and starts making her way toward the door. I can see now that she is wearing a stunning halter-dress that has a tight-fitting top, but a beautifully flowing bottom. It must be made out of chiffon or something because it is so airy and seems to hover lightly over this woman's body as she makes her way toward the door.

The woman has her long, wavy, dark brown hair pulled away from her face with a thick red and black scarf. She has big, brown eyes, a long, thin nose and enormous, pouty lips covered in deep red lipstick. Her makeup is perfectly applied—just a kiss of dark pink rouge highlights her cheek and brow bones, and her eyebrows are neatly and precisely tweezed.

"Marco!" the woman blurts out after she flings the door open. Marco lets go of my hand to embrace this woman. I watch as they kiss each other on each cheek. Her arms are long and thin, but very toned—like she works out or something. I notice Marco lightly rubbing his hands down the velvety brown skin along the backs of her arms as they break their embrace and begin talking—in Italian, of course. My first reaction is to feel jealous, but then I remember Francesca.

I hope this is another cousin, I think as I watch the two of them carry on—again, as if I'm not even here. But there seems to be more than familial affection in this woman's eyes as she nods her head and smiles at Marco as he blathers on in his native tongue. They seem to be doing a good deal of catching up as I stand off to the side, wondering how much longer I will have to wait for Marco to introduce me.

I can't seem to control my suspicion about Marco as I watch him and this new mystery woman. While it's true that every time I've doubted Marco this evening, he's proven me wrong, I still can't dismiss my feelings. And if I'm completely honest with myself, even though Marco managed to sweep me off of my feet with his whole *selfish* speech, I am not all together sure about this guy and the integrity of his words.

Finally, Marco breaks into English and says, "Christina, this is my *Eloise-ah.*"

Here we go again—I'm back to *his Eloise-ah,* and I am completely embarrassed for my doubts. I take a step forward and reach out my hand to greet Christina. She has a pleasant but slightly wary look on her face as she takes my hand in hers.

"*Buonasera,*" Christina mumbles while avoiding any direct eye contact with me.

"Christina is a long-time friend of mine," Marco interjects as the two of them exchange an uncomfortably knowing look. "She now works for my brother," he concludes as he turns his smiling face toward me.

"It is very nice to meet you, Christina," I offer in an effort to better transition myself into the conversation. Christina simply smiles at me and takes a step back into the shop to make way for Marco and me to fully enter.

"I will go and get Franco," Christina says directly to Marco, as if I'm not even in the room. She turns on her heel, glides through the room and vanishes behind a set of mirrored doors.

"Christina and I are...*friends*...and sometimes she can be a little... protective of me," Marco offers, clearly aware of the female tensions building in the room.

"I see..." I trail off, not sure how to reply. For me, the way Marco approaches his *friendships* certainly adds a dubious quality to his character.

Marco wraps his arms around me and turns me so that we are face to face. His arms hold me around the waist with a firm embrace. He looks deep into my eyes and smiles. My heart is starting to pump a little harder, and I can feel the electricity sizzling through my limbs as Marco holds me up against his long warm torso. I do my best to breath in and out. I notice that the room smells like leather and furniture polish.

"Are you having fun in my city?" he asks me with a sparkle in his eye as he continues holding me in this odd, yet exhilarating, embrace.

"I am, Marco...I really am!" I say nervously, not sure what to do here. Should I wrap my arms around his neck and shoulder area and give him a friendly hug, or should I keep my arms gathered where they are on my chest? I feel so self-aware, and so ill at ease, as Marco holds me in his arms. Is this going to be how we have our first kiss? I sure hope not—I'm still a little unsorted inside about everything, and the longer Marco holds me like this, the more confused I feel.

A thump followed by footsteps causes Marco to casually release me from his embrace. I spin around just in time to see a tall, handsome man walking through the double-mirrored doors. His face looks just like Marco's—except perhaps a few years older. But he has the same caramel-colored eyes as his brother and the same thick, wavy hair. He is wearing black trousers and a cream-colored dress shirt, which is buttoned half way up his chest. His skin is taut and creamy as it stretches over his sharp collarbones. His face is beaming as he glides toward me with his arms outstretched as he sizes me up.

"Franco," Marco says. "This is Eloise-ah."

"Ah, yes...so *beautiful*," Franco dramatically intones as his eyes travel up and down my body. I am completely uncomfortable with all of this attention, to say the least, and it doesn't help much to see Christina glaring at me from over Franco's shoulder.

"Hello," I manage to say in a raspy voice as I continue watching Franco inspect my body. He seems to be paying incredibly close attention to my legs, and I'm tempted to try my little modeling move again, but decide against it at the last minute.

"Eloise-ah, Franco designed your dress!" Marco says brightly.

Suddenly, I understand all the added attention and feel a rush of cool relief extinguishing my nerves. I instantly make the shift from feeling like Franco is a pervert to brilliant fashion designer, and now I sense the need to properly thank him for his magical creation!

"Oh Franco!" I gush. "This is the most gorgeous dress I've ever worn!" I take a few steps forward and fall into Franco's open arms. We kiss each other on the cheeks, and Franco beams with pride over my reaction.

"My brother told me you were beautiful, Eloise-ah," Franco begins with a very heavy accent after we finish our greeting. "I think this dress is the perfect match," he adds after he takes a step back to get another look at me. I stand stone still when he reaches up under the overlay and gives the hem of the silky slip dress a little tug. "It is perfection…" Franco trails off as he continues studying the dress.

Then Franco and Marco embrace with a formal hello and begin talking in Italian. As they talk, I notice Christina has returned to the shop counter and appears to be tallying up receipts. She seems a little put out by all of the attention being bestowed upon me, and for some strange reason, I immediately feel ashamed.

"Eloise-ah," Franco says to me as he wraps his arm around my waist. "Come with me, and let me show you my collection."

"Oh, my gosh! Are you sure?" I blurt out.

"I'm always sure of myself!" Franco replies with a light laugh as he guides me through the Prada showroom.

I look over at Marco who is beaming back at me. He nods his head as if to assure me that it's safe to go with his brother. I smile back at him and then turn my attention to the mirrored doors. I can see Christina's reflection in the mirrors. She's watching Franco and me from behind the counter with a smug look on her face. I do my best to shake it off, but there's just something about this woman that has me worried.

Despite my concerns, anticipation swarms my heart as we slip through the mirrored doors and walk past racks of clothing and cubbies filled from floor to ceiling with shoes, handbags and scarves. Franco takes me down a narrow brick-lined hallway that smells like must. I'm too giddy inside to really hear everything Franco is saying to me, but tiny details like the fact that he is just renting some space from Prada for now and how he is working on his own collection day and night do manage to slip into my consciousness.

At the end of the hallway, there is a thick wooden door with a round door handle directly in the center. Franco stops just in front of the door and turns to face me. He is very handsome, and I almost feel nervous about the way he is looking at me. I take a deep breath and try to keep my composure as Franco starts to speak directly to me.

"I don't usually allow people to see my work before it is finished, but Marco asked me for this favor..." he explains to me as he holds his hand to his chest in an almost feminine manner. "I am a *stilista*, Eloise-ah, and this is what I do," he continues. "I make the clothes for many other designers to put their labels on, but what I show to you now is my very own collection."

Franco wraps his fingers around the door handle and twists it. Then he gives the door a solid shove with his hip, and the large wooden panel slowly grinds open. I think I can actually hear my heart beating inside my head as Franco motions for me to enter the chamber on the other side of the door. I've never been inside the world of fashion before, and the fact that I am seeing Franco's private and unfinished collection is an overwhelming honor!

The room is flooded with sterile, white light blasting from several large spotlights hanging from the ceiling. I almost feel the need to shelter my eyes, but instead, I do my best to just squint against the blinding glare as I follow Marco into the belly of the room. For the most part, the room is kind of empty, except for a series of spindly metal clothing racks that line the outer edge of the space sort of forming a boxy half ring around the room. Each rack holds lifeless creations in various states of completion. Bolts of incredible fabrics—some colorful and light, some dark and smoldering— are propped up in a corner like a group of well-dressed women, begging to be noticed.

There is a large wooden table with an industrial-sized sewing machine perched on top and a ratty, little metal stool tucked up underneath the table. A large pegboard with dozens of brightly colored spools of thread hovers above the sewing machine on the wall. The loose ends of the thread lightly flitter in the breeze from an oscillating fan clipped to the edge of the table. Against the far wall is a long cutting table and an ironing board. Bits of fabric litter the floor below.

"So this is my *atelier*..." Franco trails off with a puzzled look on his face. "How do you say in America? *Studio*! This is my studio!" Franco says as he opens his arms and does a quick spin to better showcase the room. "This is where I do all my work—on this machine and with these two hands," he says as he holds his hands up like he's doing "jazz hands" for me.

I can't help but smile at Franco as he stands there in the middle of his tidy workshop with his hands all splayed out for my amusement. He is so sweet and so proud of his studio, and I feel very special to be standing in the room where my own beautiful dress was probably made. I take a step toward one of the clothing racks that has several brightly colored creations draped over wooden hangers. I give Franco a questioning look to get his permission to touch the garments, and he obliges my request with a smile.

"This is my first solo collection," Franco explains as he walks over and stands directly in front of the rack and carefully slides a deep green-colored garment off of a hanger. "This is a simple halter dress made of chiffon with Italian silk trims," he offers as I study the beautiful dress he is holding out for my inspection.

The dress is stunning in its simplicity. The flowing fabric looks as though it will grip a woman's body in exactly the right places, but is set free to ride the curves of her hips and dance over her legs as she walks. The silk fabric trim is an acid green color that lights the edges of the dress on fire and makes it look like pure energy is coursing through the garment. As I study the way the halter and the bodice of the dress are connected, I'm instantly reminded of the lovely Christina. If I'm not mistaken, she is somewhere on the other side of the massive wooden door wearing a very similar dress in black. A tingle of jealousy zips across my heart as I realize that she and Marco are in the Prada showroom...alone.

"This is really beautiful, Franco," I say sincerely as I do my best to shove my previous thoughts out of my mind.

"This dress is one of my favorites," he says as he slips another garment off of a hanger. The dress is a deep rose color and appears to be made from some sort of brushed cotton. It is a very basic shape—sort of like a little a-line skirt with a simple tube-top, strapless bodice. Franco hands me the dress as he starts raking through another rack in search of something. As I hold the dress, I can see that it is anything but basic. The fabric is perfectly sewn together, and inside, it's lined with a lemon colored silk. I instantly recognize the little tag neatly sewn into the liner: *FM—Florence, Italy* .

"Here it is!" Franco says with great pleasure as he makes his way back toward me. He carefully takes the rosy dress from my hands and slips it onto a nearby dress form that is attached to a rusty metal pedestal. As he gently tugs the dress into position on the tall, slender form, I notice that he has something draped over his arm—something so delicate that I can't be sure what it is. I watch as he zips the dress up on the side and then takes this fabric hanging over his forearm and unfurls it.

I take a step closer so that I can get a better look at this marvelous creation. I watch as Franco expertly drapes and folds the stunning pale pink gossamer fabric over the rose-colored dress. As I lean in even closer, I notice bright yellow details woven into the gossamer. I carefully reach out and take the fabric between my fingers—I can see now that it is the same type of embroidery that is on my own dress. Delicate knots and loops are hand-stitched in a recurring pattern that runs in concentric circles all over the fabric overlay.

Franco stops working when he notices that I am studying the fabric. He looks at me with pride and says, "I am known for my handwork."

"Yes…I can see that!" I say with a huge smile; a smile I hope will impress upon him how amazed I am by his work.

I step back and allow Franco to finish styling his masterpiece. When he is finished, I realize that I am looking at the work of a genius. Beautifully hugging the feminine shape of the dress form is a rosy, strapless dress covered in a frosty layer of pink with buds of spun gold. It's absolutely amazing.

"Franco, it's gorgeous," I say, looking at him with complete admiration. "How did you learn to do that handwork?"

"My Uncle Giuseppe wanted me to apprentice in his gold shop when I was a young boy," Franco says as he slides a wristband pincushion onto his arm and pulls up his battered stool. He begins pinning the gossamer fabric to the dress as he continues talking. "But I really didn't like working with the gold so much. I was very good at it, but it just wasn't what I wanted to do. But my...*Aunt?*" Franco looks up at me to confirm that I understand the word. I nod that I understand and he continues, "My Aunt Viola was a seamstress, and I liked to help her sometimes..." Franco sort of trails off like he is a little embarrassed by how he discovered his gift.

"Did she teach you how to do this amazing embroidery work?" I ask in an effort to help him skip the sensitive part of the story.

"She did," Franco looks up at me with a gentle smile. "She used it on wedding dresses and tea towels, and I just wanted to learn how to do it. Of course, spending time with *Zia Viola* was not what my brothers were doing, but I couldn't help it. I loved working with the threads and making beautiful things. Later on, when everyone started to see that I was serious and that my work was very good, they started to be proud of me."

I watch as Franco threads a needle, ties a little knot at the end, and beings attaching the gossamer fabric to the bodice of the dress with tiny, perfectly spaced stitches. I notice the muscles in his forearms flex as he expertly drives the needle through the layers of fabric, carefully gathering the gossamer with his long fingers as he works his way around the waistline of the dress. He seems so peaceful as he leans into his work. He is a true artist, and I feel such admiration for him as I silently study his skill from over his shoulder.

Franco finally breaks the silence with a simple question. "Do you like your dress, Eloise-ah?"

"Franco," I begin, wanting to choose my words carefully to show my great appreciation for his talent. "I don't think I have ever worn anything this beautiful in my entire life."

Franco looks up from his work and finds my face. He is smiling in a way that lets me know that he is very thankful for the compliment. "My brother was correct about you, Eloise-ah," he says as he turns his attention back to his work. "He told me that you are not only stunning, but that you have a very good heart."

"Thank you," I say in a whispered voice.

To tell you the truth, the comment about my good heart—while flattering—sort of bugs me. I just can't seem to follow this Marco Maselli. One minute, I make him want to be selfish, then the next, I'm inspiring him with my heart? And how could Marco actually know anything about my heart? I haven't shared any of my deepest thoughts or aspirations with him. I haven't even really told him a single thing about myself!

"Marco is quite happy to know you," Franco continues on the subject of Marco and me after he stops to adjust the thread on his needle. "You are the first...*amante*...?" he trails off and looks at me with a furrowed brow like he is looking for me to help in translating the word.

"I'm not sure what that word means..." I say with a nervous and curious grin on my face.

"It means...*lover*," Franco says with a seductive smile. "You are the first *lover* Marco has asked me to dress in my label," he says with raised eyebrows.

"Oh gosh!" I blurt out. I don't really have a chance to sensor myself before my reaction spills out of my mouth. "Franco, I'm hardly Marco's *lover*, I mean I just met him the other day...and this is our first date and everything..."

"It's OK," Franco says with a knowing smile. "You will be in time..." he trails off as he returns to his sewing.

I silently watch Franco as he glides his needle in and out of the folds of fabric. I'm doing my best to sort out the exchange that just took place. It's all coming at me so quickly that I am having trouble staying focused. Suddenly, I feel the need to know more about Christina—who I gather is a former *amante* of Marco's that Franco dresses in his label for his own reasons.

"Franco?" I ask in a soft voice.

"*Sì?*" Franco says as he looks up briefly from his work.

"Who is Christina?"

"Christina?" Franco asks with a strange look on his face. "Well, she works for me from time to time. She is a fit model I use, but she is also a friend of mine from a long time ago. She was a very close friend to my sister, Gia, actually..." Franco trails off at the mention of his late sister's name, and I can feel a heaviness seeping into the room.

"I see..." I mumble, not knowing what else to say. Despite how awkward I feel about conjuring up a sad memory for Franco, I can't help but feel a flash of hope in his answer for me. If Christina were a former flame of Marco's, surely he would have mentioned that, right? But instead, he only mentioned his sister's connection to Gia. This little clue leads me to wonder if what I saw between Marco and Christina had more to do with a connection to Gia than to each other. Oddly enough, this little development gives me surprising comfort!

Franco scoots his rusty stool around to get a better angle as he attaches the gossamer overlay to the lower portion of the dress. He is so steady and so precise—his stitches seem more perfect than a sewing machine. His intensity as he works is almost palpable, and it feels like the room is starting to close in on me and suck me into Franco's world.

I sense the need to add some conversation to make me feel less like a voyeur so I ask, "Franco, did you say that you used to design for other labels?"

"Correct," Franco says as he briefly looks up at me. "It is kind of a crazy story really," he begins as he shifts slightly on his stool and continues sewing on the same section of the dress. "For many years, my *Zia Viola* made almost all the wedding dresses for the women of Florence. In the summers, when the weddings were happening so much more, she would have me to help her. So I learned how to do all the tiny details and beautiful beadwork from her, and, over time, I started to add my own touches."

I watch Franco tie off the thread on his needle and reach for his spool. He measures off another line of spun gold thread by wrapping it a few times around his fingers and then cutting the thread with a pair of tiny silver scissors. He slips one end of the thread through the tiny hole in his needle and ties a tiny knot. Then he continues telling me his story.

"When *Zia Viola* retired, she left me her business. I was very good at making the gowns by then, but I was getting tired of making only what the clients wanted. I wanted to show them more of what I could do. So on my own time, I would make beautiful gowns—some for a bride and some not. But the women, they didn't want my dresses. They wanted me just to make what they wanted me to make. I was getting very... *frustrated* with this..."

Franco turns the dress form and the dress spins around with a squeaky grind. After pulling gently on the fabric a few times and spreading it out with his hands, he begins sewing again.

"My brother Andre is a banker, and he knew that I wanted to do more of my own work, so he set up a meeting with a well-known Italian designer to see if he would like to buy my dresses. After we met, the designer agreed to take some of my work and put his own label on it. As soon as he put the name *Giorgio Armani* on my dresses, they sold right away!"

Franco looks up at me with an ironic look on his face. "After that, Armani gave me a contract to design for him. Then other contracts followed. I was doing work for many labels, and, suddenly, I was too busy to even think!" His face is so animated as he says this that I can't help but smile back at him in return.

"So what did you do?" I ask, wanting to know how he got from being an Armani designer to his own label.

"Well, Andre wanted to make sure that I didn't ruin *Zia Viola's* good name, so I had to continue doing the wedding dresses and create new things for the label," he explains, with his attention now back on his work. "It was getting to be too much, so I hired one of my cousins to help me with the wedding dresses. I taught her everything, and she became very good. So in January, I sold her the business and went out on my own. Andre gave me the money to do my first collection, and this is what I have so far," Franco says as he looks up from his work and nods his head in the direction of the various racks in the room.

"That's a great story!" I say with enthusiasm. "I'm so very impressed, Franco, and incredibly honored to have one of your designs to call my own."

Franco looks up at me, and then smiles. "The dress you are wearing was a part of the collection I put together for Andre's investors. It was Marco's favorite, and he wanted you to have it. And now that I know you, I am happy for you to have it, too…"

I'm very touched. I don't know what to say in response, so I just smile appreciatively at Franco and hope he knows how much everything means to me.

"Well, Eloise-ah," Franco says as he turns the dress form back to center. "What do you think?" he says as he steps aside so I can get a clear view of his gorgeous creation.

I stand in awe as I take in this delicate creation. The gossamer fabric lightly hovers over the pink dress below with an ethereal glow. It's simply stunning. "I think it's magnificent," I say to Franco as I try to imagine how it will look when the model sashays down the runway.

"*Magnificent…*" Franco repeats as a smile slowly washes across his face. "I am so happy you like it," he says humbly as he slips the pincushion wristband off of his arm and gazes at his creation.

"I think Marco is going to wonder what happened to us," he confides when he looks back over at me. "Do you think we should go now?" he asks me with a pleasant look on his face.

"We probably should," I agree as I realize how much time has passed. "Thank you, Franco, for sharing this with me," I say as Franco steps in front of me. It is my hope that he can really understand how special this evening was for me.

"It is my pleasure," he responds as he moves toward the door. He gives the door a hard pull, and it slowly yawns open. He motions for me to step through. As I step out into the dark, musty hallway, I can feel a light pressure in the small of my back as Franco guides me along the way.

When we reach the double doors, Franco reaches around me and gives the doors a stiff shove. A blast of cool air greets us and sends a quick chill over my skin. The showroom is pretty dark with the only light coming from the spot lamps lit up in the front display window. I look around for Marco and Christina, but they don't seem to be here.

As my eyes dart around in search of Marco, I finally see him sitting on a leather sofa that is wedged into a small alcove in the far corner of the room. Christina is sitting across Marco's lap with her bare feet elegantly hanging over the side of the sofa. Her head is resting on Marco's shoulder, and her lips look like they are almost pressed up against his neck. Marco has one arm wrapped around Christina, and his other arm is resting gently across her lap.

Chapter Sixteen

I can't be sure, but I feel pretty certain that my face has just gone completely white. All the blood inside of my body seems to have pooled into my lower extremities, and I feel positively sick as my brain confirms that what my eyes are seeing is true. The fabulously gorgeous Christina is peacefully sleeping in Marco's lap, and Marco has allowed this to happen while he is on a date *with me!*

Neither one of them moves as Franco and I make our way toward the sofa. Franco stiffly clears his throat, and Marco's eyes pop open. He looks up at me with a dreamy smile. Christina doesn't move—she just stays snuggled up against Marco.

"Did you get to see Franco's work?" Marco asks brightly, without a trace of embarrassment or shame for being caught in this compromising position.

"Yep..." I say in response, a sudden heat building inside of me like molten lava oozing from a crack in my heart.

I notice that Christina is starting to stir. She stretches her long neck slightly and then rolls open her big eyes. She looks directly at me and then at Franco, but she doesn't move from her position.

"I'm sorry I took so long," Franco apologizes. "You know how I get when I'm working!" he says with a hint of nervous laughter in his tone.

"You get like a *madman!*" Christina says with a playful authority as she gives Franco a weary, affectionate smile. Franco takes a step in toward her, and she reaches out her hand. I watch as he gives her a gentle pull up and off of Marco.

"Well, it's his passion," Marco adds as he starts to stand up. "It's what he is meant to do!" Once Marco is standing, he smoothes out the wrinkles in his trousers and takes a step in closer to me. "Isn't my brother a genius?" he continues as he wraps his arms around me and gives me a peck on the cheek.

I stiffen slightly in his embrace, but he doesn't seem to notice. I'm so confused by all of this that I don't know what to do. I just stand there, locked in the moment with my limbs heavy and paralyzed. Why is everyone acting like this is OK? Am I officially going crazy? Marco steps away from my side and walks over toward Franco. The two of them begin chatting in Italian again as I watch Christina moving toward the side of the sofa.

She reaches down to pick up one of her spiked heel sling backs. Gracefully, she stretches one of her long legs out and slips the shoe onto her foot. Then she seductively looks over her shoulder, directly at me, and flips her hair out of her way while pulling her long leg in like a flamingo. I watch as she slides her finger along the inside of the sling back and finishes slipping the shoe onto her foot. The whole process is ultra-disturbing for me as I realize how out of my league I am when it comes to Christina. She manages to elegantly slip on her other shoe and then turns to face me.

Christina begins walking toward me. Her face reminds me of a regal lioness who has just gotten her way—very confident, very satisfied, and very territorial. "*Buona notte, Eloise-ah,*" she hisses at me as she saunters by.

I'm not sure what that means, but the heat from her voice lands lightly on my neck, and I feel dizzy with confusion.

"Are you OK, Eloise-ah?" Marco asks as he notices that I haven't moved from my original position.

At first, I can't speak. There is no sound in my throat, no words on my lips. I am beyond dumb-founded. I'm outside of myself, and I can't seem to find my way back in.

"Eloise-ah?" Marco asks again.

"I want to go home," I finally say in a soft, faraway voice. I can feel the prick of hot tears against the backs of my eyes, and I want to get out of here before I crack.

"But I still have so much planned," Marco protests with disappointment. "I have so many more things to show you this evening, *Eloise-ah...*" he trails off, once he realizes that I am not responding.

There is an awkward silence in the room as Franco and Christina watch Marco and me from behind the shop counter. Christina is leaning on Franco with her arm perched along the length of his shoulder. Her eyes are deep and dark and show no apologies, no regrets. She has a smug look on her face as she watches me struggle to move.

Finally, Marco steps toward me, wraps me up in his arm and starts guiding me toward the door. I can't bear to look directly at Christina—I'm too confused, too embarrassed.

"Eloise-ah..." Franco hesitates but then adds, "You are so very lovely..."

"Thank you Franco," I whisper, still doing my best not to cry. "It was truly an honor to see your work."

As we reach the door, Marco leans in and asks, "Are you sure you don't want to see more of Florence with me, my sweet *Eloise-ah*?"

"I'm sorry..." I trail off as I look into Marco's eyes. "I think I've seen enough."

Once we're outside, I tug my evening wrap around me like it's a cocoon. I feel the need to protect myself a bit, and my wrap is the only thing I have to create a little barrier between Marco and me at the moment. As we start walking, Marco gently places his arm along the small of my back and wraps his fingers around my waist. I feel myself give in a little to his touch. I want so badly to understand what he's doing with me.

The evil leather straps of my sandals are slicing into the flesh of my feet like barbed wire, and all I can think about is how much I want to go home. My mind is swirling with thoughts, but I don't even know how to sort them all out.

Marco finally breaks the silence with a question: "*Eloise-ah?* Have I done something to upset you?" His voice sounds confused and concerned, and completely oblivious.

I don't know how to answer him exactly. I keep rewinding the scene with Christina in my mind to see if I missed something. But each time, I can't seem to find any comfort in what I saw. There is really no explanation that would make sense or excuse the situation for me. I am hurt and embarrassed, and, most of all, stunned that Marco could cozy up to another woman while he is on a date with me. But after what feels like a very long pause, I finally answer Marco's question.

"I am just very confused by the way you handle your friendships, Marco," I say in a throaty voice.

As I say this, we stop walking, and Marco carefully turns my body so I am facing him. We are standing in front of a shop window filled with gorgeous clothing draped over white porcelain mannequins. Under normal circumstances, the fetching items in the window would be center stage in my mind, but, right now, I'm grasping for words to try to make Marco understand.

"You told me earlier tonight that I make you want to be selfish," I tentatively begin. "And what I thought that meant was that you wanted to have me all to yourself—that you didn't want to share me or have to be with me for any other reason than because you wanted to be with me…"

"Yes!" Marco says, his voice full of passion. "That is what I meant!" He takes his hands and grabs me by the shoulders. His face is all lit up, and I feel like he is about to pull me in for an embrace. But as my body goes rigid in Marco's hands, he softens and cocks his head with confusion.

"But Marco…for me, that means that I shouldn't have to share *you* either…" I say as I look up into his golden brown eyes.

"Ahhh…" Marco says as if the penny finally dropped. "You are worried about Christina, correct?" He pulls his hands down to his sides and then casually slides them into his trouser pockets.

"Christina, Miriam—any of the women you call your *friend* actually," I say, sort of embarrassed for being so insecure, but I just can't help myself.

Marco takes a moment to think about what I've said. His head hangs down as he studies the pavement. I can see the muscles in his jaw squeezing as he grinds his teeth in search of his next reply. Finally, after an unbearably long pause, he responds.

"I think that maybe we don't really understand each other, Eloise-ah, and maybe you are right to want to go home. Maybe it is not going to work between us like I thought it would..." Marco trails off with a bit of frustration in his voice.

"Maybe not," I add as I turn away from Marco and begin walking again. A frosty buzz builds up in my body as I realize that Marco and I just ended our potential relationship before it really even began.

I feel a flood of emotion building up inside of me now, and I really can't be sure that I won't cry this time. I do my best to be strong, but a small tear gets away from me, and I can feel it slide down my cheek, carving a hot, salty trail down my face.

Marco and I walk a few blocks in total silence until we reach his car. Francesca must have moved it because I don't recognize this part of town at all.

Marco opens the car door for me, and I duck inside. When he shuts the heavy door with a thud, I feel the same sort of thick closure in my heart. I reach up and lightly touch my fingers to the tiny gold bead hanging around my neck. Marco said the necklace was a symbol of luck and love in my life, but somehow, I feel certain I've managed to kill any chance of love there was between us in the span of just a few hours.

Maybe I shouldn't have said anything at all. I mean no one else was acting like it was odd that Marco and Christina were snuggled up on the sofa. And Franco said that Christina was a *friend* of Marco's from the past— not a *lover*. But I can't shake the look in Christina's eyes. There was a lot more than friendship in her stare, and the way she was looking at me made it very clear that she believes she has some sort of entitlement to Marco.

As Marco slides into the driver's seat, I catch a whiff of his cologne. My eyes start to well up with fresh tears as I realize how much I like this guy. The evening started out so perfectly, and I am still dizzy over how much Marco did for me. Even with this sour ending, it is still the most romantic night of my entire life. I take a deep breath in and will myself not to cry. I have so little dignity left right now, and I think if Marco actually sees me cry, things will only get worse.

Marco turns the key in the ignition, gives the engine a rev, and then he pulls away from the curb. In a matter of seconds, we are racing down the street, heading back to where we started. I look at Marco out of the corner of my eye, and I can see that his jaw is set and his facial muscles are taut. I fear that I have really messed things up, and I don't know what to do or say to fix it. I can't help the way things make me feel—I just can't! I'm not able to play the games that other women do, and that's probably why I'm still single at 33.

Marco pulls his car into the circular driveway of *Il Girasole* and then kills the engine. We both sit silently in the car for a moment. I don't know what to say, and I am hoping that Marco will know how to break the silence. When Marco says nothing, I decide to make the first move, and I slowly reach for the door handle.

"No, Eloise-ah…not yet," Marco says as he begins to shift in his seat. "I don't want this evening to end this way."

"Me neither, Marco," I say in a thick voice that is holding back a flood of tears and embarrassment.

"I am sorry that my friendships are so confusing for you, but they are a part of who I am," Marco says as he looks down at his hands. "I love people and people, love me, and I am just maybe more…affectionate than you are used to…" Marco trails off. Then he looks up at me and says, "Maybe…"

"Maybe what?" I practically beg, hoping there is some way to fix things.

"Maybe you are not ready to fall in love with an Italian," Marco says as he looks up into my eyes. His face seems pained as he looks at me with longing.

I stare back at him, unashamed to stay in his gaze. I feel drawn to him in a way that I can't explain. I want to kiss his lips and feel what I felt earlier in the evening. I don't want to cut this relationship out all together—I want to venture deeper so I can understand Marco and his heart more completely. Marco begins to lean in toward me, and I watch as his hand reaches out to cradle my face. I start to drift toward him, unsure how to stop myself from floating into his arms.

Then, just as I'm about to give in, Marco's cell phone—which is resting between us in the center console—begins to chirp. I look down and see the name *Christina* flashing in the little caller ID window. Marco quickly grabs the phone to silence it, but the damage is already done. Just seeing her name jolts me back to reality.

I feel Marco's body tighten as he slips the phone onto the floorboard of his car. He looks at me with a sorrowful expression. I shift back into my seat and stare out at a small fountain in the center of the driveway. I take a deep breath and search myself for my last remaining bit of composure.

"Marco," I finally say without even turning my head to look at him. "Thank you for the most magical night of my life." And with that, I slide my hand under the door latch and quickly push the door open. I do my best to climb out of the car with as much grace as I can possibly muster. I can hear Marco saying something to me, but I manage to shut the heavy door before he can engage me.

I make a mad dash for the gates and hastily slip through the opening. Once I'm safely on the other side of the gate, the tears come rushing down my cheeks. I heave to catch my breath, but the flood of emotions is too strong. I lean up against the inner wall of the gate, bury my face in my wrap and sob. Just outside the gate, I can hear the sound of Marco's car as he lights up the engine and pulls away.

When I wake up the next morning, my bed feels strange and foreign. It's so lonely without Sugar Ray. I miss having his big warm body cuddling into me. As I roll over and untangle my feet from the sheets, I notice my beautiful dress neatly draped over the back of the chair in the corner of the room. A sudden ache creeps into my heart, and I realize that this dull feeling weighing me down is not just because I miss my dog.

Everything that happened last night with Marco has left me feeling bewildered. I do my best to rewind Marco's exact explanation about his involvement with Miriam, but no matter how I remember the details, I still can't help but feel awful. His words do very little to help me overcome my concerns about how he approaches his relationships with women. And his *actions* don't help me at all! There truly is no way to ignore or minimize seeing Marco holding Christina on that sofa—you simply don't hold someone like that unless you have feelings for the person, that's for sure!

The thing that really gets to me is that Marco keeps expecting *me* to understand the benign nature of his friendships with women when it's pretty obvious that most of the women involved don't completely understand it either. I'm quite positive that Miriam doesn't see Marco as some simple friend—she definitely sees him as someone with whom she is romantically involved. And, judging by the way Christina was looking at me and responding to Marco, I think she is under the distinct impression that she is more than just Marco's *friend*, too.

And what about me? I'm supposedly the woman who makes Marco feel *selfish* and the woman he refers to as "*his Eloise*" when introduced! How can the same man who says those things one minute embrace another woman the next? It just doesn't add up!

And another thing: Why am I so crushed over this man? Is it because he showered me with gifts? Did Marco buy my feelings with all of his fancy presents? I contemplate these thoughts as I reach up to touch the necklace still chained around my neck. It seems like Marco gave it to me in another lifetime. I close my eyes and try to recall the positioning of the room where we ate our special dinner. I allow myself to remember the way Marco looked at me from across the table. In those moments, I felt like I was the only woman in the entire world! The way he held my hands from across the table, the way he shared details about his life—all of that was real, wasn't it?

I think it is safe to say that my affection for Marco wasn't bought with his gifts because I would give them all back right now—the dress, the necklace, and the fancy note cards—to have Marco all to myself. To have a fresh start with Marco, where we could get to know each other without all of these complications, would be worth everything to me. I've already started to fall hard for this man, and I was really starting to enjoy the trip into the great abyss of love. For some reason, he cast a spell over me, and, for a short time, I was free and uninhibited and truly ready to fall in love—even with an *Italian* man.

As I pad my way into the bathroom, I catch a glimpse of myself in the mirror. My eyes are a little puffy from crying, and my face is crisscrossed with salty tear trails. I splash some water on my face and then re-examine myself. What I see is a foolish girl staring back at me. I actually believed Marco was this amazing man even though there were so many signs to show me that he is a fraud. I guess I just overlooked all the warnings and hoped for the best because I wanted it to be my time for romance. I wanted the fairy tale for myself, and I was silly to believe that I could have it.

I take a deep breath and try to find a trace of my real self in the mirror. I know that I'm still in there somewhere—I just got a little off track, that's all. The fact that Scott had a bad feeling about Marco should have told me something. He's always been out for my best interest, and to his credit, he tried several times to point out that Marco was no good, but I didn't want to listen.

As I think about Scott, I feel ashamed for pushing him away lately. I hope there is something I can do to make it up to him. I suppose I could start by telling him everything that's been going on with me since we arrived in Florence—I'm sure he must be curious, especially since I've been so secretive. And I assume he'll understand why I fell for Marco when I tell him all about how he pursued me, and despite any concerns, I just know he'll know how to fix things for me. He's never been the kind of friend that says, *I told you so*—even though he would be totally justified in this instance. Rather, he is the type of person that helps his friends pull things back together and move on.

On the other hand, I've never actually shared anything quite like this with Scott before. We don't usually discuss dating—probably because I never have anyone to date let alone discuss! And as far as Scott sharing with me, I can't recall him mentioning any one person in particular. I guess I've never pushed him on the subject of dating out of a deep respect for his privacy. I mean, the question of his sexual orientation *is* a bit of a mystery, which, after all of these years of friendship, he still hasn't revealed. Sometimes I wish I knew for certain if he was gay or straight, but in the end, it never really mattered all that much to me. He's Scott. Wonderful Scott LaMotte whom I adore with all of my heart.

The thought of telling Scott everything gives me a certain sense of relief. Having someone to share my feelings with will help me sort out some of my emotions and help me see things more clearly. Right now, all I feel is confused and alone. And I think one of the very reasons I never told Scott anything about Marco was because I knew in my heart that what I was experiencing wasn't real. I think I knew deep down that no one could have a love-at-first-sight reaction to me. That's the kind of thing movies are made of, not real life. And Scott is a realist. He wouldn't have indulged me in my crazy thinking—not even for a minute.

After I take a long hot shower, I make my bed and tidy up my room. I take my beautiful dress and hang it up with the rest of my clothes and then carefully shut the closet doors. I dig around in my drawers until I find a pair of white chino walking shorts and a cottony navy blue halter-top. Once I'm dressed, I return to the bathroom and start combing out the snarls in my hair. Just as I'm almost finished, I hear a light knock on my front door. A sizzle of nerves flitters through my stomach at the thought of who it might be. I feel frozen stiff with the anticipation when I hear the knock for the second time, this time followed by a familiar voice.

"Elle? It's just me…"

When I realize it's Scott, I practically run for the door and fling it open. I am so happy to see him! He is standing on the front porch with two cups of something hot and steamy and a little white bag tucked under his arm. He's wearing baggy blue jeans, a long-sleeved, purple linen shirt and some brown flip-flops. His hair is disheveled on top in that perfect bed-head style, and he is wearing his big sunglasses and a huge smile. He looks so handsome and wonderful, and I feel a rush of happiness just seeing him standing there.

"Hey you!" Scott says as he takes a step closer to the door. "I thought you might be hungry."

"Oh, Scott!" I gush. "I'm so happy to see you!"

Scott just smiles brightly as he makes his way into my villa. I follow him to the kitchen and start pulling out plates and napkins. Scott wiggles off the lids of what looks like cappuccinos and places one in front of me. Then he carefully digs into the white bakery bag and pulls out two of those delicious chocolate pastries we ate on our first morning in Florence. My mouth immediately starts to water in anticipation of the buttery pastry.

As I watch Scott arranging my pastry on my plate, I feel an easy, comfortable mood wash over me, and I realize how much I've missed Scott. I have been so preoccupied with thoughts of Marco and working so hard to try to unravel what I think and feel that I've managed to shut off the most important and valuable friend in my life. Scott scoots one of the bar stools over to the end of the counter and slides his bottom onto the edge of the seat. He looks up at me and gives me a huge smile.

"Let's eat!" Scott says with vibrato as he holds his hands out to present me with our little feast.

"It looks perfect!" I say as I give Scott a sweet, meaningful smile.

We each take a sip of our cappuccino and start picking at the flakey crust of our pastries. It feels good to be with Scott again. He is like a favorite pair of shoes—as soon as you slide them back on your feet, you swear you will never wear another pair again!

"So how was the wine tasting with Sebastian and Peter?" I ask, casually trying to ease us into a conversation.

"It was actually pretty fun," Scott says as he licks some chocolate off of his thumb. "Sebastian was extra tame last night, and Peter had to limit his wine intake because of his early morning show time, so things were much more mild than usual."

"Well, that's nice," I say in a lame attempt to be a good listener before I steer the conversation to be all about me.

"How about your evening?" Scott eventually asks. "Do I dare ask how things went with you and *Capitano Amore?*"

"Well…actually, Scott…I think I need to tell you a few things about what's been going on lately…" I can't bring myself to look at Scott yet—I feel embarrassed and ashamed of myself. I don't even know how to begin telling Scott all of the details, but one thing is certain—I want to come clean.

"OK," Scott says matter-of-factly. "Fire away!" he says before he pops a big bite of pastry in his mouth. I manage to look up at him and watch as he wipes his lips with a napkin and gives me a happy smile.

"Let's go sit," I suggest as I grab my cappuccino and start walking toward the living room area. Scott follows closely behind, and we both plop ourselves down on the sofa—me on one end, Scott on the other.

It takes me a minute to figure out how to start unfolding all of the details, but Scott just sits patiently waiting for me to speak. Finally, the words just spill out of my mouth as I begin taking Scott on the emotional journey that has been my life for the past couple of days. He listens intently as I tell him about the note I found in my plant. Then he smiles brightly when I tell him about the second note under my door and the amazing dress that Marco left for me on my veranda. With every detail I share, Scott seems to be right with me—not judging me or acting disappointed—just listening to my every word and mirroring my exact emotions.

As the conversation goes on, I shift around on the sofa a bit and place my feet in Scott's lap. He gently messages my toes as I continue telling him all about the romantic dinner, the incredible artwork on the wall in the secret passageway over the *Ponte Vecchio*, the beautiful gifts and how Marco made me feel when he was holding my hands from across the table. I tell Scott every single detail that I can remember—no matter how personal or embarrassing it might be. I even tell Scott about how Marco told me I made him want to be selfish and how he noticed me when we were in the boarding area in Miami.

Then I tell him all about Franco and, of course, Christina. I tell him about how Franco made my dress and said that I was the first "lover" Marco ever asked him to dress, but how I was certain before I even went into

Franco's studio that there was something between Christina and Marco. As I recall the whole scene for Scott, the details become so vivid that I feel my face starting to well up with tears. Just telling Scott about finding Marco and the lovely Christina all snuggled up on the sofa makes it feel like it is happening to me all over again.

When I finally finish my story, my face is wet with tears and Scott is just looking back at me with a pained expression. I look down at my hands and try to figure out what it is that I want Scott to do or say to fix things. Scott must sense that I need him to do something, so he lifts my feet out of his lap and rises up and off the sofa. He silently glides across the room and into the bathroom. When he comes back out, he has a nice, wet washcloth in his hands. Then he stops in the kitchen to get a glass of water before he returns to the sofa.

When he sits down next to me, he hands me the glass of water. Then he unfolds the washcloth and tenderly wipes my face. The cool touch of the terrycloth fabric against my skin feels so soothing. I look up at Scott and see how intent he is on washing away all the traces of sadness in my face. Once he's finished wiping my eyes and my sticky cheeks, he leans back into the sofa and pulls me so that I am leaning back into his chest. He gently strokes my head as we both sit in silence.

It feels good to be here in my best friend's arms. No matter what seems to happen in my life, there is always a safe place for me right here with Scott. And no matter what Scott thinks of me—especially after what I've just told him—I know he is still willing to be my friend. My heart melts a little at the thought of how strong our friendship really is, and, for the first time since I arrived in Florence, I truly feel at home.

I can feel the steady rise and fall of Scott's torso as he breathes in and out, like the constant ebb and flow of the ocean. I drift off a bit as his fingers continue to softly stroke my forehead. I am relieved that he hasn't said anything yet. There is a huge part of me that doesn't want to know what he thinks of me—or Marco. Just knowing that he still cares for me is enough in this moment, and I think silence is all I can take right now.

When I wake up from my blissful little nap, I feel foggy-headed and hot. I shift slightly against Scott's warm chest to try to find a more comfortable position. As I roll my neck around in search of a new position, my eyes seem to be drawn toward the door as I realize that it is slightly ajar. With my eyes, I follow the crack of light between the door and the wall, and, suddenly, I see a face looking back at me. My body goes icy as I blink my eyes in an effort to see who it is. Everything around me stops when I recognize Marco's face. He is looking directly at me now with a faint, ironic smile.

Chapter Seventeen

My first flight show time in Italy is about fifteen minutes away, and, as I wait for Scott outside of his villa, I do my best to try to find my most professional flight attendant game face. In the ten years that I've been flying for *Windsong Air,* I've never had any trouble getting prepared for a flight. But today is a different story. After Scott left my villa to go get ready, I looked at my flight schedule and discovered that Captain Marco Maselli is working this flight sequence. If there was ever a time that I needed to act like a true professional, this is it.

When I first got up from my nap with Scott, I thought maybe I had dreamt that I saw Marco peeking at me through the doorway. But as Scott was leaving, I noticed that there was an unfamiliar brown shopping bag on my kitchen counter. So I waited until Scott was gone to look inside the bag—in case it was from Marco. Sure enough, it was. There, nestled deep down inside the bag, were my gift-wrappings from last night, the tiny note cards and a bottle of red wine.

When I pulled the bottle of wine out of the bag, I immediately noticed the label. It was made out of gold foil and shaped like a normal wine label, but it seemed to be handmade. In swirled black lettering, the label read: *Marco's Eloise.* So many questions came to mind as I studied the label and tried to understand the reason that Marco keeps referring to me as "his" Eloise. The whole thing made me feel queasy. I can't seem to escape this man—no matter what I do. And even though I am thoroughly convinced that I am not ready for a guy like Marco, I could feel a small measure of hope seeping back into my heart as I held that bottle of wine in my hands.

Now, as I try to prepare for another encounter with Marco, I can't decide how I really feel. We are here to work, not pursue romance, and, if I can just stay focused on the job at hand, maybe things will take care of themselves. I mean Marco is a professional airline captain for goodness sake! Surely he's going to need to stay on task in order to make sure that the plane is safe for all the passengers, right? But on the other hand, he knows that we are going to be working together today, and if he wanted to keep things professional, why did he stop by my villa with another gift?

The sound of Scott's front door creaking open shakes me out of my quiet contemplation. I quickly snap out of my funk and smile at Scott as he emerges in his navy blue tailored *Windsong Air* suit. He looks strikingly handsome in just about anything he wears, but especially in a suit. And the standard issue ruby red tie with the silver embroidered "*W's*" always looks so sharp on the male crewmembers.

"You ready to fly?" Scott asks in a forced, but peppy, tone.

"I am," I say, trying to match my enthusiasm to his. I manage to pull myself up off of Scott's front steps in one fluid motion and hang my carryon bag over my shoulder. My uniform skirt is hard to move around in—which has always seemed like a design flaw to me since, as flight attendants, we are supposed to be able to act quickly in an emergency. But *Windsong Air* is known for its fashionably dressed crewmembers; so my long, skinny pencil skirt and tailored crop jacket do help to maintain the impeccable image of Wiley Bennett I guess.

"Then let's go!" he says as he links his arm with mine, and we make our way down the cobbled walkway toward the circle drive.

"How are you feeling about everything?" Scott asks me as we pass the *Il Girasole* office.

"I don't know…" I trail off, not wanting to discuss the very latest Marco development with Scott just yet. "I checked the schedule for today and found out that Marco is going to be our captain on this sequence, and I guess I *do* feel a little nervous about that."

"Well, you don't need to feel nervous, Elle. You didn't do anything wrong last night—you just decided that you weren't the right kind of woman for

Marco's...*unusual* style of dating," Scott offers in an effort to bolster my ego while politely acknowledging our Captain's bad dating form.

"Yeah... He does have *unusual* style," I concede as I give Scott a little sideways smile, letting him know in my own way that I'm still not ready for a full on bash-fest.

Actually, to my surprise, Scott has said very little about the events that I shared with him earlier today, and what he did say wasn't as harsh as I was expecting. I was prepared for Scott to rip Marco to ribbons since it seemed clear from the beginning that Scott didn't trust Marco one bit. Instead, Scott has been quiet and managed to reserve any of his severe commentary—at least for now. But I know for a fact that if I wanted to bash Marco, Scott wouldn't hold back!

When we reach the front gate, I can see that Marta DeSoto is the only person waiting. She is sitting on a sturdy bench just outside the gate, working on one of her number puzzles. As we push through the gate, she looks up at us with a somber, weary smile on her face. I've never been that close to Marta. She's always been kind of difficult to get to know, and, lately, there's a certain sadness in her eyes that never fully goes away.

"Hi Marta," Scott says sweetly as he makes his way over to the bench. "Mind if I share this seat with you?"

"No...not at all," she says as she gathers up her purse and slides over to make room for Scott.

"How do you like Italy so far?" Scott asks Marta as she dog-ears the puzzle page in her book and closes it on her lap. Her skin is golden brown, and her short, dark hair has a silky sheen that's likely the result of a few long days in the sun.

"It's fine..." she says softly. I watch her tiny brown hands as she clips her mechanical pencil to her book and nervously smoothes her palms over the glossy cover.

"That's good..." Scott trails off, evidently tired of trying to make conversation with the ever-shy and standoffish Marta DeSoto.

We all wait in awkward silence for a few minutes, just listening to the small fountain in the center of the circular driveway that seems to be spitting bursts of water out at irregular intervals. Before long, I can hear the sounds of the others making their way up to the gate. Everyone is giggling and carrying on and once they push through the ironworks, we all start exchanging our hellos.

Bobbi Henry is the first person to greet me, and she does so in her usual bubbly way. "Sweet Pea!" she gushes as she wraps her arms around my neck. "I haven't seen you since we got here. Are you having a good time so far?" She releases her embrace and pulls back so she can see my face. Her perfume is overwhelming—just like her presence—but it's so nice to see her.

"Yes, I am," I reply with a sincere smile on my face.

"Well that's good news, my dear—really good news!" she says happily as she shifts her carryon bag around on her shoulder. Then she takes a step in closer to me and asks in a hushed tone, "Now…what about that captain that was on your tail on the flight over?" She gives me a wink and a smile as she waits for my answer.

Instantly, I can feel my face start to glow with embarrassment! How in the world did she know about all of that? I feel a mist of sweat flushing over my skin as I try to compose myself. Luckily, Bobbi doesn't wait too long for my answer and instead changes the subject.

"So did you hear about Lupe Ortega?"

"No, I didn't," I say with great interest. I'm so relieved for the change of subject that I'm sure my reply sounded rather eager.

"When the morning crew was landing here in Florence, one of the aft galley storage bins wasn't closed and locked properly and a case of tomato juice came flying out and landed right on her shoulder!"

"Oh my gosh!" I blurt out, sincerely shocked by the news. "Is she going to be OK?"

"I don't know yet—but I heard she was in a lot of pain," Bobbie offers as she begins digging around in her purse for something. "I think they took her straight to the hospital, and she's been there all day." I watch as Bobbi pulls out a small, pink compact and starts dabbing her face with a fresh coat of pressed powder.

I really like Lupe. She is Scott's neighbor at *The Wiley*—and an amazing cook. The three of us typically eat dinner together at least twice a week—we bring the groceries and she cooks. She is genuinely kind, and I hate that something bad has happened to such a good friend. Just as I'm about to ask Bobbi a few more questions, the crew van pulls into the circle drive, and I notice that Miriam Ungaro is riding shotgun.

A blast of adrenalin jolts through my body as I see Miriam climbing out of the crew van. She looks tired and irritable. She's wearing a navy blue linen pantsuit that's all rumpled around the crotch from sitting, and she has huge sweat stains half-mooning her underarms. I watch her closely as she parts the crowd of flight attendants using the clipboard in her hand and heads for a spot in the shade.

"Everybody gather round!" she shouts in her raw, raspy voice as she steps up onto a stone bench to give her a better view of the group.

Like obedient little lemmings, we all shuffle over toward Miriam and make a semi-circle around her.

"You may have heard about Lupe Ortega—she was injured this morning on the return flight to Florence. She has a fractured collarbone and a sprained wrist. Obviously, she can't fly in this condition, so we are going to be bringing over a replacement flight attendant from Miami and sending Lupe home. But, until the replacement arrives—which should be by next weekend—we are going to have to pull someone from this crew to cover for Saturday's and Sunday's flights."

As Miriam says this, I notice that she is panning the group thoroughly in search of the person that she has in mind to punish with this change of plan. As her sour face swivels around on her saggy neck, I'm almost certain the person she is looking for is me. Her eyes brighten slightly as her gaze settles on me, and I notice a nasty smile spreading across her face.

"Elle Butts!" she shouts out with authority. "You will be working both shifts tomorrow and Sunday, so be sure to get some sleep after your evening runs. The morning crew's show time is *5:00 a.m.*" Her tone is very acid, and there is an obvious note of satisfaction as she delivers the news that I am going to be taking Lupe's place.

A burning irritation rises up inside my throat as I just stand there, looking up at Miriam. She is such a petty person—a miserable, petty person.

"Now, we are running behind, so let me give everyone the specifics of today's flight to Munich and back," Miriam continues as she turns her attention to her trusty clipboard. "I've decided to mix things up a bit, so listen carefully. Sebastian, you will be flying senior today, so be sure to mark your timesheet as such."

I look over at Sebastian, who seems just as surprised as the rest of us that Miriam is letting *him* fly senior today. As a rule, Miriam has always hated Sebastian—probably because he looks better as a woman than she does, but of course that's just speculation. Flying senior means that you are in charge of the other flight attendants during the flight, and you earn about $10 more per hour since the senior has more responsibility and has to turn in all of the flight paperwork. Naturally, everyone wants to fly senior but Miriam has a short list of favorites—and Sebastian is *never* on that list!

"Scott, you'll fly up front with Sebastian and Enrique, you will be the first class floater. Suzanne, Izzy and Bobbi, you three are in the mid-cabin today and, Marta, you and *Elle* are flying aft." With the mention of my name, Miriam looks directly at me again, and in a saccharine sweet voice she adds, "Now you two in the aft be sure to close the galley bins tightly. I don't want any more accidents back there."

I can feel the heat of everyone looking at me as Miriam dresses me down. I don't know what to do other than to stand there with no reaction. Inside, I'm fuming, but I do my best not to let it show. I happen to catch a glimpse of Scott out of the corner of my eye. He is glaring at Miriam with a defiant look. I feel compelled to assure him that I don't need him to defend me, but I don't want to draw any additional attention to myself right now.

"Now, we have a fairly full flight this afternoon," Miriam continues in her obnoxious voice. "These passengers are headed for our new affiliate resort in Germany. First class is completely full so I've given catering instructions to overstock the first class galley. *However*, I demand that any extra meals be given to our *pilots*—flight attendants will *only* eat the crew meals we've provided. *No* exceptions!" Miriam gives the group an evil stare as she shifts around and revs up for her final instructions.

"Finally, there is a two-hour layover in Munich before you head back to Florence. No one is permitted to leave the airport during this layover—and

I mean it! There is a crew lounge at the airport or you can hang out in the concourse with the passengers, it's up to you. Now get on the van. You're running late," she barks irritably as she steps down off the bench with a thud and clomps off through the sunflower gate, disappearing into the shadows.

Everyone seems relieved to see Miriam heading into the resort. Sometimes, she will fly our routes with us and do these random spot checks. If she catches you doing something that is "not regulation," she can write you up and you'll be fined. I've never actually been written up before. But it seems like today, Miriam is looking for every possible reason to make my life miserable.

Something is definitely up with her. Miriam's demeanor was much more harsh than usual, and all of her "demands" seem out of character compared to her regular, apathetic pre-flight briefings. Most of the time, Miriam lets us work out the details of who works in each position, and she never gets so worked up about the crew meals. In fact, most of the time, Miriam doesn't even bother with a pre-flight briefing. She merely assigns the senior position and then leaves the rest to us. So I think it is becoming quite clear to everyone—especially me—that Miriam was making her pre-flight briefing personal today.

Even though I'm sure Miriam is strategically placing each member of the flight crew to protect her precious Marco—with all of the male crew members assigned to the positions closest to the cockpit and all of the female members toward the back—I'm kind of relieved to be flying aft today. I don't know how I feel about anything right now and working up front is the last place I need to be while I'm this confused. As the rest of the flight attendants in our crew discuss their assignments and the possible reasons for Miriam's foul mood, Bobbi Henry wraps her long, boney fingers around my arm.

"So I guess Miriam is trying to keep *you* as far away from the cockpit as possible!" she says into my ear with a conspiratorial giggle.

"It kind of looks that way…" I concede as the two of us make our way over to the crew van.

"I'm not feeling the love from Miriam for you, Baby Girl," Bobbi says as she starts climbing into the van. "You'd better watch out. I think she's got your number."

The Jetway is attached to the mid-cabin boarding door—which I personally prefer since it makes herding passengers on and off of the plane much easier. As I step on board, the familiar smell of heavy-duty cleaning compounds mixed with synthetic fabrics and scorched coffee greets my nose, and I settle right into work mode.

I give a pleasant smile to Suzanne, who is already hunched over the mid-galley beverage cart, counting out cans of soda and juice with unfamiliar labels. She flashes me a pained smile in return, obviously feeling badly about my horrible luck with Miriam. I shake it off and start making my way back to the aft galley. I start my pre-flight check as I walk down the aisle, popping open the overhead bins and checking for the safely equipment as I go.

Marta is already in the aft galley when I arrive. The tangy, pungent smell of tomato juice is overwhelming as I step into the tiny food prep area. There is an elderly Italian mechanic down on the floor digging through a tool kit. It looks like he is replacing the door to the faulty storage bin, which is directly above the left jump seat. I can only imagine how awful the accident must have been for Lupe—having an entire case of canned juice slamming into her shoulder must have been excruciating.

Marta is already organizing her side of the beverage cart, so I quickly remove my jacket, grab my apron and then stash my carryon bag in the narrow crew closet next to the lavatory. Marta and I work in silence for a while, moving various cans of European brand soft drinks and juices around in the cart until we are happy with the order. I refill the paper napkin dispenser and line an ice bucket with a plastic bag.

"What's up with you and Miriam?" Marta finally asks after the mechanic packs up his gear and leaves.

"Um…I don't know, actually," I lie, not sure I should be talking to anyone about Miriam or Marco right now.

"What if I told you I think I already know?" Marta says directly to me with one eyebrow raised.

"Well, then I'd say you probably know more than I do…" I trail off, hoping that my nonchalance will be enough to evade Marta. I do my best to act as though I'm really concentrating on my work, so maybe Marta will let the conversation pass.

"It's because of Captain Maselli, isn't it?"

Rats! She couldn't let it die! I feel my veins go icy as her question sinks in. So she knows about it already. How in the world did that happen? Darn gossips! Gossiping is almost an art form among many of my fellow flight attendants, and, while I do my best to stay out of the fray, I'm literally shocked that quiet Marta is so connected to the coconut telegraph.

OK—so she knows about Marco. But even though she knows, I don't know whether to acknowledge the subject or not. Marta DeSoto isn't exactly the type of person you want to confide in—especially when you're trying to hide a work-related romance! Her husband is a major executive at WRI, and I really don't think talking about my insane "love triangle" with Miriam and Marco is a good idea.

"Everybody knows, Elle," Marta says as she squats down to re-shelve a rack of drinks. Then she looks up at me, seemingly pleased to be in the know. But I also detect sincerity in her eyes, like she actually cares about me.

"Well…as far as I'm concerned, there really isn't much to know," I say softly, hoping that will be enough to shut down this topic of conversation.

"It's nothing to be ashamed of, Elle," Marta says as she closes the drink bin with a loud clap and stands back up. "From what I hear, he really likes you," she says as a smile starts to wash across her face.

I stare at her now, trying to figure out what she's heard, and who has been talking about me. I watch as she dips her hand into the front pocket of her apron and pulls out a folded slip of paper. She reaches across the cart to hand it to me.

My heart starts to pound, and my face begins to redden as I realize that Marco must have given Marta a note for me. As I reach for the note, Marta pulls it out of my reach. She smiles at me and says, "First, tell me what's going on."

Blackmail is the last thing I would have expected from mild- mannered Marta DeSoto! The combination of a note from Marco and this unsettling development that Marta can play so dirty really has me rattled. I take a step back and try to understand what's happening.

"Marta, it seems to me that you already know everything that's going on between Marco and me—and maybe even more—so please just give me the note!" I plead as I struggle to keep my emotions under control.

Marta leans against the food prep counter and looks as if she is contemplating the situation. She folds her arms across her chest, and I can see the white note peeking out from under her arm.

"Tell you what," Marta says in a low tone. "You tell me your secret and then I'll tell you mine. That way, we'll be even and we'll know we *have to* trust one another." With that, Marta cocks her head slightly and sends me a pleading smile.

"OK…" I begin, feeling slightly trapped, but also very intrigued by the idea that Marta has a secret. "Well…Marco Maselli took me out on a date last night, but things didn't go very well. It seems he has this habit of…*befriending* women—like Miriam for example—and leading them to believe that he is interested in them as more than just friends—even though he claims that it is not his *intention* to lead them on. He has told me he feels differently about me, but I just can't bring myself to trust him, so I am keeping my distance for now."

Marta softens slightly as she absorbs my words. I can tell she is mulling them over and comparing my story to the story she heard through the grapevine. She looks up at me with a hint of a smile. She takes a step toward me with the note in her hand.

"This note should make you feel better, then," she says as she slides the note into the front pocket of my apron.

232

I furrow my brow as I realize that Marta has already read my note. I feel offended and annoyed, but before I can say anything about it, Marta starts talking again.

"Your secret is nothing, Elle. Who cares that you're involved with one of the pilots. You're both *single* after all… My secret is much worse." Marta turns her back to me now, so I can't see her face. Her voice is sad and dark as she continues speaking. "My husband is having an affair with Michelle Maddox."

I allow Marta's words to sink in with a thud, but even after a minute of consideration, I don't know what to say to her. No wonder she looks so sad.

"Oh my gosh, Marta…I'm so sorry…" I trail off, rather stunned by her secret. "Is that why you accepted the transfer?" I add tentatively, trying to piece this whole thing together.

"I guess so…" Marta says as she turns around to face me again. "My husband made it clear to me when I got my letter about the transfer that he didn't want me to go. He said it was going to be a really difficult three months and all of this other *crap*," Marta's words sound harsh and bitter. "But when I found out that both Michelle and my husband were on the list of executives scheduled to be here for the first month, I guess I just figured if I didn't go, Oscar would be free to carry on his affair, and everyone would find out. I didn't want to be the laughing stock of the company, so I thought maybe if I accepted the transfer, he would behave, and maybe we would even rediscover our own relationship while we were spending time together in Italy."

"Does Oscar know that you know about the affair?" I can't help but ask.

"I think he figured it out. We had a huge fight about me accepting the transfer. He said that it would look bad for both of us to be here since it was not a *pleasure trip* for WRI married couples. When I pressured him on the subject and came right out and asked him about his relationship with Michelle, he got very angry. We never discussed it again. And a few weeks later, I was on my way to Florence and he was staying in Miami."

I'm shocked by all of this information. I never really thought about Marta and Oscar DeSoto all that much—although I do remember thinking once or twice that they had a sort of strange relationship. Oscar always seemed so much more outgoing than Marta. He is very handsome—with those sexy, dark Latin American eyes and his tanned and toned body—and Marta always looked so plain in comparison. But as I look at her, in this fragile state, I see that she is actually quite beautiful. Her frame is almost delicate, and her face reminds me of a doll—perfectly shaped with dark, inset eyes that sparkle when you actually take the time to look.

Now that I know about the affair, Michelle Maddox does seem like an obvious pairing with Oscar. She is polished and has a sort of glamorous side. She is very good at schmoozing with executives and has self-confidence galore. She is the literal antithesis of sweet, plain Marta. And she strikes me as one of those corporate women that use men until they get what they want, and they never think twice about the wives and children they crush in the process. If I'm not mistaken, Oscar is Michelle's boss, so who knows what's really going on with this affair.

I remember watching Michelle in the boarding area before we left for Florence. She had on all that make-up and that flashy suit. Marta must have been watching her, too, but with so much pain in her heart. At least Marta can rest easier right now—I mean if Michelle is in Italy, and Oscar is in Miami, they couldn't be carrying on their affair anymore.

"So, you must have been relieved to see that Michelle still came to Italy," I remark as I nervously rearrange sleeves of plastic cups in one of the storage bins. I can't figure out what to do with myself now that I know why Marta looks so lost and sad.

"I was until I heard she went back to Miami today," Marta says with a tremble in her voice. "*Miriam* delivered the news to me as I was sitting by the pool this morning. She told me it had something to do with Mr. Wiley needing Michelle back for some big negotiation. And I know Miriam told me this just to hurt me. She knows about the affair— sometimes Oscar uses her to help him with his cover story—and she seemed to take such pleasure when she was telling me that Michelle was gone."

Marta's eyes start to rim out with tears. I quickly draw the galley curtains to give us more privacy. Her shame and embarrassment seem to fill the tiny galley, and all I can do is pull her into my arms.

"I'm so sorry, Marta…" I coo gently in her ear. "I'm so very sorry…"

"I am just so lost, Elle" Marta sobs. "I have been married to Oscar for 12 years, and we used to be so happy. Now, I feel like I am invisible to him. It is as if he wishes I didn't even exist…"

Marta feels tiny and frail in my arms, and I don't know what to do to comfort her. I'm sure sharing her secret with me must have helped some, but I can't imagine being married to someone for 12 years and then discovering that you really don't know each other at all.

The aft galley intercom starts binging, so I gently pull away from Marta and lift the receiver.

"Elle here," I say as I watch Marta dab her eyes with a cocktail napkin.

"Everything shipshape back there?" It's Scott checking on us. His voice is lively and fun, and I wish more than anything he was flying in the back with us.

"All systems go," I say into the receiver. "Now you keep your filthy paws off those first class meals, you hear?" I say, making a dig at Miriam. I feel even more disgust for her now that I know what she did to poor Marta.

"Oh, yes ma'am," Scott replies sarcastically. "Those are for the *pilots!*"

We both laugh, and then I hang up the receiver. I check to make sure Marta has regained her composure before I pull the galley curtain back. The passengers are starting to board now, and I watch as the first few people make their way to their seats.

"Boarding," I say over my shoulder to Marta.

"OK," she sniffles. "Thanks, Elle… I needed to get that off my chest."

"Any time, Marta," I say sincerely. "If you ever need to talk, you know you can come to me," I quickly add before the first group of passengers takes their seats near the rear of the plane.

Once we're in the air and nearing our cruising altitude, Marta and I begin preparing our cart for service. It is a light load in the back of the plane, so we manage to get the beverage cart ready for service in record time. Neither one of us has said much since Marta unloaded her big secret on me, but my mind is filled with questions about how Marta discovered the affair and what she thinks she'll do next.

It isn't until I reach into my apron pocket in search of my pop-top opener that I remember the note from Marco. Part of me wants to stop the beverage service on the spot, lock myself in the aft lavatory and read it. But another part of me feels too weary to care about what Marco has to say. Marco and his silly little notes—what kind of a grown man relies on passed notes for courting a woman these days?

I look up at Marta who is diligently working on the other side of the beverage cart. I watch her as she fills up a plastic cup with ice and adds a lime wedge; then graciously hands the well-dressed gentleman seated in the aisle seat the cup along with a tiny bottle of vodka. She gives the gentleman a courteous smile and moves her attention to the next row of passengers. She is a good worker—always on time, very polite and kind to her fellow workers. And beyond that, she seems like a good person. She doesn't make any waves with others. In fact, I mostly just see her working her Sudoku puzzles and keeping to herself.

Bobbi Henry gives me the thumbs up sign to let me know that she and Suzanne have already finished serving the rest of the main cabin, so Marta and I wheel our beverage cart back into the aft galley. Automatically, we both set to work, restocking the cart for the next service run. Marta makes a fresh pot of coffee, and I refill the ice bucket, and then we both push the beverage cart back into the storage bay and lock the wheel catches down tight. I think of Lupe as I give all of the storage bins a visual check to make sure everything is locked properly in case of unexpected turbulence. Once everything in the aft galley is in tiptop shape, Marta sits down on the jump seat and motions for me to join her.

"I know I don't have to say this…but I just feel like I should…" Marta begins nervously. "Please don't tell anyone about Oscar and Michelle." Her eyes are as black as coal, and I sense her desperate need for privacy.

"I won't say a word, Marta," I promise her.

"I didn't think you would, but you know…everyone at *Windsong Air* seems to love gossip, and right now, I don't think I could handle it if everyone knew."

"I understand, I really do…" I say. "But can I ask you a question?"

"Sure…I guess…" she says as she looks up at me and takes a deep breath.

"What are you going to do? Are you going to stay with Oscar?"

"I don't know yet," she says as she looks down at her tiny hands, folded in her lap. "I mean there is a part of me that doesn't know what I would do without my Oscar, but then the other part wonders how I can stay with him when it is so clear that he doesn't even want me." She takes another deep breath and adds, "I don't want to end it, Elle, I really don't. But I worry sometimes that it isn't my choice anymore…"

The two of us just sit in silence, listening to the loud, steady hum of the jet engines. I can't imagine being in Marta's shoes. I wish that I knew the right thing to say, but I don't. I'm clearly no expert in affairs of the heart! But 12 years together is a long time. People change a lot, and I wonder if Marta even knows the man she calls her husband anymore.

"Did you read your note from Captain Maselli yet?" Marta asks in an obvious effort to change the subject.

"No…I haven't had a chance to…" I say as I contemplate the folded sheet of paper in my apron pocket. "I'm actually kind of nervous to read it," I confess, as I look Marta in the eye. "The whole Marco and Miriam thing is pretty confusing."

"Well, I think you'll understand why Miriam is being such a jerk to you once you read it," she offers. "And to be quite honest, I think it sort of shed some light on why she was so awful to me this morning, too."

What does my situation with Marco have to do with Marta? I wonder.

"Read it!" Marta says as she gives my shoulder a playful shove.

So I dig around in my apron and pull out the rumpled note. I shift around on the jump seat so my back is to Marta before I open it. I can feel her peering over my shoulder—which under normal circumstances would really annoy me—but since she's already read it, it doesn't really matter. I hold the note close to my face, and I can smell the faint fragrance of Marco's citrus cologne.

Dear Eloise-

I am sorry to have confused you last night. I want to be good to you and make you feel happy. I know now that the only way to make you happy is to belong only to you. I have told Miriam and Christina that I can no longer be close to them because I am with you now, so I hope you will give me a second chance. I know that you may also have some-one in your life that you are close to, so I hope that we can agree to be only close to one another now. I will see you after we fly.

MM

I have to read the note through a couple of times to fully understand what it says. I feel flushed and nervous as I contemplate his words. I also feel ashamed that Marco saw me cuddled up with Scott on my sofa this morning—which may not be all that different from what I saw between him and Christina at the *Prada* showroom. And no wonder Miriam is in such a horrible mood and on a warpath for me! Marco told her about us! He has drawn a line with her and Christina *for me*! He chose me! He must really care about me after all!

I fold up the note and turn to look at Marta. She gives me a sweet smile and says, "I told you that you'd like what it says."

"Well, I'm sort of surprised by it, that's for sure!" I confide as my head starts to swirl with thoughts of Marco.

"I think it's safe to assume Miriam had a bad day today—getting dumped by a hot pilot for one of your *pee-on employees* is a pretty crummy thing..." Marta trails off with the trace of an evil smile. "But it couldn't have happened to a better person," she blurts out, and we both start laughing.

"Oh, Marta," I say as I realize how she must be feeling. "I'm so sorry that Miriam was horrible to you over this whole thing with Marco."

"Don't be ridiculous, Elle," Marta says dismissively. "Miriam is just plain miserable, and she always tries to make everyone else around her feel miserable, too. I think it's fantastic that Captain Maselli is so obviously falling for you! You deserve it!"

"You really think so?" I question, not sure how I feel about any of it.

"Yes I do!" Marta says emphatically. "Falling in love is one of the greatest pleasures on earth, and a privilege you simply can't take for granted."

"So even with everything you're going through right now, you still believe in love?" I ask, hoping my question isn't inappropriate, but desperately wanting her to answer me.

Marta contemplates her answer for a moment. I watch her as she stares off into the distance, carefully mulling her words and considering the beliefs in her heart.

"I wouldn't give up one second of my life with Oscar," she finally says. "And I hope and pray that when Michelle gets tired of him and all of his whining and complaining, I will have him back again—all to myself!"

"So Oscar is the one for you, then…" I say in response.

"He always has been and always will be. I promised him—for better or for worse, Elle…" Marta says as her eyes moisten. "But I sure hope *better* rolls back around real soon!" she says with a choked up laugh.

"Me too, Marta…" I say as I wrap my arm around her shoulder.

Chapter Eighteen

The rest of our flight to Munich was extremely uneventful. Everything about it was routine and ordinary. But now that we are about to deplane for our short layover, I'm starting to feel anxiety pangs. The note from Marco was pretty clear—*I gave up my friends, now you give up yours.* For me, that's easier said than done. Scott really and truly *is* my best friend, and I don't know how I'm going to explain this whole thing to him. How do you tell the guy you've known and trusted as your closest friend for the past 10 years that you need to shelve him for awhile so you can date some guy you barely know? It just seems wrong.

I can't ignore the fact that Marco saw me cuddled up with Scott this morning. And no matter what it looked like to Marco, he didn't overreact the way I did. He simply pointed out that if he can't have a close friendship with another woman, then I can't have one with another man. Fair is fair after all, and if Marco has to give up his relationships that make me feel insecure, then I guess I should have to do the same. Of course, I have no idea how I'm going to explain this to Scott, but I know I need to do it right away. I'm sure that Marco is going to be waiting for me in the crew lounge or maybe even in the boarding area, so I really can't put off talking to Scott about this.

I watch Marta neatly folding her apron and tucking it into her carryon bag. We haven't said much since we landed—I think she must be preoccupied with her own concerns, and I really don't want to involve her in my silly problems. But now that all of the passengers have deplaned and the German maintenance crew is cleaning and vacuuming the mid-cabin, Marta finally breaks the silence.

"What are you going to say to Scott?" she asks casually as she zips up her bag.

"I don't know yet…" I trail off, surprised at how astute Marta is to figure out that Scott is my "someone" from Marco's note.

"Do you want my advice?" she offers as she sits down on her jump seat and looks up at me.

"Sure…I guess," I say, wondering what kind of advice she has about giving up a friendship for romance.

"Obviously, I'm pretty hurt and disgusted by what Michelle and Oscar are up to," she begins in a low voice. "And, make no mistake—there is no excuse for what's going on behind my back. But, as my mother always told me, you get what you give." I watch as Marta takes a deep breath and trains her focus directly on me.

"I think that sometimes you have to make a stand for what you want, Elle" she continues. "I think you have to make sacrifices and show the person that you love that you are willing to make concessions or take risks in your own life for the sake of love. Sometimes that means adjusting your life a bit here and there to create something that works for *both* of you. Maybe if I had been more open to some of the things Oscar wanted—or maybe if I had staked my claim more clearly—Michelle would not be a problem in my life right now…"

"Are you saying that you think that you could have done something different in your marriage that would have prevented Oscar's affair?" I ask, completely confused by how she could be taking responsibility for her husband's infidelity.

"I guess I am…sort of…" she says, reluctantly, as if she is in search of the meaning in her own words. "I think that sometimes, I'm too rigid with my husband. I never wanted to go along with his big ideas—even though, he's rearranged his life for me several times in the past 12 years…"

I stare at Marta, working to piece together the truth in her words. I can't help but wonder what Oscar wanted her to do, and why she didn't want go along with his plans. Did it have something to do with their careers? And how is this applicable to me? I try to understand what meaning I should be gleaning from her experience and applying to my situation with Marco, but I can't seem to find the thread.

"Marta, I'm not sure I follow what you're saying," I admit as I slide in next to her on the jump seat.

"What I'm saying is that in order to find out if Marco Maselli is your true love, you may have to make a few sacrifices—just like he did for you. You have to stay focused on what you want in this life, Elle. It's when you lose your focus or your willingness to believe in love that things slip through the cracks," she says with remorse in her voice.

I'm not sure this advice is really all that helpful to me. I mean I honestly don't know that I *love* Marco, and giving up my most important friendship to find out is a mighty big risk. But perhaps all Marta is really saying is that sometimes you have to risk big in order to win big. And maybe venturing out on my own and taking a risk on love is exactly what I need to do. Maybe it's enough to just *believe* in love right now. And, who knows, this could be the best way to find out who I really am and to discover how great it is to love and to be loved in return.

"Thank you, Marta," I say as I reach over and place my hand on top of hers. "I'm still not sure what I'm going to say to Scott, but, at least, I think I know what I'm doing."

Scott smiles brightly at me as Marta and I enter the Jetway. He's leaning against the wall just outside the boarding door with his arms casually folded across his chest. I realize now that I absolutely *don't* know what I'm doing! I'm suddenly not sure that I can go through with this. It's just too much to sacrifice. I blink my eyes hard and hope that when I open them, I'll feel differently. But as soon as I do, Scott is still standing there, looking at me with affection and concern.

"Are you OK, Elle?" he asks me as he pushes off from the Jetway wall and takes a step toward me.

"I'm not sure..." I say as I look up at him.

"What can I do to help?" Scott asks with genuine alarm in his voice. His breath is minty and his cologne is fresh and familiar as he hovers over me.

"I'll see you two later," Marta says sheepishly as she gives my shoulder a gentle pat and starts heading up the ramp of the long, narrow Jetway.

"OK, Marta," Scott says absently as he remains focused on me.

I watch as Marta disappears around a bend in the Jetway, and, suddenly, I feel so alone with Scott. But it's not a good alone. It's an awful alone. I can feel my stomach twist into a big knot as I struggle to figure out what to do. The air around us is hot and thick, and I feel dizzy. Scott clearly senses my distress and wraps his arm around me for support.

"You need to sit for a minute," he says, taking charge of the situation. He slowly guides me back onto the plane, and we settle into two seats directly to the right of the boarding door. The cleaning crew is in the back of the plane now, and I can hear the muffled sound of the vacuums.

"Thank you..." I mumble as my mind races. Maybe I can just tell Marco that I don't mind his friendships with Christina and Miriam after all! That way, I don't have to say anything to Scott, and we can just go on being friends. But just then, the image of Christina's face flashes into my mind, and I recognize the lusty look in her eyes. And it's clear that things are beyond the point of no return with Miriam. No, I have to do this. I have to wager big here. It's the only way I'll know for sure that I've given love a chance.

"Talk to me, Elle," Scott says with a worried voice as he leans in and places his hand on top of mine. The gesture is so familiar and genuine. His face is soft and kind, and I feel just awful telling him that I need to put Marco first for a while.

I pull my hand away from Scott's and dig around in my jacket pocket for the note. I give the mangled slip of paper to him and then lean my head back, close my eyes and wait for him to finish reading the words.

"I see..." is all he says after a lengthy pause.

I open my eyes to look at him, and he is still staring at the slip of paper with a furrowed brow. After another long pause, he refolds the note and places it in my hand. I can hear him pulling in a deep breath as he slides around in his seat a bit so he is facing forward. The walls of the airplane fuselage seem to be closing in on me as I listen to him pushing the breath back out, and I just wish he'd say something.

"Is this what you want?" he finally asks with a trace of sadness in his voice.

"I don't know..." I admit. "I think so, but I don't know..."

"Well...I hope it turns out the way you want it to, Elle," Scott says flatly as he turns his gaze upward. "I sure would hate to see you get hurt."

"Me, too," I say.

We sit in awkward silence for what feels like ages. I know as soon as one of us makes a move, everything becomes real. Once we step off of this plane and into the Jetway, we'll be entering into a time and place where Scott and Elle aren't best friends anymore. I can hardly imagine what that will be like, and I don't know that I'm exactly ready to stand up and walk on my own two feet just yet.

"Are you worried about what other 'sacrifices' *Capitano Amore* may ask you to make?" Scott asks with an acid tone after another long pause.

"What do you mean?" I ask, not quite sure about the question and sort of bothered by the *Capitano Amore* reference. I look at the side of Scott's handsome face and see that his jaw is tight with anger—which causes a rush of fear to barrel right through me.

"Are you willing to give him *everything* if he asks for it?" Scott says as he turns his head to look directly at me. His eyes are still soft and deep, but the anger is unmistakable.

Suddenly, I understand what Scott means by *everything*. A light chill spills down my spine as I realize that Marco may have certain expectations of me—expectations that most men have when they get romantically involved. I hadn't really thought about all of this until now. Well, I guess the thought briefly crossed my mind—specifically after I saw the dress and then again later when Franco said I would someday be Marco's "lover." But with all the other distractions and complications, I sort of lost sight of this concern.

But now, with the idea of giving my entire self to Marco front and center in my mind, I don't know what to think. What I do know is that I want to discover what a real relationship feels like, and even though I'm not sure how I will handle the subject of sex just yet, I still know that I want to venture out and explore the possibilities with Marco.

After some consideration, I finally offer a weak answer to Scott's question. "I guess I'm willing to see what happens…"

"Well then…" Scott says softly. "It sounds like you know what you're doing…" When Scott trails off, I feel profoundly sad. He has let me go—and, again, he's made things a lot easier than I was expecting. I don't know what to say to this, so I just sit and stare at an oblong coffee stain on the carpet near the boarding door. It's a bad stain that will likely never come clean.

"Good luck to you, Eloise," Scott says softly, and then he kisses me lightly on the cheek. I numbly watch as he rises up out of his seat and elegantly glides out of the airplane without even looking back at me.

My body feels like wood, and I can't seem to move. Scott never calls me Eloise. The finality and formality of his words penetrate me deeply as I fully acknowledge the choice that I've just made. Why does this have to be so difficult? Why do I have to give up Scott in order to pursue love? It's so unfair! I feel my lower lip starting to quiver, and I don't even try to stop the tears from flowing down my cheeks.

I can't seem to sort this out. I feel so hallow inside, and I fear that I've ruined everything. My decision is like that stupid coffee stain. It has changed things for good, and the damage might be permanent.

But then I think about what Marta said: Sometimes you have to make sacrifices for the sake of love. And even after everything she's been through with Oscar, she's still sure that love is worth it. It's worth the pain and heartache and everything else just to know that you are loved and to love in return.

So I know I need to do this. And if Scott is really my friend—which I'm certain he is—he'll understand in time, and he won't stop caring about me forever. Right? I mean if Marco and I are meant to be together, eventually, we will have to have enough trust in our relationship to let old friends back into the picture. I'm sure of it! And Scott will wait for me. I would wait for him if he ever needed to pursue a relationship! So our friendship isn't stained or ruined! We'll be fine!

I'm just over-reacting, that's all, and I need to stop being so dramatic. And Scott and I can still be friends—just not as close as usual for right now. I need to stop looking at this with such gloom. This is my time of discovery, and that's a good thing! It's where I am in my life right now, and I shouldn't feel badly about any of it. It's exciting, really!

I dig around in my carryon bag and pull out a pack of tissues. I blot my cheeks and wipe underneath my eyes. I fish around in my bag until I find my tinted lip-gloss. I apply a quick coat and pop a piece of gum into my mouth. Suddenly, I feel a renewed sense of confidence for some reason— confidence in Marco, in myself and even in Scott. There is so much to look forward to, and, even though I don't know how everything will turn out, I know that I am looking forward to what's ahead.

When I take my first few steps into the terminal building, I immediately notice how spotless everything is. The floors are perfectly cleaned, and the carpets are immaculate. Then I notice how every single person in the boarding area is a complete stranger, and I realize that no one waited behind for me. A little burst of panic cinches my chest as it dawns on me that I don't even know where the crew lounge is or how to contact anybody to find out.

My initial instinct is to look for Scott—he always knows what to do, and I've grown to rely on that in my life more than I'd like to admit. But there's no more Scott to fix things or to tell me what to do. I'm seriously on my own now for the first time in my life, and I'm going to have to buck up and start looking out for myself.

So I take a deep breath and try to summon up some bravery from within. I guess I could find a café inside the terminal and get something to eat. Thankfully, the layover is only a couple of hours, and soon everyone will be back in the boarding area, getting ready for our return flight. Up ahead, I can see a small cafeteria-like restaurant. The food smells great, and, as I start walking toward it, I notice that all of the tables are wiped clean and set with gleaming silverware and starched linen napkins.

"*Eloise-ah?*" comes a voice from over my shoulder. "I was getting worried." The thick, rich Italian accent is unmistakable, and I feel my knees go weak.

When I turn around, Marco is standing behind me with a gorgeous smile spreading across his face. He is even more dazzling than I remembered, and a flood of emotions fills my body as I take him in. He looks amazing in his uniform—the jacket with the four bars on his shoulders makes him look so regal and important. I don't know what to do with myself, so I just stare up at him as he moves closer to me.

"*Ciao!*" he says brightly as he reaches for my hand. Once he takes a hold of it, he brings it to his lips and gently presses a warm kiss right in the center.

"Hi," I whisper back as an uncontrollable smile takes over my face. I feel as though I'm beaming, and my body begins to feel flush.

"Do you have your papers with you?" he asks me.

"My papers?" I question, not sure what he means.

"Your passport and your crew cards?" Marco specifies, as he looks me in the eye.

"Oh! Yes, I do," I say, wondering why I need my passport.

"I am going to take you someplace where we can be alone for a little while," Marco explains as he wraps his arm around my waist and starts guiding me into the main concourse.

"OK," I manage to say before I start to notice my body melting into Marco's. That floating sensation that seems to come over me when Marco casts his spell is starting to kick in once again, and I can't seem to feel my feet as we walk down the main concourse toward a set of slate gray double doors.

Marco slides his ID badge through a badge reader next to the door. The heavy doors open with a loud buzz and Marco pulls on the handle and guides me inside the dark hallway. It smells like tobacco and floor polish on the other side of the doors, and as we walk further down the hall, I realize that we're entering some sort of private lounge. I turn my head to look inside some of the rooms as we pass. One room has plush seating and a large television along with a juice bar and line of vending machines.

Another room seems to be filled with monitoring screens. Everywhere you look inside that room, there are TV monitors displaying moving images that look like radar reports and various forms of flight information. As we pass, a gentleman wearing a thick navy blue sweater with a fancy patch on the sleeve looks up at me and gives me a grave look. Suddenly I feel nervous that Marco is taking me into a zone of the airport that is forbidden to common flight attendants. I automatically stiffen with this thought, and Marco tightens his embrace.

"It's OK, Eloise-ah. You are not going to get in trouble for being here as long as you are with me, and you have your papers," he whispers into my ear, sending a cascade of chills down my entire body. Suddenly any fear I was feeling has vanished, and I can't wait to be alone with Marco.

Finally, we reach a door near the end of the corridor. Marco slides his ID badge into the badge reader, and, again, the door opens with a buzz. This time, when Marco opens the door, we enter into what feels like a glass room that is simply lit up by lights coming from a dozen or so runways and landing strips on the other side of the glass. As we step inside, the room starts to rumble and shake as a huge 747 takes flight, launching with a massive roar into the black horizon. I watch as the plane rises up and over the windows and off into the distance, headed for some unknown destination.

There are overstuffed lounge chairs neatly positioned along the front of the room, and Marco guides me over to a set of chairs in the far corner. I notice several pilots stretched out in lounge chairs, perfectly situated for watching the next plane as it queues up for take off. Some of the pilots look like they are sleeping, while others are fixated on the runway and the huge airplanes moving around like pawns on a chessboard.

Marco pushes two of the lounge chairs closer together and motions for me to take a seat. I do my best to gracefully sit down in my tight skirt and, then, turn my body to be leaning back into the cushy chair. Marco removes his jacket, drapes it over the back of his lounge chair, and then carefully lowers his body next to mine. He slides his arm behind my neck, and I scoot in next to him so his shoulder cradles my head. I feel giddy inside as I take a deep breath and settle into my new place in Marco's arms and in his life.

"What *is* this place?" I ask after another huge plane growls off the runway and into the pitch-black sky.

"It's an observatory of sorts," Marco says in a low whisper, directly into my ear. "It's a place that really only captains are supposed to go, but I made arrangements with one of the airport directors to bring you with me for a little while."

"Let me guess," I say in a soft voice. "The director is your cousin?"

Marco smiles down at me and says, "Something like that!"

A dart of wonder stabs my mind as I consider the vagueness in his answer. Could the director actually be a gorgeous woman, perhaps? Who happens to owe him a favor?

No! I can't do this again! I have to fully trust myself now and stop constantly questioning every single thing about Marco. He keeps finding ways to bring me to places that are forbidden for regular people, so he can show me how special I am to him. That's it! And it doesn't matter who it is that pulled the strings for us to be here because Marco is doing it all for me. As I watch the tiny wheels of a gigantic plane bump against the distant landing strip and kick up a swirl of smoke, I decide not to question anymore. It's time to just enjoy the ride.

"Eloise-ah?" Marco asks after a few minutes of silent observation.

"Hmm?" I hum as I tilt my head up to see his face.

"May I give you something?" he asks with a twinkle in his eye.

"Depends on what it is," I say with a playful tone. The truth is, I sincerely hope it's not another gift. All of his presents just seem to confuse me and make me worry even more about his expectations. So I hold in my breath slightly as a wait for his reply.

"I want to give you a kiss," he says with a smile. "A *real* kiss," he adds so that I know what he means.

"OK..." I whisper as my mind starts to vaporize. My heart starts pounding as I realize how much I've wanted him to kiss me.

Marco shifts his body around in the lounge chair to face me, and, he slides down so his face is even with mine. He looks at me softly and reaches his hand up to cradle my cheek. He smiles and whispers, "Don't forget to breath..."

I smile back in return and pull in a sharp breath. I don't know how to prepare myself for this moment, so I don't. I just let it unfold on its own. My eyes float shut as Marco moves in toward my mouth. I can smell his clean skin as his lips gently press against the side of my face, and, then, with soft, nip-like little kisses, he finds my mouth. His lips feel soft and smooth. I allow myself to literally drift into his being as he pulls my mouth into his. A thunderous roar shakes the room, and I can't be sure if it's just a plane taking off or if it's actually me letting go and letting Marco carry me away.

When Marco and I reenter the main concourse, we still have about 45 minutes left until our show time. So we decide to get something to eat in the cafeteria near our gate. I don't know if I'm even all that hungry—and, quite frankly, I think I could have just stayed in that observatory forever and survived quite nicely on Marco's kisses. But practicality ruled, and Marco suggested food, so here we are, at the cafeteria with the clean tables and starched white napkins.

As I slide a cup of steaming hot beef stew, a buttery dinner roll and a tall glass of ice water off of my tray, I realize that maybe I am hungry after all. I watch as Marco arranges his food on the table—roasted red potatoes and a thick slab of roast beef along with a crispy green salad and a cup of some sort of fruit strudel for dessert. Now I sort of wish I had been paying more attention to the selections. But my mind is off kilter, and I think I might still be walking on air. Our first kiss was beyond magical, and just recalling it makes me quiver!

I take a spoonful of the hot stew, and the flavors bring me back to reality. It is perfectly salty and thick, and I'm so grateful that we decided to eat! I watch Marco as he digs into his potatoes. He looks up at me with a smile. I swoon at him and take another bite of my stew. I feel so happy right now—so very happy!

"I understand that you were chosen to take over for the injured flight attendant on Crew 1," Marco says between bites. His face tells me that now he fully understands why I was so concerned about his relationship with Miriam.

"Yep…" I trail off as I think about the fact that I have to get up at 4:00 a.m. tomorrow *and* Sunday morning, *plus* fly the evening routes! I do my best to push the thought of it out of my mind so I can stay in this moment, but I'm sure my face is reflecting my annoyance over the whole situation.

"I wish there was something I could do, Eloise-ah," Marco says apologetically.

"It's OK, Marco," I quickly reply. "And besides, I think anything *you* try to do will only upset Miriam even more, and who knows what will happen then!" I smile at Marco in an effort to let him know that I'm fine with everything.

"Well, I need to make it up to you!" Marco says brightly.

After giving it some thought, I playfully respond, "You know what? You're right! You *do* need to make it up to me!"

Marco just smiles at me for a moment. I beam back at him, feeling flushed and incredibly happy to be swallowed up by his presence. I can tell that his mind is whirling and plotting, and it makes me giggle when I think of all the things that Marco Maselli seems capable of doing.

"I *will*," Marco promises as he reaches across the table and takes my hand. "And you can be sure that I will spoil you and treat you like a queen!"

I stop to absorb his words for a second. My first reaction is to protest and tell him that it's unnecessary to spoil me, but then a new idea pops into my head. Maybe it *is* necessary! So I just smile at Marco with a raised eyebrow, and we both start laughing.

Chapter Nineteen

In between all the kissing, flirting and eating, Marco and I do manage to discuss the subject of how we should handle our relationship in front of the others. I was quick to point out that Miriam is already seriously upset, and I don't really trust the members of our crew to keep things quiet. As of right now, I'm working my tail off this weekend because Miriam is punishing me, and I don't put it past her to keep on punishing me—especially if she learns from the others that Marco and I are enjoying ourselves too much while we're working. So we decide to keep things on the down low. I plan to work in the aft galley when Marco and I are flying together, and we agree that we should always do our layovers with the rest of the crew.

So with all that settled, we decide it would be best for us to split off and arrive at the gate separately. Marco takes it upon himself to go first—he has to check the weather and do some other captain-like things, and I need a minute to compose myself. But just before he leaves, Marco leans across the table and gives me a seductive peck behind my ear. Then he rises up from his seat and heads off toward the gate. I watch as he confidently walks out of the cafeteria and strides down the concourse.

I'm overwhelmed with my feelings of attraction for this man, and for the first time since we met, I'm completely willing to believe that I really am *Marco's Eloise*. We belong to each other now, and I have never been so happy! This is the first time I've ever felt this way, and I want to savor every moment. I absently reach up and touch the place on my neck where he just kissed me, and shivers race down my spine.

I dig around in my bag and take out my tinted lip balm and give my lips a fresh coat before I gather up my things and get ready to join the others. I rework my hair into my standard up-do for flying and straighten my skirt when I stand up. Then I pull in a deep breath and slide my carryon bag over my shoulder. Even though I'm not walking next to Marco at the moment, I still feel as though I'm floating on air! I don't recall ever feeling so tingly and alive inside.

As I approach the gate area, I can see Marco out of the corner of my eye. He is leaning against the podium, talking to the gate agent—who is a thick German woman in her late 40's. I happen to notice that she's beaming at Marco as he flirts with her. A tiny twinge of concern comes over me, but I decide to let it go. I'm beginning to understand that Marco is just a flirtatious guy, and I'm going to have to get used to it if we're going to make this thing work. I do my best to shake it off and keep my focus set on all of my fellow flight attendants seated in the gate area.

Scott and Bobbi are sitting near the boarding door, and Scott is shifted in his seat so that his back is toward me. A rush of remorse washes over me as I realize that I can't go over and sit next to Scott right now. I pretty much ended that privilege a couple of hours ago, and I'm still wondering how I'm going to be able to survive without my best friend. It's practically automatic for me to hang out with him, so I have to make a conscious effort to steer clear of him as I enter the gate area.

Luckily, Marta is sitting off to the side in a row of seats that faces outward, toward the concourse walkway. She is sitting very still, with a paperback novel resting in her lap, but staring off into the distance. As I approach her, I see that she is deep in thought, so I stop short and quietly wait for her to notice me.

"Oh... Hi, Elle," Marta finally says as she reenters the present.

"Hey. Are you OK?" I ask tentatively.

"No... I'm not," she says in a deep, husky voice. Her whole body seems still, but I can see something wild smoldering in her eyes as she looks up at me and continues. "I just tried to call Oscar on his cell phone—it's like 3:30 in the afternoon in Miami right now, so I figured I'd catch him while he's still working. The only problem is, some *woman* answered his phone instead..." Marta's voice trails off into a whisper as she tries to stop herself from crying.

"Oh no!" I blurt out in disbelief. "Are you sure you dialed the right number?" I ask, wanting to make sure that Marta considered all of the possibilities before jumping to conclusions.

"Oh I'm sure," she says bitterly. "I could hear *Oscar* in the background asking the woman that answered his phone to tell him who was calling and then laughing when she said she didn't know. Then, when I tried to call him back, Oscar had turned off his phone." I can tell she's doing her best to hold back her tears, and I feel my nerves igniting as I try to think of what to do to help her.

I drop my carryon bag on the floor and slide into the seat next to Marta. I do my best to use my body to block Marta from the rest of the crew seated on the far side of the gate area. I'm careful not to touch her as she breaths in and out, trying to regain her composure.

"I don't think it was Michelle," Marta continues in a low whisper as she stares intently at a random spot on the floor. "It didn't *sound* like her anyway. And besides, Miriam said that Michelle left this afternoon and was stopping at our new base in Paris before she heads back to Miami," Marta looks at me now and leans in close as she continues. "So on our layover, I checked to see if I could find out which flight she was on. The main gate agent said that Michelle didn't take a direct flight from Florence and isn't due to land in Paris until tomorrow."

"Did the gate agent mention where Michelle is laying over?" I ask, hoping that if we have all the information, Marta can somehow put her mind at ease.

"She started to get a little suspicious about my snooping around, so I didn't want to push my luck," Marta admits as she pulls in a tiny sniffle.

"Oh Marta…" I don't know what else to say. I can't even begin to understand how she must be feeling, and there is really no appropriate response to offer. The two of us just sit there in dazed silence.

"So not only is my husband cheating on *me*; apparently, he's also cheating on *Michelle*," Marta concludes acidly. "That's just perfect!" she practically spits as tears start to rush down her cheeks.

"Elle! Marta! Come on!" comes a voice from behind us. As I look over my shoulder, I see Suzanne Keller standing just outside the boarding door waving her arms wildly at us in an effort to hurry us along. It looks as though everyone else is already on board, and we are the last three crewmembers in the waiting area.

"We better go," I say to Marta as I scoop up my carryon bag and quickly sling it over my shoulder.

I watch as Marta wipes the tears off her cheeks and straightens her skirt. Then she shoves her novel into one of the deep side pockets of her bag, runs her fingers through her hair, and rises up from her seat and falls into stride beside me as we make our way toward the boarding door.

"Are you going to be OK?" I whisper to her as we rush toward the boarding door.

"I'll have to be," she says with a final sniffle.

The German gate agent that was flirting with Marco is holding the door open for us, and she looks annoyed. I try to get a good look at her as I pass by. I can see from her nametag that they call her Elsa. She is about three inches taller than me and has thick blonde hair pulled back with tiny-jeweled bobby pins on both sides. She glares directly at me as the three of us enter through the doorway, and I feel slightly nervous when she starts scolding me in German for being late.

Once we enter the Jetway, Elsa slams the heavy boarding door and engages the alarm. I feel a skittle of nerves racing around in my stomach for no real reason other than the fact that I hate being scolded, and it seems like Elsa is making this rather personal.

Neither Marta nor Suzanne seems too concerned with the whole exchange, so I do my best to shrug it off and act casual as we make our way down the ramp toward the plane. As we round the final corner, I'm startled to see Marco entering the Jetway and heading for the ramp door. His hair is swept back and sexy, and I feel myself go all wobbly inside at the sight of my man. When he sees me, he doesn't even try to hide his feelings as his face washes over with big grin.

"*Buonasera*," Marco says as he turns his body toward us and leans his back against the ramp doorway. Then he trains his eyes on me and gives me a little wink.

"*Buonasera*, Captain Maselli," Suzanne says with great formality as the three of us slow to watch him step onto the metal staircase just outside the door to complete his final walk-around.

My heartbeat is thick and steady, and I feel so silly for reacting this way, but I can't seem to help myself. I'm so completely infatuated with this man, and even the subtlest gesture from him has the potential to turn me into a giddy idiot! I feel my face go flush, and I will myself to return to normal, but it's no use. I'm too happy!

"So, Elle..." Suzanne begins as we make our way onto the plane. "Where were *you* during our layover?" There's a trace of playful sarcasm in her tone as she raises an eyebrow and waits for me to answer.

"Um..." I stammer around, in search of something good to say. "Around..." I trail off, not sure how else to handle the details of my layover. But I can't seem to stifle the smile on my face as I avert my focus from Suzanne and start making my way toward the aft galley.

"I see," Suzanne says, smiling to herself and shaking her head.

Marta and I both manage to stay completely focused on our work during the return trip to Florence. I decide not to press her with questions about Oscar and who she thinks the other woman might be—even though my mind is filled with wild ideas of my own. And for whatever reason, Marta doesn't ask me anything about what happened with Scott, or what I did with Marco on the layover. It seems like we're both willing to throw ourselves into our work in order to avoid getting too personal right now.

But for me, all it takes is a single recollection of kissing Marco in the observatory, and I'm all in my head anyway. I feel myself slipping away from reality from time to time to think of how it felt to be in Marco's embrace. I'm sure Marta notices that I'm slightly distracted, but she's good enough not to mention it. I sort of want to tell her how I'm feeling and give her some of the details about my layover, but all things considered, I decide against it. It just doesn't feel right for me to be so happy when Marta is obviously reeling inside over the latest situation with Oscar.

When we finally land in Florence, it's after midnight. Marta and I are the last two crewmembers to step off the plane, and we scramble to catch up with the others as they make their way onto the crew van. As I look around, I feel a flash of disappointment that I missed Marco, but in truth, I also feel relieved. Scott is seated in the far back of the van, and, as I climb aboard, our eyes briefly meet. He gives me a weak smile and quickly looks away. As I shift my body and slide into my seat, a bittersweet feeling consumes me as I think about what I've given up to gain Marco.

I unlock the door to my villa and dread washes over me as I realize that in less the four hours, I'll be heading back out for the morning flight. Apparently, Miriam has found a loophole in the system that makes it "legal" for me to fly with less than eight hours off. European flight attendant regulations are quite different from American standards, and, as long as I have *some* time off, Miriam can legitimately work me. Although I'm quite certain that my flight schedule for this weekend isn't actually permissible, even by European standards, I don't have the energy to fight it, and I'm determined to make the best of a bad situation.

The glow from the hood light over the stovetop gives me just enough light to keep me from tripping on my way into my villa. I manage to toss my carryon bag into the overstuffed chair to the left of the door and kick off my shoes all in one spastic motion. I'm just about to turn around to shut and lock the door behind me when I feel a gentle touch on my shoulder. My body seizes up as a catch a whiff of the citrus cologne.

When I turn around, Marco is standing in the doorway. He's still wearing his uniform, but his tie is loosened around his neck, and his jacket is wide open. I take a step forward and fall into his arms. He kisses me on the top of the head, and I pull in a deep, delicious breath. I feel myself relax into his warm body, and all I can think of is how happy I am.

"*Eloise-ah...*" Marco says as he exhales, his voice thick and rich like velvet.

Gently, Marco takes me by the shoulders and pushes me so that he can see my face. As I look up at him, I literally feel dizzy with desire. Everything about him is perfect, and I want to stay glued to his side for the rest of my life. He takes his hand and reaches up and rests his fingers in the nape of my neck.

"What am I going to do with you?" he asks me with a playful look in his eye. "You have taken me by surprise, *my Eloise-ah*," he says as he rests his forehead against mine. I look up into his eyes, and I do my best to stay steady.

On impulse, I rise up on my tiptoes and press my lips against his. My eyes float shut, and my mind begins to swirl as Marco pulls me in close to him and wraps his arms around me with longing. The kiss is deep and soft and the most magical one yet. I can feel my body shudder as Marco runs his hand down my back and presses it into the small of my back.

When we pull apart, I catch a look in Marco's eye that takes my breath away. I can see more than desire in those caramel-colored eyes—he looks ravenous! Suddenly, I don't know what to do. I think things may be escalating faster than I can handle, and, as Marco starts to step into my villa, I feel panic overtaking me.

"Marco!" I say in alarm, rattling us both into a sober moment.

I can't seem to steady my nerves, and I feel like a frightened little animal that is in way over her head. I'm confused and completely unsure of myself. I love the kissing and the holding, but I don't know if that's going to be enough for Marco.

Marco stops just inside the doorway and looks at me with concern. I stammer to try to find the words to smooth things over. I don't want to ruin the moment, but I know that I have to be decisive.

"Sorry…" I fumble to find my words. "I'm just…" I trail off, not sure what to say.

"It's alright," Marco says as he steps closer to me, his face alight with a smile. He looks normal now, and I feel myself relax as he approaches me. "You need your rest."

He takes my hand in his and gives it a kiss. He looks at me with a sweet smile on his face and whispers, "*Buona Notte.*"

I watch with a mixture of sadness and relief as Marco turns on his heel and slips out of my villa, gently closing the door behind him.

I lug my carryon bag down the dimly lit cobbled walkway toward the front gate of the resort. It's 4:45 a.m., and my feet are sore and tired, and my eyes sting from lack of sleep. That was by far the shortest night's sleep ever. I had so much adrenaline pumping through my body from the intense moments with Marco that it took me ages to finally fall asleep. Plus, I couldn't stop thinking about Marco and the way he overtakes me with his presence. My whole body is feeling things for Marco that I've never really felt before, and, quite frankly, it scares me.

The crew van is waiting in the driveway when I arrive, so I take a deep breath and climb aboard. So far, there are only three people inside—Peter Jameson, Nina Harrison and a girl we all call Pocahontas—who's real name is Jenna Raymond, but she looks just like a dainty Indian girl with long, shiny, black hair and coppery brown skin. We all sort of mumble sleepy hellos as I settle into the last row of seats. Peter reaches over and kneads my shoulder with his hand and gives me a weary, sympathetic smile.

"She's got you working your little bum off, doesn't she?" Peter remarks in a low whisper. I nod my head and smile weakly as I work to rid my nose of the stench of his sour coffee breath.

"For what it's worth, we're glad to have you with us," Pocahontas says over her shoulder as she stifles a yawn.

"Thanks, Pocha," I say in response.

"So did you hear about the weather back home?" Peter asks no one in particular.

"No," I manage to grunt as the three of us all train our attention on Peter.

"I guess the tropical storm they were expecting in Miami turned into a Category 1 hurricane," Peter says with authority. "Luckily, it took a turn and hit somewhere north of us—near Jacksonville, I think. I talked to my sister, and she said they got loads of rain in Miami."

Instantly, my thoughts turn to my family—specifically Sugar Ray. I sure hope that Violet was able to keep my boy safe from all the heavy winds and rain. He hates bad weather, and, right now, all I can think of is how much I miss him.

"My sister said there's another storm brewing out in the Atlantic, and so people are pretty much bracing for the worst this hurricane season," Peter adds before the van door swings open.

I drift off into my thoughts as the rest of the crew climbs into the van. I think about my dad—the hurricane tracker extraordinaire—and my mom—who worries so much whenever these storms approach. Right now, I couldn't feel further from my home. A homesick feeling washes over me as I try to remember who I am and how I got here. Between the lack of sleep and my longing for Sugar Ray, I feel as though I could cry. I do my best to pull myself together before anyone can notice, but Peter seems to have picked up on my emotions.

"You OK?" he whispers to me, blasting me with another hit of his hideous breath.

"Yep," I say as I hold my breath. "Just tired," I add for believability.

I manage to make it through the morning flight to Madrid with no real issues. Peter and I work together in the aft galley, and, despite being incredibly tired, I manage to have a good time. He and Sebastian—whom he calls *Bass*—can be kind of over the top for me sometimes, but one-on-one, Peter is actually pretty great. And once I got a stick of gum in his mouth, his close-talking ways didn't even bother me.

It's bright and sunny when the crew van drops us off at *Il Girasole* around 2:30, and everyone from Crew 1 is headed for the pool to unwind. But not me—I only have a short window of time before I have to leave with Crew 2 for the evening flight, and I need to try to catch a power nap.

As I make my way down the cobbled pathway to my villa, I freeze mid-step. Up ahead, I see Scott walking toward me. He and Sebastian are walking together, and it looks like they've been at the pool all day. Scott's skin is glossy and brown, and, when he sees me, his smile fades slightly. I give him a little wave, and he waves back.

"Elle, have you seen Pete?" Sebastian asks when he sees me.

"Yeah, he went to his villa," I reply, but I can't take my eyes off of Scott.

"Thanks!" Sebastian says as he takes off toward Peter's villa. "See you guys in the van," he hollers over his shoulder.

Scott watches Sebastian as he dashes around a corner. His face looks sad, and I sense that he's uncomfortable being alone with me.

"Did you have a good day?" I ask Scott, hoping to ease the tension between us.

"I did," he says as he looks down at his feet. "How 'bout you?" he asks without looking at me.

"It wasn't bad," I say, trying to stay positive. "I'm kind of tired though," I add with a nervous giggle.

"I bet," Scott says with a sigh.

I just stand there as this awkward chasm builds between us. How strange it is to try to make small talk with my best friend! Scott looks hurt and confused, and I don't know what to do to fix it, so I don't do anything.

"See you later," Scott finally says as he starts walking toward his villa.

"OK," I whisper as a lump of sadness wells up inside of my throat. Scott lightly brushes my shoulder as he passes by me on the cobbled walkway, and I almost reach out and grab his arm. But I don't. I just stand there and feel his absence increasing as the sound of his footfalls grows fainter and fainter.

I start walking toward my villa, feeling so alone and confused. Why does this have to be so complicated? As I reach the steps leading up to my villa, I'm not at all surprised to see Marco sitting in the bistro chair on my porch. Suddenly, my gloom and confusion lifts, and a smile works its way onto my face.

Marco is wearing a pair of faded jeans, a light blue T-shirt, dark sunglasses and a pair of leather sandals. He appears to be reading a magazine, but, as I approach, he closes the magazine and flashes me a huge grin.

"I thought we were going to be keeping things on the *down low*!" I chide him in a harsh but mocking whisper. "What if Miriam sees you on my porch?" I say, only partially scolding him for his indiscretion.

"I had to see you," he simply responds as he stands up, pushes his sunglasses onto the top of his head and reaches for my hand to guide me up the steps. "I'm not flying with you tonight, and I *had to see you*,"' he repeats.

"Well, when you put it that way…" I say as a silly smirk spreads across my face. "But let's get inside," I say as I drop his hand and rush toward the door.

Once we're inside, I take a few moments to freshen up. I brush my teeth, wash my face and put on another coat of deodorant. Suddenly, I'm not the least bit tired! When I step out of the bathroom, I see that Marco is barefoot in the kitchen pouring two glasses of chilled water. He looks up and smiles at me as I enter the room.

"Feeling better?" he asks.

"Much," I reply as he hands me a glass of water.

"Come," Marco says as he leads me from the kitchen into my bedroom.

My heart starts to pound with a heavy thud as I watch Marco set his glass of water on the bedside table and, then, begin removing all of the throw pillows from the bed with care.

We are about to stretch out on my bed! I think as a cascade of nerves riffle through my body.

"I'm impressed that you made your bed," Marco remarks with a silly grin.

I just smile and let out a nervous giggle. Despite the fact that I only gave myself 20 minutes to get ready for my flight this morning, I still managed to make my bed before I left my villa. Probably not a priority for most people, but it's just who I am. I'm not sure if Marco is poking fun at me or truly impressed. I decide it doesn't really matter as I watch him rolling onto the bed and reaching for me to join him.

I set my glass of water next to his and take a step in closer to the bed. I manage to kick off my shoes before Marco gently pulls me into his arms.

In one gloriously graceful motion, my body is lengthwise next to his, and my face is within inches of his yummy lips.

"Hi," I whisper as I feel my body relax.

"*Ciao*," he whispers in return. Then he closes his eyes and moves in to kiss me.

Chapter Twenty

The past two-and-a-half days are nothing but a blur to me as I make my way to the crew van for my final flight sequence of the weekend. I've averaged about two to three hours of legitimate sleep each day, and between the lack of rest and the adrenaline rush of falling hard for Marco, my body is jittery and unstable. But I only have the flights to Paris and back remaining, and then I have four glorious days off. I try to bolster myself with this thought as I climb aboard the crew van for the ninth time in three days.

With my head leaning against the window of the van, I work hard to fight off sleep. Marta is seated next to me, and the rest of the crew is climbing into the van. Everyone except for Marta and me seems to be in a jovial mood, but I'm simply too tired to join in all the fun. And despite the fact that my beloved Marco is our captain on this sequence, I'm all tapped out in the energy department. I've already blown through my second, third, fourth *and* fifth winds, and there just isn't anything left.

"Elle Butts!" blasts a familiar raspy voice from the doorway of the van. My body jolts upright, and, suddenly, an unexpected sixth wind blows through my system, and I'm as alert as I can be. Miriam is glaring at me, and I can feel myself quivering in my seat. "No sleeping!" she shouts.

My face starts to redden as anger begins to boil in my stomach. I can't stand the sight of Miriam Ungaro as she leans her shapeless body into the threshold of the van door. Marta gently places her hand on my knee and gives me a little squeeze. I pull in a deep breath to try to calm my nerves, but it's safe to say, I'm more than just a little frazzled.

"Listen up people," Miriam continues sourly as she peers into the van for a better view of the rest of the crew. "As you know, we're going to begin training our permanent flight attendants based here in Florence this week, so you can expect to see our trainees shadowing you on upcoming flights. This means that they'll be watching and learning *from you*, and I won't tolerate a bad example."

Miriam shifts her weight from one foot to the other and launches into the rest of her speech.

"So tonight, you will have the *pleasure* of my company on board the flight to Paris and back, so that I can do a thorough spot check of your procedures and protocol. I expect to see five-star service from you people, and, if I *don't*, there will be consequences—of that you can be sure."

A sober hush falls over the crew, and I'm sure we're all thinking the same thing: *This flight is gonna be hell.*

Marta and I quietly set to work in the aft galley, preparing the beverage cart for the first leg of our trip, and we do our level best to follow every rule. So far, Miriam hasn't been back to check on us, but it's only a matter of time. On our last flight together, Marta was positioned in the mid-cabin so we haven't had a chance to reconnect, and I am incredibly curious about how she's doing. But with Miriam on board, I'm not sure I should say anything. In the end, my curiosity wins out, and after taking a quick look into the cabin to make sure no one is there, I clear my throat and ask Marta my first question of the day.

"So how are you doing?" I ask in a soft, concerned voice.

Marta looks up from her work, and I can see deep sorrow in her eyes. She looks tired and frail, and I'm not sure if she's going to answer my question with words, or if I should draw my own conclusions about her well-being from her dull expression.

"He called me," she finally says after much deliberation. "When I got back to my room on Friday night, he'd left a message." Marta's voice is hoarse and weary, and I stop moving the cans around in the top drawer on my side of the beverage cart and give her my full attention.

"What did he say on the message?" I ask, doing my best to gently prompt the story out of her.

"Just that he missed me so much and that he was sorry he missed all my calls. Then he said that Mr. Bennett sent him to *Greece* unexpectedly, and his cell phone doesn't work very well over there," she says flatly as she turns her attention to a baggie filled with lime wedges from the catering box.

I watch as she pulls the baggie open and dumps the wedges into a plastic cup and pulls the baggie over the top of the cup. She opens her top beverage drawer and rearranges a few cans and shoves the cup into the space. When she looks back up at me, she seems quite angry.

"So I guess you're not buying it..." I trail off, not sure if I should be commenting on the situation.

"Oh, I'm sure he was in Greece, but the fact that his cell doesn't work well over there and that he had no time to call me to let me know where he was going is another story," she replies tersely as she shoves the top drawer shut with her hip. "At least now I know where Michelle was headed before she went to Paris," she adds.

An awkward silence fills the galley. I don't have the energy to sort out all of the details, but Marta is ice cold on the subject of her unfaithful husband, and it really doesn't seem like she wants to discuss it further. So I slide the ice buckets into an open compartment on the beverage cart and then help Marta glide the cart into the storage bay and lock the wheel catches. I look around the galley to make sure we didn't miss anything and then confirm that all of the bins on the galley wall are properly locked and secured for take off.

When the aft galley intercom starts binging, Marta looks up and then slides past me so she can grab the receiver mounted on the wall. She seems rather eager to answer the call, so I step back and watch her as she brings the receiver to her ear.

"Aft galley, Marta speaking," she says pleasantly as she rolls her eyes at me. This is the way Miriam expects us to answer the intercom system—

which no one ever does—so I feel a wash of relief spilling over me that Marta answered the phone.

"Yes…" Marta says as she listens intently to the voice on the other end of the line. "I'll be right up," she concludes with a friendly tone that doesn't fit her expression.

"Miriam wants me to work the mid-cabin door during boarding," Marta informs me as an irritated look overtakes her face. "She says that Enrique is 'critiquing' Scott and Sebastian on their first-class pre-flight service protocols, so he can't do the greeting."

We both pull annoyed faces at this news, and I breathe a selfish sigh of relief that Miriam is picking on Enrique right now instead of me. Marta slips off her apron and hands it to me before she leaves the galley. I just smile at her as I carefully fold her apron and place it on the food prep counter. As I watch Marta make her way down the aisle toward the mid-cabin door, the aft galley intercom starts binging again, and this time, I'm prepared to answer it properly.

"Aft galley, this is Elle," I say in my most pleasant voice.

"It's just me," says a female voice on the other end of the line. I have to rewind the voice in my head a few times before I realize that it's Bobbi. "She's on her way back to the aft galley. She just stepped off the plane for a minute to let the gate agent know we're ready to board, but I wanted to let you know before she got to you."

"OK…" I say into the receiver as panic starts to race through my body. "Thanks for the heads up, Bobbi!"

"Sure thing, Cutie. Hey, are you gonna be OK?" she asks in her motherly voice before she hangs up.

"I hope so…" I say with a quiver in my voice before I hang the receiver on the hook.

I look around the galley to make sure everything is perfect. I grab a handful of paper towels from the lavatory and run some water over a few, so I can wash and dry the outside of the bins and the front of the beverage and meal service carts. My mind is swirling as I bump around the galley, trying to cover every detail and doing my best to remember all of the things that

Miriam will be looking for. I complete my work and shove the used paper towels in the garbage chute just as Miriam enters the galley.

"Elle Butts," Miriam says with a smirk. "How are things going in the *aft galley?*" Her tone is patronizing and miserable, and I do my best to stay pleasant and polite.

"Very well," I say with a hint of a smile on my face.

I notice that Miriam is dressed up more than usual this evening. She's wearing a pair of loose-fitting black trousers with a wide leg and a purple knit sweater that hangs low around her hips. The scoop neck of the sweater dips down across the cleft in her cleavage, and a tiny diamond pendant suspended from a thin gold chain wobbles around in the valley of her shriveled boobs when she moves. From her pointy-toed shoes to her over-coiffed hair, Miriam looks as though she's trying to work it, and I can't help but wonder if her choice of clothing has anything to do with the fact that Marco is working this flight.

Miriam looks at all of the bins and checks the wheel locks on the beverage cart. Then she leans against the food prep counter and looks directly at me. Her stare is intense, and I don't know what to do. So I uncross my arms and tuck my hands into my apron pocket and wait for her next comment.

"Elle," she begins with a weary sigh. "Do we wear our *aprons* during boarding?" Her tone is filled with venom, and I feel the sting of her words as I instantly recognize my first mistake of the day.

"No ma'am, we most certainly do not," I say quickly. I notice Miriam blanche when I say the word "ma'am," and I instantly regret saying it. I guess that's going to be my second mistake of the day.

Miriam pulls in a deep breath as she sizes me up. I'm doing my best to remove my apron quickly, all the while trying to make sure that my blouse doesn't come untucked in the process.

"You know, Elle, we've had a few complaints about you this weekend," Miriam begins frostily. "Elsa, the German gate agent, said that you were late and nearly held up the boarding process in Munich on Friday. And several of the other flight attendants on *this* crew are concerned that your head is…*in the clouds,* so to speak."

I look up at Miriam with a furrowed brow as I try to figure out which flight attendants would complain about me. I can't say I'm terribly surprised about the Elsa comment—I knew she was singling me out with her guttural scolding! But who else would say something negative about me to Miriam?

"You look confused—like maybe you're wondering which one of your fellow crew members is unhappy with you right now," Miriam says in a mocking voice. "I guess it might come as a shock to you that one such complaint comes directly from your formerly true blue buddy, *Scott LaMotte.* Apparently, he's unimpressed with your work ethic and your *loyalty*...to the company," she says as she trains her eyes directly on me.

"Scott?" I say as the shock of her words sink in.

Scott is complaining about me to Miriam? My whole body goes numb as I consider the validity her words. As I stand there in front of her, I'm pretty sure that all the color has drained from my face. I can feel the prick of hot tears behind my eyes, and I pull in a sharp breath and pray that I can keep it together.

"Yes. It seems that he feels like you aren't able to...*focus* on your work," she confirms as a nasty smile stretches across her face. "And Scott *is* one of our finest flight attendants, and if *he's* concerned about you, well, I need to take note."

I just stare up at Miriam, completely dumbfounded. Normally, I wouldn't believe a word she was saying about Scott, but under the circumstances, maybe he really is unhappy with me. Maybe he isn't even my friend at all anymore. I steel myself against that thought and do my best to stay composed as Miriam continues.

"The bottom line is, I simply can't have you around my trainees, Elle. It's not good for *Windsong Air* or our image. So here's what I'm going to do," she says as she pulls a slip of paper out of her trouser pocket. "I'm going to permanently move you to Crew 1, and Lupe's replacement will fly in your position on Crew 2. Since I will be setting up my trainees to shadow only on the evening flights, I can prevent them from being exposed to your...*slack ways*. And once we return to Miami, I can deal with you more...*appropriately*."

Miriam hands me the slip of paper, which is a yellow carbon copy with the *Windsong Air* corporate insignia on top. It's a standard document that we use whenever we swap a trip with another flight attendant, and, as I hold the slip in my hand, I can see that Miriam already filed the change order with crew scheduling in Miami.

"So next weekend, you'll officially be on the early crew," Miriam says with a spiteful smile. "Oh, and, by the way, you should be sure to thank Marta when she returns to the aft galley—she's done a *marvelous* job cleaning and securing this area for take off," she adds before she turns on her heel and exits the galley.

I can't move. I feel completely frozen. Even my mind can't work out the details of this exchange with Miriam. How could Scott betray me like this? It's just too much for me to take in. I can hear the sound of Miriam working her way down the aisle toward the front of the plane, doing her best to casually slip by the boarding passengers with a forced politeness. Once I'm sure she's gone, I duck into the aft lavatory, and the tears instantly start streaming down my face.

When we land in Paris, my mind is raw from thinking too much. I didn't want to tell Marta about my conversation with Miriam because I'm pretty sure if I try to talk about it, I'll end up crying. So I just kept to myself during the flight and did my best not to mess up during the service. And the truth is, I don't think Marta even noticed me anyway—she seemed to be gnawing on her own thoughts, and I can't really blame her for not wanting to open up while we're working.

As usual, Marta and I are the last two people to deplane, and as we lumber up the Jetway, the Paris maintenance crew pushes past us with all of their cleaning supplies in tow. I wish I could just curl up in one of the first class seats and take a quick nap, but, obviously, that's not going to happen. So I hold the flimsy handrail inside the Jetway and pull myself up the ramp and toward the open door.

I'm feeling nervous about catching up with the rest of our crew during this layover, especially since Miriam said that "several" people were complaining about me. I try to tell myself that it's just Miriam making things up in an effort to punish me over Marco, but I can't totally be sure. Scott can't even look at me anymore, and every time I come near him, he turns and walks the other way. He and Sebastian are spending all their time together, and, now, even Sebastian seems to be avoiding me.

Plus, I don't know how I'm supposed to act around Marco with all of this stuff going on. I secretly want him to wait for me in the gate area, so we can spend our layover together, but I don't think that's a good idea. It would be best for us both if we completely limited our contact on this sequence—especially with Miriam lurking about. I hope he just went on to the pilot's lounge, so I don't have to act like I don't notice him when I'm with the rest of the crew.

As we enter the actual boarding area, a frosty blast of air blows over us, and it takes me a second to adjust. Then, with no warning, Marta grabs my arm and stops abruptly. I look over at her face and I see an expression of shock mixed with joy and confusion. When I follow her gaze up ahead, I think the same expression washes across my own face.

"Marta!" Oscar shouts as he rushes toward his wife with outstretched arms.

"Oscar?" Marta gasps as she blinks her eyes in disbelief.

From where I'm standing, I can see that she's trembling at the sight of her husband bounding toward her. As soon as he reaches her, Oscar scoops tiny Marta up into his arms and swings her around like a rag doll. She weakly wraps her arms around his shoulders as he covers the side of her face with kisses. I watch in disbelief as Marta struggles to keep her composure. Oscar begins speaking to her in Spanish—all the while nuzzling her neck and smiling from ear to ear.

When Oscar finally puts Marta down, I can hear her ask, "Oscar, what are you doing here?" Her face is flushed, and I can't tell for sure if she's happy to see him or not. Her body language is taut and restricted, and I watch her shift in place trying to sort out the details in her mind.

"I couldn't bare to be away from you, so I came to surprise you!'" Oscar says as he catches his breath and continues beaming at his wife. "And judging by the look on your face, I've done it!" he laughs as he pulls Marta into his arms and kisses the top of her head.

I start to feel uncomfortable just standing there, gawking at them as they reunite, so I quietly step aside to give them some privacy. Up ahead, I can see Enrique and Suzanne ordering drinks at a nearby coffee stand. I realize that I could use a cup of something hot, so I head in their direction, leaving Marta and Oscar alone in the boarding area.

"Hey Elle," Enrique says as I approach. "How you holding up?" he asks after he gives me a little hug.

"I'll be fine once we finish this last leg," I say, not meaning to be so sour, but unable to restrain myself.

"It's weird to see Oscar DeSoto here," Suzanne remarks as she flicks a packet of artificial sweetener with her finger and then adds it to her coffee. "I heard he was sleeping with Michelle Maddox and that he and Marta were over," she says non-chalantly.

I follow Suzanne's gaze and see Marta and Oscar sitting in the boarding area. Oscar is cooing something into Marta's ear, and her face is lit up with happiness. I can't help but feel sad as I consider Suzanne's comment. Even though right now she looks so happy, Marta would be crushed if she knew that people were talking about her husband and Michelle.

"Well, judging from all the PDA going on over there, it was either a false rumor or *somebody has a guilty conscience*," Enrique says in a singsong voice as if he is an expert on these matters.

"I think we're looking at a guilty conscience for sure," Suzanne says to Enrique, and he nods his head in agreement. "I'm just surprised that Marta looks so happy to see him," she adds in a hushed tone.

As I make my way to the front of the line at the coffee stand, I feel rather edgy. I'm so tired and ruffled from all the personal dramas swirling around me that I can't seem to find my center. I order a hot herbal tea and watch as the young clerk fills a small, Styrofoam cup with steaming water.

"So how did it go up front with Miriam?" I ask Enrique over my shoulder as I wait for the clerk to hand me my tea. I'm shocked that I just brought up the subject of Miriam, but I can't think of anything else to ask at the moment, and, as Marta's friend, I feel compelled to change the subject.

"Oh God," Enrique gushes. "It was awful! She had me *judging* Scott and Bass on their service techniques! And I swear, I couldn't find anything either of them did wrong, but it was like Miriam was testing me and expecting me to *find* something!" Enrique dramatically takes a sip of his coffee as he and Suzanne wait for me to pay for my tea. "It was *completely* awful," he adds.

"Wow," I remark, trying to show some empathy for Enrique.

"Luckily, she pretty much vanished during the flight," Suzanne says after I join them at the condiment counter and look for a lid for my tea. "We were all pretty relieved that she seemed so focused on the pilots after take off because trying to brace ourselves for her visit to the mid-galley, and not knowing when she'd surface, was very unsettling."

The three of us walk to the dining area and then huddle around a table near the coffee stand. I can feel my face start to redden from Suzanne's remark about the pilots, so I keep my head tilted low, as if there is something really interesting on the lid of my cup.

"Yeah," Enrique adds. "She spent most of the flight up in the cockpit making sure *Captain Maselli* was comfortable."

Anger spills into my system as I picture Miriam trying to move in on my man. I boil inside as I think about how coniving and rotten she is. Then my mind shifts to thoughts of Marco, and I start to wonder where he is right now. I thought I didn't want to see him in the boarding area or in the crew lounge, but now I just wish I knew where he was! Jealousy grips my heart as I wonder if Marco sneaked off with Miriam for some private time with her on this layover.

"Elle," Suzanne tentatively begins as she rattles me out of my thoughts. "What's going on with you and Captain Maselli?" she asks with her eyebrows scrunched together. I notice Enrique sliding forward in his seat to involve himself more directly in the conversation.

"Nothing…" I sheepishly admit. "I mean, I've gone on a date with him if that's what you're asking about…" I trail off, worried that I have said too much.

"That's what we've heard, but I just wanted to make sure—you know how unreliable rumors can be," Suzanne says as she looks back over toward the boarding gate. I follow her gaze and notice that Marta and Oscar have disappeared.

"So is that why Miriam is all over you?" Enrique asks, always a fan of romance and drama—especially when it involves someone else.

"I guess so," I say as I pull off the lid on my drink and stare down into the Styrofoam cup. "Miriam and Marco were friends during his training in Miami, and I think she is kind of… *possessive* of him now," I add, feeling the need to at least clarify a few things.

"Ewww!" Enrique interjects. "I'm sorry, but Miriam Ungaro is just nasty! I can't believe Captain Maselli would go for her!"

"He didn't!" I snap defensively. "He was just nice to her, and she got the wrong impression," I add, trying to soften my tone a bit.

"OK…" Enrique says with his hands up. "I didn't mean to say it like that."

"I know you didn't," I say in an effort to smooth things over. "It's just that Marco and I agreed not to talk about things with the crew."

"Well, this certainly explains a lot," Suzanne says as she stirs another packet of sweetener into her coffee. "We heard up front that Miriam is removing you from our crew and putting you on the morning crew. Is that true?"

"Yep," I say as I work to fight off my irritation that Miriam is letting the rest of the crew know in her own way.

"She must really want to keep you away from Captain Maselli in a bad way," Suzanne adds with a laugh of disbelief.

"That's how it seems," I say, fighting the urge to tell them about how Miriam said people on our crew were complaining about me.

"The funny thing is that Captain Maselli is nice to her and all, but he was completely ignoring her when I saw them before the flight," Suzanne says.

"Yeah, and while I was up front 'critiquing' Scott and Bass on the pre-flight service, the captain seemed irritated when Miriam kept offering him food," Enrique adds.

I don't know what to say, but a flood of relief spills into my stomach with the news that Marco was annoyed with Miriam. I think maybe even a little smile washes onto my face as I do my best to keep my focus downward so Suzanne and Enrique can't see.

After a bit of a pause, Enrique asks, "So I think I understand why Miriam is being such a bitch to you now, but does your thing with Captain Maselli have anything to do with why you and Scott aren't friends anymore?" He leans in slightly as he waits for my answer.

"We're still friends..." I say weakly, knowing that they can both see directly through me.

My heart pounds a little harder now with the mention of Scott. The truth is, I really don't know if Scott and I are friends anymore. I mean before, I thought we were, but now, I'm not so sure.

"Did Scott say we weren't?" I sheepishly ask, grasping for some proof about Scott's real feelings toward me.

"No," Enrique says. "I just noticed that you two don't seem to hang out anymore, and Scott seems so edgy whenever you're around."

"Oh..." I say, somewhat relieved by his answer, but also very sad that others are noticing the rift between us.

"Your secret's safe with us," Suzanne assures me as she folds all of her empty sweetener packets into a napkin and looks at Enrique. "I mean about Captain Maselli," she adds for clarity.

Enrique nods in agreement and then says, "It's not really a secret, exactly, but we won't tell anyone that you confirmed the rumors."

I give them both a weary smile and take a long slow sip of my hot tea and pray that this night ends soon.

Marta isn't on board yet, so I set to work alone in the aft galley. I'm eager to get this flight over with so I can fall into my bed and get some quality sleep. I'm just about finished with all the prep work when Enrique enters the galley with a big grin on his face.

"It's you and me in the back, Baby!" he says with a bright smile and his arms open wide in a happy gesture.

"Really?" I question, thankful to see someone with so much energy joining me for the final leg.

"Yep!" he confirms. "Miriam is letting Marta fly up front since her husband's on board, so she switched us," he says as he double checks the wheel locks on the cart and starts looking around the galley for things to do.

"Well, alright then," I say in a weary but pleasant voice.

"Don't worry, Elle," Enrique adds. "I did some checking, and this flight is practically empty."

A wash of relief comes over me as I say, "That's great news." I look at Enrique and smile.

The aft galley intercom is ringing, so I make my way over to the receiver and pull in a deep breath. "Aft galley, Elle speaking," I remember to say at the last second.

"*Ciao,*" comes a deep, sexy voice on the other end of the line. My body flushes over as I realize Marco's calling me from the cockpit.

I automatically turn my body so that I'm facing into the corner of the galley and then say, "Hey you…" A smile instantly brightens on my face, and I can feel a few tingles zinging through my stomach.

"I miss you," he says in a husky whisper. I can hear the sound of the co-pilot confirming something in the background.

"Me, too," I say, hoping that Enrique isn't looking at me or listening in. "Where were you during the layover?" I can't help but ask. I need confirmation that he wasn't with Miriam.

"I went to the pilots' lounge with my first officer and thought about you," he says in a sexy voice that makes me go weak in the knees.

"You did?" I ask, sounding like a little girl, I'm sure.

"Yes…" he trails off. "I must go, but I will see you at your villa when we get back."

Before I can say anything else, Marco hangs up, and the line goes quiet. But my heartbeat is banging in my ears, and the rush of feelings from that silly little call has done more to enliven me than ten cups of coffee.

"Who was that?" Enrique asks with a sheepish smile on his lips.

"Nobody," I answer smugly and flash him a similar smile.

Enrique just laughs at me and then ducks into the cabin to watch the passengers as they board.

Chapter Twenty-One

I'm just about to give up on Marco when I hear a faint knock on my front door. When I look through the peephole, I can see that it's him, and I finally start to relax. It took him forever to get here, and I was getting worried that he wasn't going to show. I know that I'm overtired and irrational, but I just wanted him to hurry up so I could get my good night kiss from him and fall asleep.

As the door yawns open, my heart skips a beat as I look at Marco, dressed in baggy cotton shorts and a well-worn gray T-shirt. I'm sure he must be disappointed to see me in my thick terry cloth bathrobe with my hair tied back into a loose ponytail, but as I take him in, he doesn't seem to react to my clothing. His face is peaceful and kind as he greets me with a wide grin and soft eyes.

He takes a step into my villa and pulls me into his arms. He smells good and feels even better, and I can't wait to fall asleep in his arms. After what seems like minutes, Marco kisses the top of my head and then gently pushes me away from his body, so he can move inside and close the door. Without saying a word, I pad into my bedroom and start removing the throw pillows from my extra fluffy bed. Marco stands just inside the doorway of my room and watches me as I place each pillow on the window seat with care.

"Do you want some wine?" Marco asks.

"Do you?" I ask, sort of surprised by his question.

"I think it will help me relax—and it might help you, too," he says with a smile.

Honestly, I don't think I can *relax* much more, and I'm just so eager to climb into my bed and fall asleep that I hesitate to give him an answer.

"I will open a bottle and bring you a glass," he says as if he knows what's best for me.

I just smile to myself as I watch him move from the doorway and head into the kitchen. I can hear him opening drawers in search of the wine opener, and I don't even have the energy to shout out to him that it's in the drawer next to the stove, but I'm sure he'll figure that out soon enough.

My bones are weary as I pull the covers back on my bed and fluff the pillows. I peel off my bathrobe and hang it on the hook by my closet. I'm wearing a two-piece cotton pajama set with a light pink camisole top and purple knee length bottoms. It is by no means sexy, but that's precisely why I chose it. I don't know if it's the best idea to be inviting Marco into my bed—especially since I don't know what his expectations are physically—but I really wanted to see him tonight. And I figure it'll be fine since we're both so tired.

When I crawl into my bed and lean back against the pillows, my body and mind start to drift off. I can feel the blood slowly moving through my veins, and my heartbeat seems to be pounding from my feet instead of my chest. I'm sure if I close my eyes, I'll instantly fade away, so I train my gaze on the picture of Sugar Ray on top of my dresser.

A leap of happiness fills my heart as I realize that tomorrow is finally Monday. That means that Violet will be expecting my call. I can't wait to talk to her to find out how Sugar Ray is doing and to make sure that she's made solid plans in case one of these bad storms turns into another hurricane. I wish more than anything there was a way to talk to Sugar Ray, but knowing that's impossible makes talking to Violet the next best thing.

"Here you are," Marco says as he leans in over the bed to hand me a glass of red wine.

"Oh, thank you..." I say as I try to steady my hands so I don't spill wine all over my bed.

I take a tiny sip and feel the ruby red liquid melting into the back of my throat. It's warm and soothing and smoothes off whatever edges remain in my body on its way down. Marco is standing next to the bed, looking at me with a big smile on his face.

"I'm relaxed…" I say as I look over at him with a smile and hooded eyes.

"*Buono*," Marco says softly.

As I press my head back into my stack of fluffy pillows with my wine glass in hand, I watch Marco as he places his own glass on the bedside table. Then, in one fluid motion, Marco crosses his arms in front of him and lifts his T-shirt up and over his head. My jaw drops as I see Marco, standing there in the yellow glow of the tiny lamp by my bed, with his muscle-rippled stomach and wavy rope-like arms. After he drops his shirt to the floor, he rakes his fingers through his golden brown hair and looks directly at me.

He is the most beautiful man I've ever seen! His caramel skin looks silky and smooth, and I imagine my body pressed up against his while I drift off to sleep. But then I start to feel my body seize up as Marco begins unbuttoning his shorts. I don't know what to say or do because I was honestly hoping that Marco was just going to snuggle up beside me—while wearing most of his clothing—and literally sleep with me! But now that I am seeing all this skin and watching his hands fumbling with the button on his waistband, I feel panicky.

When his shorts drop to his ankles, I'm beyond relieved to see that Marco is wearing boxer shorts low and loose across his hips. And as he steps out of his shorts, his face no longer looks wanton, but, instead, looks tired. He easily slides his body next to mine on the bed and slips his long, brown legs under the covers. He reaches for his glass of wine and shifts around slightly so he's facing me. He raises his glass in preparation for a toast, so I raise mine to meet his.

"To overcoming the obstacles of love," he says with a sweet smile as he looks into my eyes.

I clink my glass to his and take a sip of wine without taking my eyes off of Marco. I watch as he takes a deep pull of wine between his soft lips. His mouth is so perfect, and I can hardly wait to kiss him. Marco must have the same need as he reaches for my wine and places both of our glasses on the bedside table. Then he slowly turns toward me, and we both slide down and sink into the pillows.

As we roll onto our sides and stare at each other face to face, I feel content. His eyes are bright and clear. He's right—we've been forced to overcome many obstacles to be together, but when I look into his face, I feel nothing but happiness. All of the punishment I've endured from Miriam and even the loss and betrayal of a great friend seem to be insignificant irritations compared to the way I feel about Marco right now.

Marco takes a deep breath and closes his eyes for a moment. When he opens them again, he smiles at me and presses his lips to mine. His kiss is soft and slow at first but it grows more passionate as he pulls my mouth into his. I feel his arm wrap around me, pulling me in closer to his body. His skin is warm, and I can feel his muscles rubbing up against me through the thin fabric of my pajamas.

Marco wraps his leg over my hips and slides his hand up underneath my camisole and runs it down the length of my back. I feel my body tighten slightly, but it feels too good to protest too much. Marco must sense my concern, so he gently pulls his hand out from underneath my nightshirt and draws it up to my jaw line instead. With his leg still wrapped around me, he caresses my face with his hand as he kisses me deeply. Then he pulls his lips away from mine, and we both open our eyes. He looks at me with a weary smile and rolls over to turn out the light.

When the room goes dark, Marco folds me into his smooth chest and wraps his hand around my head, cradling it very gently. I feel like I'm wrapped up in a thick, warm vine. He sighs deeply and kisses me on the forehead. A wave of exhaustion washes over me as I breathe in the scent of Marco's skin and allow myself to drift off into a deep sleep.

When I wake up, I'm alone in my bed. The room is very bright, like maybe it's already mid-day. I roll around and try to untwist myself from my sheets, so I can climb out of bed and see what time it is. As I pad my way into the bathroom, I check the clock on the microwave on my way past the kitchen. It's almost 2:30 in the afternoon! I can hardly believe I slept that long, but, the truth is, I needed it. I still feel groggy, but I can't possibly sleep another minute. I need to get up and get moving, so that I don't ruin a perfectly good day.

I brush my teeth and wash my face, hoping that both of these daily rituals will be enough to pull me out of my cloudy mind. I think maybe I'll go for a long run—or maybe just a walk, depending on how hot it is outside today. That usually gets my blood flowing again. I drag a hairbrush over my long tangled locks and do my best to gather my hair up into a tidy ponytail. As I look at myself in the mirror, I still look tired, and my face is a bit slack from sleep, but I'm too happy to waste the day sleeping.

When I reenter my bedroom, I notice that Marco must have cleared away the wine glasses before he left because the bedside table is empty. I didn't hear a thing and can't even recall him leaving. He must have slipped out earlier this morning and didn't want to wake me. As I begin making my bed, a smile washes over my face, and I think of what a complete gentlemen Marco was last night and how incredible I feel when I'm kissing him.

I've known Marco for less than a week, but so much has happened between us that I feel like I've known him much longer. In the beginning, I had my doubts about this man, and to some extent, I was certain I couldn't trust him. But there's a part of me now that's willing to trust him with my whole heart, and, as I think over the way he's been so careful with me, I feel fairly sure that I'm falling in love.

With the bed made and a pair of green running shorts and a yellow jog top on my body, I think I'm ready to face the world. After I lace up my running shoes, I decide to grab a bottle of water to take with me on my workout.

When I open up the refrigerator, I let out a giggle of surprise. Inside the fridge, there's a gorgeous fruit basket directly in the center of the rack. A gift card with my name neatly printed on it is tied to the handle of the basket with a rose-colored ribbon. A huge smile warms across my face as I snatch the card off the basket and flip it over to read it.

Eloise-

I know you need your rest today, but I want to see you. I would like to take you out this evening, so be ready for a light dinner at Giardino Di Boboli. I will see you at 6:00.

MM

I can't stop smiling as I reach into the basket and pull out a velvety peach and then grab a bottle of water from the door rack. I close the fridge and search the countertop for my key. I'm giddy inside as I step out onto my porch and feel the hot afternoon sun on my shoulders. After I lock the door and hide my key under the cushion of the bistro chair, I take a long swig of my water and start making my way over the cobbled pathway toward the front entrance.

As I suck on the luscious, juicy peach, I wonder where the *Giardino Di Boboli* is. It must be someplace pretty romantic! Marco definitely has a way of making everything so amazing and so special. When I pass Scott's villa, a tiny tingle of nerves rushes over me, but I'm determined to let it go. Right now, I'm quite sure nothing can wreck my day. I'm finished flying for a few days; I'm all rested up; Marco is taking me to dinner; and, when I get back from my walk, I'm going to call Violet. I feel plain cheery at the moment! I can't remember a time when my life has been any better.

Talking to Violet was a mixed blessing. On the one hand, I was so happy to hear that the bad tropical storm Peter told me about didn't cause any major problems for Violet or Sugar Ray and that *The Wiley* weathered the storm just fine, too. And I guess I should be happy that Sugar Ray is doing so great—he's eating well and tags along with Violet wherever she goes. But I sort of wanted to hear that my dog was lonelier for me. My heart aches for my furry companion, and, while I don't want him to be miserable without me, I do wish there were more signs that he was missing me.

Violet did tell me that she and Sugar Ray stay at my apartment every night, and she thinks that's partly why he's so happy. I picture him resting his head on Violet's foot as she talks to me on the phone, and I wish I could reach out and touch him. Before we hang up, I make sure for the hundredth time that Violet is going to call my dad if a bad storm is heading toward Miami, and she promises she will. So with everything said, I reluctantly say my goodbyes and hang up the phone. As I flop down on my bed and stare up at the ceiling, I pray with all my heart that Sugar Ray knows how much I love him.

The odd thing is that while I'm sure my heart aches because I miss my dog, I can't help but notice a loneliness welling up inside of me for Scott. For ten years, Scott has been my closest friend, and we've never let anything come between us before. I'm still reeling over the idea that Scott could stab me in the back with Miriam, and, while I honestly can't imagine him saying all of those things, his body language makes it crystal clear that he doesn't want to be around me one bit.

I hate that when we see each other in passing, he so obviously turns the other way. I didn't want things to be like this—I just wanted to be able to have a normal, healthy relationship with Marco without his ambiguous friendships getting in the way. But it's gotten so complicated. And even though I am still pretty upset that Miriam moved me to the morning crew, I think it will actually be easier on me emotionally to be on a crew that doesn't have Scott or Marco assigned to it.

And then there's Marco. My heart is doing crazy flips for him these days, and thinking about him is pretty much the only remedy for missing Sugar Ray and worrying about Scott. But I also have a nervous pit in my stomach about how quickly things are happening between us. Last night was amazing—sleeping next to Marco was the most wonderful experience, and whenever I'm away from him, all I can think about is the next time we'll be together. But I have to wonder how long it will take for Marco to tire of just kissing and hugging. He's a grown man, after all, and I seriously doubt he's used to women holding him at bay when it comes to sex.

And the truth is, I'm starting to want more than just kisses and hugs, too. My mind is flooded with thoughts of what it would be like to give myself to Marco. When he touches me, I quiver with desire, and there is certainly a part of me that is considering what it would be like to let this relationship evolve to a level I've never known. But as soon as I allow myself to think about letting go of my convictions and non-negotiables about sex, I feel lost and confused. It's like I can't imagine respecting myself after the heat of the moment passes, and I feel disappointment building up inside me over the thought of losing something that I've protected for all these years.

I ponder this thought as I look through my closet in search of the perfect outfit for this evening. Marco will be here in about a half an hour, and I'm all showered and my hair is blown straight. Figuring out what to wear is my final hurdle, and I want to be sure to pick something that looks great but isn't too suggestive. I finally pull out a brushed cotton sundress from my closet and slip it over my head.

It's one of my favorite dresses, and I feel sad as I remember that it was Scott who actually picked it out. It's light blue with tiny white flowers and a brush of khaki in the background. It has tiny braided straps that crisscross in the back, and it feels super soft against my skin. I pair it with dark brown, braided leather flip-flops and my jean jacket in case it gets cool. When I look at myself in the full-length mirror in my room, I'm happy to see how perfectly the dress looks with my tan skin and freshly washed hair. I look like summertime through and through, and I hope this dress is appropriate for my "light dinner" with Marco.

After I put a dab of jasmine-scented perfume behind each ear and on both wrists, I put on a pair of gold hoop earrings and my gold necklace from Marco. With the chain clasped around my neck, I gently reach up and roll the tiny gold bead between my thumb and forefinger. Marco said the neckace was a "gesture of deepest friendship," but what I feel growing inside of my heart is beyond simple friendship. I think I'm falling in love with Marco, and that thought is both frightening and exhilarating at the same time!

With only ten minutes left before Marco arrives, I decide to fill out a few postcards to send out tomorrow. So I quickly scribble a note to my parents, one to my sister and one to Nora. I feel so happy right now that all I can say in each note is: *Having a wonderful time! Wish you were here!*

This time when I slide into Marco's car, I'm already prepared for letting go and enjoying the ride—as well as getting in and out with a bit more grace. So as he fires up the engine, I simply smile at him with anticipation. As we peel out of the driveway, I feel a sense of freedom overtaking me, and I realize that I'm actually starting to trust Marco.

"You look perfect," Marco says as he takes his eyes off the road to look at me.

"Thank you," I say as a blush of color washes over my cheeks. "You do, too," I add as I notice what he's wearing. He has on an easy pair of faded American jeans and a starched white cotton dress shirt. The leather belt wrapped around his waist matches the leather of his Italian loafers, and he looks so handsome and well-groomed.

"I'm taking you to one of my favorite places in the entire city," he says as we take a fast corner. "*Giardino Di Boboli* is our central public garden, and it is absolutely amazing in the summer," he says as he looks at me out of the corner of his eye. Then he adds, "And it is the most important place to take someone you love…"

"Oh," I say as a huge smile spreads across my face. I think Marco just told me he loves me! My heart is pounding wildly inside my chest as I savor this moment. I sink down into my seat slightly as I fight off the urge to shout out that Marco Maselli just said he loves me!

"In the summertime, the gardens stay open after sunset," Marco continues talking as if he didn't just send me to the moon. "They allow musical performances in the amphitheater, and I thought we could listen to some music before we eat."

"That sounds perfect!" I say as I beam up at Marco. I feel so happy that all I can do is smile.

In a matter of minutes, Marco slides his car into a narrow parking space along the side of the road. He hops out of the driver's side and opens my door for me. As I emerge from his car, I realize how excited I am to be with him in his city again. He closes the car door and pulls me into his arms.

"It was difficult for me to leave you this morning without a kiss," he says playfully as I look up into his eyes.

"It was?" I question, not knowing what else to say.

"You were so peaceful, and I didn't want to disturb you, but all I've been able to think about all day are your lips," he says, his words landing softly on my face.

I just smile up at Marco, completely lost in his words and wondering how he could be any more romantic. Then, he slowly moves in and kisses me—as we stand right in the middle of the sidewalk! The kiss is long and deep, and I get lost in it. Right now, there is no one else in the world that matters except for Marco Maselli. He consumes me, and I don't even care about the consequences of my feelings. I want to stay lost in the moment and enjoy the power of my desires.

Marco said he loves me, I think as his arms pull me in closer to him. *Marco said he loves me...*

Giardino Di Boboli is enormous! It's like a lush green oasis in the middle of the cobblestone city, and it is the most beautiful place I've ever been. As we make our way through the main entrance that extends off the rear of the *Pitti Palace,* there are couples strolling arm in arm, nuzzling each other while sitting on stone benches and admiring the elaborate gardens.

"Over here is the Amphitheater," Marco explains as we ascend into a large tiered area. "It was designed so that the Medici family could see different circus performances and spectacles."

In the center area of the amphitheater, there is a small group of people setting up instruments and moving chairs around. I can see string instruments mostly, but it also looks like there are some electric guitars and drums off to the side.

"They are still setting up for the concert," Marco says as he turns his attention toward the center of the amphitheater. "I want to show you more of the gardens, and then we'll come back to listen." Marco takes my hand and pulls me toward a lovely tree-lined walkway.

All around us are shaded alcoves and manicured walkways with canopied greens and lush foliage. It's like no other garden I've ever visited, and, as Marco gently pulls me under his arm and leads me down one of the garden nooks, I feel myself slip into a dream.

We follow a small pathway that leads to a pavilion that Marco says is called the *Kafeehaus*. It's shaped like a boat with a prow and a deck, and, as we make our way up the rise, there is a stunning view of Florence. The pink and orange shadows of the setting sun magnify the beauty of the city, and I see her in all of her glory, outstretched before me.

"I will be right back," Marco says to me as he gently kisses me on the top of the head.

I watch as Marco walks toward the small bar area over in the far corner. I notice people milling around the deck with small bottles of wine and various summer drinks. The breeze is fresh and light, and I'm carried away by the amazing views.

When Marco returns with two plastic wineglasses filled with dark red wine, he points out several sights for me to take in—like the lovely ancient villas, and the lush, ripening vineyards and olive groves. It's exactly what I'd imagined Tuscany would look like. He explains that up ahead is the *Belevdere Fort* which is shaped like a six-point star.

"My parents were married there," Marco says as he nostalgically gazes off toward the glowing building. He's leaning next to me on his elbows on the thick stone railing, and I'm aware that our shoulders are lightly touching.

"They were?" I ask pleasantly, hoping to gently prompt him into sharing more of the details.

"Yes, they were," he confirms softly. "Once, my father told me that he and my uncle were visiting the fort and standing up on the ramparts. When he saw the beautiful view from up above, he realized that he wanted to be with my mother for the rest of his life. So, they had to make their vows on that very spot," Marco says as I catch a twinkle in his eye. "It is not normally open to weddings, but as you know, *the Maselli's have connections,*" he says with a smile as he looks over at me.

I just smile back at Marco and look out over the stunning views. It's the kind of sight that makes you want to plant some roots with someone you love and grow a life among the rolling hills and ancient buildings. As I pull in a sip of my wine, I close my eyes and do my best to burn this image into my memory forever.

"Eloise-ah?" Marco whispers into my ear. A rush of chills spreads down my legs as I slowly turn to face Marco. "I love you," he says with an intense, meaningful look in his eyes.

He said it again! Only this time, there is no mistaking it! He just told me he loves me! I swallow deeply as I try to comprehend it! How could he know that he loves me so soon? And what do I say in return? In an instant, my mind is flooded with thoughts that I don't know how to control, so I do the only thing I can do. I lean in toward Marco and press my lips to his.

Marco gently kisses me in return with his warm mouth open and ready to taste my kiss. I close my eyes as Marco softly nibbles my lips and gently pulls me closer to him with his arms. He slowly moves his kisses across my cheek and down my neck, and I feel my body give into desire. I'm completely lost in the experience of being loved by Marco.

A passing couple shakes us out of our private moment, and we pull away slowly and enter the real world once again. I take a step back and adjust my sundress while Marco turns to the side and runs his fingers through his thick, wavy hair and smiles to himself. I lift my plastic wineglass off of the railing and take another long, slow pull. The heat from the wine moves down my throat and slows my heart rate to a lazy, thick thud.

"The music must be starting soon," Marco finally says after he takes the last sip of his wine. "Shall we go and listen?" he asks with a sweet smile on his face.

"We should," I say as I smile back at him.

Marco takes my hand, and the two of us make our way back toward the amphitheater. I can hear the music as we get a little closer, and it sounds like a combination of jazz and classical music fused together.

We find a couple of seats in the back row, and we settle in for a good long listen. Marco wraps me up in his arms as I lean into him and let the music fuse into my mood. The sun has whispered its final pink thoughts for the day, and the evening shades of purple and gray are taking over.

"Are you getting hungry yet?" Marco asks me after we've sat in silence for at least thirty minutes.

"Yes, I am," I say, after I allow myself to think about food for the first time in hours.

"Let me take you to a quiet place," Marco says as he shifts his body and carefully moves me so I can stand up. "We can walk there," he adds as he guides me in a new direction that is away from his car.

I'm too in my head to even talk, but Marco's "*I love you*" is all I can think about. No one has ever said those words to me—other than my family of course, and they don't count! When they say those three little words, they don't fog your mind or cause your heart to swell. As I look over at Marco, silently strolling next to me with my hand in his hand, I feel a warm, foggy rush of emotions.

"Marco?" I ask in a soft voice.

"*Si, Eloise-ah,*" Marco says as he slows his pace and turns his attention toward me.

"I love you, too," I say with a smile.

A huge grin spreads across Marco's face as he stops and pulls me into his arms. He lifts me up off the ground and spins me for one rotation. I can hear him laughing as I bury my face into his shoulder.

Chapter Twenty-Two

After the host guides us to a dimly lit table in the far corner of the restaurant, I'm a bit startled when Marco slides right next to me in the booth instead of sitting across the table from me. At first, it feels very awkward sitting up against Marco, but as soon as the host leaves the table, Marco wraps his arm around me and then gently reaches for my face with his other hand. He kisses me passionately, and I'm literally hypnotized.

When Marco pulls away, he says, "I can never get enough of your face and your lips."

I give him a shy smile in response. The things he says to me often leave me speechless. His confidence and ease when it comes to courting me is hard for me to handle because I never know what to expect. He's romantic and exciting and, to tell you the truth, if it didn't sound so corny, I'd tell him his lips are pretty darn addictive, too!

But as Marco slides his body even closer to mine, it triggers a wash of nerves throughout my system. It just seems like, all of a sudden, Marco is making things a lot more physical than before, and I'm starting to feel like maybe we're moving too fast. My heightened alertness makes me feel self-conscious and a tad bit sweaty—which are two things you don't want to feel when you are kissing and cuddling. So in response, I quickly reach out my arm to grab a menu.

"Do you think we should order?" I ask while I do my best to act like this was a very natural move on my part.

"Good idea," Marco says as he reaches for his own menu. "When I'm around you, I sometimes forget that I need to eat," he says with a light laugh.

When we entered the restaurant, Marco mentioned that it was one of his favorites. The owners are friends of his brother Andre, and so no matter what it is, Marco claims the chefs will prepare it for me. This is kind of tricky for me because I'm not a very adventurous eater. I like plain, regular food—nothing fancy—and I'm more than just a little worried that Marco is going to have the chef make me another pile of tripe, or some other outrageous dish just to be impressive! I decide I can't let this happen, so I do my best to figure out what to eat on my own.

As I look over the menu, all of the dish descriptions are neatly printed in Italian. I quickly run my eyes down the selections in search of one or two words that I can recognize. Finally, about halfway down the page, I see *Bolognese*. Thank God! Something I know I like! Once I see what I'll be having, I close my menu and place it back on top of the table.

When I look up, I realize that Marco has been watching me the entire time. I flash him a nervous smile, and a grin widens across his face. As I look at him, I'm amazed at how handsome Marco is—his face is so perfect, and his teeth are so white and straight. And when he smiles at me the way he's smiling at me now, I have to pray that I don't melt into a soupy puddle on the floor.

Just then, a long, gangly waiter approaches us. He stops short of our table and then yells, "Marco!"

Marco turns to look at the waiter, and shouts happy hellos in return. Marco slides out of his seat next to me, and I watch as the two men greet each other with pecks on the cheeks and a warm embrace. I continue watching as they start talking in Italian. Marco is very animated, and it's clear that these two have not seen each other in some time and that this is indeed a happy reunion.

Finally Marco turns his attention back toward me. He says something about me in Italian to his friend, and both of them start laughing and nudging each other playfully. I'm not sure what Marco said, but the reaction is making me feel nervous. Are they making fun of me?

"Eloise-ah," Marco finally says. "This is Roberto—the little brother to one of my closest friends. He has been hearing all about you from his brother, and now he is pleased to meet you."

"Oh!" I say, immediately regretting my concerns. "It is nice to meet you, Roberto," I offer in slow, deliberate English as Roberto reaches out for my hand.

"*It is-ah nice to meet-ah you, too,*" Roberto says with a very thick accent. Then he starts rattling off something in Italian to Marco, but keeps his eyes trained on me.

"Roberto thinks you are even more beautiful than he was expecting," Marco translates for me. "He said his brother was sure I was lying when I described you to him!" he adds with a huge smile.

"*Grazie,*" I say directly to Roberto as my face flushes over. These Italian men sure do know how to compliment a woman!

Marco and Roberto start talking again, only this time, Marco doesn't translate. So I try to key in on all of their expressive hand gestures, and I make my own conclusion that Roberto is telling Marco about *his* new girlfriend. To me, it seems like Roberto is tracing the outline of a very voluptuous woman that he wants to cover with rose petals or something else that he can pluck and sprinkle on top. Then he describes how he will kiss the woman and set her free. I watch in amazement as these two men carry on with such bravado and color and a blur of hand gestures. It's like watching a foreign puppet show with no puppets!

Finally, Roberto smiles at me, and Marco slides back into my side of the booth. I watch as Roberto gives me an odd little bow, then turns around and heads toward the kitchen.

"I took the liberty of ordering something really special for us," Marco says as he settles back into his place right next to me. "Roberto's brothers are the best chefs in all of Tuscany, and I wanted them to create something *really* nice for you." Marco turns his attention to my face now and plants a petal soft kiss on my nose.

I do my best to hide my disappointment over the idea of eating another "specialty" dish. I flash Marco an insincere, but appreciative smile and say, "That sounds wonderful."

"*You* are wonderful," Marco says as he moves in closer. "You are so wonderful that I can't help but love you," he adds as he looks deep into my eyes.

And suddenly, tripe, sautéed pig intestines or even Tuscan road kill all work for me because Marco Maselli *loves* me!

Roberto's brothers are indeed the best chefs in all of Tuscany as far as I'm concerned! I've never eaten such delicious creations in all my life! (However, this dinner was anything but *light*!) And Marco was such a proud Italian as he described every dish in glorious detail as it arrived.

The *Prima*—or first course—was a vegetable and bread soup called *ribllita* (that Marco said his mother believes makes you stronger) and a pasta dish called *strozzipreti* (which Marco translated as "priest strangler" made of pasta, cheese, and spinach, baked in the oven and smothered in a homemade red sauce).

The *Secondi*—or second course—was called *bistecca alla fiorentina*. This was a huge charcoal grilled T-bone steak served with lemon and drizzled olive oil. It was the most delicious steak I've ever eaten—the outside was crispy and full of flavor while the inside was perfectly pink and juicy. Roberto also brought us a smattering of what Marco called the *Contorni*— or side dishes. There were three in all: *carciofini fritti* (fried baby artichokes); *fagioli all'uccelletto* (boiled white beans sautéed with tomato and sage); and *Insalata mista* (which was the most delicious, fresh mixed green salad).

Roberto kept our wine glasses filled at all times with the most gorgeous selection of red wines while Marco filled my mind with stories of his family and of his life growing up in Florence. I was mesmerized by everything Marco said—the way his mouth moved when he talked and the way his eyes would light up when he looked at me. It was like I was consuming this man along with each delicious bite of my food.

Now, with my belly full and my mind swirling from all the wine and amazing stories, Marco shifts his body in the booth seat so he is turned toward me. I do my best to shift as well, and once we're facing each other, a strong sense of contentment washes over me

"Tell me about your family, Eloise-ah," Marco says after he takes a deep sip of his wine.

"My family?" I ask, realizing that this is the first time Marco has actually asked me to share anything about myself. "Well...first of all, they're great!" I begin as I settle in and try to figure out what to share.

It doesn't take me long to start rambling on and on about how wonderful my parents are and how incredible my sister is. I tell him about Edna Pearl and how I am planning to visit her in England sometime before I go back to Miami. And of course, I tell him all about Sugar Ray and how I talked to Violet today. I blather on and on about how much I miss my dog and how difficult it is for me to be away from him for so long. The more I talk, the more homesick I become, and I start to feel a big lump forming in my throat.

"You miss your pet very much I see," Marco says with deep compassion in his voice.

"I know it's silly, but I really do," I say in a thick voice. With all the wine and the heavy food, my body is fully out of whack, and I do my best to try to find my composure, but it's nowhere to be found.

Marco reaches for my hand and kisses it softly. I feel embarrassed by my emotions. I never expected this to happen right in the middle of this perfect dinner.

"I have an idea," Marco says as he leans his head in closer to mine. "My mother has a Boxer named Chianti. Let's go to the vineyard for the day tomorrow, and you can meet my family, eat dinner with us and spend some time with your dog's long lost...cousin!"

"Oh Marco," I gush, barely able to contain my emotions. "That would be amazing!"

Marco's face is filled with amusement over my reaction. I feel myself start to blunder about, but then stop, as Marco reaches for my face. He tilts my head up by gently lifting my chin and moves in for a lingering kiss. When he pulls away, he smiles at me and I feel so understood.

Marco offers to buy me some gelato on the way back to his car, but I'm simply too full to eat another bite. So we stroll along the cobbled sidewalk, arm in arm, and I listen to the sound of Marco's voice as he tells me intricate details about his life in this city. He tells me about where he went to school and how he knew from the age of six that he wanted to be a pilot. He shows me the spot near a small fountain where he had his first scooter accident and the gelato shop where his father used to take him for important conversations. With each story he tells, I feel myself falling more and more in love with this man—this amazing, gorgeous man.

As Marco pulls into *Il Girasole*, I realize that I don't want this night to end. Marco shuts down the engine and removes the key. He drops the key to the floorboard with a tiny chink, and I realize that Marco isn't ready to end the night either.

When I turn to face him, Marco's sexy smile nearly takes my breath away. I want to kiss him and feel his body next to mine so badly. Marco holds me in his steady gaze, and I feel myself quiver slightly from the thoughts I'm entertaining.

"Wait right there," Marco says as he reaches for his door latch.

I watch him as he pulls himself out of the car and walks over to my side and lifts the handle. When the door swings open wide, Marco reaches for my hand and lifts me out of my seat like I'm filled with helium. In one silky motion, Marco pulls me into his arms and shuts the car door behind me. Then he backs me up against the door and begins kissing me passionately. The kisses are intense and a bit frantic and it surprises me at first. But then I catch a whiff of Marco's citrus cologne, and, suddenly, everything changes.

My eyes float shut while my mind races with thoughts that are taking me to places I don't usually allow myself to go. I can feel Marco's body swelling against my thigh, and I'm torn between giving in and holding out. Our kisses are starting to spin out of control as Marco moves his hands up and down the sides of my body. He knowingly moves them over my breasts, and I feel a spasm of desire coursing through my heart.

"I love you, Eloise-ah," Marco whispers into my ear as he wantonly kisses me down the side of my neck.

I lean my head back with my eyes closed and savor his words and his kisses. I feel myself tremble as Marco starts kissing me along the rib of my collarbone. I notice his hand wandering down the side of my body toward my legs. A rush of panic grips me when Marco begins grabbing the fabric of my sundress and starts to pull my skirt up the length of my thigh.

"Marco," I say in a breathy voice. "It's too fast…"

Marco ignores my voice and continues his exploration of my neck with his lips while he pushes his thigh firmly between my legs and continues guiding his hand up and under the fabric of my dress. His hand is warm on the side of my thigh as he squeezes and kneads his way up to my buttocks. I can feel the heat from his body radiating on me, and his breath is hot and steamy as he works his way around my neck and back up to my lips.

"Marco," I plead, trying my best to slow him down without totally ruining the moment.

"Let's go to your villa," Marco suggests between kisses.

"I don't know…" I say as I pull away and look up at his face.

"It will be more comfortable," he gently reasons. "We can just sit on the sofa and kiss…" he trails off and then kisses my mouth.

I feel myself giving into him as he rhythmically works his lips over mine. It's the kind of kiss that scrambles your brain and makes it impossible to think clearly. Marco adjusts his footing slightly and forces his weight against my body, pressing me firmly against the side of the car. I push back on Marco, afraid I'm about to loose my own footing, and Marco pulls back with a jerk.

"Are you alright?" Marco questions, a wash of concern moving over his face.

"I am," I say as I try to gather my thoughts and pull myself up so I don't slide all the way down the side of the car.

"Let's go," Marco says emphatically as he peels his body away from mine.

This time, Marco isn't making a suggestion. He takes my hand in his and starts guiding me toward the entrance gate, and I obediently follow, not sure what else I can do. As he leads the way through the gate, my mind is swirling. I'm totally conflicted. I want Marco so much, but I don't think

I'm ready for things to move as quickly as they are. But I'm nervous about telling Marco that I'm not ready. And with each and every step, we move closer and closer to my villa. Once we're inside my tiny apartment, I don't know if I'll be able to stop myself.

"Marco, wait!" I finally say as we make our way past the office. "I need a minute."

It was the only thing I could think of to say. I'm sobered by the alarm in my own voice, and I realize that I'm even less ready for this than I thought. Marco turns to face me, and I look away from him like a scared child. I sense a softening in his demeanor as he steps in closer to me.

"Eloise-ah…" Marco says as he tucks a loose strand of my hair behind my ear. "I'm not going to hurt you."

"I know…" I trail off, too embarrassed to look him directly in the eye. "It just feels like we are moving kind of quickly, ya know?" I say, looking up at him for the first time since I stopped the passion train.

"It is not too quickly for me, but if it is too quickly for you, we can slow it down," Marco says with an amused smile on his face.

"We can?" I ask, feeling a wash of relief spilling through my body.

"Of course we can," Marco laughs lightly as he pulls me into his arms.

His embrace feels wonderful as I allow myself to relax and enjoy the safety of Marco's arms. When we pull apart, I look up to check Marco's face. His face is calm and relaxed, and I'm reassured that I didn't totally ruin the night.

After we go up the steps to my villa, Marco leans his shoulder against the door jam as I dig around my purse in search of my key. When I unlock the door, Marco carefully guides me inside and shuts the door behind us. I switch on the lamp next to the door, toss my purse and jean jacket into the overstuffed blue chair, and make my way into the kitchen. Marco casually kicks off his shoes and moves over to the sofa.

"Do these villas have a…radio?" Marco asks as I finish filling two glasses with water.

"Over by the fireplace," I say over my shoulder while I put the bottle of water back in the fridge.

As I walk toward the living room, I can see Marco stooped down on the floor, trying to figure out how to turn on the stereo system. He fumbles around with a few buttons, and the speakers crackle and hiss while he dials the tuner into one of his favorite local stations. He turns the volume down a bit, and soothing music fills the living room with a sexy, silky beat.

I watch Marco as he rises up and glides toward me. He takes both glasses of water out of my hands and places them on the coffee table. Then he takes me in his arms and slowly starts moving his body to the sway of the music. I lean my face into his shoulder and allow myself to float around the room with Marco.

Marco kisses my forehead, and, when I look up, he smiles at me. Then he gently moves us toward the sofa, moving his hips and legs in time with the music. In one fluid, dance-like motion, Marco swings me around, and I fall softly into the sofa. I smile up at Marco as the cushions cradle my woozy body. He smiles back as he begins unbuttoning his dress shirt.

I watch as he effortlessly moves his fingers down the center of his shirt, parting the fabric down his smooth, brown chest. He slips the shirt off of his shoulders and works the buttons on the cuffs, one at a time. He looks down at me, and I can feel a shiver of desire skittering through my thighs.

Shirtless, Marco lowers his body on top of me, and I can feel the heat from his torso through the cotton of my sundress. Marco perches himself up on his elbows so his full weight isn't directly on me. He tenderly tucks my hair behind my ears and smiles sweetly.

"You are perfect in every way," Marco says in a dreamy voice.

"Thank you," I say, immediately regretting such a dumb reply. For some reason, I don't know what to do with all of these compliments.

Marco smiles and then says, "*Prego.*"

Then, he moves in and begins kissing me. At first, the kisses are soft and sweet, but gradually, the lust between us starts to build, and, before I know it, Marco is consuming me with his mouth. His hands are moving around my body wildly, and I can't decide what to do to stop him—and, truthfully, I'm not completely sure I want him to stop!

I can feel his fingers tugging at the tiny braided straps on my sundress, doing his best to pull them down over my shoulders, but they're crisscrossed in the back, so they won't slide down. When he pulls away from my mouth, his eyes look fierce, and I can see that hungry look that makes me want to run and hide.

"I want you, Eloise-ah," Marco says lustfully when he pulls back briefly to look into my eyes.

I look back at Marco, feeling breathless and somewhat terrified. I can't deny how badly I want him, too, but there is just something gripping me and keeping me from completely giving in.

"I want to look at your body and feel your skin against mine," Marco adds as he lifts himself up off of me and stands over me as I melt into the sofa cushions. "Take me to your bed," he says as he reaches his hand out to help me up and off the sofa.

Just then, we're both shaken by a loud, persistent knock at the door. Now I can hear a muffled voice calling out my name. I look up at Marco, and he looks back at me with surprise on his face.

"Are you expecting someone?" he asks as he reaches down and grabs his shirt off the floor.

"No," I say as I try to figure out who it could be.

I quickly lift myself off of the sofa and walk toward the door as Marco slips his shirt on his back and falls into step right behind me. I take a quick look through the peephole and see Marta DeSoto standing on the porch, her face wet with tears.

"It's Marta," I say over my shoulder to Marco. "She looks like she's crying," I add as I quickly work the lock on the door so I can let her in.

"Elle!" Marta says as steps into my villa and practically falls into my arms.

"Oh my gosh, Marta! Are you OK?" I ask, even though I can clearly see that she isn't.

"No, I'm not OK," she sobs into my shoulder. "And I never will be again!" she bellows like she's in great pain.

I look over at Marco, and he looks stunned. I don't know what to do, so I just continue to hold Marta's in my arms until she manages to calm herself down enough to notice that we're not alone.

"Oh, Captain Maselli," Marta says with a thick, juicy sniffle as she works to compose herself. "I didn't realize you were here," she adds as she chokes back a sob.

"It's OK," Marco says earnestly as he works his foot into one of his loafers. "I was just leaving."

"Please..." Marta starts to protest. "I should go—you two were trying to be alone and...I should go..."

"No, Marta, no!" I say as I look over at Marco with pleading eyes.

"Marta, I really was getting ready to leave," Marco assures her. He looks over at me with compassion on his face. "You must need to talk to Eloise—ah, and I have a *whole* day planned with her for tomorrow," he says with a genuine smile.

"It's OK, Marta," I say in agreement, hoping it will work to calm her down until I can get Marco out the door.

Marta looks at both of us with her puffy, red eyes, and I feel the need to protect her. She looks tiny and frail, and I can tell that whatever happened tonight has ripped her heart out and left her bleeding.

"Marta, just go into my room, and I'll be right in," I say in a soft voice. I watch as Marta nods her head, steps around Marco and enters my bedroom.

Once I'm sure she's gone, I look up at Marco and mouth the words, "I'm sorry." He nods his head like he understands. He takes me into his arms and kisses me on the top of the head.

"Your friend really needs you," he says in a soft, deep voice. "I really *want* you, but your friend really *needs* you," he clarifies with a little laugh.

"Well, we still have tomorrow," I remind him as I pull away to look up at his face.

"That we do!" he says brightly. "I will pick you up at noon, OK?"

"Perfect!" I say with a smile.

Then Marco kisses my lips softly. "Remember," he says into my ear. "I love you..."

Before I tend to Marta, I take a moment to refresh myself in the bathroom. Things were getting pretty heated with Marco, and I feel flushed and filmy, so I splash some water on my face hoping to rinse off some of the confusion I'm feeling at the moment.

I don't understand how I can be so divided inside. A huge part of me wants Marco as badly as he says he wants me, but I just can't let it happen. I have tingles and desires the likes of which I've never felt before, and these feelings are much more powerful than I ever realized they could be. It's like every now and then, I lose my mind and start slipping away from myself, but at the last second, I come to my senses just in time to take control.

And it doesn't help my state of mind that Marco keeps telling me that he loves me. No guy has ever said those words to me before, and hearing them only confuses me. I haven't really known Marco long enough to believe that he really means it, but, then again, maybe he's found his soul mate in me. I've heard people say that when you meet your soul mate, you just know. And I've been so preoccupied with so many other things lately that maybe I haven't been centered enough to realize that Marco is *my* soul mate, too. I contemplate this as I study my face in the mirror.

Could Marco be my soul mate?

I dry my face off on a fluffy white towel and turn my attention back to Marta. Whatever's going on with her is serious. I put a line of toothpaste on my toothbrush and start brushing my teeth, all the while wondering what Oscar could have done to upset his wife so badly. When I saw them together at the pool this afternoon, they looked like the picture of happiness.

As I get ready to leave the bathroom, I look under the sink for a box of tissues but only find a spare roll of toilet paper. So I grab the roll and dig around in the vanity drawer until I find a travel tube of aspirin. I make a quick stop in the kitchen to get a couple glasses of water, and I quietly make my way toward my bedroom.

When I enter, I see Marta, flopped across my bed, face up. She looks almost catatonic as her glazed eyes focus on some undetermined spot on the ceiling. She's wearing a pair of white cotton shorts and a pink lace camisole. Her tiny leather sandals are dangling from her feet as her honey brown legs hang over the side of my bed.

"Marta?" I whisper, not wanting to startle her out of her deep state.

"Yes," she whispers hoarsely without changing her gaze.

"I brought you some water and aspirin," I say as I move in toward the bed.

Marta shifts around until she's sitting on the edge of my bed. I slide in next to her and hand her a glass of water. I place the roll of toilet paper and my glass of water on the bedside table and try to open the top of the aspirin tube. After several tries to outwit the childproof cap, I succeed. I turn toward Marta and tap out two tiny white tablets into the palm of her hand. She gives me a grateful smile and washes the pills down her throat with a long swig of cold water.

"Thank you," she says with a weak smile.

"You're welcome," I reply as I slide up onto the bed. I move the pillows around to make room for Marta to get more comfortable. She slowly follows my lead and kicks off her sandals and moves in so she's leaning against a stack of pillows with her tiny hands folded across her stomach. She seems calm now, but I worry if I try to rush her with the details of her story, she may come unglued. So I just sit and wait.

Finally, Marta breaks the silence. "Oscar left me," she says plainly without any emotion.

"What?" I ask not sure I heard her correctly.

"Michelle is pregnant," she adds as she turns her head toward me so she can see my reaction.

"What?" I ask again—only this time with more shock.

"Oscar said they were *trying* to get pregnant…" Marta's words trail off as she rolls her eyes up toward the ceiling while a single fat tear spills down her cheek.

"What do you mean they were *trying*?" I ask, doing my best to follow the bizarre details of this situation. *Michelle Maddox? Pregnant?* Who would have ever guessed she'd *try* to get pregnant!

"Elle," Marta begins as she changes her gaze so she can see my face. "Remember when I told you that things with Oscar may have been different if I had tried to be more *open* to the things he wanted?"

I nod my head that I remember.

"Oscar wanted children," she says and then looks away. "And I didn't."

"So he and Michelle decided to make a baby?" I say, trying to figure out what's going on.

"Kind of," she says as she readjusts her back against the pillows. "Oscar and I have been fighting about having children for the last year or so. He says I'm being selfish, but I don't think I am. I just know that I wouldn't make a good mother, and, when I married Oscar, he told me he didn't want to have any children either. But then things started to change about two years ago after Oscar's brother and his wife had a baby. Oscar was sure that being around Julio and Carmen's baby would change my mind—but it didn't."

I watch Marta as she reaches for her glass of water and takes a long, deep sip. Then she grabs the toilet paper roll and pulls off several squares and dabs her eyes.

"When Oscar showed up in Paris, he told me he wanted to give our relationship another try," Marta continues. "He said that he wanted to end things with Michelle because he realized he was just trying to punish me for not wanting to have a family with him. He said he didn't love Michelle—he loved *me,* and he wanted to make things work. He told me if I would forgive him, we could start a new life together—with or without children. So I agreed to put everything behind me, and I promised that I would think about becoming a mother. Oscar seemed so happy, and we were making love every spare second of the day," she says as the tears start to flow down her cheeks.

"I thought everything was going to be so special and that Oscar and I could go back to the way things were when we first got married," she says in a thick voice. "But this afternoon, Michelle showed up. Oscar told me he needed to break it off with her in person, so they went somewhere in a taxi, and they were gone for hours. I felt like a caged animal waiting for Oscar to come back. And when he did, he looked so different."

I reach over and place my hand on Marta's arm. I can tell that recalling the order of events is only making this more difficult, so I wait patiently for her to continue telling the story.

"He told me that Michelle was pregnant. She wasn't sure until yesterday—she went to a clinic in Paris because she was feeling ill. So there's no chance it was a botched pregnancy test or anything, and she's *certain* the baby is his. Michelle flew to Florence today because she wanted to tell Oscar about the baby in person," Marta says bitterly, and I can feel the hatred in her tone.

"Oscar told me that he feels like now, he needs to *do the right thing!*" Marta practically spits the last few words as a flood of tears pour out of her eyes. She rolls her body into mine, and I hold her as she heaves and sobs into the pillows.

"Oh Marta..." I say softly as I rub her back. I can feel the heaviness of her grief, and I don't have a clue how to comfort her. So I just hold her and gently run my hand up and down the length of her back.

When Marta pulls away, she presses her nose into a wad of balled up toilet paper and does her best to blot away the grief. "They left about an hour ago," she says through hiccupped sobs. "They're headed back to Miami. Michelle wants to find a nice home in Coral Gables."

"Oh my gosh, Marta, this is just awful," I finally say, feeling overwhelmed with all this information and helpless to find a way to make Marta feel better.

"Oscar was just so matter of fact about it all," Marta continues as her eyes take on that glazed look again. "He just came in and told me and then left. He didn't even take his stuff, Elle... He didn't even take any of his things..." I watch as Marta's face cracks and the tears flood down her face.

Exhaustion finally takes over, and a few hours later, Marta and I are both tucked under the covers of my bed. I can hear the quiet rhythm of Marta's breathing as she pulls in short shallow breaths. The heaviness of her heartbreak permeates the room, and I can't seem to make sense of it all. Yesterday, when I saw Marta by the pool, she looked so happy. Oscar wanted to rebuild a life with her, and that's all she needed to hear to forgive him. She trusted him and even managed to somehow put his infidelity behind them. And then suddenly…a baby changes everything.

Once I'm sure Marta is asleep, I slip out of the bed and take off my sundress. It is completely rumpled and looks as tired as I feel. I toss the dress into my laundry basket in my closet and pull a clean nightshirt over my head. I do my best to climb back under the covers without shaking the bed. Once I lean my head into my pillows, weariness soaks through my body.

As I stare up at the ceiling, I wonder how Marta could have taken Oscar back in the first place. I know she said that he convinced her that he had a change of heart and that he realized how much he loved her, but how could she really trust him after all they'd been through? I guess it's easier to believe that Oscar was telling the truth about his *changing heart*—look how quickly it changed again as soon as Michelle turned up pregnant!

People tell you all of the time to "follow your heart" when it comes to matters of love, but how can you be sure you can trust it? And if you can't trust your *own* heart, how can you possibly trust someone else's?

When my thoughts turn to Marco, a mixture of excitement and fear stirs inside of me. He kept saying that he loves me—and I want to believe him. But we barely know each other. And as much as I think I might love him, too, it feels like I still need to do some more "falling" before I know for sure.

Chapter Twenty-Three

I'm up early today. I woke up around 6:30 when I heard Marta leaving. I didn't know if I should hop out of bed and rush after her or not. She had a pretty difficult night, and, I'm sure, if she needed to talk, she would've let me know. Marta is a very private person, and the fact that she's let me in is still a bit of a surprise. She's going through a horrible time in her life, and she needs to have someone to talk to—and, truthfully, so do I. We are a very unlikely pair, but she's become one of my only friends now that Scott and I don't talk. It's an odd friendship, but it's a friendship nonetheless.

It's a gorgeous day outside, and I'm looking forward to meeting Marco's family and spending more time getting to know him. The impact of what happened to Marta has me questioning everything, and, despite my excitement over Marco—and the fact that he keeps saying that he loves me—there is a layer of skepticism over my heart that I need to break through. I'm hoping that spending some time with him and his family will help me see *the real* Marco and give me some insight into my own true feelings.

After my long morning run, I still have about two hours to kill before I need to get ready to go to the vineyard. So, I decide to go out to the pool area and soak up some early rays. I slip on my bathing suit, grab a towel, my book and a peach from Marco's basket and make my way toward the pool. It's still too early for most people to be up and moving, and there's a sleepy hush over the resort that compels me to tiptoe down the cobbled walkways.

The pool decks are completely empty as I make my way over to a set of chairs on the far side of the pool. They're perfectly positioned to catch the early morning sun. Once I'm settled into my lounge chair, I reach for my book and look for the dog-eared page somewhere toward the middle. Once I find my place in my book, I reach for my peach and start devouring it as I read.

I'm fully engrossed in my book and my peach when I hear the scraping sound of someone moving a lounge chair across the deck floor a few feet away. When I look up, I have to blink hard to be sure that my eyes aren't playing a trick on me. When I open them again and push my sunglasses up onto the top of my head, a powerful zing of adrenaline pulses through my body.

"Hello, Elle," Gabriel Menendez says with an acid-like tone. "You look surprised to see me," she says as she drops a colorful canvas bag onto her lounge chair. She has an evil look on her face, and her beauty sort of takes my breath away.

"Gabby! Hi!" I say as I grope for words. "What are you doing here?"

"I'm Lupe's replacement—didn't you know that?" she says smugly as she starts sliding her bathing suit cover-up off her shoulders and eventually over her perfectly shaped hips.

"I guess no one mentioned anything to me," I say as a nervous tremble rides up my spine.

I haven't seen Gabby since the night her crazy boyfriend tried to make a move on me at dinner. I feel so awkward, especially since I purposely avoided her and made no efforts whatsoever to find out if she was mad at me before I left for Italy. Judging by her frosty demeanor, I think it's safe to assume that she was indeed mad, and, now, her anger has turned into a grudge.

"When did you get here?" I ask in an effort to make polite conversation.

"This morning," she says as she lowers her amazing body down onto the lounge chair.

I watch her as she digs through her bag and pulls out a bottle of suntan oil. She snaps the top of the bottle open and pours the oil onto one of her thighs and begins messaging it into her skin.

"I'm all mixed up from the time change, so I decided I would sit by the pool for awhile until my body relaxes," she finally says, which at least makes me feel like she's willing to try to make conversation.

"Well it's great to have you here," I lie in an obvious effort to placate her. The coconut smell of her suntan oil is wafting over in my direction. It smells like Miami to me, and a rush of homesickness momentarily washes over me.

Gabby laughs and continues rubbing oil into her skin. "Make no mistake, Elle," she says as she squirts more oil onto her stomach. "We aren't friends anymore, so I'm not going to *pretend* that I'm happy to see you, OK?" When she looks up at me, I feel like she's attempting to shoot daggers at me out of her mocha brown eyes.

Stung by her words, I just look at her as all the blood drains out of my face. I don't know how to respond to her, so I don't. Gabby reaches into her bag again and pulls out a hot pink iPod and shoves the speaker buds into her ears. She leans back on her lounge chair and closes her eyes. All I can seem to do is just sit there in awkward silence, watching Gabriel Menendez tapping her perfectly polished toes to the beat of the music in her ears.

I pretend to read my book for a while and hope that Gabby will just fall asleep. I don't want her to see me leave—then it might seem like I have a guilty conscience or something. And I don't! The truth is, I'm completely shocked that Gabby still seems to believe that I was responsible for Manny's behavior at dinner that night. I thought for sure Manny would tell Gabby about my virginity, and, if anything, Gabby would be laughing at me, not hating me. The whole mess is as surreal to me now as it was when it happened.

I hate to admit it, but it really bothers me that Gabby is here. Why didn't they pick the replacement person in order of seniority? Gabby started a couple of years after I did, so surely there had to be someone senior to her that wanted to take this transfer. And the thought of having Gabby on the evening crew is the thing that makes me feel the worst. Even though she's Lupe's replacement, thanks to Miriam, Gabby is really replacing *me*. That means she'll be working with Marco. Suddenly, I feel incredibly insecure and nervous, and I have to leave the pool area right away.

So I quickly gather my belongings and pull myself up off of my lounge chair. I'm kind of unsteady as I try to straddle the width of the chair with all my stuff in my arms. I do my best to silently waddle down to the end of the chair, but my leg accidentally knocks the side of one of the low tables positioned between my lounge chair and the chair to the right. The result is a loud clatter as the tabletop jiggles inside the frame. My heart starts pounding from the adrenaline rush of possibly waking Gabby, but I'm comforted to see that she didn't even stir.

Once I'm on the other side of the pool gate, I feel like I can finally breath. I feel shaky as I totter down the walkway, so I take a deep cleansing breath and try to find my center. I head toward my villa and do my best to put this situation into perspective. *Yes*, Gabby is gorgeous, and *yes*, she will be flying with my Marco. But Marco said he *loves me*—and that doesn't just happen! There has to be chemistry and a connection, not just physical attraction. Besides, I think Marco and I might be soul mates, destined to be together forever.

A warm feeling comes over me as I think about how I had to come all the way to Italy to find my soul mate. When I found out about this transfer, I knew that something big was on the horizon for me, but little did I know it was finding the love of my life!

When Marco turns onto the road that leads to *Marbello Vineyards*, my heart is racing with excitement over meeting his family. I've heard so many wonderful things about everyone, and the fact that Marco wants me to meet them must mean that he sees a future for us. I manage to steal tiny glimpses of Marco while he's driving. I love the way his mouth forms the sound of each and every word he speaks and how animated his face becomes when he's talking about his passion for this country. I don't know for sure what it feels like to be in love, but as I listen to Marco and breathe in his presence, I think I'm starting to find out.

Marco explains to me on the drive that since it's a weekday, the vineyard should be nice and quiet. But on the weekends, it can be very busy.

There are wine tastings and food pairings each weekend in the summer, and people from all over the world stop by to tour the vineyard. His two brothers, Angelo and Lorenzo, run the business side of the vineyard while his mother is the master blender *and* the heart and soul of *Marbello*. Marco's mother invited the rest of his family to join us for dinner tonight—so I'll be meeting *everyone*—but during the day, Angelo is going to show us around.

The dirt road is packed and rocky, but a cloud of sandy yellow dust billows around us as we snake our way up to the main house. Neatly planted rows of grapes stretch beyond my view on either side of the car, and it is unquestionably the most beautiful place I've ever seen. As we approach an open clearing in the road, I notice a rustic, barn-like structure to one side and a beautiful, blonde, brick house that just barely peeks through a leafy canopy of trees.

"Welcome to *Marbello*," Marco says with pride.

"It's *beautiful*," I say as I try to absorb every detail.

"No...*you* are beautiful," Marco says as he shuts down the engine of his car and then moves in toward me.

I'm drawn to his lips and, when we kiss, every feeling I have for Marco is affirmed. I *do* love him. There is no question for me now.

As we pull apart, I whisper, "I love you..."

Marco just smiles at me and then says, "Good!"

We both laugh lightly as Marco reaches for his door latch and slips out of the driver's seat. I watch him elegantly glide around the front of the car to open my door for me. He's wearing a pair of tan shorts and a white, gauzy linen shirt. When he opens my door and gently takes my hand, I feel like a princess. I'm wearing a simple, mid-length, purple sundress with thick straps and a pair of flat sandals, but something about the way Marco dotes over me makes me feel like I'm elegantly dressed and in a movie or something! I can hear the sound of a dog barking off in the distance, and I wonder if it's Chianti. I smile up at Marco, and he smiles back.

"Are you ready to meet my mother and my brothers?" he asks brightly.

"I am," I say as a fresh tingle of nerves flutter through my stomach.

"I told my mother that she needed to be sure to give Chianti a bath—she has work to do with one of our guests," he says as he takes my hand and gives it a little squeeze.

I just smile at the thought of meeting this dog, and I hope that being around another Boxer will help me with my homesickness for Sugar Ray and not make it worse. As we round the corner of the barn and start walking toward the house, I can see a beautiful woman dressed in a floral skirt and white shirt walking toward us. I smile when I notice that she's wearing rubber work boots with her skirt, but, for some reason, it looks perfectly natural.

Running along beside her is a fawn-colored dog with a familiar square face and stumpy tail. My heart instantly melts as Chianti comes running toward Marco with a happy hello and a shimmy of joy to share with us. Marco reaches down to give Chianti a loving rub on the head and scratch behind the ears. I stoop down to meet Chianti and finally get a good look at her face. She is adorable! Her soft brown eyes have a familiar quality that sends a rush of relief to my aching heart. Chianti immediately greets me with a show of affection and a few misplaced slobbery kisses.

I'm laughing as I stand up and work to wipe the slobber off my hands and my shoulder, and that's when I get my first good look at Marco's mother. She's stunning. She has stark white hair pulled back into a tight bun, and the olive brown skin of her face looks young and fresh. She has light green eyes that have flecks of gold, and her nose is thin and her lips are full and rosy. She gives me a stiff and reserved smile as Marco begins our introductions.

"Mama, this is my *Eloise-ah*," he begins as he turns his attention toward me. He is beaming with pride, and I can't tell if he is proud of me or proud of his mother.

"*Buongiorno, Eloise-ah*," she says with very little warmth or emotion. "My name is Sofia," she says as she takes my hand and presses her lips into a tight smile.

I'm instantly aware of the reservation in her tone and in her gestures, and I wonder what I've done to set things off to such a frosty start. But I do my best to find my manners, and I give her a gentle smile in return.

"It is very nice to meet you, Mrs. Maselli," I cautiously venture in, hoping to score some points for sincere respect.

"Now it seems you have a new best friend," Sofia says with her thick accent as she turns her attention to Chianti, who is still wagging her bottom around and doing a little dance to get some more attention.

"That's just fine by me," I say with a huge smile, doing my best to endear myself to Marco's mother as I reach down to rub Chianti's back. She's much thicker and quite a bit shorter than Sugar Ray, but just having some of her unconditional dog love around me right now gives me hope that I can handle this situation.

Marco and his mother start walking toward the house, and I notice how gently he wraps his arm around her. It's obvious that Marco deeply respects his mother, and I can tell that she is very fond of her son. I'm sure she must be skeptical of the women he dates, and I wonder if her icy reaction toward me is a common first response to a newcomer. I just hope I can figure out how to thaw her heart and prove to her that I'm Marco's soul mate. Her son said he loves me, and that has to make me worthy of her friendship at least. Right?

I can hear them conversing in Italian, and I don't even try to figure out what they're saying. I just lag behind a few paces as Chianti loafs along beside me. As we make our way up to the main house, I can smell the aroma of fresh baked bread and roasted garlic. Marco opens the side door for his mother and then turns to look at me. He smiles at me like he's really happy that I'm here. I quicken my steps a bit, and Marco wraps his arm around my shoulders as he guides me into the house. The screen door closes with a slam, and I can hear Chianti let out a little whimper.

"Can she come in the house?" I ask Marco.

"No, she can wait for us outside. My mother is making her gravy for dinner tonight, and Chianti gets too excited from all the smells," Marco explains with a light laugh as we make our way into the kitchen. A smile broadens across my face as I imagine how Sugar Ray would react to the heavenly aromas wafting from this kitchen.

When I enter the kitchen, I'm surprised to see how enormous and bright it is. There are pane glass windows stretching across one whole side of the room and fancy, modern appliances spaced out all along the other side. A long wooden table with bench seating stretches down the center of the room, and a clear glass vase filled with purple and orange wild flowers is placed right in the center. The room is a combination of Old World charm and present-day sophistication.

Marco releases my hand, and I watch as he greets his brothers who look like they were both eating lunch at the table. I can tell they must be his brothers because they both look like older versions of Marco. I watch as these men greet each other with kisses and hardy slaps on the back, and it makes me smile when I think of what a close knit family this must be. I notice Sofia snatching a wary glance at me before she lifts the lid on a huge pot of sauce simmering on the stovetop. She gives the sauce a gentle stir, replaces the lid and then turns her attention to her boys.

"*Eloise-ah*," Marco says as he reaches his hand out for me. "Come to meet my brothers!"

I take a few tentative steps closer and grab Marco's hand. He guides me around to the other side of the table and perfectly positions me for the introductions.

"This is my brother Lorenzo—he is the one who *makes* all the money for the vineyard—and this is my brother Angelo—who *spends* all the money we make at the vineyard," Marco says as he dodges a fake slap on the face from Angelo.

"It's wonderful to meet you both," I say as I nervously reach out my hand and give it to Lorenzo. I'm not sure at first what to make of Lorenzo. He seems incredibly serious, and there is something very sad in his eyes as he says his hellos.

I shift my attention now to Angelo, who has a much happier face and disposition and seems to be bubbling over in anticipation of meeting me.

"It is a pleasure to have you with us today at *Marbello, Eloise-ah*," Angelo says sincerely as he takes me in. "We have been hearing so much about the lovely American girl who has stolen our brother's heart!" he says as a wash of joy overtakes his face.

I just smile in return, not sure what to say, but feeling a flood of happiness over the fact that Marco has already told his family about me and that they think I've stolen his heart! But then I watch as Angelo's eyes quickly dart toward his mother and then back to me. When I cautiously look at Mrs. Maselli, she is tying an apron around her waist with a bitter look of distaste on her face. A heavy feeling settles in my stomach as I return my eyes to Angelo and give him a weak, forced smile.

"Angelo has a lovely lunch planned for you," Sofia says in a business-like tone from the other side of the room. "He is going to take you and Marco to one of my favorite *vistas* for a picnic and, when you return, I will take you on a *personal* tour of my winery."

"How wonderful," I say to her, doing my best to send her my most appreciative smile. A wash of nervous tingles cascades through my body as I think of being alone with this woman who seems to already dislike me quite a bit.

"I'm hungry," Marco says, interrupting my mild panic attack. "Angelo, hurry up and take us on our picnic!"

Angelo laughs at his younger brother, and I can tell that these two are the clowns of the family. I watch as Angelo drains a glass of some type of lemonade, gathers up his plates and walks toward the kitchen sink. After he deposits his dishes, Angelo grabs his mother in his arms as he passes by and dips her back so he can plant a kiss on her face. Sofia's laugh is big and loud, and you can't help but feel the joy she has for her boys.

Lorenzo seems to be trying to ignore us. I notice that he is reading a newspaper with his lunch, and it looks like an Italian version of *The Financial Times* or something. He barely even looks up when his mother laughs, and he shifts around a bit in his chair after he takes another bite of his sandwich. As Marco and I follow Angelo out of the kitchen, I can't help but wonder why Lorenzo seems so sad.

"Lorenzo is in a good mood today," Marco says in English, probably for my benefit. He lets out a loud whistle, and Chianti comes barreling around the corner of the house.

"Ah, you noticed!" Angelo says with a huge grin. "You see, *Eloise-ah*, our brother is a *very serious* man, and so it is my job, and Marco's job, when he is here, to make Lorenzo laugh!"

"Oh, I see…" I reply lightly as I pat the side of my thigh in hopes of getting Chianti's attention. The simple gesture does the trick as she runs up beside me and starts nuzzling my leg as I follow the guys toward the barn.

"Yes—it is my mission in life to find ways to…make Lorenzo smile," Marco continues, as the two brothers seem to find great amusement in teasing their more serious and moody brother.

"Sometimes it is more difficult than other times—it all depends on the day," Angelo says over his shoulder as the three of us enter the barn. "Today, it will not be so difficult," he surmises.

"Why is that?" I ask, curious about what could make the difference.

"Because *you* are here," Marco says brightly.

I just look up at Marco and give him a quizzical smile. "What do I have to do with anything?" I finally ask.

"He will be on his best behavior with a beautiful woman around," Angelo answers for Marco. "He will be hoping you have a single sister," he adds with a peel of laughter.

Both Angelo and Marco start laughing, and I don't really get the inside joke, but I guess it's safe to assume that Lorenzo doesn't have much luck with the ladies. At any rate, Marco and Angelo seem to be enjoying themselves, so I laugh along and act as though this all makes sense to me.

Then I add, "I do have a few single friends from work I could introduce him to."

"*Oh Marco!*" Angelo says with great interest. "That could be just the thing!"

"No!" Marco says emphatically. "I don't want anyone I work with dating my miserable brother."

"What about your not-so-miserable brother?" Angelo asks after a short pause. Then he laughs out loud to break the tension.

"We'll see," Marco says to Angelo with a smile as we all make our way into a wide open section of the barn.

There is a small four-wheeler with a flatbed on the back sitting in the middle of the space. A thick pad and a cream-colored blanket are spread out over the flatbed, and a tan wicker basket is resting in the center.

"Go ahead and climb on," Angelo says to me as I stand and stare at the arrangement. "It is a long drive uphill to get to the vista."

I look over at Marco, and he smiles sweetly and gives his eyebrows a quick raise. I watch as he walks over to the flatbed, puts one leg up on the back wheel and extends his hand out for me.

So I follow him and take his hand, and he helps me climb onto the platform. He climbs on board, and we both settle in with our backs toward the open cab of the vehicle. Angelo hops into the driver's seat and fires up the tiny engine.

"Do you want Chianti to come?" Marco asks.

"Can she?" I sheepishly request.

"Of course," he says. Then he lets out a quick, sharp whistle, and Chianti jumps up onto the flatbed and positions herself right between us. "OK, you can stay there for the ride out, but when we get there, *I'm* sitting next to Eloise-ah," Marco says to Chianti as he runs his hand down her back.

"She doesn't speak English, Marco, so you may have to translate," Angelo says from the driver's seat.

Marco looks at me, and we both laugh. I enjoy the banter between Marco and his brother. He looks so much like Marco, except for his bright blue eyes and his paunchy belly. But he's still quite handsome and interesting, and I can't help but like him.

It's a bumpy ride out to the vista, but the views are spectacular. Marco singles out several points of interest to me as we roll and wobble up steep hills and down winding paths. The countryside is literally lush with vineyards and wooded areas, and it looks like a tapestry made up of dark greens, deep yellows and honey-colored grasses. We pass old stone structures that Marco says were checkpoints his grandfather used in order to survey his crops when the vineyard was still considered young.

"This vineyard is in her prime now," Marco explains. "She is producing some of Tuscany's most important wines. These grapes over here are all our *Sangiovese* grapes—which is the most important grape used when making our Chianti," Marco says as the dog nestled between us pops her head up at the sound of her name. Marco rubs her head lightly and then continues talking.

"My mother is a third generation winemaker, and she has become quite good at blending the grapes and knowing how long to age them," he says with great pride. "And she is famous for being a good judge of character—in both wine and people," he says as he surveys the land around us.

"Marco?" I tentatively ask.

"Yes, Eloise-ah," he replies as he turns his attention toward me. His face is soft and handsome, and I'm almost afraid to speak and ruin this lovely moment.

"I'm worried that your mother doesn't like me," I blurt out as my face crunches up a bit with insecurity.

"She will…" he assures me. He gives me a smile and looks up at the sky as we continue to bounce along the rutty trail.

His words don't bring me much comfort, because in a way, he's acknowledging to me that he knows his mother doesn't like me, and that I was, in fact, correctly picking up on her dislike back at the house. I feel no relief from mentioning my concern, so I decide to change the subject altogether and let this latest information marinate inside me for a while.

"So did you and your brothers and sisters grow up on this vineyard?" I ask, as I look around at all the amazing places to run and get lost as a kid.

"Some of us have never grown up!" Angelo interjects over his shoulder.

"That is very true," Marco says with a light laugh. "Angelo still lives here, and Lorenzo just built a villa on the other side of this hill," Marco says as he points uphill.

"Yes…it is true…I still live with my mother," Angelo jokes from the front seat.

I just laugh at him while I try to imagine what it would be like to live in such in spectacular place. As we work our way down a tiny embankment, I can smell the fresh scent of the lavender that lines the edge of the path and other earthy fragrances that are too plentiful to decipher.

"We did live here when we were growing up, but only in the summers," Marco continues. "As children, we used to play in the vineyards and sometimes have grape wars with the rotting fruit we found on the ground. And sometimes we would play a game of...*hide and you find me?*"

"Hide-and-go-seek?" I suggest with a giggle.

"Yes!" Marco says as his eyes twinkle with the memories.

"Well it's just magical out here, Marco..." I trail off as I do my best to memorize the scenery.

"We are here!" Angelo announces as he brings the four-wheeler to an abrupt stop.

When I turn around to see where Angelo has taken us, my eyes can't seem to drink in the splendor fast enough. In the far distance, I can see the city of Florence nestled into rolling hills that partially swallow up manmade works of art with God-inspired beauty. To my left, a gently sloping field covered in red flowers sways in the breeze, and a tree-lined vineyard down below bakes in the heat of the early afternoon sun. It's beyond breathtaking. It's perfection.

By the time I turn back around, Marco and Angelo have already set up our picnic. The cream-colored blanket is spread out beneath a tall shade tree, and the wicker basket is resting off to the side. Chianti is busy sniffing out a trail along the edge of the clearing. I take a deep breath and close my eyes. I want to remember how I feel right now for the rest of my life.

"I will be back to get you in *two hours*," Angelo says as he climbs back onto the four-wheeler and gives the engine a rev. "So you two behave," he adds with a happy laugh as he pops the clutch and sputters away.

Marco motions for me to join him, so I make my way over to the blanket. When Chianti notices me, she bounds toward me with a stick in her mouth, and I can't help but think about how having her here makes this moment even more complete. Marco takes my hand, and we both kick off our shoes and then step onto the soft, cottony blanket.

"We are lucky to have such cool weather. Sometimes when I've been out here, it feels like the sun will roast you alive," Marco says as he lowers himself down onto the blanket.

"So do you come out here often?" I have to ask the question—even though my doubts about Marco have nearly disappeared. I carefully sit down on the blanket and fold my legs up underneath my dress and wait for Marco's answer.

"It is my mother's favorite place in the vineyard," he says as he pulls the basket onto the blanket and starts digging out various wrapped items. "She and her brothers and sisters *did* grow up on the vineyard, and this particular spot has very special meaning to her. So when I was a boy, she used to take me here for picnics."

"You and your mother seem very close," I observe as I help Marco unwrap some of the food. So far, everything looks pretty delicious—there are dried fruits, cheeses, and some sort of panini-looking sandwiches along with several types of grapes.

"We are—maybe more so than the others," Marco says as he looks off into the distance. "I think it is because I am her youngest. There is just something about a mama and her youngest boy," he says with a smile.

I smile back at him and try to resist the urge to leap over the food in the middle of the blanket and kiss his lips. Chianti creates a momentary diversion for my lust as she presses her wet face up against my shoulder and wags her tail. When I look down by my hand, I see that she's brought me the stick, and wants me to toss it. I indulge her and then return my attention to Marco.

"Thank you for bringing me here," I say. A gentle breeze catches my hair, and I can feel a long skinny strand stretching across my face.

"You are so beautiful, *Eloise-ah,*" Marco says in return. I watch as he shifts his body around on the blanket so he is able to reach for me and draw my face in close to his.

When his lips touch mine, my eyes drift shut, and I'm transported to a place where there is no need for food or water—just Marco and his kisses.

Everything in the picnic basket tasted so amazing, but there certainly was a lot of cheese. As I eat my last bite of some sort of brie-like spread on a thin salty wafer, I notice that my stomach feels rather thick and bloated already. As I wash the bite down with a final taste of red wine, I say a desperate prayer that the wine will settle my stomach.

I do my best to shove my worries about my bloated belly and Marco's mother to the back of my mind as we both stretch out on the blanket. Marco is resting his head on the upturned basket, and I have my head cradled in the angle of his shoulder. Despite my best efforts to ignore my stomach, I'm aware of an uncontrollable gurgling sounding bubbling inside of me. I gently fold my hands across my abdomen, hoping that this will at least muffle the sounds a bit.

Marco doesn't seem to notice my gastro-intestinal distress as he starts talking about family and how it is the most important thing. I listen to his words as they lull me into a state of contentment, and, even though I can't help but worry about his mother's icy reception, I try to think positively that she will come around and see me for who I am: *The woman Marco loves!*

Every now and then, Marco pulls me into his arms, and we kiss. And these kisses are some of the most delicious kisses so far. There is no lust or aggression, just soft, passion-filled licks and pecks that make me feel safe with Marco.

"Your friend...Marta? She was very upset last night," Marco says tentatively during a lingering lull in our conversation.

"Yes, she was," I say, wondering how she's doing. I feel a ping of guilt that I didn't make time to check in on her before I left today.

"Her lover...he left her for another woman, is this true?" he asks somberly as he lightly brushes my forehead with the tips of his fingers.

"Yes, but how did you know?" I have to ask, feeling slightly protective of Marta and what other people might be saying about her.

"I just guessed—pain like that is usually easy to recognize," he says matter-of-factly.

"It is the worst kind of pain, I think," I add, trying to figure out how Marta will ever recover.

"My brother Lorenzo knows this pain," Marco shares in a soft voice. "His wife left him recently."

"Oh, that's terrible," I say as I tilt my head to look up at Marco.

"It was," Marco agrees. "He was not so happy in the marriage, but he loved her so much, and, when she left him, I think she took his smile along with her."

I understand everything completely now. I feel a sadness welling up in my heart for Marta and Lorenzo—two wonderful people who are grieving the loss of their greatest loves.

"I hate that they are going through all of this pain," I say quietly, wondering how people survive a loss like that.

"Yes, but it is a part of life and love, I guess," Marco replies in a matter of fact tone.

"Maybe…" I say, kind of sobered by his words.

"Better to love and be broken than not to love at all," Marco says brightly as he kisses my forehead.

I try to sort out this exchange and not read too much into it, because in my haze of emotions, I know if I take the time to carefully analyze it, I might not like what I see.

"Maybe we should introduce your brother to Marta some time," I suggest, hoping to change the direction of the conversation.

"Maybe," Marco says, like he might actually be considering it. "We'll see," he adds just before he rolls over on top of me. "I don't want to talk about sad people right now," he says, as his mood turns lively. "I just want to kiss the woman I love!"

I hold my breath as the weight of Marco's body presses into my bloated, cheese filled belly, willing the gas building up inside of me to stay in and not slip out. The pain is horrendous, but I can't ignore the beautiful man on top of me, staring into my eyes. I give Marco an awkward smile and playfully wiggle out from underneath him. I turn myself upright and straighten my dress. Marco follows my lead and sits up, too, and then reaches for my hand. He gently kisses my wrist, followed by a series of pecks that lead up my arm, to my shoulder and then onto my neck.

Oh wow… I think as I relax and allow myself to enjoy every second of this affection.

When Angelo pulls the four-wheeler back into the barn, I see that Sofia is waiting for me by the gate. She waves her hand as we roll past, and Marco blows his mother a kiss. I watch as she catches it in the air and pretends to tuck it in her pocket.

"She likes to save my kisses for later," Marco says to me with a smile.

When the four-wheeler comes to a halt, Angelo walks around to the side to help me off the platform. He's smiling from ear to ear, and I can't help but feel happy when I'm around him.

"Mama is going to take you on a tour of her cellar now," Angelo says. "Be sure to ask her if you can taste something from her *Riserva,*" he whispers to me as I step past him. "It will make her day!"

"OK," I say with a smile as I try to commit to memory the word *Riserva.*

My palms are already sweating as I try to prepare myself for time alone with a woman who doesn't seem to want to like me.

"I will see you soon, *Eloise-ah,*" Marco says as he sidles up next to me and walks with me toward his mother. "Don't worry—once she gets to know you, she will love you as much as I do," he assures me. "She is amazing," he adds before he gives me a kiss on the forehead and walks off toward the house, leaving me alone with his gorgeous but stoic-looking mother.

"Did you enjoy the vista?" Sofia asks me without even a trace of a smile.

"Oh, yes. I really did," I gush, trying to force my charms on her so she will warm up to me.

"Good. Now I want to take you into my world and try understand what my Marco sees in you..." she says in an even, dry tone.

Yikes! I think as I do my best to deflect her verbal barb with as much grace as I can muster.

Sofia takes my arm and gently wraps it under hers as she guides me toward a large, cobblestone structure with a huge wooden door. The gesture is mixed with reassurance as well as domination, almost as if Sofia is letting me know that she is in control—of our conversation as well as who her son falls in love with.

My heart is beating wildly, and my stomach is a mess. I'm terrified that Marco's mother won't approve of me, and this thought does nothing to quell the bubbling caldron of gases and acids mixing together deep inside my belly. I haven't had much of a chance to prepare myself for being impressive, and in my current condition, I'm bracing myself for the worst.

As we enter through the wooden door, I can smell the pungent fragrance of wine and wet wood. Once my eyes adjust to the dim lighting, I can see that there are huge wooden barrels stacked up in wide rows all the way down the length of the building. It's cool and calm inside, and I can't believe how small I feel with the peaked ceiling and the wide beams that stretch across the room. There are simply too many barrels to count so I don't even try, but I do my best to fathom the greatness of the bounty in this room.

"This is where we age our wines," Sofia begins flatly as she guides me past the first row of barrels. "My father and I set up this room, and I have done my best to keep exactly the way he left it for me," she says with a hint of pride in her voice.

"It's incredible," I say as I follow her down one of the rows, drinking in the aroma of the room. I don't want to say too much, but I certainly want to compliment her every chance I get.

Sofia begins telling me about how she makes the wine, and I do my best to follow along, but it's all very confusing to me because sometimes I'm not sure if she is speaking English or Italian! But when she's talking about winemaking, her voice is round, soft and pleasant, and I can see a love in her eyes that isn't there when she is simply looking at me. So I do my best to stay in the moment with her as she reveals her passions to me.

She takes me to a tasting barrel and uses an ancient-looking wooden ladle to dip out a taste of her most important wine—the *Riserva*. As I taste the wine, Sofia watches me with pride. I carefully take a sip and allow it to roll over my tongue. Sofia tells me how to breathe it in on its way down, so I can truly experience the taste. I close my eyes to better explore the flavors, and, when I open them, I'm speechless. The flavor is rich and full, and it makes my body float as it makes it way down my throat.

By the time she's finished with the tour, I don't really know any more about winemaking than I did before, but what I *do* understand is that the wines of *Marbello* are quite special. She takes me past her blending table and shows me how she decides which grapes will be blended to create each of the wines of *Marbello*. The *Sangiovese* grapes—that Marco pointed out to me on the way to the vista—are among Sofia's favorite, and she tells me how a good Tuscan red begins with a deep knowledge of these glorious grapes.

Sofia is so elegant. And even though I barely understand a word of what she's saying, her accent and the passion behind her words are riveting. She reminds me so much of her son when he's talking about Florence—there is a love and a connection they seem to feel that they both have a deep need to share. After she checks a few things and adds a few notes to a tattered leather-bound book on her blending table, she looks up at me with a weak smile and a gentle sigh.

"Come," she says as she reaches for my hand. "I want to learn more about *you*," she says with resignation as I gently place my hand in hers. She guides me out of the aging cellar and toward a pair of rustic wooden chairs just outside.

"This is where I like to sit and think," Sofia says as she leans back into her chair. "That is one of the things that is so magical about *Marbello*— there are so many wonderful places to be alone with your thoughts," she says to me with her first truly kind look of the day.

"Yes…I can see that," I say appreciatively as I lean back into my own chair and pull in a deep breath. The view from here is nothing short of spectacular. The sky is growing more yellow and orange with the close of the day drawing near. I allow myself this moment of reflection and lose my worries in the wispy, cotton-candy clouds.

We both sit for a while in blissful silence. Chianti eventually finds us, and after giving her mama a kiss, she rests her boxy head in my lap for a little scratch behind the ears. I feel so happy to see her. She gives me added courage to face Marco's mother, who seems to be waiting for me to start the conversation.

So slowly, and cautiously, I start sharing the smallest details about my life. In no time, Sofia asks me specific questions about my family and my background, soaking in the information with interest, but with no emotion. I do my best to answer the questions succinctly and with care, but nothing seems to be changing Sofia's impassive attitude about me—the woman her son claims to love.

Chapter Twenty-Four

The rest of the evening is a blur. When Sofia and I join Marco and his brothers, the chaos of setting up the table for dinner and welcoming a never-ending stream of family is well underway. There are so many people in the kitchen—everyone kissing and hugging and jabbering in Italian— that all I can do is stand back and observe.

Marco's three sisters arrive with their husbands. There's Rosa, Marco's oldest sister, and her husband, Guy; his middle sisters, Bella and Gina, who both brought their husbands, Piero and Ricco. Franco arrives with *Zia Viola*, the aunt who taught him how to embroider, and they both coo and cluck over me in Italian. The last to arrive are Andre and Marco's father, Giorgio.

Giorgio is quite handsome. With a thick head of silver hair and a long lean body, he looks like he could be an Italian movie star or something. I watch him carefully as he cuts through the room and takes Sofia into his arms and kisses her deeply. Even though she's distracted with preparing for the family feast, Sofia allows herself this moment of indulgence with her husband. It makes me smile as I can see the love between them is still so strong after years of marriage and raising such a big family.

For the most part, all of the Maselli men seem to approve of me, but there's a constant heaviness in the room whenever Sofia is around. Her disapproval of me is literally palpable. And I know I'm not the only one who feels it. Even Marco seems to be keeping his distance from me and doesn't even protest when his mother seats me between his two oldest sisters at the dinner table. I'm conscious of the weighty, watchful eyes of Sofia, as she seems to monitor my every move.

Luckily, the dinner is incredible—and this time I mean it in a *good* way! There's Sofia's famous red sauce and homemade pastas, and a decadent dish called *Osso Buco*, which is veal cooked with vegetable and is positively *out-of-this-world delicious*! And each of Marco's sisters brought *contorni* (side dishes) that taste fabulous. There's an eggplant dish and another white bean dish that I could easily eat every day for the rest of my life and be very happy! And the wine—well, the wine is amazing!

When the night is nearly over and I'm helping Sofia and Marco's sisters with the dishes, I struggle to stay calm. My stomach troubles still haven't quieted down, and Sofia hasn't softened toward me one bit—even with the distraction of her entire family around her. And while Marco's sisters were much more interested in getting to know me, I still feel certain that I haven't managed to do anything to win Sofia over. I feel a wash of disappointment in myself that I was unable to make a connection with Marco's mother. It's obvious to me that her opinion matters very much in this family, and I'm pretty sure she's decided I'm not right for her son.

My heart is heavy as I carry the last of the dishes into the kitchen from the dining room, and I hear Sofia and her daughters laughing and carrying on. I want to join in so badly, but even if I could speak Italian, I'm quite sure there's no room for me in that circle of women.

As Marco and I start saying our goodbyes, I wish things could have gone a bit differently with Sofia. I want more time to try to get to know her and to show her how much I love her son. But it's getting late and I can tell Marco's ready to be alone. So I give Sofia a weak hug goodbye and thank her for her amazing hospitality. She gives me a polite smile and wishes me a good night. It's rather anti-climactic to say the least, but I can't help feeling a sense of relief that this day is just about over.

When we step outside, the air is fresh and cool. It smells of cut grass and wildflowers, and, as I breathe it in, I try to swallow all the emotions billowing up inside of me. Marco's mother doesn't like me. And that hurts me…very much.

As we make our way toward Marco's car, I feel something bump up against my leg. When I look down, Chianti is walking next to me with a stick in her mouth. She's wagging her stumpy tail for me, and I simply melt at the sight of her. So I stoop down and take her head into my hands.

"Chianti," I say with a thick voice as my eyes well up with tears. "You be a good girl, OK? I know you don't speak any English, but I hope you know how much I loved meeting you." I pull in a sharp breath and will myself not to cry anymore.

On the drive back to Florence, I feel heavy and burdened with my thoughts. I can't stop wondering why Marco's mother seemed to resist getting to know me. My cheeks feel scratched with redness and embarrassment over the idea that I failed so miserably to impress Sofia Maselli. And to make matters worse, Marco hasn't said a word to me. His silence is strange and makes me uncomfortable, so I just stare out the window of the speeding car, and watch the countryside disappear into the distance. I wish he'd break the silence or reassure me that, even though his mother didn't seem to love me, *he still does.*

When we finally turn into *Il Girasole*, Marco parks his car along the side of the road and climbs out. This time, when he opens the door for me, there's no question we're going back to my villa. But I'm not worried. I think I need the reassurance of Marco's physical affection tonight, so I silently take his hand and allow him to lift me out of the car.

When we enter my villa, I quickly excuse myself, and slip into the bathroom. I need some time to freshen up and regain my composure. I wash my face, brush my teeth and put on a fresh coat of deodorant. Then I search my vanity drawers for a roll of TUMS in a final effort to calm my stomach. These small efforts do wonders to make me feel better about myself, and, suddenly, I'm looking forward to spending some alone time with my Marco. I guess in the end, it matters most what Marco thinks of me, not his mother. And there's plenty of time for her to get to know me down the road. If we're going to build a life together, she'll have to let me in, right?

When I come out of the bathroom, a little rush of nerves grips my still uneasy stomach. At first, I look around, and I don't see Marco. My initial thought is that he left. He couldn't handle the fact that his mother hated me, so he left! My heart sinks with shame as I realize that maybe it really does matter what his mother thinks of me—so much so that he can't even be around me anymore!

But then I notice that there's a light on in my bedroom. Relief rushes over my bruised ego, and I realize that I need to let the Sofia thing go and make a better effort to reconnect with Marco. I can't let this woman haunt my mind and ruin this amazing thing I have with my soul mate. So far, nothing about falling in love with Marco has been easy, but maybe that is the very thing that makes this love so worthy and so powerful.

As I step into my room, I see that Marco has placed all of my throw pillows on the window seat. And when I look to my right, I see that Marco is already under the covers in my bed. All I can see is his naked body from the waist up, and he is leaning up on one elbow looking directly at me as I enter.

"Take off your clothes…" Marco says with a steamy, lust-filled voice. His torso is smooth and muscled, and he looks so very handsome flexed on his side in my bed.

I'm frozen in place. I don't know what to do exactly. I can't just take off my dress and hop in the sack with Marco—that's too much! So I just stand there and stare at him, trying to decide how to slow things down without ruining everything yet again.

"*Eloise-ah,*" Marco coos. "I won't hurt you—just come to me," he says as he pats the open space in the bed next to him.

I take a step toward the bed. Marco reaches out his hand for me so I take it, and he carefully pulls me onto the bed. Once I'm next to him—on top of the covers—I take a second to kick off my sandals and then roll over onto my side so I am facing Marco. He smiles seductively and pulls my body closer to his. The only thing separating me from his naked lower half is my dress and the blankets from my bed. I can feel my heart pounding wildly as Marco presses his body close to mine.

"*Oh, Eloise-ah,*" Marco moans. "I've been wanting you all day…"

He moves in for a kiss, and I allow myself to be pulled into his lips. He's gentle and careful as he takes my mouth in his, and we find our rhythm. His kisses reassure me that nothing has changed for him—I'm still *his Eloise* and he still loves me. My heart eases into this idea as I allow myself to follow his kiss into a dreamlike world of indulgence.

Marco slides both of his arms around me now and rolls my body on top of his. I can feel the heat from his chest through the fabric of my dress, and when his hands start moving down my back and over my buttocks, I'm suddenly torn between my insecurities and my convictions.

Marco lifts up my dress up and slides both of his hands up the length of my hamstrings, while gently working his way up to caressing my bottom. His hands are warm and smooth, and I can feel my muscles tighten with pleasure as he starts to explore my form. Then he rests his hands softly on my hips. He starts to work his fingers under the sides of my panties as he kneads my flesh between his fingers and tries to pull my panties down.

My body lurches, and I firmly place my hands on top of his. Marco tries to gently push my hands away, but I keep fighting him.

"What are you doing?" Marco asks as he pulls away from kissing me and laughs lightly at my behavior. "I want you so badly, *Eloise-ah*," he says as he nuzzles my neck. "Don't keep me waiting..." he adds as his lips momentarily find my earlobe.

I don't know what to say or do, and when Marco starts kissing me down the length of my neck, I weaken slightly. Marco takes advantage of the moment and begins to slide his hands up my sides again, going for a second try at my panties.

This is when the panic sets in. I'm not ready for this, and I can't let this thing get too far out of hand. So I lift my body up and off of Marco and flip myself around so I'm sitting next to him while he remains stretched out under the covers.

"Marco, I can't," I say as I pull my hands up to my face in an effort to hide myself from his eyes. But I keep my fingers lightly spread so I can see the look on his face.

"What do you mean, *you can't?*" Marco says, like he really doesn't understand my words. He turns his body to the side and rests his head against his fist. He looks confused and maybe a little annoyed.

"I just can't," I say as I try to figure out what I can do to prevent this from becoming a major scene. I take my hands away from my face and rest them on my thighs.

"Do you have your...*blood*...or something?" Marco asks with hope in his voice.

Totally embarrassed by his question, I feel my face go scarlet as I answer with an emphatic "No!"

"Then what is it?" he says as confusion washes over his face.

"This is just too fast for me," I try to explain as Marco looks at me with those caramel eyes and those dreamy lips.

Marco rolls over onto his back now and lets out a long slow sigh. I can feel the air in the room thickening, and I'm not sure what to do to lighten it. I just sit there with a painful expression as I wait for Marco to say something.

"What does this mean, *'too fast'?*" Marco asks as he stares up at the ceiling.

"It just means that I don't know if I'm ready for all this yet," I say after I take some time to consider my answer.

"You mean for making love to me?" Marco asks as he turns his head to look at me.

I nod my head in affirmation.

"*Eloise-ah*, I love you, and ever since the first time I saw you, I have wanted to make love to you," he says as he rolls onto his side. He reaches his hand over and rests it on top of my hand, and I can see that his eyes are pleading with me to understand. "I want you to be my woman. *I want to make love to my woman*," he concludes, a faint smile of hope on his lips.

I'm taken aback by his words, and each time he tells me he wants to make love to me, I feel nervous and confused. That is such a serious term—*make love*. That's the kind of thing that is done with some weight and meaning. Most of the time in Miami, guys don't use that term—they have *sex* with girls or they get *laid*. But making love—well—that's an entirely different idea.

And that's exactly what makes this situation such a big deal. Instead of just saying no to the passing, fleeting notion of sex with someone I barely know, what we have here is much deeper. We have actual feelings for each other—passionate feelings of love and respect.

But…I can't deny that I have some red flags.

How can you know you want to make love to someone the first time you ever see them? Doesn't that seem more like lust than love?

But what if Marco and I are soul mates? What if we were just meant to be together, and we can't deny it? What if Marco is just more in tune with his soul than I am, and he knew right away that he was meant for me, while I'm still trying to work it all out?

I realize now that I've left him hanging, and I need to say something. So I take a deep breath and slide onto my side so I am facing Marco, but with a slight gap between us. I reach over and run my fingers through his hair. His face softens as he slowly blinks his eyes and then opens them to look at me.

"I just need you to be patient with me, Marco," I finally say. I feel Marco release a sigh of disappointment. He gives me a weak smile and then closes his eyes.

"There is an old Italian proverb," he says when he opens his eyes again. "It goes like this: *He who is not impatient is not in love.*"

I mull the words over, trying to figure out the double negative and what it actually means. Does it mean you're not in love if you're patient? I repeat it in my mind several times trying to find the meaning, but I'm at a loss.

"It means that love is passionate, not patient, *Eloise-ah*. It means that you can't have the kind of love that makes you weak in the knees if you are being too cautious, too careful," Marco explains as he trains his gaze on me.

"But what if you jump in and only later discover that you were too quick? What if you are impatient and then discover that if you had taken your time, you would have seen that things wouldn't last?" I ask, being the devil's advocate to his passionate proverb.

"You cannot help it when you fall in love," he says. "It comes on you with white hot heat, and if you hesitate, it might…slip away…"

I don't know what to say. I'm stumped. He might be right—if I hesitate, maybe love *will* slip away, but if I'm too hasty, it might barrel right into me and then leave me broken-hearted and burned in the process.

"I don't want to pressure you," Marco says as he reaches over and touches his fingers to my chin. "I want you to be ready to experience my love, but you cannot expect me to wait forever," he says as he moves in for a kiss.

"I know…" I trail off before his lips reach mine.

When we turn out the lights, I do my best to fall asleep, but I can't seem to relax. I'm riddled with worry. First, there's the fact that Marco's mother disapproves of me, which clearly I can't control. *And* I've come to an obvious impasse when it comes to my convictions and my desires. This relationship is the biggest thing I've ever experienced, and I'm in so deep that I can't even touch the bottom of this pit of emotions. My heart and my head are at such odds at the moment, and, as I listen to Marco's steady breathing and feel the warmth of his body next to mine, I'm not sure how long I can do this.

Something has to give…and I'm not sure if I'm ready for that yet.

I've been in Italy for a total of three weeks now, and so far, things have been pretty intense. I've had some major transitions in my life since I arrived, and, when I think about it, I'm really surprised at how well I'm handling everything. I'm no longer on the crew with all of my closest friends, so I've had to learn to make new friends and carry on. I don't have Scott around to help me navigate my way through life, but somehow, I seem to be doing just fine. I have a serious boyfriend—which is completely new and exciting—and so far, I'm holding things together very well. So, even though things aren't exactly the way I thought they'd be, my time in Italy is proving to be a wonderful adventure and a time of discovery.

My first weekend on the morning crew took some getting used to. The show time is so early, but when you're finished, you still have a whole afternoon and evening to rest up. Peter and I are getting much closer and always pair up to work together in the aft galley. He is incredibly entertaining, and there's something comforting to me about spending time with him since he often hangs out with Scott on our days off. Every now and then, he'll let a little something slip about how Scott's doing, and in some small measure, it makes me feel less guilty when I hear that Scott is doing well.

Miriam has even started to lighten up on me. So far, since she moved me to the morning crew, I've only seen her a few times. She isn't exactly friendly or glad to see me, but at least she hasn't done anything malicious toward me. We've all met some of the Italian flight attendants in the past few weeks, and it seems that they've figured out the secret to making Miriam a tolerable person. The rumor is that they introduced her to a one of the baggage handlers here in Florence, and Miriam is falling in love! Whether the rumor is true or untrue doesn't really matter to me. As long as she continues to leave me alone, I'm happy!

And I haven't had any further run-ins with Gabby, thank goodness. I've seen her in passing a few times, and every now and then, I'll see her at the pool, but for the most part, we keep our distance. It makes me feel sad that I can't clean things up with her, but how do you make amends for something you didn't do? I think Gabby just made up her mind to dislike me, so I'm better off just letting things go. I've seen her getting ready to go out a few times, and from what I've heard, she's working her way through the Italian co-pilots at the moment. I don't care what she does as long as she doesn't mess with Marco.

Marta and I have become very close. Needless to say the past few weeks have been pretty difficult for her, but she manages to hold her head high despite the fact that everyone seems to be talking about Oscar and Michelle. Marco and I have taken her out to the vineyard several times, and so far, she and Lorenzo seem to be slowly developing a friendship. I wish I could say the same was true for Sofia Maselli and me. She seems to keep her distance when I'm at the vineyard, but I'm always aware that she's watching me. The truth is, I would really rather avoid going to the vineyard altogether, but Marco keeps insisting that it's good for Lorenzo.

At first, I was worried that it might be too soon for Marta to consider spending time with another man, but each time she's joined us, she seems happier. The last time we visited, Lorenzo actually smiled when Marta climbed out of the car. I'm not sure Cupid's involved yet, but I think having someone to talk to with the same heartache is helping Marta get over her loss, too.

Marco and I have been spending every spare minute together—going to the vineyard, taking tours of museums and going shopping all over the city. I feel like things are evolving rather nicely, and whenever I'm around him, I feel like I'm falling more in love. But I can't deny that things are still a bit strained in the "*making love*" department.

While Marco is doing his best to be patient, I'm still struggling with the conflict of my desires and my convictions. We've had two tiny fights over the subject, and I can tell that Marco is tiring, but I still don't know what to do. Sometimes I wish that I didn't have this conviction because I have such a longing to be with Marco. But each time I let my guard down a little, a huge wave of concern takes over, and I feel myself pull back out of fear and uncertainty.

I've been considering giving into Marco more so lately than ever. Even after only three weeks together, I'm growing so close to him, and I think I might actually see a future with him. He is nurturing and loving, and even though lately, he's been a little less attentive, he dotes on me more than anyone I've ever known. If I knew for sure that we were going to end up together, maybe I would feel differently, but I think it's still a bit early to tell for sure. And even though I trust Marco much more than I did in the beginning, it is very difficult for me to get around his overly friendly demeanor with women. His flirtations typically cause me to feel invisible, and, if I'm being totally honest, there are times that I wonder if Marco is actually faithful to me.

This thought has been crossing my mind recently, ever since Marco started dropping me off so early from our dates. For the past week, we've spent all of our days off together, but Marco either drops me off right after dinner, or just before, telling me that he has a few things to take care of for Franco. I know things are crazy right now for Franco because he is in the final stages of getting ready for his first solo show in Milan, so I believe that Marco and all of his siblings are pitching in to help. But it just seems like Marco is helping a lot more at night. I always offer to come and pitch in during the day, but Marco always seems to have some reason that won't work.

Anyway, I'm doing my best not to let my suspicions get the best of me, but it isn't easy. I think that Marco must sense that I'm worried, and so the past two nights, when he's needed to get away to help Franco, he's been very verbally reassuring. He tells me he loves me so much that I have no other choice but to believe him. But there is a part of me that wonders if these are somewhat empty words.

Tonight, Marco is taking me to a tiny, intimate restaurant for an early dinner. He told me that he needed to talk to me about something, and he wanted to do it over a nice, quiet dinner. As I stand in front of my closet, figuring out what to wear, I try to imagine what Marco wants to tell me.

On the wild side of my imagination, I wonder if Marco is going to propose to me! It's not all that far-fetched an idea. After all, Marco says he really loves me and he always introduces me as *his* Eloise. But on the more practical side, I don't feel like that's it. Even though we're still incredibly close, I feel like things might be slowing down some or cooling off a bit. I try not to think about that too much—those are the kind of thoughts that make women seem needy and insecure, and I refuse to let myself look like that (even if maybe I am).

But these conflicting thoughts make it difficult to choose the right clothing for this evening. I don't want to wear anything too plain, in case this is the big moment! But if I'm too dressed up, and Marco's announcement is something more unremarkable, I'll feel silly all dolled up. Finally, after tremendous consideration, I pull out a black jersey strapless pantsuit. It is one of the most flattering outfits I own—the tube-like top has a layer of draped jersey fabric across the front that gives me a lovely shape, and the legs of the pants are wide and airy when I walk.

I add a thick turquoise necklace, some tiny silver drop earrings and a thick black and blue bracelet. I can hear Marco on the front porch just as I finish strapping on my tall, sleek, black sandals. When I open the door, I notice that Marco is dressed rather casually—he has on an easy pair of chinos and a light yellow open collar shirt. When he sees me, his face widens into a bright smile.

"You look gorgeous," Marco says as he takes a step in and pulls me into his arms. "And you smell fantastic, too," he adds as he nuzzles me around my neck.

"Thank you," I say as I pull away. I worry now that maybe I'm overdressed, and as I stand there considering this idea, I nervously twist my earring around in my ear.

"Are you OK?" Marco asks lightly with a wash of amusement on his face.

"Well, maybe I should change before we go," I say

"Absolutely not!" Marco says emphatically. "You look perfect! I had to dress down a bit since I need to help Franco load some boxes tonight. He is shipping some of his wares for the show in Milan and he's a nervous wreck," Marco explains as he pushes by me and heads into the kitchen.

I watch as he opens the fridge and looks around for a bottle of water. Once he snags one, he twists off the top and drains the bottle in one tilt. When he's done, he looks up at me with a smile.

"Are you ready to go?" he asks before he tosses the empty bottle into the trashcan underneath the counter.

"Sure," I say with a weak smile.

The restaurant is nearly empty since Marco and I are eating so early. Even the host seems surprised that we've arrived at such an early hour for dinner. We follow him as he takes us to a table next to a large picture window that looks out over a lovely courtyard. Marco waits at the end of the table for me to slide into my side of the booth and hesitates before he slides in on the side across the table from me.

I try not to make a big deal in my mind about how usually when we sit in a booth, Marco sits next to me and wraps his arms around me while we wait for our food, but in my heart, it's kind of a big deal. I look at Marco from across the table and try to read his facial expressions as he looks over the menu. He looks relaxed, but focused, as he moves his eyes up and down the menu selections. When he looks up, he catches me staring, and I immediately divert my eyes.

"Eloise-ah—is something the matter?" Marco asks as he puts the menu down and reaches across the table for my hands.

"No," I say like I can't understand what he is talking about. "Everything is perfect," I say in a sweet, upbeat voice.

"Good," Marco says with a smile. Then he raises his hand to summon our waiter.

As soon as the waiter arrives, Marco orders us some wine and flat water, then pauses to look at me. I oblige and place my order of *spaghetti ala Bolognese*. Then Marco orders his dish—which I think is some sort of lamb dish. When the waiter finishes taking our order, he walks away and leaves Marco and me alone.

"So, Eloise-ah, I do have something I need to tell you," he begins as he nervously fidgets with his fork.

"OK," I say with a pleasant smile while I try to brace myself for the news.

"Franco has asked me to go to Milan to help him with his show," he begins tentatively.

"Well that's great, isn't it?" I ask as confusion over why this is such a big deal comes over me.

"Yes, it is great," he says as he leans forward in his seat. "But it means I will be gone all next week."

"Oh," I say, trying to act like this is no big deal. "Well, it sounds like it is an important thing for you to do, so I think you *have to* go," I add to assure Marco that I'm OK.

"Ahh…" Marco says with a sigh and a light laugh, as if he is so relieved by my supportive reaction. "I was so worried that you would be upset that

I cannot take you with me and that we would have to spend an entire week apart," Marco explains as his face fills with relief.

"I understand that this is a really important opportunity for your brother," I say as his words only now start to sink in. He *can't take me with him.* We have to spend *an entire week apart.*

Our waiter arrives with our wine and water and a loaf of hot garlic bread. Marco reaches for the bread first and offers me a piece. I take it from him quickly and try to put the conversation into perspective.

It bothers me that Marco can't take me and that we'll have to be apart for an entire week, but what bothers me the most is that Marco knew this would bother me! Have I already started to become the needy woman? Have I shown all my cards of insecurity? I can't let this be how he sees me. I have to do something to save face here.

"Actually, Marco, I had something to tell you, too," I say as I pop a bite of hot bread into my mouth. I do my best to look mysterious and confident as I brace myself for my own big announcement.

"Oh really?" Marco questions as he trains his eyes on me.

"Yes—I'm doing some traveling on my own next week, too," I say like this was planned for ages. "I am going to Essex to see my grandmother, and I was a little worried about telling *you*," I say with a breathy laugh like I'm so relieved that the cat is finally out of the bag.

The last part is a bit of a lie. Of course I was planning to go see Edna Pearl, but it wasn't exactly all planned out yet, and I most certainly wasn't *worried* about telling Marco. In fact, I was going to see if he wanted to come with me! But it makes me feel better to pretend all those things. At least I don't look as needy.

"Well, then, it all works out perfectly!" Marco says as a wash of happiness comes over his face.

"Yes—perfectly!" I concur as I take a deep swig of my wine.

Chapter Twenty-Five

My flight to London is very uneventful, except for the fact that my mind is racing with thoughts of Marco. Things between us seem strained, and I can't figure out if it's just me, or if there's something up with Marco. I don't like the way things ended between us yesterday afternoon. We met for a hurried lunch in the city after I got back from my morning flight and before Marco had to get ready for the evening run to Paris. During the lunch, Marco snapped at me twice and, then, immediately apologized. He claimed that he was just a bundle of nerves because this fashion show is such a big deal for his brother. But in my heart, I know it's more than that.

While our kisses are still quite frequent, and our confessions of love for one another continue to rally my spirits, there's a knowing inside of me that Marco's interest is fading. We've only known each other for just under a month, and it seems reasonable to expect that things would still be fresh and new at this stage in the game. And, while I'm thankful that Marco isn't pushing me on the subject of *making love*, I know he leaves me at the end of every date wanting more. It kills me inside to let him down in this way, but I feel myself growing more and more protective of my heart.

I just wish that I trusted Marco, but I can't. It seems like he's not as willing to rearrange his life for me as he was in the beginning, and, as a result, I feel like he's hiding something from me. Initially, I thought maybe he'd started something up with Christina behind my back. That was an easy conclusion since he's been spending so much time at Franco's studio lately. But when I brought her up in a round about way, I learned that the whole reason Franco is short-handed is because Christina left and is no longer working as Franco's assistant. As relieved as this news made me, I still can't help but feel like something's going on.

The last time Marco came over to my villa after a date, I asked him if he was all right. I just wanted to take a temperature reading, and to my surprise, things escalated rather quickly. Marco vehemently defended his demeanor by reminding me that *I'm* the one who's keeping *him* at bay. He blamed me for the growing distance between us, and said if I would just let my guard down and allow him to love me completely, all of this trouble would melt away. As much as I'd like to believe him, I feel certain that a month of waiting isn't too much to ask. My heart is telling me that I need to continue holding out, while my mind is grasping at straws, trying to figure out how to remain loyal to myself while still pleasing Marco.

I take a taxi from the airport to the Liverpool Station and catch the next train to Essex. As the train rumbles through the outskirts of London, I feel a wash of sadness running over me. My thoughts are miles away with Marco. He left for Milan very early this morning so there wasn't any time to say goodbye. I know it sounds silly to be missing him this way—we're only going to be apart for a grand total of three days. But I really think something big is about to happen to our relationship, and that makes me scared.

My grandmother sent a car to the train station to pick me up, and once I climb inside the warm cab, I start to feel excited about seeing Edna Pearl. I haven't seen her in over a year, and I can't wait to sink into one of her cozy armchairs and eat some of her lovely scones and shortbread biscuits. Right now, I think Edna Pearl is the best possible person for me to spend time with—especially since I'm so confused. She's always helped me gain perspective and direction in my life, and right now, those are two things I'm sorely lacking.

As the driver slowly rolls the car out of the train station, I watch as some of the familiar houses pass by my view. Essex is such a lovely old town, and I remember, when I was a child, imagining my mother as a little girl walking up and down the sidewalks. When we turn into Edna Pearl's estate, I see her climbing down the front steps so she can meet me by the car. She grabs the hand railing and leans her body carefully as she makes her way down the steps. Her face is already beaming in anticipation of our reunion.

As I open the door and pull my body out of the car, I can hear her clucking and shouting as she makes her way down the driveway. She's wearing a frilly floral dress (or *frock* as she calls it) and a light yellow cardigan over her shoulders. She hasn't changed one bit—she's still slightly plump with glossy silver hair neatly curled and tucked away from her face. She's wearing large gold earrings and her signature half glasses perched on top of her head, hiding among the curls. As she pulls me into her arms, the familiar smell of *Aquanet* and *Rosemilk* lotion fill my nostrils and remind me that I'm safe and at home with Edna Pearl.

"Oh Love," she says as she tightens her embrace around me. "Look how *lovely* you are!"

I can't even respond because I'm too happy right now, all folded up in my grandmother's arms. I realize now as I allow my body to relax into her embrace that this is exactly where I need to be right now.

It doesn't take long for me to settle into my room upstairs in the main house. After I change my clothes and freshen up in the bathroom, I can hear Edna Pearl humming to herself as she prepares a tray of tea and fresh baked scones. I pull on a pair of soft, cotton sweatpants and a plain white T-shirt. I dig around in the closet until I find the pair of flannel bedroom slippers that I left on my last visit. When I slip them on my feet, I'm surprised they still fit. It's always such a comfort to know that if you leave something at Edna Pearl's house, it'll be there waiting for you—even if you don't return for years!

As I thump my way down the sweeping staircase, I see that Edna Pearl is already waiting for me in the living room. She's seated in her favorite yellow armchair, and, as I approach her, I notice that she's fussing around with a remote control for her CD player.

"This silly bugger must need *battries*," she says as I enter the room. She taps it against her knee and presses the play button again. "Bugger…" she says under her breath.

I punch the play button on the CD player as I pass by and look over at Edna Pearl with a smile. She gives me a happy grin as she places the remote control on the side table next to her chair.

"Who needs *battries* when you're around then?" she retorts brightly as Billy Holliday starts singing a jazzy tune that fills the room.

I just smile at her as I take my seat on the flowery settee. For as long as I can remember, Edna Pearl has had the same furniture. Nothing ever changes here—it's like a magical time warp where you can reconnect with your past while still living in the present.

"Pour us some tea, would ya, Love?" Edna Pearl asks before I settle into my seat.

"Certainly," I say as I reach over and gently pick up a tea cup from the serving tray.

In true British fashion, Edna Pearl has already prepared the tea with the perfect amount of milk and sugar before she filled up her serving kettle. As I pour my grandmother the first cup, my mouth is already watering in anticipation of the warm, creamy, slightly sweet mixture. When I hand Edna Pearl her cup and saucer, she motions for me to give her a scone, too. I oblige with a smile.

"This looks fantastic," I say as I pour myself a cup of tea. "I've been looking forward to proper tea and scones all day!" I say brightly after I take my first delicious sip.

"Well, I'm simply delighted that you're here, Love," she says as she wipes the corners of her mouth with a white linen tea napkin. "Now, before you settle in for a good long chat, your mum's been ringing me today. She wants you to ring the house in Miami straight away."

"Is everything OK?" I ask, concerned about my mother and father all of a sudden.

When I was packing my bag for my trip, I was listening to the BBC channel and they were talking about a series of big storms that are expected to get even bigger and hit somewhere along the East coast of Florida. I

344

didn't really zero in on the details since they were rather patchy at best; plus I had so many other things on my mind.

"Well dear," Edna Pearl begins with her eyebrows raised. "Your father is quite concerned that a rather nasty storm is heading their way," she says and then takes a sip of her tea.

"Well...that might just be dad," I say as I try to placate my own concerns. "He's such a hurricane nut that sometimes you have to take his predictions with a grain of salt."

"I wouldn't know, Lovey, but they've been talking about it all day on the telly," she says as she takes a tiny nibble of her scone. Her eyes look a bit worried, and I can tell that she wants me to call my mother so she'll feel better, too.

"I guess I better call," I say as I look around the room for a phone.

"In the kitchen, Darling," she says as she looks up at me with concerned eyes. "And take your tea—don't want it to go cold," she adds with a sweet smile.

It takes me a few tries to remember how to dial the number, but once I figure it out, the lines are all busy. I try several times before the line finally rings through. When my mother answers the phone, I can hear the strain in her voice, and it makes me nervous.

"Mom?" I say into the line.

"Oh, Eloise!" she gasps. "I was worried you'd have troubling ringing through."

"I did, but I just kept trying. What's going on?" I ask as fear starts to pump through my veins.

"Well, Sweetheart, there are some bad storms headed our way," she begins to explain as calmly as she can. "The first storm—the one called Debbie—looks like it is going to hit somewhere quite a bit north of here— possibly in the Carolinas. But the storms they call Ernesto and Florence could end up hitting South Florida with a *one-two punch*."

"Oh, my gosh," I say as I try to imagine what two hurricanes in quick succession could do to our area. "What does Dad think?" I ask, wondering if my father has anything more hopeful to say.

"Well, you know how these things go—all of these different weather models come up with different predictions and in the end, it's anyone's guess. I'm convinced that the weather is really the last thing God still knows more about than we do," she says ironically, like she's already exhausted from all the useless predictions.

"Do you guys have to evacuate?" I ask as I start to run down my list of questions.

"So far, there are no mandatory evacuations in effect, but they are encouraging people to do so voluntarily so that the roads won't jam up if they do have to issue mandatory controls," she begins. "But your father wants to hold out a bit longer. He has a plan, as you might have guessed."

"I'm sure he does, but, Mom, you have to make sure that Dad gets in touch with Violet. I don't know if she has a safe place to go, and I'm so worried about Sugar Ray!" I say with a sudden rush of emotion.

"I'll make sure, Darling, but you mustn't worry yourself too much. The storms are still days away." I can tell she's shifting gears now to try to keep me from getting too upset. "And I'm quite sure your father and Violet have spoken, and if things look like they're getting too dangerous, we'll make sure Violet and Sugar Ray can come with us."

"*Please, Mom!*" I plead with her. "Don't forget to call her and *make* her bring Sugar Ray over. I don't think she has a reliable car, and I'm not sure if she'll feel comfortable taking mine. The last thing I want to have happen is for either of them to get stranded…"

I can feel the lump of fear growing in my throat, and I wish more than anything I were at home, making sure that Sugar Ray was safe. But I'm all the way over in Europe, and there is absolutely nothing I can do.

"Oh, Darling—we'll do our best to make proper arrangements, but you mustn't worry," she says, her voice pleading with me to relax.

"I just feel so far away with all of this going on, Mom," I say as I struggle to stay strong.

"I know, Love. I know," she says with great compassion. "But we all have to be brave and just stay on track," she adds to try to get me to snap out of my upset.

"I'll try," I promise her as I take a sip of me tea.

"The main reason I wanted you to call us today is because your father purchased a satellite operated telephone of some sort," she says, getting down to business. "It is supposedly the most important thing to have in your hurricane kit. But, anyway, it will work even if the phone lines are down, and I wanted to make sure you had the number. Let me get your father to come on the line to explain it," she says as I hear her calling my dad's name in the background.

"OK," I say as I frantically look around Edna Pearl's kitchen for a scrap of paper and a pen. I find a flowery paper napkin on the countertop and a marking pen hanging from a string on the refrigerator door and then wait for my dad to start talking.

"Elle?" my dad says in a loud voice.

"Yes—hi Dad!" I say surprised at how happy I am to hear his voice.

"We gotta a lot going on down here, Sweetheart," he begins like he's some sort of rescue hero, ready for action. "I was hoping that Florence wasn't going to come and get us, but she may very well be the one that does us in…" My dad trails off, and I can hear my mother yelling at him in the background to stop being so dramatic and just give me the phone instructions.

"Dad," I say firmly, trying to get him to focus on me. "If things look like they're gonna get really dangerous, you have to promise to call Violet and make sure she and Sugar Ray are OK—you got that?" I feel so desperate right now over the thought of a bad storm and losing Sugar Ray that I'm pretty single-minded.

"I got it, Sweetheart," he assures me. "And I think that your mother spoke to some woman at *The Wiley* about your apartment. So everything should be worked out. And who knows, a weather system from the North may push both storms down and around the tip of the state and end up in the Gulf of Mexico," he says like the optimistic weatherman that he is.

"Well if that doesn't happen, I'm counting on you to help me out, OK Dad?" I say in a shaky voice.

"Will do, kiddo," he says. "Now here are those instructions for my new sat phone…"

Edna Pearl and I spend the rest of our afternoon together trying to find news coverage on the weather in Florida. After searching and scanning through nearly every station, we finally find one program that gives us some satellite images and forecasts. Watching the three huge blobs of spinning color hovering hundreds of miles off the East Coast of Florida does little to calm my nerves. And there is little consolation in the fact that the National Hurricane Center is predicting that the first storm, the one called Debbie, is likely only going to be a tropical storm. It's the other two storms—Ernesto and Florence—that appear to be the biggest threat.

I try to call Violet several times at my apartment on the two different phone numbers she gave me, but she isn't answering. So I decide to call the front desk at *The Wiley.* Finally, Dan, one of the most tolerable of all the Snoops answers the phone after about 20 rings.

"*The Wiley,* this is Dan," he says into the phone. He sounds like he's been running and is out of breath.

"Dan? It's Elle Butts," I say as relief washes over me.

"Elle?" he says with a surprised voice. "Aren't you in Italy?"

"Yes, but I heard about the storms, and I wanted to call to see if you could give me some information," I say, desperate to launch into my need for him to find Violet, but wanting to pace myself a bit.

"They're evacuating us right now, Elle, so things are really crazy," he says distractedly into the phone. In the background I can hear a lot of commotion. "But I know that they'll call your emergency contact person with all of the details about where they're storing your belongings and stuff," he adds like he wants to hurry me off the line.

"OK, that's fine, but Dan? Have you seen my dog sitter, Violet, and Sugar Ray at all?" I ask with my fingers crossed and my eyes pressed shut in hopes of hearing some sort of news that will help to put my mind at ease.

"Oh yeah—the lady with the mullet?" he confirms.

"Yes!" I say, happy to hear that he's at least seen her at some point.

"I saw her over here yesterday, and she had a bunch of stuff from your place for your dog," he says. "I didn't talk to her though. I just know that she took your car and your dog. Hey, Elle, I'm sorry, but I gotta go," he says as the commotion starts to increase in the background.

"OK. Thanks, Dan!" I say before I hear the line go quiet.

When I hang up the phone, I feel a small measure of relief knowing that Violet is still OK and that she is taking my car and my precious dog somewhere out of harm's way. I wish now that I'd left a note or something with Dan to give to Violet in case she returns, but I doubt that will happen—especially since they're evacuating *The Wiley*. I just have to rest assured that things are going to be fine. The weather forecasters think the big storms are still days away from impacting the coast of the United States, and now that I know Sugar Ray is safe, I should try to relax.

When I come back into the living room, Edna Pearl is reading a paperback with a crocheted quilt over her lap.

"Did you have any luck, Love?" she asks as she looks up from her book and lifts her half glasses up and onto the top of her head.

"Yeah, I guess so," I say as I sigh and plop myself down on the settee. "It sounds like they're getting everyone out of our building and that Violet already took Sugar Ray somewhere safe."

"Well, that's brilliant news!" she says in an obvious effort to bolster my spirits. "I'm sure everything will work out, Love, you just have to have some faith."

"I know…" I trail off, feeling fairly certain that I don't have nearly enough faith in me to keep me from worrying.

"Rudy and Quinn are going to bring a chicken curry takeaway to the house in a bit," she says, her voice filled with hope and excitement.

Rudy and Quinn are my cousins. They both go to University of Essex and live in a tiny flat near the school. It's been ages since I've seen them—their father is some sort of high-ranking officer in the British Navy, and they've always moved around a lot.

"Oh, that'll be nice!" I say as I make an effort to change my attitude. I don't want to spoil my time with my grandmother, so I need to pull it together. "I think the last time I saw the boys they were still pre-teens!"

"They're all grown up now," Edna Pearl says with pride. "They're good looking young men, and they're both doing so well in university," she adds for good measure.

"It'll be fun to see them again," I say as I realize how truly nice it will be to reunite with my cousins.

"Eloise," Edna Pearl begins softly. "Why don't you try to relax a bit. All of this fuss with the weather is taking it out of you, Love," she says with such concern in her eyes.

"Maybe I'll go rest up a bit in my room," I say after I consider her words. "I do feel kind of tired, and I don't want to be in a bad mood when the boys get here."

"I think that sounds like a lovely idea," Edna Pearl says. "Just close your eyes and think happy thoughts."

"OK," I say as I get up and start walking toward the stairs. But, first, I stop and plant a kiss on my grandmother's cheek.

"And, when the boys are gone, we can have some time alone to talk about what's *really* eating at you, my Darling," she says with a smile after I pull away.

Dinner with my cousins was just the happy distraction I needed. They've turned out to be the most wonderful people, and I thoroughly enjoyed every minute of our time together. Rudy, the oldest, is studying to be an art historian, and Quinn is only in his first year of university but thinks he may want to become a doctor. They both have the best personalities, and their British sense of humor is dry and unexpectedly funny.

The entire evening was filled with comical stories about Edna Pearl and our moms growing up in Essex. It was exactly what I needed to get my mind right and to help me feel more connected to my roots. I hardly thought about the impending storms or about Marco the entire evening, which was a welcome relief. It was just all laughs and lighthearted conversation.

When Rudy and Quinn were leaving, Rudy promised to keep tabs on the weather in Florida for me via the Internet. He said he'd call me if he found out any information that might be helpful. It was such a thoughtful gesture, but honestly, I know for a fact that having more information about the progress of the storms is only going to make me worry. However, he was incredibly sweet, and it helped me to know that he cares so much about my feelings.

When I join Edna Pearl in the living room, she's already placed a mug of hot chocolate with marshmallows on a thick coaster on the side table next to an empty armchair. This is her signal that it's time for girl talk. So I grab a quilt from the hall closet and snuggle myself into my chair with my mug of cocoa. After I take my first sip of the gooey chocolate drink, my grandmother wastes no time getting to the bottom of things.

"So who is this *Marco* person that you mentioned with such a flush at dinner?" she asks before I can even swallow. Her eyes are trained on me like she's expecting a specific kind of answer, so I know I can't dodge her without eventually getting cornered.

"He's the man I've been seeing in Florence," I begin tentatively.

"I see," she says as she lowers her head a bit and waits for the rest of my answer.

"OK, here's the story," I say as I shift around in my chair. "He's one of the pilots—he's actually a captain—for *Windsong Air* in Italy, and we met on the flight over to Florence."

"So you've only known each other for about a month then?" she asks, tallying up the details, as she likes to do when listening to a story about your life.

"Yes," I affirm and then continue. "Anyway, he spotted me and made a real effort to get to know me—he left me notes and even gave me a few special gifts—until I agreed to go out on a date," I say, wishing I would have chosen my words more carefully.

"Go on," she says.

"Well, we've been spending all of our time off together, and he's introduced me to his family—his mother owns an important vineyard outside of Florence and she's shown me around and stuff—and it feels like we're falling in love!" I say, trying to jam all the highlights into one big sound bite while omitting all of the other stuff on purpose.

"My goodness, Love," she says with a smile on her face. "That is a lot of detail muddled all together. Why don't we take this nice and slow, so I can learn what's really going on."

I take a deep breath and try to figure out how to tell her everything without actually telling her *everything*. I don't want to share too many of the negatives with her—she'll only discourage me because she won't understand the whole thing the way I do.

"I don't know what to say, Gran. I just know that I think I'm falling in love with Marco, and he's already told me his feelings are the same," I trail off, completely unsure of how to explain all of this to her.

"I see," she says again as she squints her eyes like she's trying to understand. "Does Scott like this chap?" she finally asks.

"I don't know," I say as adrenaline jolts through my body. I *really* don't want to explain to her how Scott and I aren't friends anymore *because* of Marco, so I do my best to come up with some other explanation. "Scott and I...are not spending much time together anymore. We just...sort of shifted things a bit," I say, hoping she'll let it go at that.

"I see," she says yet again, making me feel fairly certain she's not buying it. "Does this sudden *shift* between you two have anything to do with your new boyfriend?" she asks, obviously more tenacious than I'd like her to be right now.

"Kind of. Marco and I just decided that if we are going to be together, we need to keep our opposite-sex friendships to a minimum so that there isn't any confusion or hurt feelings," I say, proud of my matter-of-fact answer.

"So are Scott's feelings hurt by this at all?" she asks, cutting right to the core.

"I don't really know," I lie, feeling her questions closing in on me from all sides.

"OK, then," she says. "Let me see if I understand this. You and this Marco chap are falling in love, and you've decided that in order for that love to grow, you can't carry on your friendship with Scott. Is that about right?" she asks.

"Well, it isn't *exactly* like that, but sort of...I guess," I say, hating the way she made that sound.

"And you say that Marco has told you he loves you?" she asks pointedly.

"Yes, he has," I say, feeling proud that I don't have to lie about that.

"And he's known you for just about a month, then, right?" she confirms.

"Yes…" I say, feeling a bit uncomfortable about where she's going.

"And you say that you *think* your falling in love—but you don't *know?*" she attempts to clarify.

"Actually, I do love him, but it's just that this has never happened to me before, so I'm just trying to be careful with my words. But the answer is yes—I do love Marco," I say, feeling like my resolve needs to look strong for Edna Pearl's sake.

We both sit in silence for a moment as Edna Pearl considers her next round of questions and as I brace myself to come up with the proper answers to satisfy her curiosity.

"Would you say that Marco is more of a friend or a love interest only?" she asks.

The question seems safe enough to me, but I still take a moment to consider it before I answer.

"I'd say he's both," I reply as I mentally sort through my reasons for my answer to back it up. "He is the best tour guide in all of Italy, and he's shown me things and taken me to places that normal people aren't even allowed to go. He's made arrangements for me to spend time with his mom's dog because he knew I was lonely for Sugar Ray, and he is always telling me how beautiful and great I am," I blather as I try to convince Edna Pearl that Marco is amazing.

"He sounds like quite a lad," she says sincerely. "Is there some reason he didn't tag along on this trip to meet me?" she inquires with pointed interest.

"His brother, Franco, is a fashion designer, and he had his first solo show in Milan this week, and Marco went along to help him—but he couldn't take me because it was just too much stress and everything, and so I decided to come and see you on my own instead of waiting to come see you when he was available…" I know that my answers are sounding weak, and no matter how I try to deliver the information, I sound pathetic.

"I see," Edna Pearl says for like the fiftieth time. "Eloise, this is not sounding right to me, Love. Why am I worried about this?" she finally asks.

"I don't know," I say, trying to sound like I have nothing to hide. "I guess since this is my first real boyfriend, it's just more unusual to hear me talking about a guy," I offer up as a possible suggestion.

"OK—perhaps that's it, but my next question is a really important one, so I want you to take your time in answering it," she says, followed by a long pause and a steady gaze. "Does Marco meet *all* of your non-negotiables?"

Oh rats! She had to bring up my darn non-negotiables! I sort of knew this was coming, but I'm not ready to talk about *my list* with her right now. I don't even want to think about my list at all. I hate that I ever even wrote a list because, to be honest, until I met Marco, I actually believed that my non-negotiables would help me *find* my soul mate, not *keep me from* him. So far, all of my rules and regulations have done nothing but strangle me and destroy my ability to fully love Marco. So right now, I don't even know if I believe in my list anymore.

I want to tell Edna Pearl that I've found my soul mate in Marco. There are loads of confirmations that we're meant to be together, and I want her to accept that I've found my life partner and we're deeply in love. I want her to understand that for the first time in my life, I want to give myself to a man and not wonder if I've done things the right way or wrong way. Because how could it be wrong when you're in love?

But I know that if Edna Pearl knew the thoughts I've been having and the way I've been feeling about Marco for the past few days, she'd never believe that Marco is my soul mate. From the outside looking in, things may seem clouded, but when you're on the inside, things are clear. Well, actually, that's not true—but they have the *potential* to be clear because when you're on the inside, you can *feel* the relationship. And even if the feelings are shaky, you still have a knowing that simply can't be explained or denied.

"He does fulfill my list…in a way," I finally say after much consideration. "I actually think he might be my soul mate," I **add**, hoping that this will convince her that Marco is quite special.

"Your soul mate?" she says with great interest. "Well, Love, that is a pretty amazing thing. I wonder, though, could you tell me what *exactly* makes him your soul mate?"

I start to feel my stomach boiling with anger at the way Edna Pearl is grilling me on this subject. Why can't she just leave it alone? Why must I defend all of my feelings to *her*? No matter what I say, she won't understand, and I can tell she's going to challenge every comment and every explanation I give! Why can't she just believe me that I'm in love?

"He just understands me," I finally say with a touch of acid in my tone. "He's just the most amazing man, Gran. He makes me feel so special, and he treats me like a queen!" I say with perhaps a bit of drama for added emphasis.

"Well, then…" Edna Pearl trails off. "I'm sure he must be very lovely," she adds as she folds her hands in her lap in defeat.

"He is," I say, trying to soften my tone a bit. "I just wish you trusted me here," I plead. "I just wish you had more faith in me and my ability to see things for what they are, Gran."

"Oh Love, I have *tremendous faith* in you," she says with her head cocked to the side. "And I *trust you* so very much. But I understand that right now, you simply can't see things clearly. You don't know the two-faced nature of love—one minute you're sure you're looking into the purest emotion God ever bestowed upon man, and the next, you're being eaten alive by the burning heat of lust," she says as her voice turns deep and somber.

"You'll fight your own instincts when it comes to lust," she continues. "You'll find ways to rearrange the facts so you can sleep at night, but deep inside, you'll know that you've fallen for an imposter. In the early throws of a relationship, it is difficult to see the difference between lust and love, but Eloise, my darling, I trust that you'll know the difference when the time comes."

That night, when I went to bed, I felt something change in my heart. I felt angry toward Edna Pearl for not being more willing to find the joy in my newfound love. I just wanted her to be like a normal grandmother who loads you up on sweets and tells you all the things you want to hear. But instead, she wouldn't let up on the subject of my relationship with Marco.

If ever there was a time that I needed her support, it is now. I'm already confused enough, as it is, by the way things are going with Marco at the moment, and all I wanted Edna Pearl to do was affirm my feelings of love. Instead, she fueled my growing doubts and made me question things. As I drift off to sleep, I picture Marco in my mind, wrapping his arms around my body and holding me tight. That's what's real—the love between us, and nothing else. What we have is the real deal, and I don't have to defend it to anyone—not even to my grandmother.

The remainder of my trip to Essex was a bit strained. Between watching the weather reports and dodging the topic of my new relationship, I felt like Edna Pearl and I were both walking around on eggshells. We took the train into London to do some shopping at Harrods one day, and we visited with my cousins one more time on the day before I had to leave. But the truth is, there was no easy flow between us like there usually is, and that made me feel so sad.

Now, as I pack my bag to head back to Italy, I realize that I've actually been counting the hours until I leave. This has never happened to me before at Edna Pearl's house—I've always dreaded leaving because it just feels so warm and safe when I'm with my grandmother. But now, things have changed, and I don't feel warm and safe anywhere. I just want to get away from this place and hole up in my villa so I can think in peace.

When I'm loading my bags into the back of the hired car, I can hear the click of Edna Pearls shoes on the driveway as she approaches me. I don't want to turn and look at her because I'm afraid I might cry. But I can see her out of the corner of my eye as I do my best to act like I'm busy shoving my bags into the trunk of the car.

"Can you get everything to fit in the boot?" she asks as she approaches.

"Yep," I say as I give the trunk a slam. I take a deep breath and turn to face her. I do my best to plant a sweet smile on my face so she won't know that I'm a mess inside, even though I know she sees right through me.

"It was wonderful having you here with me for a few days, Love," she says as she steps in close to me. She's wearing a red dress with black buttons running down the front. The arms of a black cardigan hang lightly over her shoulders.

"I had a nice time, too," I say as I soften toward her.

"I have something for Scott. I know you two don't spend much time together, but I couldn't resist sending him a tin of my honey and lavender scones," she says as she hands me the tin that she was holding behind her back.

"Oh, I'm sure he'll love these," I say immediately feeling a stab of guilt in my heart. Scott adores my grandmother, and I feel just awful that I came to visit without him.

"Keep me posted on things, Love," Edna Pearl says as she engulfs me in a big embrace. "And remember, there is never anything you could ever do that would make me love you less," she says as I melt into her bosom.

"I know," I say as I fight off a sudden urge to cry.

As the car rolls out of her driveway, I see Edna Pearl standing on the bottom step of her porch, waving at me with a huge smile on her face. I know she's telling me the truth that she loves me, but I'm just too mad at her right now to let it in. So instead, I let the sadness of being away from Sugar Ray and my parents wash over me.

By the time I board my flight back to Florence, I feel more certain about things than I have all week. When I get back to Italy, things are going to be different. It's time for me to let go of my silly little list of rules. I wrote that list of non-negotiables when I was 15 years old, for crying out loud! I'm a woman now, and those rules may have served me well in my teens and twenties, but they don't apply to the growing needs I have inside for physical intimacy with a man. I love Marco, and he loves me, and if I'm going to discover the meaning of true love, I need to stop holding back. I need to surrender to my own desires and stop analyzing everything based on a few promises I made when I was just a young, gangly girl.

And even though I can't stop thinking about how tense things have been between Marco and me, I believe in my heart that it will all change once I completely give myself to Marco for the first time. There's no doubt in my mind that this is what I have to do. As I settle back into my seat for the flight back to Florence, I picture what it will be like to actually make love to Marco.

Chapter Twenty-Six

Marco is coming over tonight. It will be the first time we've seen each other since we both returned to Florence, and I'm all giddy and nervous about seeing him again. I feel like I'm a new person inside—ever since I decided to let my guard down and completely give myself to Marco. It's almost like Red Hot Elle is back, but this time, she's not so naïve. I know what I want, and I know that I'm ready to experience the desires I've been holding at bay ever since I met Marco Maselli. I'm certain this is the right thing for us—for our relationship.

I've already planned out what dress I'm going to wear—and what I'm going to wear *underneath* it! It's really the only sexy dress I own. It's a strapless, sapphire blue dress with an empire waist and is made of buttery soft chiffon with lace trim. I've actually never worn it, but I bought it when Scott and I were shopping in Coconut Grove before we left for Italy. It was on sale, and, when I tried it on, Scott practically forced me to buy it. He promised if I bought a dress like this, the occasion to wear it would suddenly arrive. Well, he was right. The occasion is here, and I know it will be the perfect way to present myself to Marco for my first time.

Marco said he'd be here about 6:00 to pick me up for dinner, so I have the whole day to myself to get ready—physically and mentally. So after my run, I decide to take care of a few things around my villa. The maid service at *Il Girasole* is great, but they don't do any laundry, so I start shoving all of my dirty clothes into one of my pillowcases so I can lug it over to the laundry room. Then I rummage through my purse for the laundry card I bought—the machines don't take change like they do back home. You have to use these special cards, and, for some reason, I can't seem to keep track of mine.

After searching every possible place I could've put my card, I give up and decide to go to the office to buy a new one. So I slip out of my villa and head over to the office. When I pass by Scott's villa, I can't help but look over to see if there are any signs of life. It's still and quiet, and a pang of guilt hits me right in the stomach. I really do miss Scott—I miss talking to him and knowing what's going on in his day. Clearly I'm still hurt over the whole situation with Miriam, but I guess I sort have to blame myself for that. I rejected Scott, and he retaliated.

I can hear laughter and voices as I round the corner to the office entrance. Once I make my way up the steps and through the door, I stop dead in my tracks when I see Scott, Sebastian and Peter all talking to Bruno at the front desk. I don't know if I should run and hide until they leave the office or just push on ahead and see how things go. I don't even have a chance to decide on my best strategy because Peter sees me first and starts walking toward me.

"Elle!" he says in a friendly voice. "What are you doing up so early?"

"Peter—it's almost 11:00," I say kind of rudely. I feel so nervous that my mind is muddled, and I don't really know how to act.

"Well girlfriend, that's early to me!" he says with a huge laugh.

I carefully look over Peter's shoulder while he's laughing and catch a quick glimpse of Scott and Sebastian. They're exchanging some money with Bruno I think.

"So what are you guys up to today?" I ask as I return my focus back to Peter.

"Shopping," he says in a happy tone. "We're planning to hit some of the fancy shops down on *Via de Tornabuoni*—I hear they have Prada *and* Gucci!" he says with such enthusiasm.

The mention of Prada makes my stomach do a flip. I wonder if Franco is in the showroom today. I wish I could tag along so I could find out for myself. And it would be so much fun to hang out with the guys and shop, but, obviously, that can't happen. So I just try to smile and hide my true feelings and emotions about missing out.

"That sounds great," I say brightly. "It's unbelievable down there. Marco took me one time and the shopping is incredible," I add, just in case Scott is listening. I know it's spiteful, but I can't help it.

"That's the buzz on the streets!" Peter says with a smile. "So how was your trip to London? Did you have a good time with your grandmother?" he asks rather loudly.

"It was fine," I say, feeling a rush of nerves cascading over me. I guess I figured Peter would tell Scott that I was going to see Edna Pearl, but I really didn't want to rub his nose in it—especially since I originally invited Scott to come with me.

"Good," Peter says. "You know, there's nothing like spending time with your family."

"Yep…" I say as I notice Scott and Sebastian walking toward us.

"Hey, Elle," Sebastian says.

"Hi Bass," I say and then I look at Scott.

He just gives me a weak smile and then looks away. We all four just stand there in awkward silence until Peter graciously breaks the tension.

"Well, my dear—have a great day! And wish us luck on finding some great sales!" Peter says with a flare, as the three of them start moving toward the door.

"Good luck…" I say, fighting a sudden urge to cry.

My mind is a mess as I fold my clean laundry on my bed. Between the unsettling exchange with Scott and the constant flow of disturbing information on the TV about the impending storms in Florida, I feel unsteady and nervous inside. So far, the forecasts for Ernesto and Florence haven't changed much in the past 12 hours. They both seem to be stalled out over the tropics, but the longer they sit, the more strength they build. I know I should just turn off the TV and give myself a rest, but for some reason, I can't seem to get enough.

Finally, after all my clothes are neatly put away and the news coverage of the hurricanes starts to get more spotty, I decide to rest my mind and go sit out by the pool. It isn't as packed as I was expecting. There are clusters of people all along the lower deck, but for the most part, the pool is quiet. So I climb up to the upper deck and find a lounge chair.

Once I'm slathered in sunscreen and stretched out on my back, I close my eyes and think about my life. I can't get over how much things have changed for me since I arrived in Italy. Marco came out of nowhere and literally swept me off my feet. But his presence also swept my life clean of my most important and trusted friend. It makes my heart ache whenever I see Scott, and he turns the other way or avoids looking at me altogether. I know I've really wounded him, but, honestly, it seems like he's being a bit dramatic about it.

The more I think about it, the less sad I feel, and the angrier I am that Scott can't even be civil with me anymore. He's acting like I've done something unforgivable! I've never stopped him from dating anyone—that I know of, anyway. Just because he's never chosen to pursue a love interest in the time that we've been friends doesn't mean that I wouldn't have supported him. And, yes, I realize that I told him we couldn't be close right now, but you'd think he'd be more understanding about it. You'd think he'd at least take advantage of those moments when we do innocently bump into one another to find out how I'm doing.

I guess he's not the person I thought he was. I don't really know what's happened to him over the past few weeks. He hangs out with Sebastian and Peter all the time, and who knows what those three talk about and do. Scott has changed as much as I have, and I can't allow myself to believe that all of this awkwardness between us is solely about Marco. Scott's finding himself, too, and so I can't take on all of this responsibility for the dramatic changes in his personality. Maybe I should just stop expecting anything at all from Scott when I see him in passing. Maybe I just need to avoid him, too, and shut him down, just like he does with me.

The sun feels so good on my skin, but my anger is starting to make me boil up inside. So I decide to take a quick dip in the pool and then come back and read my book. I lift my body up off the lounge chair and make my way to the swimming pool. It's cool and clear, and as I dive into the deep end, I can feel the salty water rinsing away all of my negative thoughts and feelings. When I come up for air, I'm refreshed and recharged and ready to put my old thoughts behind me. I want to look ahead to my future with Marco. Tonight, everything between us is about to change, and, for the first time in my life, I'm going to experience the act of making love.

When I pull myself out of the pool, I see that Gabby is just arriving. A surge of nerves grips me, but I do my best to keep my cool as I walk up the sundeck toward my lounge chair. I can't help but notice how amazing Gabby looks in her bathing suit and sarong. She's wearing a deep rose-colored string bikini with a light pink gauze-like wrap around her waist. As she saunters into the pool area, it seems as if everyone stops to look at her. I'm entranced by her beauty—her long dark hair is piled up on top of her head and her dark sunglasses make her look so chic and elegant.

I dig around in my bag in search of my book, but when I look up, Gabby is standing only a few feet away from me. I stare up at her in stunned silence and watch her as she pulls her sunglasses down so I can see her eyes.

"Is this seat taken?" she asks in a husky, aloof voice.

"No—not that I know of," I say, sort of shocked to be talking to Gabby.

I watch as she drops her bag onto the lounge chair right next to mine. My heart starts to beat with a heavy bang inside my chest.

Why is she sitting next to me? I have to ask myself as I watch her pulling things out of her bag.

She takes out a long, colorful beach towel and a bottle of suntan oil and places it on the table between our chairs. Then she unfurls her towel across the lounge chair and looks up and gives me a wicked smile.

I give her a quick smile in return and then do my best to look as though I'm intrigued with my book. But I can't seem to take my eyes off of Gabby. She looks so gorgeous as she fixes her hair and puts on a coat of hot pink tinted lip protection. I watch as she carefully unties her sarong. It's so beautiful with tiny embellishments and ornate stitching cascading all down the length of the fabric. The detail work is exquisite. Once she has it untied, Gabby carefully folds her sarong and hangs it over the back of her lounge chair.

"How have you been, Elle?" Gabby asks.

Her voice rattles me, and I don't really know what to say so I simply stammer, "Fine—how are you?"

"I'm *perfecto*," she says with a mock Italian accent as she begins oiling up her skin with her coconut-scented oil. "I think Italy agrees with me," she says, flashing me a sultry smile.

"That's great…" I say, stumped by her sudden acknowledgement of me. I'm not sure how to handle this sudden change in her demeanor—I mean the last time I really saw her, she made it perfectly clear that she didn't want to be my friend.

"I heard you went to see your grandmother in London," she says, clearly trying to make conversation with me.

"Essex…actually, but yes, I did," I say as I struggle to figure out how she knew where I was. She's rubbing oil on her thigh now, and she thoroughly works the glossy mixture into her pores before she squeezes more oil to the palm of her hand. "How did you know I went to see my grandmother?" I finally ask, unable to keep my curiosity at bay.

"It's not like people don't know what everyone else is doing around here, Elle," she says with a look that makes me feel stupid. "Why—was it supposed to be a *secret?*" she adds as she returns her attention back to her oil application.

"No, I was just surprised you knew about it, that's all," I say as I try to play the whole thing off like it was no big deal.

I watch as Gabby starts smoothing the oil down her shin. And that's when I notice something familiar gracefully wrapped around her ankle. It's a very thin gold chain with an oblong gold bead dangling off to the side, and the sight of it makes my blood run cold. As I zero in on the delicate anklet, I can see that it is identical to the necklace Marco gave me on our first date.

"Do you like my anklet?" Gabby questions in a mocking tone when she notices me eyeing it.

"It's…pretty," I say as I try to keep myself from jumping to conclusions. "Where did you get it?" I finally ask, terrified of her answer.

"It's from one of the gold shops on the *Ponte Vecchio*," she says with a knowing smile.

I don't know what to think. Did she *buy* it herself or did someone *give* it to her? Before I can even decide if I want to know, Gabby reaches down and rolls the bead between her fingers.

"It's really special. The goldsmith who made it for me—I think his name was Giuseppe or something like that—told me it is a Florentine *amuleto* that represents luck," she offers up and then looks at me out of the corner of her eye. Her smile is mean and eerie, but I'm too confused to respond.

"Oh," I say as my mind starts to race, and my heart pounds inside my ears.

"Elle? Are you OK?" Gabby asks with mock concern. "Because you look like you just saw a ghost."

I watch as an evil smile spreads across Gabby's face.

Chapter Twenty-Seven

I can't stop thinking about Gabby and her anklet. I don't want to feel suspicious about it, but I really can't help it. As I clasp my own version of this Florentine bobble of hope around my neck, I try to remember my Marco and how passionately he loves me. I try to keep in mind how many times I've misjudged him since we met, and I realize that this might be just another time that I am misconstruing all of the facts. I want to believe that it's just a coincidence and that Gabby bought herself a similar gold keepsake. But I know in order for me to believe it, I'm going to have to force myself to leave it alone.

As I give myself a final check in the mirror, I can't believe that tonight will be the night that I give myself to Marco. The thought of making love to him has been the only high point in my day. I've tried to imagine how it will happen. I've always stopped things so abruptly with Marco that now, I don't know how much time he'll take pulling me in, and quite honestly, I'm not sure how long I'll last myself! I feel a flush of anticipation settling in my thighs when I hear the light knock on my front door.

When I fling the door open, Marco is standing on my porch wearing a pair of black trousers and a white linen shirt. His smile is bright and happy, although he does looks a bit weary. But once he focuses in on me in my amazing dress, his smile perks up. I watch him as he takes a step into my villa.

"*Eloise-ah*," he says with great emphasis on my name. "You are..." he can't seem to find the right word, so he just smiles and takes me into his arms and gives me a long kiss.

I feel so relieved that nothing's changed. He's still in love with me and I'm still his Eloise! As I allow him to kiss me and pull me in close, I realize how perfectly right it is that I should make love to this man tonight. Now is the time, and, if I hesitate again, Marco may be gone.

As Marco pulls away, he just looks at me again and smiles sweetly. I feel a blush spreading across my cheeks as I beam back at Marco.

"How was Milan?" I finally ask, wanting to ease us back into the present.

"It was fabulous, but I am so very tired," Marco says as he shifts his demeanor a bit. I watch him as he moves over toward my sofa and sits down.

"Was the show great? Did everybody love Franco's work?" I ask as I try to hold myself back from attacking Marco for details about the big show. I slide in next to him on the sofa, and he takes my hand.

"It really was fantastic—Franco was the toast of the town," he says as his eyes glaze over a bit. "I'm so exhausted from all of the parties we went to—*Dolce & Gabana, Versace, Armani*—everyone wanted to spend time with my brother!"

"You must have been so proud," I say as a twinge of jealousy settles into the pit of my stomach that Marco couldn't work it out for me to tag along.

"I was…" Marco trails off.

He seems distracted and tired, and I try not to let this get to me. This is going to be *our* night, and I don't want to ruin it for us both with my insecurities and my wild imaginations. So I lean into Marco's warm body and give him a sweet kiss on the side of the face.

"Marco," I whisper into his ear. "I have a surprise for you tonight," I say, hoping this will pique his interest and blow some wind into his sails.

"You do?" Marco says with a light laugh as he cranes his neck to look at me.

"I want you to make love to me tonight," I say, still in disbelief of my own words.

Marco just looks at me, his face rather blank, in fact, and I don't know what to think or feel about his reaction. So I try again.

"I've decided that I'm ready now—I want to give myself to you completely," I say, hoping to conjure up a more fitting reaction from him.

Marco shifts around on the sofa so that now we are both leaning forward, and he is able to get a clear look at my face.

"Eloise-ah," Marco says. "I don't know what to say."

"Say, 'that's wonderful—I want to make love to you, too,'" I offer up, feeling nervous that this isn't going very well.

Marco closes his eyes and leans back into the sofa and lets out a deep sigh. I'm not sure what to make of all this. I thought this news would make Marco so happy. I thought he would wrap me up in his arms and carry me off to the bedroom before I could change my mind. But never in my wildest imagination did I expect this sort of reaction.

Marco lifts his hands to his face and rubs his eyes. "Why don't we go and eat something and see where the night takes us, OK?" he finally suggests after a painfully long silence.

I feel a flush of complete shame and embarrassment washing over me, but I don't want to let Marco know how I'm feeling. So I give him a sweet smile and rise up off of the sofa and say, "Just let me get my purse."

When we arrive at the restaurant, Marco still seems distracted, and I still feel awkward and embarrassed. I wish I hadn't have said anything to him back at my villa. I wish I could go back in time and start all over. This time, I'd just drop big hints during our dinner and allow Marco to pursue me the way he has in the past. Then I could've surprised him by giving in. But I can't go back in time and change it. So I need to try to come up with a new strategy. Maybe if I don't say anything else about it, Marco will come around. He knows now that I'm ready, so maybe his mood will shift over dinner and everything will turn out fine.

Marco has never taken me to this restaurant before—it seems a bit commercial and touristy for Marco's taste. But it's very nice, and once we're seated at a table in the center of the restaurant, I do my best to stay upbeat and cheery as I allow my new plan to unfold.

"Shall I order us some wine?" Marco asks as he reviews the wine list.

"That sounds perfect," I say as I peek at Marco from over the top of my menu.

"Why don't we go with something white tonight," Marco suggests as he studies the list more intently. "I tire of the reds now and then—maybe this will change things for us a bit, yes?" he expounds for my benefit before looking up at me.

"That's fine with me," I say, trying to stay on course with my cheeriness, but feeling so uncomfortable.

Marco orders a bottle of some sort of white wine, and I do my best to decipher the menu selections. I'm not a fan of white wines at all, but I do know that white is usually good with fish, so I scour the entrée listings in search of the word *pesce*. Suddenly, a tall woman with dark burgundy-colored hair and pale green eyes approaches our table. She's wearing a flowing purple, low-cut dress with gold jewelry draped all over her entire body. When Marco sees her, his face lights up for the first time since we arrived at the restaurant.

"Marco!" the woman says with a deep, seductive voice.

"Bianca!" Marco says as he rises up out of his seat.

I watch as the two kiss each other in greeting and start chatting in Italian. This is a very regular scene for me when I'm with Marco in public—it seems that everywhere we go, people know Marco Maselli. But for some reason, this time, I feel very nervous as the gorgeous young woman in purple touches Marco's shoulder and laughs at whatever it is he's saying to her in Italian. After what feels like a ridiculous amount of time, Marco finally gets around to introducing me to his latest long lost friend.

"Bianca, this is Eloise-ah," Marco says as he steps aside so Bianca can get a proper look at me.

"Hello," I say, as an icy chill races down my spine. He just introduced me as plain old Eloise! He's dropped the "my" and now I'm just regular Eloise! I can feel heat rising up to my cheeks as I try to keep my composure in front of this Amazon goddess called Bianca.

"Bianca is a friend of mine that…manages some of my assets," Marco offers as he and Bianca both laugh. I fail to get the joke, but my mind starts whirling with possible meanings as a wave of nausea ripples through my stomach.

"*It is-ah good to meet-ah you, Eloise-ah,*" Bianca says with a sultry smile.

She and Marco wrap up their chat in Italian as I just sit there, suddenly feeling very alone and vulnerable. I feel self-conscious in my amazing blue dress, and I wish that I could somehow disappear into thin air. I don't know how to handle myself at the moment, and I'm working so hard to keep the hot tears building up behind my eyes at bay. When Marco returns to his seat, I watch as the happy grin on his face begins to fade. I feel a wall go up between us as he lifts his menu off the table and begins studying it with great intensity.

When the waiter returns with our wine, I watch intently as Marco tastes the wine before he allows the waiter to pour me a glass. Then Marco orders for us both—in Italian of course. I didn't even get to tell him what I wanted, but, truthfully, I don't care about the food right now anyway. I'm completely suffering inside with confusion, and no matter what the waiter brings, I doubt I'll be able to eat it.

Once the waiter is gone, Marco lifts his glass for a toast. But instead of a toast to love or to anything in particular, Marco simply says, "*Salute.*"

I tap my glass against his and feel such a lump of disappointment building inside of me. What's happening to us? Why has a short time apart changed everything so dramatically? What did I do to ruin such a perfect romance? These are all questions I'd love to ask Marco; but instead, all I can do is sit across the table from him, acting as though nothing's wrong.

We seem to be running out of small talk right about the time the food arrives. My dish is something called *branzino*—which Marco translates for me as sea bass. It is light and delicious, but, honestly, I have zero appetite. So I simply move my fish around on my plate while I struggle to figure out what to do. When I look up at Marco, he seems to be devouring his food—some dish called *pesce azzurro* that looks like a bunch of different kinds of fish all tossed together in some sort of lemon and oil mixture. He is literally wolfing his food as if it's been ages since he had a good meal.

When he looks up and sees me staring at him, he sends me a weak smile and continues eating. His body language and his sudden personality change are starting to break my heart, and I don't know if I can bare it much longer. I don't want to make a scene in the restaurant, but I have to know what's going on.

"Marco," I say as I watch him scoop up a big bite of fish and shovel it into his mouth. "What's happening to us?" I ask with a quiver in my voice.

"We are eating," Marco says with a blank look on his face as he chews and swallows his food.

"I know that," I say as I try to say it another way. "I mean, why are things so strange between us all of a sudden?"

"I don't know..." he trails off, only this time his face tells me that he knows exactly what I'm talking about.

"Did I do something wrong?" I ask, hoping that his answer to this question will give me some insight into these sudden changes, so I can fix it and we can go back to the way things were.

Marco ponders my question for a minute before he answers. I can feel my feet growing cold, as all the blood in my body has started to pool around my heart. I'm terrified to hear his answer, but I need to know what's going on.

"I don't know, Eloise-ah," he begins as he lifts his glass of wine and swishes it around distractedly. "You just have so many rules—and so little passion."

"What do you mean?" I ask, wanting desperately to understand what that means.

"It is like the pillows on your bed," he begins as he sits his wine glass back on the table and leans forward on his elbows. "Everyday—no matter the time you must rise—you make your blankets and line up the pretty colored pillows along the bed. And every night, you take the pillows off and place them on the bench so they don't touch the floor."

"Things are changing between us because I make my bed?" I ask as confusion swarms my mind. What does making my bed have to do with anything?

"No," Marco says with a light laugh. "You are not listening to me. What I mean is that you live your life with all sorts of rules and reasons, and you don't know how to live with passion. You are so worried about being right and safe that when the time comes to express your passion, you don't know how," he says as he takes my hand and kisses my fingers lightly.

I just stare at him with a confused look, not knowing how to respond or what to think. I don't know what to say, so I just stare across the table, trying to see into Marco's eyes as he continues his explanation.

"Eloise-ah—you are so beautiful, and I was unable to help myself when I first met you. Your long blonde hair, your pure face, and your gorgeous body pulled me in," he says as he pauses to look at me. "But you never really allowed me in. You shut down my love because you don't know how to unleash your own passions," he says like he's lecturing me now.

"But I told you before dinner, I'm ready now! I'm ready to feel my own passions," I say as my eyes begin to rim out with tears. I do my best to blink them back, but it's no use.

"I know what you said, but I don't think it can be for us now," he says with an earnest look on his face. "It is too late for me. I warned you not to hesitate," he adds with a pained look on his face.

I gently pull my fingers from his hands and lean back in my chair. I feel as if I may throw up. This is all so upsetting, and I can't seem to make out the truth of what's happening here.

"Passion is not something everyone knows how to handle," Marco continues from across the table. "It is something that must come naturally. But for you, it is something that you are keeping up on a shelf, hoping that someday, everything will be just so. All of your rules—they are so unnatural. They make it too difficult for me, and I find that I cannot be so patient anymore," he says as he looks at me with a somber face.

"So it's too late for me, then?" I ask in a thick voice, wanting to make sure that I'm understanding everything exactly how he means it.

"My parents have been married since they were 17 years old," he responds. "And there has never been a single day when my mother and my father have not found time to demonstrate their love. They are both very passionate people—as am I and the rest of my family. *Passione*—it is not something that you try on, Eloise-ah. It is who you are," he says like he's finished.

I don't know what to say now because I'm certain that if I utter another word, the floodgates will open up, and I won't be able to stop crying. So I take a deep breath and look at Marco one last time.

"Maybe...you should take me home now," I manage to say in an even voice.

The drive back to *Il Girasole* is incredibly difficult for me. It seems as though Marco has already moved on from me and made up his mind that I'm incapable of passion. He seems content in his decision as he zips through traffic and takes tight turns like he can't help but enjoy the ride. As he pulls the car into the circle drive of the resort, he keeps the engine running and slips out of the driver's side. He walks quickly to my side of the car and pops open the door—almost like he's in a hurry to get rid of me.

When he helps me out of the car, he pulls me into his arms for one last embrace. At first, I tighten my body against his, but no matter how I fight it, I give in one last time. I feel myself melting into his arms as I breathe in his citrus cologne for what I'm sure is the very last time. When we break apart, I look up at Marco, and he smiles kindly at me.

"Marco, I have one last question," I say as I steel myself against my emotions.

"What is it?" he asks sincerely and in a calm, dreamy voice.

"Are you already seeing someone else?" I can't help but ask this question. I feel as though I need to know the answer to help me close the door.

"Eloise-ah," Marco says softly. "You are not easy to replace for me—I loved you very much..." he says with a pained smile.

"You did?" I ask in a whispered voice.

"Yes...I *did*," he confirms, with great emphasis on the "did."

I don't know what to make of his answer. There are so many things to consider here, and it wasn't exactly what I was looking for in the way of clarity. But before I can even come up with a follow-up question, Marco pulls me closer and kisses me on the forehead. Then he takes me by the shoulders and smiles.

"You are beautiful, Eloise-ah—don't ever forget your amazing beauty," he says as he releases me and walks around the front of his car.

I stand there in a daze as I watch him slide into the driver's seat and shut the door. He gives the engine a light rev and pulls out of the driveway. I watch as his taillights vanish into the distance. Once I know I'm alone, I allow the tears that have been building all night to roll down my cheeks, and I turn and start walking back toward my villa.

As I hang my gorgeous blue dress in my closet, the tears stream down my face and huge, heaving sobs of pain rise up my body and out of my mouth. The ending of this fairytale romance is so devastating to me, and I feel quite certain that I may never fully recover.

I can't believe how stupid I am! I actually believed that Marco was different from other men I've known in the past. I thought he was my soul mate! He made me feel things I've never felt before. And he said he loved me! How can his love for me change in a matter of three days? And how could his feelings for me be love if he can let them go so easily?

None of this makes any sense to me. I guess I could understand it if he hadn't said he loved me. Sometimes, you might think you love someone, but you never say it unless you're sure. And Marco seemed so sure! I felt it in his kiss and saw it in his eyes every time he looked at me. He showed me around his town and introduced me to his family, and he repeatedly uttered the words *I love you* in my ear!

As I look at the throw pillows on my bed, a fresh flood of tears spills down my face. I move in toward my bed and take the first pillow and fling it into the air. Then I take the rest of the pillows and pull them all into my arms. I tightly wrap my arms around the bundle as I sob into them, trying to understand how making my bed and caring about where the pillows are stored makes me a passion-less person. It angers me to think about what Marco said, and I can't make my heart feel any better. So I release my arms and let the pillows fall to the floor. I take my feet and kick at the pillows like a two-year-old having a temper tantrum.

I know I'm a passionate person—whether I make my bed or not! I know in my heart that I feel things as deeply as Marco and the rest of his wine-soaked family! How can he say those things about me when all I've ever felt for Marco was passion and desire? How can he assume that I don't have heat in my heart or a longing like his? So I wasn't ready to express my passions the way he was—but it doesn't mean I don't have real feelings!

I can feel a rage growing inside me that I've never felt before. I'm beyond hurt—I'm destroyed. I was going to give myself to Marco tonight, and part of me is terrified that, if Marco were to knock on my door right now, I'd still do it, just to prove that I am filled with passion and love. I don't know who I am anymore—I've lost sight of everything that matters to me in the span of four short weeks. I've lost my soul mate—if he ever was my soul mate—and I've lost my best friend in the process. I feel so lost and so alone, and I don't know where to go.

But I know I can't stay here in my villa. This was supposed to be the happiest night of my life. I was supposed to be here, alone with Marco Maselli, making love to my soul mate for the very first time. When I woke up this morning, I never imagined myself tossing my throw pillows around the room and literally collapsing from a broken heart. All I know is that I have to get out of here for a bit. I need to give myself a chance to breathe and sort this all out.

So I pull on a pair of running shorts and a jog top. Once I slip on my running shoes and lock the door to my villa behind me, I walk with purpose toward Marta's villa. I need to have someone with me for a bit—someone who will understand my feelings. As I climb the steps to her villa, I can hear her TV and smell the aroma of something baking.

When Marta opens the door, she looks happy. I haven't seen her smile like this in such a long time that I almost wonder if I'm at the right villa. But her face is easy and fresh, and she looks like a totally different Marta than the one I've been spending so much time with lately.

"Elle!" she says with great alarm as her soft face changes into one filled with worry. "Are you alright?"

"No—Marta, I need you," I say as my face cracks and tears spill down my cheeks.

"Oh, my God, Elle—come in," she says as she steps aside.

As I enter her villa, I can see that she is baking. It smells wonderful, whatever it is, and I can't seem to help but drift toward the kitchen. I slide up onto one of her bar stools and try to figure out what she's working on. It looks like some sort of bread. Marta joins me in the kitchen and sidles up on the other side of the counter.

"I'm baking some Italian style bread," she says in explanation of the mess on her counter. "I love to cook, but I haven't done it for such a long time, so I decided that today, I was going to make something using only Tuscan ingredients," she explains as she lifts a pan of freshly baked bread off of a cooling rack for me to see.

"Wow, Marta—that looks amazing," I say, temporarily shifting my mind to something other than myself.

"Elle, I know you didn't come over here because you smelled my bread baking, and, judging by your face, something went terribly wrong tonight. Talk to me," Marta says with a concerned look on her face as she dusts the flour off a section of her countertop and then leans down onto her elbows.

"I think Marco broke up with me tonight," I say to her after a long pause. Just saying it out loud to someone else feels miserable, and I can feel new tears forming in my eyes as soon as I finish saying it.

"Oh, God, Elle, I'm so sorry," Marta says as she walks around to my side of the counter and puts her arms around me.

"It all happened so out of the blue, and I don't know what to do with myself now..." I wail into her shoulder, trying to control the flood of emotions without any luck.

"Oh my poor sweet Elle," Marta coos into my ear as she gently rubs my back. "Do you want to talk about it?" she asks after a long pause.

"I need to get some air," I say as I pull away from Marta's shoulder. "Will you go for a walk with me?" I ask.

"Sure, Chica. I'll go for a walk—just let me change my clothes," Marta says as she moves away from me and heads for her bedroom.

My head is pounding from all the tears and pent up emotion, and I look around Marta's kitchen for some aspirin and a glass of water. I find something that looks like pain reliever, only the label seems to be printed in Italian. I pop open the lid and tap out two tablets into my palm and wash it down with a swig of Marta's lemon water. I wish that a couple of simple pills could take away the pain my heart is feeling right now because this is the most awful feeling in the world.

"You ready?" Marta asks as she steps out of her room. She's wearing leggings and a T-shirt and a pair of Keds.

"I am," I say as I make my way out of the kitchen, and we both begin walking toward her door.

When we step outside, I try to steady myself with a few cleansing breathes. But to my surprise, there simply isn't a way to reverse the upturned feeling of being dumped—not even for a second. All the fragrant smells of *Il Girasole* make me think of Marco, and, before I even manage to say my first word, a sob from deep inside works its way up and out of my mouth.

The walking and talking helps a little, and by the time Marta and I walk to the *Ponte Vecchio* and are starting to head back, I've managed to fill her in on how things went from amazing to non-existent in a matter of three days. Marta is gracious and keeps her questions to a minimum—even though I know it's a shocker for her when I reveal that Marco would be my first, and how I've managed to hold onto my virginity until age 33. She offers very little in the way of advice. Rather, she just listens to me and seems to make all the right faces, groans and moans to make me feel so understood and heard.

As we round a familiar corner that I pass nearly every day on my run, she finally asks me her first question. Her voice is steady and calm, and I feel so lucky to have a friend that has so much experience with this type of pain and suffering.

"So when you asked Marco if he was already seeing someone else, all he said was that you were difficult to replace?" Her question is one that I've been stalled out on myself.

"That's what he said, but Marta, I know he must've moved on. It was too easy for him to walk away from me tonight—he didn't even seem to hesitate," I say as anger rises up my throat and settles in my voice. "And there are just too many things that make me know it in my bones."

"Like what?" Marta asks in a breathless tone as she slows our pace down a bit. I don't think Marta is much of an exerciser, so I do my best to keep my steps a little closer together.

"Well, you'll probably think I'm crazy when I tell you this," I say, nervous all of a sudden about what Marta thinks of me.

"No I won't," she says emphatically.

"OK," I say as I reluctantly reveal my deepest suspicions. "Today, when I was at the pool, Gabby all of a sudden started being nice to me. She came over to my area and pulled up a lounge chair and then started making conversation with me."

"Gabby?" Marta clarifies with little surprise in her voice.

"The one and only," I say. "I thought it was strange, especially since she made it so clear that she didn't want to be my friend when she first arrived. But as she was applying all her tanning oil, I noticed an anklet that she was wearing. It was a thin gold chain with an oblong bead just like the necklace Marco gave me on our first date. When she noticed me looking at it, she seemed to turn evil on me—like she *wanted* me to see the anklet. Then she told me that the jeweler who made it told her it was a Florentine *amuleto* given for good luck! *And* she said the jeweler's name was *Giuseppe!*"

"So?" Marta says as confusion crosses over her face.

"Marco said that his *Uncle Giuseppe* made my necklace, Marta, *and* he told me that the necklace had the same exact meaning!" I say as if this should be totally obvious to Marta.

"So what are you thinking is happening here?" Marta asks, almost as if she is expecting me to already have all the answers.

"A few weeks before we left for Italy, Gabby wanted me to meet her new boyfriend, Manny, for dinner at *Grazie*," I say after a deep sigh. "To make a long, painful story short, Manny is a gynecology intern who works at the clinic where I get my checkups. Earlier that day, I had my annual checkup, and Manny was there and learned through one of his fellow interns that I was still a virgin. Then at dinner, Manny realized I was the patient the interns were talking about, and he started to make a move on me. Gabby misinterpreted the whole thing and accused me of making a move on her boyfriend."

"How bizarre!" Marta says with a laugh.

"Tell me about it," I concur.

"So now you think Gabby wants you to think that she is making a move on your boyfriend as a form a retaliation for what happened that night in Miami?" Marta sums up.

"It makes perfect sense," I say as I start to see things more clearly.

We walk in silence as we both ponder the story. I can't say putting these pieces together makes me feel any better, but, at least, if there is something going on between Marco and Gabby, it makes it easier for me to hate him.

"Elle…" Marta says in a faraway voice.

"Yes," I say, wondering why she's acting funny.

"I have something to tell you, but I don't want you to freak out, OK?" she says as she slows our pace down even more.

"What is it?" I ask in a low voice, feeling the tiny hairs on my arms dancing in anticipation of what I can only expect is bad news.

"I've kind of noticed Marco and Gabby flirting a bit on our flights," she begins slowly. "I didn't really think much of it because Marco seems to flirt with every female—the gate agents, the van drivers—any female that he comes into contact with."

"And your point is?" I say as I feel myself begin to cringe at the thought of how much Marco's flirting bothers me.

"Well, on the last flight to Munich," Marta begins in a sheepish tone. "I happened to see Marco and Gabby coming out of this set of double doors that I think lead to the private pilots lounge. Gabby looked kind of disheveled and they were both laughing. Then I saw Marco sort of tap Gabby on the butt before they took off in separate directions. Later, when

I saw them pass each other in the boarding area, they seemed to be eyeing one another in a sort of conspiratorial way."

Glacial doesn't begin to explain the kind of cold that is running through my body as Marta shares this seemingly strange exchange she witnessed between Gabby and Marco in Munich. My heart is nearly incapable of pumping blood to the rest of my body because it's frozen with shock. How could I be so stupid? Of course Marco has another woman. Gabby.

Chapter Twenty-Eight

Marta and I stop and sit on a random bench outside of a closed bakery. I needed a minute to sit and take it all in—Marco is seeing Gabby. That's why he was able to leave me so easily, and why he made such a point to tell me that he *did* love me. Now he has his sure thing, and he can unleash his stupid passions with *her* because *I* hesitated. I'm literally blown away by this turn of events. I went from wanting to give Marco my virginity to wishing I'd never met him—all in the span of a few short hours.

"I can't believe he took Gabby to the pilot's observatory," I finally say after what feels like hours of sitting in silence. "That was the most romantic moment of my life."

"Really?" Marta asks as though her interest is piqued.

"It was this totally glassed in room where you could see the planes taking off and landing," I explain as I revisit the scene in my mind. "It was where Marco gave me my first real kiss, and I'm telling you, it was the most incredible kiss, Marta. It brought me to my knees."

"Wow," Marta simply says as she leans back into the bench.

We sit in silence for a bit longer as I mull the details of the situation over and over in my mind. I knew I was in for trouble when I saw Gabby by the pool that first morning. I knew she had it in for me, but I guess I didn't realize that she could be so vindictive. And that's assuming that this was all her doing. I mean, did she pursue Marco to hurt me, or did Marco pursue her because I hesitated? Either way, I'm the loser in the end.

"You gotta admit, Elle," Marta says with a light laugh. "Marco is kind of cheesy."

"What do you mean?" I ask, trying to figure out what would make her say such a thing.

"Well, he didn't do anything very original for Gabby—he gave her the same kind of gold bobble, took her to the same secret pilot's hide out—he probably gave her a dress and fancy note cards, too. I mean, Elle, it sounds like he's just using the same moves on Gabby that he used on you!" she says, as if this will make me feel better.

As I allow her words to sink in, I realize that she may be right. Maybe all of the things he did for me are standard dating protocols for Marco. Maybe none of it was special at all. I wish this thought brought me comfort, but it actually makes me feel worse. I mean, to me, everything Marco did was incredibly amazing, and it seemed like he was trying to make every second so special, just for me. He was calling in favors from family members and taking me to places regular people can't go. It was all so magical, and the thought of it being a part of Marco's standard dating routine makes me feel like I've been fooled. It makes me feel like a poor, naïve sap that will fall for anything.

"I feel like such an idiot," I confess to Marta after a long pause.

"Well, you shouldn't," Marta says in a matter-of-fact voice. "Oscar courted Michelle with several of his *signature moves,* and it made me hate him for having such a limited imagination," Marta confides as she stares up into the black sky. "I found a few receipts in his pockets for dinners and gifts—and they were all from the same bag of tricks he used to lure me into his life all those many years ago."

"Oh brother," I say as I roll my eyes and then join Marta as I lean back into the bench. "So you know exactly how I'm feeling right now..." I trail off as I shut my hot, puffy eyes.

"Yep—sadly, I do," Marta says followed by a long sigh.

When Marta and I near *Il Girasole,* I realize how exhausted I am and how I only have about four more hours until I need to start getting ready for the morning flights. I wish I didn't have to work today—I just feel like disappearing for a while. I don't want to have to face my co-workers or deal with my emotions anymore. But I know I have to try to accept things and get on with my life. At least I only invested a month of my life in this relationship—and not 12 years like Marta. And while it was an intense month, I have to keep it all in perspective.

"Are you feeling any better?" Marta asks like she's out of breath from the walk.

"I guess so," I say to her as I grab her hand and give it a little squeeze. "Thank you so much for walking with me," I add as I give her a sidelong smile.

"Hey—what are friends for?" she replies as she leans down and rests her hands on top of her knees. She pulls in a deep breath and then lets it out with a loud push.

I can smell the lavender plants in the garden around the fountain. I pull in a deep breath and stretch my arms, hoping that I'll be able to sleep for a few hours. When I twist my torso so that I can stretch my lower back, my eye catches something that makes me freeze. As I squint my eyes to get a better view, I see Marco's Ferrari parked along the side of the road, just beyond some leafy trees that line the outer edge of the *Il Girasole* entrance.

"Elle?" Marta asks as she looks at me with concern. "What's the matter?"

I take a lunging step forward so I can take a closer look at the car. My veins go icy as I confirm that what I'm seeing is real, and I start to walk quickly toward the car. I can feel Marta following me, her breathing labored and heavy. When I reach the car, I take my hand and place it on the hood. The engine is still hot—like Marco recently arrived after a fast spin around the city.

"Who's car is this?" Marta finally asks.

"Marco's," I practically spit as I pull my hand away from the engine. I'm so angry right now all I can see is red. I spin around and start heading for the front gate, my pace strong and purposeful.

"Oh, God, Elle, no!" Marta says with panic in her voice as if she can read my mind. "You can't go over there. You can't go to Gabby's," she says like she pleading as she chases after me.

But I have to see this for myself! I have to see if he is with her. I've pieced everything together based on clues and gossip, but for this whole thing to be real, I need to see it with my own two eyes! As I slip through the sunflower gate, I start to head in the direction of Gabby's villa, ready to confront the two lovebirds in the act. But just as I pass a clump of trees, I feel Marta's body slamming into mine, and we both come crashing to the ground.

"Elle!" Marta says in a harsh whisper. "You can't do this!"

"Marta! Get off me!" I say as I struggle to turn myself right side up. "Are you crazy?" I manage to ask her as she untangles her legs from mine and then grabs my wrist.

"You can't do this to yourself, Elle!" she warns in a hot and heavy whisper. "You'll only regret it," she adds as she catches her breath.

"But I have to see it for myself! You don't understand!" I say adamantly as I fight to break away from her grip.

"No—that's where you're wrong. I *do* understand," she says in a shaky voice as she pulls me into her view. "You will regret having that image in your head, Elle, and there will be nothing that can stop you from replaying it and replaying it. The memory will torture you, day and night, and you'll wish you only left it to your imagination," she says as her face crumbles right in front of me, and the tears start pouring down her cheeks.

Suddenly, I feel sobered by her words. As I focus my eyes, I can see the hurt and regret in her tears. I can actually feel the pain she's endured from learning too many of the intimate details of Oscar's affair. In my heart, I know she's probably right. And if it would help for me to see what's going on with my own two eyes, I'm sure Marta would want that for me right now.

"OK, Marta," I say as I try to calm myself down. "I understand."

"Good," Marta says as she lifts her hand to her face and wipes away her tears.

I reach for Marta and pull her into my arms and do my best to comfort her. I can feel her tiny body shaking. I know that what she's been through is even worse than what's happening to me right now, and I want to be strong for her sake. I want to move on without creating even more haunting memories for myself—even though the temptation to spy on Gabby is so powerful.

"Promise me you'll go back to your villa and try to sleep," Marta says once she's gained her composure.

"I promise, Marta," I say with a whisper. "I promise."

I feel as though I'm floating outside of myself. The only sensation that feels real is the cold, dew-soaked grass on my bare feet and the cool night air as it wraps around my exposed shoulders. The moon casts an eerie glow over the resort, and, as I tiptoe along the cobbled pathway, the sound of my heartbeat is pounding out a steady rhythm in my ears.

When I reach the villa, I silently climb the steps. The porch is cold and smooth on my feet, and a tiny shudder of nerves mixed with a chill shimmy up my spine. The plantation shutters are tightly pressed down on all of the windows but one. The one nearest the front door is cracked open, just enough to spill golden light from inside onto the porch. The unsteady pool of light flickers as though it's coming from a candle or maybe even a fire in the fireplace. I watch the light dance across my toes as I allow my feet to step into the glow.

I can hear soft music—jazz I think—humming through the walls of the villa. As I rest my ear against one of the covered windows, I can also hear voices—one deep and one high. I close my eyes and try to listen to what the voices might be saying, but all I can hear are deep vibrations and high pitched moans.

Quietly, I slide my body down to the ground and lean my back up against the wall just beneath the window. I sit there, crouched up into a tiny ball and allow my breathing to steady. I close my eyes and absorb the vibrations of his voice and the smooth notes of the jazz music as it escapes through the walls.

When I open my eyes, I take a deep breath. Then I slowly turn my body, keeping myself low and close to the ground to prevent any sudden movements from giving me away. Once I'm positioned just perfectly, I slowly lift my torso up, guiding my body in tiny increments until my eyes are even with the first opening in the slats of the plantation shutter.

At first, I can't see anyone. The room is dancing in candlelight and there is a small fire burning in the fireplace, but there's no one within view. I carefully lift my body up so I can see through the second opening in the slats. This time, I can see much more clearly. I allow my eyes to adjust first, and then engage my brain so that I can understand exactly what I'm seeing.

I can see a man's back—brown and muscled. His shoulders are round and thick, and I can see the shape of his hips as they taper down and just out of my view. His dark hair is disheveled, and the golden highlights sparkle in the dim light of the room. His arms seem to be gathering up a woman, and I can see his muscles flex and the back of his neck tighten and relax as he consumes the woman with his embrace.

Her arms suddenly wrap around his shoulders, and she seductively moves her fingers along his spine and then over his shoulder blades. I watch as her arms pull him toward her, and her legs rise up and wrap around his waist. Seconds later, I see Gabby's face rising up over his shoulder. She tucks her chin on top of his shoulder and smiles with the look of sheer rapture and pleasure. When she opens her eyes, she sees me peering through the window. She looks at me with a sultry smile, and then tosses her head back and moans in ecstasy.

A shockwave ricochets through my body as I flail my arms around, blindly batting the air in search of my alarm clock. When I finally connect, the alarm is silenced, but my head begins to pound and thump in its place. As I peel my eyes open, the room seems blurry and dim. I fight the urge to shut my eyes again and fall back to sleep, but I know I need to act now. So I roll out of bed and pad into the bathroom.

When I turn on the light, I'm horrified by my reflection. My eyes are red and puffy, and my lips are swollen and chapped. As I take a closer look at myself, a sick feeling washes over me as I remember that last night, Marco dumped me. The reality is even worse this morning, and I wonder how long I'll have to carry this painful burden in my heart.

I turn on the shower and let it get hot while I step out of my pajamas and dig through my vanity drawer in search of a new bar of soap. When I rip open the paper wrapper on the soap, I take a deep pull of the citrus body wash, and tears instantly flood my eyes. I'm not sure I'll ever be able to smell citrus again without crying.

The hot water stings my skin as I step into the steamy shower, but I want it to hurt. I welcome the pain right now because it's the pain that tells me I'm still alive. As the water cascades down my hair, I swallow a sob that seems to have risen up in me from out of nowhere. I massage some shampoo into my scalp and try to stimulate my brain cells in the process. I lean my body against the wall of the shower and watch the bubbles from my shampoo wash down the drain.

Once I dry off and run a brush through my hair, I at least feel more human again. I wash my face and brush my teeth, and to my relief, I notice that my shower seems to have helped my puffy face a little bit, and by the time I finish blow drying my hair, I'm starting to look a bit more like myself. I finish getting reading in the bathroom and then head into the kitchen to grab some water and something to eat. When I see the clock on the microwave, I realize I'm running out of time.

I make a mad dash into my room and pull on my underwear and my uniform as quickly as I can. Then I yank on my stockings and shove my feet into my shoes. As I kick one of my throw pillows out of the way, a sick feeling comes over me as I fight the urge to make my bed. Or maybe I fight the urge not to make my bed. I can't be sure. All I know is that my heart aches as I consider the disarray of my room which pretty much mirrors the current condition of my heart.

I decide to just leave my room as it is and gather my carryon bag and flight credentials. I lock my door and wobble down the pathway toward the front gate, feeling unsteady and on the verge of tears. I do my best to bolster my emotions because I don't want anyone to know how badly I'm hurting. Knowing this crew, everyone probably already knows about Gabby and Marco, and I'd hate for them to discover that I was actually the last one to find out.

When I push my way through the front gate, everyone is already on the crew van, and I quicken my pace so I don't keep everyone waiting. The gang offers up weary hellos as I slide into the van and lean up against the window. I do my best to keep my face upbeat and bright, and, if anyone asks about my eyes, I'm going to lie and say I'm fighting allergies.

Once everyone's on the van, the van driver lurches us out of the circular drive. As we roll passed the entryway of the resort, my eyes fall upon the spot where Marco parked his car last night. A thud of emotions sinks into my stomach as I see that his car is gone. I remember putting my hand on the hood—and it was still warm—but I can't remember if I saw Marco and Gabby together or if I dreamed it. The whole night is fuzzy, and I feel confused—like maybe I'm losing my mind or something.

Chapter Twenty-Nine

I feel like a zombie. My head is pounding, my arms and legs feel thick, and my stomach is riddled with nerves and waves of nausea. I do my best to hide it from Peter, but when you're working that closely to someone in such a confined area, they're bound to notice things. Peter is gracious enough not to ask me while we're setting up for service. And he's amazing during the service, too. He seems to be covering my every mistake like a real pro without comment or irritation.

When all of the passengers in our area have had their morning coffees and juices, Peter and I wheel the cart back into the aft galley and start restocking it in silence. After we've put everything away and the cart is locked into the storage bay, I try to act like I'm focusing on the catering paperwork. But the truth is, I can't concentrate. All I can think about is Marco, and if I really saw him with Gabby last night. Did I actually get up in the middle of the night to go and spy on them? And if I did, was the guy that Gabby had her legs wrapped around even Marco?

"Elle," Peter says as he stands directly behind me. The sound of his voice startles me. "Why don't you let me do the catering order. You look like you might be tired."

I don't even have the energy to protest, so I turn around and face Peter and say, "OK...thanks, Pete."

"Are you gonna be OK?" he asks as he looks at me with great concern. "You don't look so good."

"Allergies," I lie as I shrug my shoulders and hand him the paperwork.

"What are you allergic to?" Peter inquires as he takes a closer look at my face. "Hunky pilots who cheat on you?"

"What?" I say, alarmed by his words. My face feels hot with shame as I stare at Peter, trying my best to make it look like I have no idea what he's talking about.

"Oh, Honey...come here," Peter says as he pulls me into his arms.

I'm so stunned that Peter knows that I just numbly stand there as he wraps his arms around me and says "there, there" into my ear. When he pulls away, I look at him with a blank expression, not sure if I should confirm or deny his comment.

"Come sit," Peter finally says as he makes his way over to his jump seat. He pulls the seat down and scoots over to the very edge to make room for me. I watch him as he stuffs the catering paperwork into his apron pocket and focuses on me.

Slowly, I walk toward Peter. I feel dead inside and incapable of tapping out one more bit of emotion. I'm weary and confused, and I don't think talking to *Peter* is going to make things better. But knowing him, avoiding the subject is not an option. So I reluctantly slide in next to him and let out a heavy sigh.

"Girl, we're all so worried about you," Peter says as he wraps his fingers around my low-slung ponytail and runs his hand down the length of it. "Scott is a mess right now—not knowing for sure if you're OK..." Peter trails off like maybe he wasn't supposed to mention Scott's name.

"I'm fine," I lie—very unconvincingly, I'm sure.

"No, you're not fine, Elle!" Peter says emphatically. "You've been played for a fool by some Euro-trash pilot, and it's just terrible."

"No, I haven't!" I reply defensively.

"And Gabby—the way she just swooped in and did her little thing, and then, *poof*, she's stolen herself a man," Peter blathers on as if to himself.

"So it was Gabby that pursued him?" I can't help but ask.

"Bass said she had her eye on your man from day one—but it didn't take long for good old *Capitano Amore* to notice her and start making his move," Peter says.

As I sit there, listening to everything he's saying, I wonder if Peter forgot who he's talking to. His delivery seems so blunt and harsh, and that *Capitano Amore* dig feels like his words are actually punching me in the stomach. Even though it's technically gossip, what he's telling me is the first real confirmation I've had that Gabby and Marco are together, and I feel my last remaining shred of hope for things to somehow turn around slipping away.

"Well, I don't know *all* the gory details, Sweetheart," Peter says after he notices that I'm starting to fall apart in the seat next to him. "All I know is that everyone thinks what he did to you is just horrible," Peter says as he drops his hands into his lap and stares straight ahead.

"So everyone already knows?" I ask as my voice starts to thicken with hurt and shame.

"Well, certainly everyone on the evening crew," Peter adds in a softer, more sensitive voice. "But everyone's on your side, Elle—we all love you—even Scott."

"Yeah, right," I huff at the thought of Scott still loving me.

"He *does*, Elle, and he's so worried about you right now," he says, sounding a little defensive himself.

"Well, he didn't love me a few weeks ago when he told Miriam Ungaro that he thought that I was disloyal to the company and that my head is always in the clouds and that he felt I should be removed from Crew 2 because of it," I snap back as acid rises up into my throat.

"Oh please, Elle," Peter laughs. "You don't honestly think Scott said those things to Miriam, do you?"

"Well, I wasn't sure at first, but it seems like Scott can't even so much as look at me whenever I see him," I say, feeling very frustrated and confused.

"Honey, he can't look at you because he's hurt," Peter says as he turns his body slightly so he can see my face. "And that whole exchange with Miriam went down very differently than she told you it did," Peter says with authority.

"It did?" I ask in a weak voice.

"Girl, he came to your defense when Miriam started blaming you for different things that were out of place in the first class galley," Peter says moving his hands dramatically as he gears up his story. "She kept saying that you were the first person to stock the galley when we left Miami and that you set a bad precedent for the others to follow. Scott told her she was crazy and pounced on her and said that she was being too hard on you—that you were so tired you could barely focus and to leave you alone."

"Really?" I say feeling relieved to hear this version of the story.

"Yes! And Scott had nothing to do with her decision to move you to the morning crew," Peter says emphatically. "Just face it Elle, Miriam was looking for reasons to punish you because you moved in on her crush—sort of the way Gabby did to you, I guess," Peter says, like he just realized the pattern himself.

"Oh, thanks, that makes me feel fantastic," I say to Peter as I roll my eyes. I hate the thought that I suddenly have another thing in common with Miriam. We've both been passed over by Marco for someone else.

"Well, it certainly does show you the quality of man *Marco Maselli* is—he'll lead a girl on, get what he wants from her and then move on to his next victim," Peter says, like he's such an expert on the subject of how Marco dates. "He's scummy and evil, Elle, and so is Miriam… *But Scott isn't,*" Peter says in conclusion as he looks me dead in the eye.

I take a moment to think about everything Peter's just told me. It makes me feel better to know that Scott didn't say all those terrible things about me to Miriam. But at the same time, it's hard for me to believe he would defend me when he's up against Miriam, but go out of his way to be indifferent toward me whenever I'm around.

"Well, that still doesn't explain why Scott's also avoiding me," I add, hoping there is some decent explanation for that as well.

"*Hello!* May I remind you that *you* told him that the two of you couldn't be friends," Peter says in a singsong voice.

"I didn't tell him that he couldn't be *friendly* toward me when we saw each other in passing," I bark back, feeling incensed by the fact that Peter is making this out to be entirely my fault.

"Come on, Elle," Peter says chidingly. "You hurt him pretty badly when you basically said you'd rather have Marco Maselli—some egotistical, glorified Italian bus driver—in your life, rather than him."

Peter's words settle over me like a heavy blanket. I guess I knew that my decision to pursue my relationship with Marco hurt Scott, but I didn't realize how much. Now, a new layer of emotions floods into my body, and I feel tears of regret over what I did to Scott welling up inside of me.

"Do you think he'll ever forgive me?" I ask Peter after I swallow hard to try to keep the tears from spilling out of me.

"I don't know," Peter says as he stands up and starts fishing around in his apron pocket for the catering paperwork. "I'm sure he will someday—but I think it's gonna take awhile," he says as he looks over his shoulder at me. "Just give it some time, Elle."

"OK," I say in a whispered voice.

I sit still for a few moments, watching Peter count sodas and check things off of the catering forms. I can't believe how horribly I've messed things up in my life in such a short amount of time. I just wish I could take it all back. I wish that I'd never signed up for the transfer. I feel forever changed and damaged in some way from this experience. I feel so lonely and I don't even have Scott to help me piece things back together.

When we get back to *Il Girasole*, I agree to meet Peter down by the pool. Part of me just wants to go back to my villa and hide under my blankets and shut out the rest of the world. But Peter insists that if I'm going to save face with everyone and keep the rumors from spiraling out of control, I need to act like everything's normal. I'm not sure it exactly matters to me what everyone thinks, but minimizing my humiliation over the Gabby factor would be nice.

So I slide on my bathing suit and gather up my pool gear. I flip on the TV to find out the latest about the hurricanes—unfortunately, the news coverage in the middle of the day is pretty spotty. But I figure if there isn't any breaking news, things must still be OK back home, and I decide to try and table this worry for later.

It's a relief to put on my big Jackie O sunglasses because they hide some of the puffiness in my eyes. As I take a quick look at myself in the mirror, I see a tired version of myself that looks defeated, but not destroyed. I know I can get through this, but I just have to figure out a way to stay strong. My biggest priority right now is fixing things with Scott. It won't be easy, but if he really cares about me as much as Peter seems to think he does, maybe he'll decide to forgive me in time.

The pool is packed with people. Everyone from the morning crew is just arriving as the evening crew is preparing to leave. I can see Scott and Sebastian sitting together on the upper deck, but I don't feel ready to approach them—especially since Peter's not with me. So I find a chair near the entry gate. I don't want to draw any attention to myself by looking for a lounge chair with better positioning, so I settle for the closest chair in sight.

After I spread my towel down over the chair, I take off my cover-up and neatly fold it and put it in my bag. Then I sit down on my lounge chair and pull out my book and pretend to read. My body is rigid with nerves, and, while I'm sure it's just my imagination, I can feel people staring at me from across the pool. I do my best to act like I'm perfectly fine, but I just wish Peter would get here. Each time the gate swings open, I quickly peek over the top of my book to see who it is. I finally decide that if he's not here in the next ten minutes, I'm leaving.

Suddenly, I feel a shadow spreading over my legs, and as I slowly lift my eyes, I'm stunned to see Gabby standing at the foot of my lounge chair.

"Hello, *Elle*," she says in a frosty tone.

"Gabby," I say in an even tone—even though my heart is beating wildly inside my chest.

"What are you reading?" she asks as she stands there, shifting her weight from one leg to the other.

"Just a novel," I say as I do my best to look like I'm unmoved by her presence and that I'm actually reading the said novel.

I don't want to look directly at Gabby, but I can see from my peripheral vision that she's wearing the same rose-colored bikini and frosty pink sarong cover-up. It's all I can do to keep from looking up, but it doesn't seem like she's planning on moving any time soon. So I decide I better take action.

"Is there something I can help you with, Gabby?" I finally ask as I lower my book. Now I have a full-length look at Gabby, and she nearly takes my breath away she's so pretty.

"No, I was just wondering what you were reading," she says as she unties her sarong and gives it a shake.

The sarong is gorgeous. It has the most brilliant detailing—tiny iridescent beads are delicately tacked to the fabric with intricate knots of silky thread. As I look more closely, I realize how familiar the handwork looks. That's when a rush of cold sweat sweeps across my body. It's one of Franco's designs!

I watch as Gabby reties the sarong low and loose across her perfectly shaped hips. I feel my lips go numb as I realize that literally every special thing Marco did for me, he's also done for Gabby. I feel actual hatred sweeping over me for both Gabby and Marco. I want to stand up and push her into the pool, but I can't do anything because I'm stuck to my lounge chair. My arms and legs feel like they're weighted down. All I can do is stare at Gabby's beautiful sarong in disbelief.

"Isn't this detail work *amazing*?" Gabby asks me after she notices that I'm staring at her sarong.

I nod my head in agreement, not sure how to handle the swirling emotions coming at me from every side.

"I got it a few days ago when I went to a big fashion show in *Milan*," she says, as a knowing smile spreads across her face.

The confirmation of her words slam into me with great force, and I feel a heave of air rush out of my mouth. I don't know what to do or what to say, but I know for a fact that I have to leave. So I push myself off of my lounge chair and rush past Gabby.

I quickly make my way toward the gate, and, as I approach, someone else is about to enter. I firmly grip the handle in my hand and fling the door open with force. When the door peels back, I'm stunned to see Miriam Ungaro, wearing her big red hat and a white terrycloth sundress. We both look at each other in surprise, and before I can control myself, tears start flooding down my face.

I manage to whip past Miriam and run all the way back to my villa without seeing anyone else. Once I reach the steps to my place, I realize that I left my key in my bag at the pool. So I just sit down on the steps and bury my face in my hands and sob.

Once I'm sure the coast is clear, I decide to go back to the pool area to gather my things. I know I made an awful scene, but it all happened so quickly that I hope people didn't notice. When I open the gate and enter the pool area, I can see that my things are still on the lounge chair and they appear to be untouched. I give a quick look around and see Peter waving at me from the top deck. I wave back and then pull out my cover-up and pull it over my head. I gather the rest of my things and make my way toward Peter.

"Where've you been?" Peter asks with genuine alarm in his voice. "Bass and Scott said you had a run-in with Gabby and you took off."

"Oh, great—so people noticed?" I say in a sheepish voice.

"*Hello!* Of course they did," Peter says in a way that doesn't make me feel one bit better.

"Perfect," I say as I plop down on the lounger next to his.

"Where did you go?" Peter asks with a very puzzled look on his face. "I practically knocked down the door at your villa, and no one's seen you for hours."

"I left my key in my bag, so I couldn't get into my villa," I explain. "So I climbed the wall to my veranda and just crashed there until I was sure the evening crew was gone."

"Oh, God, what a drama, eh?" Peter says as he takes a sip of his Diet Coke with lemon.

"I guess so…" I say, not wanting to talk about it.

"Bass said that Gabby was trying to provoke you or something, and you just had to get away," Peter says matter-of-factly—almost as if he is reporting on some event that didn't involve me.

"Something like that," I say blandly.

"You OK?" Peter finally asks after a long pause.

"I will be," I say as I smile up at him.

Chapter Thirty

The rest of the weekend is very hazy for me. I'm completely numb, and there really isn't any further pain or humiliation in this world that could make me sink much lower. The topic of the end of my relationship with Marco is clearly sizzling gossip at the moment. I can tell because every time I walk up to a group of my co-workers, they seem to abruptly stop their conversations and then flash me pained, sympathetic looks. I can't stand it, but what can I do?

I've been spending my time between flights with Peter for the most part—which isn't exactly my number one choice. He tends to say things the way he sees them, without much care or concern about his delivery. And he's told me things about Marco and Gabby that I wish I didn't know. I've learned that they are out in the open now with the evening crew, and the stories of their exchanges make me feel jealous and heartbroken at the same time. And according to Sebastian, Gabby hardly works the flights at all. She just rides up in the cockpit with Marco after take off and orders everyone else around. It makes me sick inside that I completely misjudged Marco. I thought he was a person with a quality heart. I thought he was a kind, thoughtful man who understood me without explanation. But how could he be all of those things and then suddenly turn into a man that finds *Gabby* so fascinating?

Peter claims that the more I know about what Marco's doing with Gabby, the quicker I'll get over the humiliation of it all. His philosophy is that, if I can be mad at Marco, it will hurt less. In some respects, I think he might be right, but what he isn't factoring into his thinking is how disappointed I am in myself. Each time I learn a new detail about Gabby and Marco, I realize how many times I ignored my own red flags. I dismissed so many things that concerned me about Marco because I wanted him to be perfect for me. I wanted to believe that he loved me the way I want to be loved. And even though there were countless things that scared me, I thought that the unfamiliar feeling in the pit of my stomach was actually love.

And something else Peter can't understand is how much I changed inside for Marco. I lost my head over this guy—so much so that it wasn't even that difficult for me to ditch my best friend or lose sight of my own values. I stopped questioning things around me and started believing my own voice wasn't worth listening to anymore. And when I think about my visit with Edna Pearl, and how I evaded her questions and knowingly edited the truth for her benefit, I feel sick. I can't believe how much I was willing to sacrifice for Marco—my family, my friends, my beliefs and even my virginity—all because I thought he loved me.

Then there are all my "what if" thoughts. What if I did have sex with Marco? Would that have been enough to keep him from responding to Gabby's advances? What if I'd been willing to jump in the sack with Marco the very first time he crawled into my bed? Would that have made him *really* fall in love with me? Or would it have made me hate myself more than I already do?

And then there's Scott. What I've done to him hurts me the most. Peter says that Scott will come around, but I don't know. I've seen Scott a few times over the weekend, and even with him knowing everything that's going on in my life, he hasn't even made one attempt to talk to me. I can't blame him, I guess. If the tables were turned, I might want Scott to feel the natural consequences of his choices, too. But at the same time, I just wish he'd say *something* to me to let me know that there's room for forgiveness—even if it will take some time.

When the crew van drops us off from our final flight of the weekend, I tell Peter I'll meet him for an early dinner. I really want to avoid the pool today—it seems like ever since my run in with Gabby, I don't feel safe out in the open until the evening crew is gone. So I head toward my villa, feeling a bit sad and lonely.

But as I climb the stairs, a surge of adrenaline hits my thighs when I notice a white note wedged into my doorjamb. My mind starts whirling and I feel my hands go clammy as I stare at the note. I almost don't want to move. I just want to stare at it in anticipation. This is how it all started with Marco in the first place. Does this note mean that Marco wants me back?

My heart is beating wildly when I finally grab the tiny slip of paper and unfold it. The handwriting is unfamiliar and very shaky, but I think it says that I need to come to the front office for a message. When I try to decipher the signature, it looks like it says Bruno. My heart sinks with a huge thud, and I feel a deep depression sweeping over me. My eyes fill up with tears, and I'm surprised by how much hope still lives inside of me for Marco.

As I unlock the door to my villa and push my way inside, I can't control my emotions for a second longer, and with a big heave, I allow myself to burst into tears. The ache in my heart over all that I believed about love and about Marco is overwhelming. I adored every second of being courted— and even if Marco used the same moves on Gabby, it doesn't matter. It was the first time in my life that someone made me feel so special.

After I take off my uniform and pull on a cotton sundress, I flop back on my perfectly made bed and stare up at the ceiling. I wish that I could stop loving Marco as easily as he's stopped loving me. I know I wasn't imagining the intensity between us. There was something there—I know it! The way he looked at me, and kissed me—that had to be love.

Or was it just lust?

When I close my eyes and try to think over the many times Marco told me he loved me, and why, I do start to see a pattern. The first time he told me of his feelings was when he said that I make him want to be selfish. He said that he took one look at me in the airport in Miami and knew he wanted me all to himself. I remember him telling me he wanted me to know my own beauty. And on the night when he broke up with me, he only mentioned the physical things he liked about me—like my hair, my face and my body. Add to this the fact that he wanted to sleep with me so quickly, and maybe what he really felt for me wasn't love at all. Maybe he just wanted me to think that, so I'd give myself to him completely.

These revelations don't make me feel much better. They make me feel like a fool. I thought Marco was so different, but I was wrong. So maybe it *was* lust between us. Maybe it was just a fleeting, shallow relationship that wasn't meant to last. I don't know. But whatever it was, it meant the world to me when it was unfolding and right now, a huge part of me wishes I could have it all back. I know I lost myself, and I changed too much, but it was amazing having someone adore me the way I thought Marco did.

As I roll over onto my side, I try to remember what it was that I liked about Marco. Was it his looks? Of course—he's gorgeous. Was it his personality? Yes—he was so romantic and full of life that it kind of took me by surprise. Was it the idea of love? Absolutely. The first time Marco said those words to me, I was forever changed. For me, there were so many things that lured me in, and now that it's all over, I don't know if I can trust myself anymore. What I thought was love turned out to be a house of cards that was easily knocked over with a tiny puff of wind. I feel like a flattened deck, and I don't know how I'm ever going to get over this.

When I enter the office, Bruno is sitting in a broken down wicker chair, reading a book. He looks so at ease with his legs crossed at the ankles and his reading glasses perched on the tip of his nose. But when he sees me walking up the steps that lead to the front desk, he quickly jams a bookmark into his book and hops up out of his seat.

"*Signorina!*" Bruno says animatedly as he scurries around the desk. "You-ah have come for-ah your *messaggio?*" he asks with his eyebrows raised.

"*Si,*" I say as I give Bruno a sweet smile. I watch him bumbling around behind the long counter, trying to pull what looks like an answering machine around so it can sit on top of the desk. When the cords don't reach, Bruno motions for me to come around the desk.

"Come to listen," he says in his broken English as he continues waving his hands at me as I step around the side of the desk.

"*Grazie,*" I say as I move in closer to Bruno. I can see that his fingers are slightly yellowed, and I can smell the ripe stench of wet tobacco as I lean in close so I can listen to the message.

Bruno hits a few buttons, and I can hear the scrambling sound of a tape rewinding. Then, with his thick, dirty finger, he hits *play* and the machine grinds and sputters. I can hear a woman speaking in Italian first, and Bruno shakes his head in frustration as he hits the *fast forward* button. When he hits *play* again, I can hear a loud beep followed by a very familiar voice.

> "*This message is for Elle Butts. This is Violet Harper—her dog sitter. I need to let her know that it looks like the hurricane's headed this way and it's gonna be pretty bad, so I'm trying to find a shelter that allows animals. I can't get in touch with her dad at all, so I wanted to leave word that Ray and I are on the move, but we'll call as soon as the storm passes. Thank you.*"

When the message ends, Bruno pushes the stop button and looks at me with a worried face. I can't move as I absorb the words of Violet's message. I can feel a rush of panic sweeping over me as I consider the fact that as of right now, I have no way of knowing for sure where my precious dog is—or my parents. If Violet couldn't reach my parents, does that mean they've already evacuated without sending word?

"Bruno—when did this message come in?" I ask in a panicked voice. Bruno just looks at me like he's desperate to understand my words. "When did this message arrive?" I ask again, only this time, I'm speaking slowly and deliberately, and I've added a series of hand gestures to help him understand.

"This *messaggio?*" Bruno confirms as I shake my head up and down, trying to get him to tell me something I can understand. "I-ah listen…to the…*messaggio…l'altro ieri…*"

"*L'altro ieri?* What does that mean?" I shriek as I struggle to understand Bruno.

Bruno looks panicked as he tries to figure out how to explain when the call came in. He looks around the desk for something, tossing papers around, and digging through a pile of notebooks like he's thought of a way to tell me his thoughts. Finally, he pulls out a calendar and starts flipping through the pages. Then he slams the calendar down on the counter and points.

"Here," he says as he looks up at me. I look down at his hand and see his big, yellow finger pointing to the date for yesterday.

"Yesterday!" I say, happy to have solved the mystery, but overwhelmed by the fact that I'm just now finding out.

"Yesterday!" Bruno says with a huge smile on his face.

I feel tempted to grab Bruno by the shoulders and yell at him for not finding me sooner, but there's no time. I have to try to phone my parents right away and see if they can find Violet before the storm actually hits. So I shake off my urge to scold and start moving around the desk.

"*Grazie*," I say to Bruno as I race out of the office. I don't even turn around to look at him on my way out—I just want to get back to my villa and start tracking down my family.

As I blast through the front doors, I slam right into Peter. Suddenly, our arms are all tangled up, and my body is reeling from the shock of the impact. When I look up, Peter's face is white and his eyes look worried.

"Elle!" he says, his voice loud and animated. "My God, are you OK?" he asks as he grabs me by the shoulders.

"The storm...it's hitting...Sugar Ray and Violet..." is all I can say as fear fully grips my heart. In an instant, my face is gushing with tears as I fall into Peter's arms.

"I know, Elle," Peter says as he holds me up. "I was coming to find you. There's a meeting about what's going on in Miami at the pool," he explains into my ear as I sob into his shoulder.

When we arrive at the pool, everyone is spread out all over the decks, but no one seems to be relaxing. The evening crew is dressed for work, and they all seem sort of out of place sitting on the lounge chairs in uniform. There is a palpable tension in the air, and, as Peter and I take a seat near

Bobbi Henry, I do my best to regain my composure. Miriam Ungaro and Maria, the gate agent we work with here in Florence, are looking over some sheets of paper and quietly talking while the rest of us wait in agonizing anticipation of the big announcement. My mind is racing, and I wish they'd just start talking so I could leave this meeting and get on with my mission to contact my parents.

Finally, Miriam turns to face the group. She's wearing a plain white T-shirt and a pair of tight, acid-washed blue jeans. Her hair is pushed back away from her face, and, right away, I can tell that she's nervous. She takes a step forward and clears her throat. A hush falls over the pool area as we all look and listen intently.

"As you may or may not know, there's been some serious hurricane activity in Miami this week," Miriam begins in a somber tone. "The first storm hit several days ago and turned out to be a strong tropical wave, but the second storm—which was called Hurricane Florence, oddly enough—was much bigger and hit Miami full force early this morning."

I can hear a kind of collective gasp as Miriam takes a brief pause until the group quiets down. My heart is beating loudly inside my head and the tears are damming up behind my eyes as I focus on Miriam.

"We've gotten word from Miami that things are looking pretty bleak," Miriam continues with a slight wavering in her voice. "The destruction is pretty serious and early reports are that *The Wiley* is gone."

The news hits us all with a rush of emotions and questions. People start reacting and moving around, but I can't move. I'm literally shocked to the core. It's as if this news was the final straw. I feel my face go slack as I sit in stunned silence. Hot tears stream down my cheeks and sting my skin with a trail of wetness. All I can think about is Sugar Ray and my parents. Miriam calls for our attention once again as she struggles to keep her own emotions on track.

"We've heard that everyone was safely evacuated from *The Wiley* a day or two before the storm hit, and that they were able to secure some of your personal belongings as well," Miriam continues, doing her best to get through this. "Mr. Bennett has provided temporary housing for all residents of *The Wiley*, so none of your fellow employees are stranded. But the situation is devastating for people in and around the entire coast of South Florida."

Miriam pulls off a pair of reading glasses hanging from the collar of her T-shirt and then slides them on her face and begins reading her notes. "Understandably, you have many questions, but, unfortunately, we don't have a lot of answers. We do know that Mr. Bennett set up an emergency information website before the storm hit, and as soon as they can restore power or hook up to a generator, they will begin posting information for you. I will let you know the second any new information is available, and we will have daily briefings so you know what's going on back home."

I watch as Miriam folds up her notes and then removes her glasses. I can't take my eyes off of her as the rest of the group starts moving around and shouting questions at her. It's all a blurry scene for me as I just sit there in shock over the losses of the past few days. But what happened today is the biggest loss of all.

When I get back to my villa, I dig through my stuff in search of the napkin with my dad's satellite phone number. After rummaging through every bag I own, I finally find it on top of my dresser next to my picture of Sugar Ray. I lift the phone off the cradle and begin punching in the numbers the way my dad told me to, but all I get is a rapid busy signal each time I try. I place the call several times, but I can't ring through.

So I try to call my sister in Chicago. I leave her a message on her answering machine, hoping that she'll call me back right away. I just pray that she has some idea where my parents are, or that she's been able to get the silly sat phone to work. I can feel myself starting to slip into a deep, dark place as I contemplate the magnitude of the disaster. When I turn on the television, every single station is showing pictures of the destruction. Even in Italian, the message is clear: *Miami was destroyed by Hurricane Florence.*

As I lean back into the thick pillows on my bed and try to recognize the images flashing before me, I hear a loud knock on my front door. I take a quick look at the clock and realize that it's probably Peter coming to get me for dinner. So I reluctantly roll off of my bed and make my way toward the door. But when I look through the peephole and see who it is, I'm not sure I want to open it.

It's Miriam. I can't decide what to do, but then I realize she may have information for me, so I take a deep breath and open the door. Once we're standing face to face, I notice how drained she looks. Her eyes are bloodshot and her skin looks pale and greasy. She really looks awful, but then again, so do I.

"Hello, Miriam," I finally say after we've stood there for a moment, awkwardly looking at each other.

"Hi, Elle," she says flatly. "Do you mind if I come in?" she asks.

"Sure, come on in," I say nervously. I step back and allow her to enter my villa.

Miriam makes her way over to the sofa, and I follow her and sit myself down in the big blue armchair. Once we're both seated, we sit in silence for a moment. I can hear the sound of Miriam breathing in and out. I can tell she's nervous and burdened, and, for the first time ever, I feel sorry for her.

"Can I get you some water?" I ask, hoping to break the silence in the room.

"You got any wine?" she asks with a sheepish grin.

"Sure," I say, completely surprised by her question. I jump out of my seat and head toward the kitchen. "I only have red. Is that OK?" I ask as I grab two wine glasses.

"That's perfect," she answers over her shoulder as she adjusts her posture on the sofa.

I quickly pour us some leftover wine I have in my fridge and carry both glasses to the living room. When I hand Miriam a glass, she takes it from me and looks up at me with a grateful smile. I smile back, wondering what's going on between us. I settle back into my chair and take a deep swig of my wine. I can feel the heat rolling down my throat and easing my tensions as I sit quietly and wait for Miriam to begin talking.

"Elle, I know that things between us have been rather… personal since we arrived in Italy," she begins after taking a sip of her wine. "I was hurt and I took it out on you, and for that, I'm sorry," she says as she looks up at me.

I stare at Miriam in disbelief, not sure if I should respond or if I should just let her continue talking. I shift around in my seat and take another nervous sip of my wine as I watch Miriam swirling her wine around in her glass.

"But we have to let bygones be bygones," she continues as she watches the burgundy liquid spiraling like a funnel cloud inside her glass. "I know that you are going through a lot right now, and with the news of the disaster in Miami, I wanted to talk to you personally about an option Mr. Bennett is making available," she says, training her eyes back on me.

"OK," I say, trying to understand what just happened and where she's heading.

"I have a few tickets to Miami that Mr. Bennett issued for crew members that need to get back right away to deal with their affairs," she confides in me. "We have enough of the Florence based flight attendants trained now that I am authorized to send three people home. I wanted to offer one of the tickets to you, Elle—that is, only if you want it," she says as she looks up at me with kind eyes and a soft, genuine smile.

"Miriam," I say in a soft whisper. "Are you sure?" I ask in disbelief.

"I'm sure," she says with a reassuring look. "I can tell that you're not here anymore anyway. I mean, none of us is with the news of the hurricane. But you, you seem to need to get back home...so you can find yourself again."

"I don't know what to say," I respond after a long pause. "I'm overwhelmed, Miriam. I really am!" I say as my eyes brim out with tears. "I'm not sure I'll be able to find myself among all the wreckage in Miami, but at least there, I might have more luck finding all the pieces..." I trail off as my emotions grip my heart.

"I know," she says as she looks down at her hands. "It won't be easy to deal with all of that, but I'm not sure it will be any easier if you stay," she adds.

"No, I'm sure you're right," I say with a sniffle. "Miriam? I'm sorry, too," I say out of the blue. "I hated the way things happened," I add, feeling out of control with my words.

"Me, too, kiddo," she says in a soft voice. "I don't think Marco Maselli was worth it in the end, do you?" she asks after a bit of a pause.

"No…not at all," I say, feeling a wash of relief spilling over me that at least Miriam and I will be OK.

"Poor Gabby," Miriam says followed by a laugh.

And suddenly, I can't help but laugh too!

Miriam told me what little she knew about the situation in Miami before she left me to pack my bags. The airport is already open, shuttling people out of Miami and transporting needed supplies in. Mr. Bennett has agreed to lend his equipment and his crews to aid in the relief efforts, and so things back at *Windsong Air* are very busy indeed. I will likely be assigned to a relief crew when I return, so there won't be too much time for me to search for my family and Sugar Ray. However, Mr. Bennett is making all of his resources available to his employees who are looking for lost loved ones and trying to pull their lives back together.

I ask Miriam if she's offered the ticket home to anyone else and she said no. She said she knew that things had been especially difficult for me since Gabby arrived, and she wanted to give me an out. Then she revealed that, so far, I'm the only person who even knows there are any such tickets. So I promise Miriam I will keep my mouth shut and allow her to handle any questions after I'm gone. There isn't much time for me to tell anyone anyway—my flight leaves at 5:00 a.m. tomorrow.

After Miriam leaves, I cancel my dinner plans with Peter. I just tell him I'm too tired and need to be alone. Then I start the process of packing. As I look around my villa, I feel a new sense of sadness. I'm leaving Italy so soon and with so much disappointment in my heart. This adventure I was so looking forward to has come to such a painfully abrupt ending. When I arrived, I was filled with hope that this experience would broaden me and make me a better person, but instead, I feel destroyed inside—like I was hit by my own personal Hurricane Florence. As I slowly begin to gather up my things, my heart starts to ache as I think about leaving this beautiful villa.

Repacking everything into my suitcase is much more difficult than I expected. Not just because I've accumulated a few things along the way, but because it really means this adventure is over. As I fold all of my clothes and take things off the hangers, I realize how much I still want to stay. There are so many shops I wanted to visit, and so many gifts I wanted to buy. But I figured all that could wait. There was always tomorrow. But tomorrow is no longer an option and I realize that I got greedy with my time here. I didn't make the most of every minute like I'd planned to. I was too busy thinking about Marco.

When I take my beautiful *Franco Maselli* dress off the hanger, I hold it up to my body and look at my reflection in the mirror. It's still the most gorgeous dress I've ever seen, and, no matter how horribly things ended with Marco, this dress will always mean so much to me. I can't help but smile a little as I remember the way I felt when I first put it on—so special, so regal. It was a Cinderella moment for me, and I will never forget it.

When I look around my room, it seems like I've always lived here. It almost feels like home now. And in the midst of all this sadness, that's what my heart craves the most—a sense of home. But when I stop packing for a moment and watch the haunting images on the TV of Miami in the hours after Hurricane Florence blew in, blew up, and blew out, I realize that once I leave this villa, I'm essentially homeless.

As I tuck my picture of Sugar Ray into my satchel, I realize that home is in my heart, and finding him will help me find myself again.

Chapter Thirty-One

It's after midnight and I just finished packing the last of my things. But I have left over food and wine that really shouldn't go to waste. So once I'm sure the evening crew is back, I tiptoe across the grass with a shopping bag clutched in my hand. When I climb the steps to Marta's place, I see that a light is on in her room, so I gently knock on the door.

When Marta answers, she looks fantastic. Her face is bright and fresh, and her eyes seem to sparkle when she sees me standing on her front porch. She's wearing a pair of cotton shorts and a tank top, and she looks the best I've ever seen her.

"Elle!" she says cheerily. "What are you doing up so late?"

"Can I come in for a minute?" I ask nervously, wanting to get inside before anyone else sees me.

"Sure," she says as a worried look crosses her face. "Is everything OK?" she asks as I walk past her and head for the kitchen.

"Yep," I say as I heave the bag of food up onto her countertop. "I just wanted to drop off a few things for you," I say as I start unpacking the bag. "I've got wine, some incredible cheese I bought down at the market, some Italian chocolate, some bottled water and a bag of amazing nuts," I say as I hold up the tiny white bag filled with pistachios.

"Why are you giving me all this stuff?" Marta asks as she joins me in the kitchen. She leans her hip against the side of the counter and waits for my reply.

"I'm actually leaving," I say as I nervously fold up the empty paper shopping bag. "But you can't tell anyone," I add, feeling sort of crummy that I'm betraying Miriam by telling Marta what I'm doing.

"Leaving? What do you mean?" Marta asks with the look of confusion on her face.

"It's a long story, but Miriam made it possible for me to go home to Miami to look for my parents and Sugar Ray," I say rather quickly, trying to gloss over all the details of how Miriam and I made up.

"Wait a minute. Is she *sending* you home, or is this something *you* want?" Marta asks with a suspicious tone.

I take a deep breath and decide I better share the details with her. Once I explain how Miriam apologized and gave me this chance to go home, Marta seems to soften a bit. She grabs for the bag of pistachios and sifts out a handful. She listens to me talk as she snaps open the nuts and discards the shells in a neat little pile.

"Wow, what a turn of events," Marta comments when I've finished my story. "I would've never guessed Miriam even *had* a heart," she adds with disbelief as she wipes her hands on a dishtowel and heads for the living room.

I follow Marta and sit down next to her on the sofa. "It was quite a shock for me, too," I admit once I'm settled in with my feet propped up on the coffee table. "But I'm glad it happened the way it did. It just never felt right to be at odds with my boss over a guy."

"So...when do you leave?" Marta asks.

"In a few hours, actually. I have to meet the crew van at 4:00 a.m.," I say as I pull a face. "But I guess it's better that way—no long drawn out goodbyes," I say with a smile as if this would be a problem for me, all things considered.

Marta shakes her head like she understands. We both sit quietly for a moment, watching the small TV in the corner of Marta's living room. More pictures of the devastation in Miami flash up on the screen. Marta has the sound muted but there really are no words—English or otherwise—to describe the aftermath.

"Are you nervous about going back?" Marta asks in a somber tone as she shifts in her seat.

"Yes...I am," I say as the cameraman focuses in on a street sign for Ocean Boulevard. It's twisted around a nearby palm tree with half the letters sandblasted off. "But I can't stay here anymore, Marta—I have to get home and find my parents and my dog," I say as some fresh tears start to flood my eyes.

"I understand," Marta says as she gently grabs my hand and gives it a squeeze. "Bass told me that Peter was worried about you and your missing dog."

"I feel like my life here is ruined, and so is my life back home, but I'd rather be there than here," I admit as the tears start to roll down my cheeks.

Marta doesn't say anything. She just allows me to cry as she holds my hand. The images on the TV continue, and, as I watch, I can barely recognize the flooded streets of South Beach.

"What about you, Marta? Have you heard anything from Oscar or anyone back home?" I ask with a sniffle as I wonder if she's feeling the same sense of loss that I am right now as I stare at the miserable images on the TV.

"No—I don't return Oscar's calls," she begins with a frosty tone. "I have no idea if he's safe or not, and I really don't care," she adds.

"So you're moving on then?" I ask, wondering how she managed to do that so quickly.

"Actually, Elle, I've been wanting to tell you something, but I haven't been able to find the right time," Marta says as she shifts to face me. "I'm actually seeing Lorenzo," she says as she looks at me with a pained expression.

"You are?" I ask in surprise.

"Yeah, and I really like him," she adds with a smile. "We have so much in common, and we have the best conversations," she says as her face starts to beam with happiness. "And he loves my cooking—which Oscar never did—and he is so fascinating and well-read," she blathers on with excitement.

"That's wonderful!" I say with sincerity. "I think that's really great," I add, wanting her to know that I approve.

"Is it?" she questions sheepishly.

"Of course! Why wouldn't it be?" I ask, feeling embarrassed that she would think that I'm that petty.

"It's just that Marco is Lorenzo's brother and all, and I didn't want you to feel badly…" she trails off as she starts to nibble at a hangnail on her index finger.

"No…it's good, Marta. I think Lorenzo needed you," I say, thinking back over my first impressions of him.

"And I needed *him*," Marta says with a big smile.

"Well, then, things worked out for a reason," I say as I stare at some arbitrary spot on the coffee table. "At least something positive came out of my relationship with Marco," I add as I think of the irony of the situation.

"Lorenzo actually feels terrible about what his brother's done," Marta says, almost in defense of Lorenzo. "But Elle, I think this is a regular pattern for Marco, and Lorenzo says he's just waiting to see how long it will take for his brother to tire of Gabby," she adds, as if for my benefit.

"Time will tell," I say with a sigh, wishing that this bit of information would make me feel better, but for some reason it doesn't. "Does Mrs. Maselli like Gabby?" I ask tentatively, hoping that maybe *this* piece of information will placate my insecurities.

"Honestly, Elle, I'm not sure Mrs. Maselli likes any of the women her sons date—including me," Marta says as she looks at me with a furrowed brow. "She isn't exactly a warm person to begin with, but I think Marco brings so many women to the vineyard that she has grown pretty wary of the tours he asks her to give," Marta adds.

"Oh…" I say, feeling even worse for knowing that even that special day was completely standard procedure, too.

"Are you going to tell Scott that you're leaving?" Marta asks in an obvious effort to change the subject.

"I haven't decided yet," I say as I think of my former best friend and how odd it is that I have to *decide* to tell him something this major. "Miriam wanted me to keep things hush…" I trail off, knowing my reasoning is lame.

"I'm going to miss you, Elle," Marta says sincerely after an awkward pause. "You are a really great friend," she adds.

"I'll see you in a couple more months—when the crews come back to Miami," I say, surprised at her comment.

"No, you won't," she says as she looks me in the eye. "I'm not coming home," she adds with her eyebrows raised.

"Oh," I say as the penny drops.

"As soon as my divorce is final, I'm leaving *Windsong Air* and moving in with Lorenzo," she continues. "This is my home now, Elle," she says with a little smile.

"Well then," I say as a pit starts to form in my stomach. "That's great news!" I say as I try to sound sincere.

As I drag my bags down the front steps of my villa, I take a moment to reflect on everything that's happened to me since I arrived. I look at the potted sunflower quietly resting on the bistro table. I can almost see Marco's note tucked among the leaves. A smile washes across my face as I think of the magical moments Marco gave me. And even if they didn't last, they were real. I place the key under the cushion of the bistro chair as Miriam instructed and start making my way toward the circle drive. I pull in a deep breath of air, and the smell of lavender and buttercups dance around me. It's a sweet smell I'll never forget.

When I pass Scott's villa, I pull out the tin of honey lavender scones Edna Pearl made for him. I place it on the doorstep along with a note. I used one of the special cards Marco gave me from his sister's paper shop. It took me so long to figure out what to write. I wanted to say so many things, but nothing sounded right. So in the end I went with something simple:

Dear Scott,

Edna Pearl made these for you. She wanted me to tell you that she misses you. For what it's worth, you were right. Maybe in time, you will find a way to forgive me.

Be well,
Love Elle

I feel my heart cinch with sadness as I continue walking down the cobbled pathway. I wish I knew how to fix things with Scott, but, right now, that relationship is just one of the many things that are broken and destroyed in my life. I miss him terribly. But I know that the damage is already done.

The crew van is waiting for me, and as I slip through the gate for the last time, the driver starts the engine. As I lug my bags into the van and settle into my seat, the driver gives me a weary wave and then puts the van in drive. When we pull out of the driveway, I glance back for my final look at *Il Girasole*. In the predawn light, it looks lovely and still. I feel a wash of sadness rinsing down my cheeks as I focus on the sunflower gate for the final time.

Chapter Thirty-Two

The flight to Miami is uneventful so far. Maria, the gate agent, upgraded me to first class, so at least I'm able to stretch out and sleep for most of the flight. However, it's a fitful kind of rest. All the emotions coursing through my body make it difficult for me to really unplug and relax. I'm sad and nervous and scared, and I can't seem to think of any part of my life that feels safe and settled. Aside from reeling over the emotions of being dumped by the man I thought I loved, I feel lost inside and un-tethered to anyone or anything at the moment. I miss Sugar Ray and my parents, and I don't even know how to begin looking for them. It's all too much, and my body feels exhausted with worry.

As I lean back into my wide leather seat, I watch the thick, dark clouds pass by my window as the pilot begins the decent. Most of the passengers on board are either returning to see what's left of their lives or flying to Miami to search for missing relatives and loved ones. I can feel the collective anxiety building as the flight attendants pass through the cabin and start making their final preparations for landing.

When the plane banks to the right, I have a perfect view of the ground below, and I struggle to understand what I'm seeing. Instead of the familiar urban sprawl, all I can see are mounds of wreckage swallowed up by water. I can make out the twisted beltways of some of the main roadways leading into Miami, but there are literally sections of road missing and covered with water. As the plane slowly turns to line up with the runway, I can see trees and light poles upturned and bent; there are homes that have no rooftops and buildings half crumbled to the ground. The normally packed streets are empty, and a dozen or so cars are piled up against an embankment where it looks like the flood-waters deposited them before receding.

When our plane touches down, I notice that even the airport terminals look battered and torn. Thick pieces of plywood replace the large panes of glass along the passenger concourses, and I can see the twisted remains of a Jetway crumpled and piled up like a discarded tin can against the side of the terminal. Random branches and all sorts of unidentifiable debris are smattered across the airport grounds, and the eerie darkness of the clouds above makes it feel like we are about to enter a most ominous place.

As I gather up my belongings and prepare to leave the comfort of my first class seat, I do my best to steady my nerves. Many of the passengers are tearful as they make their way toward the boarding door. The magnitude of the destruction that we all saw from up above is surreal, and trying to find the pieces of your life within all that wreckage seems impossible. As a tall blonde woman wearing a teal blue tracksuit walks down the aisle, I can hear her crying. And in that moment, I realize that in my grief, I'm not alone.

The customs area is quiet and calm. The normally bustling terminal seems deserted and empty. Only two customs agents are working the booths, and so we all line up and wait in silence to be cleared to enter Miami. I flash my crew credentials to the elderly man working the booth, and he gives me a weary smile and says, "Welcome home." I smile at the irony of his words. Home. What does that word even mean?

Miriam told me that there would be a driver waiting for me when I arrived in Miami. She said to wait near our regular terminal, and someone would find me. So I drag my suitcase and my carryon bags over to a bench just inside the terminal. I sit and watch people milling around, looking for their connections, while airport security patrols the area with a heavy presence. The usually electric atmosphere in the airport is waterlogged and somber. People seem nervous and forlorn. Up above, I can see the dark, cloud-filled sky through a huge hole in the ceiling. I watch as a tired maintenance man moves a hydraulic lift into position so he can secure a thick plastic tarp over the hole before the sky opens up with rain. The image is haunting. I pull in a deep breath and wonder how things will ever be the same.

"Elle Butts?" I hear a man's voice saying my name.

When I turn to look, I see that it's Abe Rosenthal—Mr. Bennett's personal driver. He's about sixty years old with stark white hair and a thick peppered mustache. Abe is a long-time WRI employee and seeing him standing there in the terminal makes me feel safe and protected for the first time since I arrived. He smiles at me as I take him in, and he opens up his arms like a dear old grandfather.

"Abe!" I say as he gathers me up in his arms. He smells like tobacco smoke and Ben Gay.

"How's our girl?" he asks me in a soft whisper.

"Overwhelmed," I confide as I continue resting my head against his chest.

"There's a lot of that going around these days," he says with a light laugh as he breaks his embrace and looks down at me with a gentle smile. "But we gotta do what we can to get through this, OK?" he says with a twinkle in his eye.

"I know," I say as I fight the urge to cry.

Abe loads my belongings into the back of a huge black Range Rover. When he climbs into the driver's seat, he gives me a sincere smile and starts the engine.

"Are you ready for this?" he asks as he looks over at me. His face is somewhat blank, but I can tell by his eyes that what I'm about to see is heartbreaking.

"I guess," I say nervously.

"Most of the roads are closed, so I have to maneuver my way over to headquarters using side streets, so just bear with me," he says before he puts the truck into drive.

"OK," I say, already noticing a haze of emotions moving through me.

"Miriam sent word that you're looking for your parents," Abe says as he expertly guides the Range Rover over a steep pile of rubble. The overhang of the main departure terminal looks like it gave way, creating a serious roadblock for regular cars.

"Yes—I can't seem to reach them," I say as my body bounces around in the front seat. The tires of the Range Rover seem to easily grind over the pile of debris, but I'm at a loss for how. "Abe, this is unreal!" I can't help but say as I start to see the amount of damage that surrounds the roadways leading away from the airport.

"I know—the front edge of the hurricane belted this area pretty good," Abe says as he concentrates on the road. "It was a monster, Elle, a real monster…"

I can't even respond to his words as I take in the destruction. None of the traffic lights are working as we approach our first major intersection, so there are barricades with stop signs posted at all four points. When Abe rolls to a stop, I notice that one of the thick, steel street lamps to my right is folded over like it was made of tin. To my left, the wires from a downed telephone pole strangle a tree that was uprooted from a nearby median planter.

As Abe drives on, I can barely comprehend the damage that surrounds me. Awnings from familiar buildings are ripped aside and tossed along the edge of the road like crumpled paper napkins. Gas station overhangs are peeled away like the tops of sardine cans, but, somehow, the pumps still seem to be working. A long string of cars line the side of the road, waiting for a turn to fill up.

"I'm sure you heard about *The Wiley*," Abe says in a low, somber voice.

"Miriam said it was hit pretty badly," I say as I look over at Abe and wait for his response.

"Humph," Abe laughs. "It's worse than that—sections of it aren't even *there* anymore," he says like he's still in disbelief.

Numbness settles in my bones as I realize that nothing will ever be the same. The place that I've called home for the past ten years is gone—wiped away and swallowed up by a hurricane named Florence.

When we finally reach the makeshift WRI headquarters, I'm surprised by how sturdy everything looks. The building looks like an old U-shaped hotel that used to have a pool in the middle, but now there is a lovely garden complete with stone benches and a fountain. I can see that the structure did suffer some wind damage, but for the most part, everything looks like it's in working order.

"We moved crew scheduling and the corporate staff into this side," Abe says as he directs me toward the left side of the building. "This is where we have the generator pumping so we can run the computers and satellite phones," he explains as we near the entrance.

"Are people already working?" I ask in disbelief.

"Oh yeah," Abe confirms. "Mr. Bennett wanted to get the relief efforts moving right away, and, once he moved all the residents of *The Wiley* to one of his properties up in Margate, there really was no reason not to," he says as we follow the sidewalk toward the first door. "People need to get their lives back to normal, and getting up and going to work actually really helps," Abe adds as he looks at me with a smile.

"I guess you're right," I concede, dreading going back to work in my current emotional condition.

On the other side of the door, there is a long table with computers and printers spaced out at even intervals. Several of the guys I recognize from crew scheduling are talking on the phone and to each other as they shuffle flight plans and computer printouts back and forth. It's a literal beehive of activity as we enter the room, and I actually do feel a spark of hope as I watch people pulling together to get things back on track.

"Elle, do you know Harvey?" Abe asks as we approach a middle-aged man, who happens to have a very unfortunate case of male-pattern baldness, sitting in front of a large computer. I look at him closely, but I can't seem to recognize his face.

"No, I don't believe we've met," I say. Then I extend my hand and introduce myself. Harvey flashes me a weary smile as he leans back in his chair and looks up at Abe.

"Harvey is the person that Mr. Bennett has assigned to help employees with displaced family members and such," Abe says as he pulls up an empty chair next to Harvey. "Is this a good time to talk to Elle?" Abe asks Harvey, almost as an afterthought.

"It's as good a time as any," Harvey says as he scoots his chair over a bit to make room for mine.

"Thank you so much," I say as I sit down. I feel an eagerness washing over me as I settle into my seat.

"Yep," Harvey says as he starts clicking his mouse and popping up windows on his computer.

"Elle, I have to check in with Mr. Bennett's office," Abe says as he starts moving toward the door. "But I'll be around to take you to the temporary housing complex when you're done with Harvey."

"Alright," I say as a little nervousness spills into my stomach. "See you soon, then," I add. I felt so safe with Abe by my side, and I was kind of hoping he wouldn't leave.

"So, when was the last time you talked to your family?" Harvey asks as he opens up a colorful program on his computer.

"Well, it was a few days ago, I guess," I say as I try to remember when we last spoke. With all the time changes and everything that's been happening, I can't seem to give him a very good answer.

"And did they tell you where they'd go if they had to evacuate?" Harvey asks like he's ready to get down to business.

"Well no," I say as I struggle to remember my dad's exact words. "But my dad has a satellite phone—which I couldn't seem to work when I was in Italy—but maybe I was doing something wrong or maybe it just doesn't work in Europe," I blather on, flooding Harvey with more information than he likely bargained for.

"Do you have the number?" Harvey asks as he looks up at me. His eyes look tired, and I realize that his job must be a little like looking for a needle in a haystack right now.

"I do," I say as I dig through my satchel and produce the rumpled napkin. "My dad gave me some instructions over the phone on how to dial the number, but I must've done something wrong..." I trail off as Harvey takes the napkin from me. I watch as his brow slightly furrows when he focuses on the numbers.

"Well...let's give it a try," he says as he reaches for an odd looking phone sitting on the desk next to his. It's a large, brick-like phone that reminds me of an early cell phone, except there is some sort of strange antennae attached to the side.

I watch carefully as Harvey punches in the numbers, slowly and methodically. Once he's done, he holds the phone up to his ear and listens intently. When there's no activity, he resets the phone and tries again. I watch him try to place the call several times, each time with no luck. My heart starts to tighten with worry as I realize that it may not be that easy to find my parents.

"Not working. Your dad may have forgotten to charge it before the storm hit," he says after he's accepted defeat with the sat phone numbers.

"That's unlikely," I say without thinking. "You don't know my dad," I add as my mind wanders to the image of my father. He lives for this kind of crisis, so it is unimaginable to me that he would forget to charge the battery!

"Do you have any family outside the Miami area we could contact that might know where your parents are?" Harvey says after he gives me an irritated look.

"My sister!" I say with a burst of relief. "She lives in Chicago! I'm sure my parents would've contacted her if they were going to leave the area!"

"Let me open up a line for you," Harvey says as he reaches for a different phone. He hands the phone to me and then says, "Dial the number."

"OK," I say as I take the phone and punch in the numbers for my sister. I listen quietly as the phone clicks and then connects. "It's ringing!" I say to Harvey after the first ring.

"Great," Harvey says like he doesn't really mean it.

"Hello?" my sister says into the phone.

"Abby! It's Elle!" I say, thrilled to hear her voice.

"Elle! Where are you?" she says with obvious worry in her voice. "I've been calling you in Italy and no one knows where you are!" she blathers like she's half mad at me, half ecstatic to hear my voice.

"Abby, listen," I say as I try to calm us both down. "I'm in Miami."

"What?" I can hear the shock in her voice and I can almost see the look on her face as she tries to sort out what I'm saying.

"I came home early. I don't know where Violet took Sugar Ray, and I couldn't reach Mom and Dad," I say as the words start tumbling out of my mouth.

"So you flew all the way home to look for them?" Abby asks in disbelief.

"It's a long story, but yes, I did," I say as I struggle to keep this conversation on track. "Do you know where Mom and Dad are?" I finally bring myself to ask.

"Yes. Mom called this morning," Abby says calmly. "She and Dad are fine."

"Well, where are they?" I ask as I feel tears of joy mixed with anxiety pricking the back of my eyes.

"I don't know exactly," Abby says like she's choosing her words carefully. "Elle, Mom said that the house is gone." Her voice sounds hallow and sad, and I can tell now that she's been crying.

"Gone? What do you mean, *gone*?" I ask, trying to get my brain wrapped around the idea that my childhood home could be *gone*.

"That's all Mom said about it," Abby says with a quiver in her voice. "She and Dad are working at a rescue center somewhere down there. I don't know exactly where, but Mom said people need them, so they're staying put for now," Abby says, clearly upset by all that's happening to her family.

"OK," I say as I struggle to comprehend the reality of her words. "Do you know where they're staying?" I ask, hoping Abby will be able to get more specific.

"I think they are staying at the rescue center," she says, sounding a bit unsure of her answer.

"OK, that's a start," I say as I picture my parents rolling up their sleeves to help out.

"What about you, Elle? Where are you going to be?" Abby asks like a second worried mother. "Will I be able to call you?" she adds before I can even answer her first two questions.

"Mr. Bennett set up temporary housing, and as soon as I have more details, I'll call you again," I promise my sister as I watch Harvey give me the "wrap it up" sign with his finger.

"OK, Elle. I love you and please call me when you can so I know you're OK," she says as I rush her off the phone.

"I will...and I love you, too," I say before I hang up the phone and hand it to Harvey.

"I know where you're parents are," Harvey says as he looks up at me.

"You do?" I ask in disbelief.

"When I heard your sister say they were working at a rescue center, I pulled up the three main sites, and your parents are both listed as relief workers," Harvey says as he pulls up the web page for me to see. "Your dad is working as a grief counselor, and your mom is a triage nurse," he says plainly as he points to the information on the computer screen.

"Can we call over there?" I ask, overjoyed at the thought of hearing my mom's voice.

"Yeah..." Harvey says as he scrolls down the page in search of the contact information. "Actually, they don't have a phone—we'll have to use a radio," he says as he gets up out of his chair and ducks into a closet.

When he returns, he has a big, black walkie-talkie style radio. He consults the computer screen one more time and then turns the frequency dial to the correct channel. I can hear the squawk of radio traffic as Harvey turns up the volume.

"Rescue Center 3, this is WRI HQ—do you copy? Over," Harvey says into the radio. He pulls the speaker away from his mouth and waits for a response.

Seconds later, I hear a male voice crackling through the speaker, "This is Rescue Center 3—go ahead. Over."

"Do you have a…" Harvey trails off as he looks at me to fill in the blank with a name.

"Dr. Butts," I quickly say, wondering how he forgot my last name after he just looked up my parents on the website.

Harvey gives me a funny look and then says, "Do you have a *Dr. Butts* there? Over." I can tell that Harvey is fighting off the urge to laugh, so I give him a pained expression and just shrug my shoulders, hoping to let him know that I understand the name is pretty bad.

After a few more seconds of crackling dead air, a familiar voice fills my ears. "This is Dr. Butts—Over."

It's my dad! Harvey hands me the radio and shows me how to hold down the talk button. My hands are shaking as I try to steady myself. I take a deep breath and carefully push the button down and draw the radio up to my mouth.

"Dad—it's me, Elle," I say slowly. Then I add a quick, "Over."

"Eloise? Over." I can hear the confusion in my dad's voice.

"Yes! Um, Over." I can feel a smile spreading across my face and some tears of joy spilling from my eyes.

"Are you in Miami, Sweetheart? Over." My dad sounds confused and overjoyed as we continue this jerky conversation filled with few words and lots of *overs*.

"Yes, Dad, I am. I flew home today. Over."

"Are you safe? Over."

"Yes. I'm fine. Over."

"Where are you staying? Over."

"Somewhere in Margate at Mr. Bennett's temporary housing complex. Over."

Something cuts into the frequency, and I can't hear my dad's voice anymore. The voice of a female police dispatcher comes on and all I can hear is crosstalk between dispatch and a police unit responding to a call about some looting in Liberty City. Harvey motions for me to wait a second. Once the police exchange is complete, he gives me the signal to try again.

"Dad? Are you there? Over."

"Yes, Elle, I'm here. We'll find you soon. Over."

"OK, I love you, Dad! Over."

"Love you, too, Sweetheart. Over."

I feel much better as I sit in the front seat of the Range Rover on my way to the temporary housing complex. I've spoken to my sister and my dad, and Harvey is scouring the local shelters for any word on Violet and Sugar Ray. At least I know my parents are safe, and Harvey promised he'd contact me right away if he finds my beloved dog and his sitter. I actually feel myself relax for the first time in what feels like days as Abe slowly drives down a desolate road.

As we move further away from the coastline, things appear to be more normal. Aside from the broken tree limbs littering the roadway, massive puddles of water and all of the boarded up windows, it looks as though Hurricane Florence spared this area of South Florida—for the most part anyway. But there is an eerie calm all around, and it almost feels like people are still in hiding, waiting for real confirmation that it's safe to return.

When Abe turns the truck into a gated entry, I'm surprised to see how nice the temporary housing complex looks from the outside. Abe explains to me that Mr. Bennett was in the process of turning this facility into a corporate convention-style hotel, but stopped production when he realized that he would need to evacuate *The Wiley*. So the rooms are in various stages of renovation, but he assures me that it is a dream compared to other alternatives around the city right now.

After we unload my suitcase, Abe leads me into the complex. The lobby is going to be quite stunning when it's completed. But in its current state, the exposed concrete floors and the partially painted walls seem to emulate the raw qualities of life after a hurricane. Abe finds an envelope with my name on it behind a semi-constructed wrap desk near a bank of elevators. We both let out a little moan when we discover that my room is on the sixth floor—and no power means *no elevators*. So we make our way to the stairwell and start climbing.

When we reach my room, Abe graciously opens the door for me and lugs my bags into the room. There's a queen-sized bed with no headboard in the center of the room. It's dressed with a simple quilt and two pillows. A small bedside table with three candles and a book of matches is positioned next to the bed, and a tall, slender dresser is pressed up against the wall across from the foot of the bed. Two overstuffed, canvas-covered armchairs are shoved into the far left corner, and a large desk is pushed off to the right. It looks as though the furniture was haphazardly added to the room with no thought or attention to detail, but, all things considered, it looks perfect to me.

There is a bathroom to the right of the door, and, when I peek my head in, I see a standing shower *and* a bathtub. Abe places my suitcase and my carryon bags next to the bed and takes a look around.

"Welcome to your new home, Elle," he says with a smile. He's still slightly out of breath from climbing six flights of stairs with my suitcase in tow. "It may not be pretty, but it's clean and dry, and that's a lot when you think about it."

"You're right," I say as I let out a sigh and make my way over to one of the armchairs. "This will do just fine," I add as I look up at Abe and smile.

"There are a few things downstairs that you should know about," Abe says as he walks over to the second armchair and takes a seat. "There is a computer that's hooked up to the generator and has satellite Internet access, and there is a small kitchen with some coolers in case you have any food you want to store."

"Good to know," I say as I think about how hungry I am.

"There's also a pizza and sub delivery in the evenings since there's a curfew in effect right now, Mr. Bennett is supplying food to keep everyone on site," he explains as the thought of a hot, delicious slice of pizza enters my mind. "Oh, and you'll need this," Abe says as he hands me the envelope with my room keys and such. "Your flight schedule is in there, along with an extra key to your room."

"My flight schedule?" I ask, wondering what he means.

"Yeah," Abe says like he's surprised by my question. "Mr. Bennett is helping the rescue efforts by lending his planes and his flight crews."

"I know that part, I just didn't think I'd be flying so soon," I say as exhaustion literally grips my body.

"You've got time to rest," Abe says knowingly. "So I suggest you use it wisely," he adds with a wink. Then he stands up and starts heading for the door. "By the way," he says as he turns to look at me. "What on earth did you do to make *Miriam Ungaro* such a huge fan of yours?"

I have to smile at the question. Considering everything that's happened in the past month, it seems more than ironic to hear someone come to this sort of conclusion about my relationship with Miriam.

"Let's just say we bonded a bit over some shared adversity," I say as I look at Abe and smile.

About six hours later, I've taken a nap and a chilly shower, and now I'm on the hunt for food. So I wander downstairs, hoping to find something decent to eat. When I reach the lobby area, I see several people sitting on two sofa's still covered in plastic wrap. As I approach, I see that one of the people is Lupe Ortega. She has her arm in a blue sling, and she looks exhausted. But when she notices me walking toward her, she almost looks as if she's seen a ghost.

"Elle! Is that you?" she questions as she squints her eyes at me.

"Hey Lupe!" I say as a smile washes across my face. "Hi everyone," I add, not to be rude.

"What are you doing here? Aren't you supposed to be in Italy?" she asks as the rest of the people shift around to look at me with confusion.

"Yeah…well, I needed to get home," I say, hoping they don't bombard me with questions.

"Did you come back alone?" Barbie Denton asks. Barbie is from New Jersey and is one of the newer *Windsong Air* hires, so I don't know her very well.

"Yes. It's just me. Everyone else will be back in about six or eight more weeks," I clarify as Lupe scoots over to make room for me on the sofa.

"Well, are you OK?" Lupe asks with concern as I slide in next to her. She uses her good hand to rub me on the back, making me feel welcomed and loved.

"Yeah, I just needed to get back to deal with my family," I say as I wonder if I have enough energy to keep up this question and answer session.

"Did they get hurt?" Lloyd Rubin asks me with great concern. Lloyd tends to be very dramatic and always seems to be in the middle of every company controversy.

"No, but I guess their house—well, my house from when I was growing up—is destroyed," I say as I zero in on my own words. I still can't quite comprehend how the little yellow house where I've lived all my life could be wiped away.

"Did you hear about *The Wiley?*" Barbie asks as she leans back on the sofa and flashes me a look of disbelief.

"I did," I say as I look down at the floor.

"Totally destroyed," she confirms with her thick New Jersey accent. "My God, we are so blessed that Mr. Bennett had the good sense to move us," she adds as she inspects one of her acrylic nails.

Everyone starts sharing their own stories of what they saw during the hurricane and how the storm has impacted their lives and the lives of their friends and families. We polish off two pizzas and at least three liters of Coke, and it actually feels good to be together, venting and crying. I'm amazed at how terrifying the actual storm was for these friends of mine, and I can't help but wonder how anyone ever fully recovers from a storm like this.

When night falls, Barbie lights a few candles, and I watch as she expertly flicks the lighter and touches the flame to the wick without catching her long, fake fingernails on fire. I look down at my own fingernails for a quick inspection—the nailbeds have only recently started to look a little better. A quiet smile washes over my face as I think about all the ridiculous things I did for Marco. Then I think of how badly he broke my heart.

I have to fight off the urge to cry as I think about how much loss I've endured in such a short period of time. I've lost my first love, my best friend, my beloved dog, my childhood home *and* my current home all in the span of about four weeks. I feel as though I have nothing left—just a bunch of heartache that I don't know how to deal with. Everything in my life has been stripped away, and the things I used to count on are gone.

And isn't it all so ironic? Hurricane Florence—the powerful tropical weather pattern that pummeled the city of Miami with 140 mile per hour winds for three straight hours—not only left me homeless, but it may have separated me from Sugar Ray for good. And Hurricane Florence—the powerful *emotional* hurricane that ripped through my heart—not only left me bewildered and crushed, but it's caused me to question everything.

Chapter Thirty-Three

It's been five days, and there's still no news on the whereabouts of Violet or Sugar Ray. I've done everything I can think of to find them, but no one knows where they are. Every shelter in our area has put out alerts and posted signs so if Violet *is* around, she'll know that I'm looking for her. Harvey has gone out of his way to help me, but even he seems like he's starting to lose hope.

I've met up with my parents at the rescue center. Things are slowly starting to return to normal for many of the people in the area, but my father is working around the clock with his grief counseling efforts. So many people who didn't heed the warnings to evacuate are suffering the loss of loved ones, and there are tremendous feelings to deal with when you consider that most of the people at the center are homeless, and many, penniless, too.

My mom seems to be holding up quite well, all things considered. She and one of the relief workers managed to get confirmation that our house is indeed destroyed. Tropical Storm Ernesto—which doused the area with massive rains three days before Florence hit—caused the canals to swell so much that the hurricane actually swallowed up entire neighborhoods in one gulp. As I sit on a dingy cot in the makeshift triage unit, I watch my mother check on one of her patients. He's a fellow rescue worker who accidentally cut off one of his fingers with a chainsaw.

"Mom, how can you do this job?" I ask after the patient leaves with new, crisp-white bandages carefully wrapped around his hand.

"You mean looking at blood and broken bones?" she clarifies as she looks at me with her soft green eyes. Even covered in filth, my mother looks so beautiful and strong.

"I guess…" I say, not exactly sure what I mean.

"It's important to me to help people, Love," she says as she washes her hands using some water from an Igloo cooler. "Most of the people that need services from a shelter like this don't have insurance or any money to get proper treatment at a hospital, so they need people like me—and your father—to help them in times of trouble." She dries her hands on a white paper towel and then sits down next to me on the cot.

"Any word on Sugar Ray?" she asks gently as she smoothes a few pieces of hair away from my face.

"No…" I say as my face crumbles, and the tears begin to fall. "And Harvey says that with each passing day, the odds of finding him get even worse," I moan as my mom pulls me into her chest.

"Oh, Love," she softly coos into my ear. "I'm so sorry…"

"I feel as though I've done nothing but cry for days on end," I bawl as I pull away from my mom's embrace and wipe my eyes. "There's just so much to clean up and so much about my life that feels up in the air that I'm starting to lose my faith that anything good can ever happen to me again."

"Well, it's natural to feel this way, Eloise—*for a season*," she says as she places her fingers under my chin and turns my face so she can look into my eyes. "We've all been through a lot—no doubt about it. And things are bloody awful right now! But we can't take on this belief that things are always going to be this way."

"But Mom, how can you be so calm and stay so positive when your house is under water and everything you own is ruined?" I ask, my voice hoarse with pain.

"Because, Love. Those are just things," she says with a light laugh. "Things can be replaced. And a home is not only the four walls and the roof over your head—its what's in your heart," she adds, like she really believes what she's saying.

"I hear people say that all the time, but I don't really know if I believe it," I say bitterly as I turn away and look down at the dirty floor.

"Ah…well, *I* think you do believe it," she says with a certain knowingness in her voice. "If you didn't, you wouldn't have wanted to come all the way *home* from Italy—where it was safe and sound—to find your family and your dear dog in the midst of all this rubbish," she says with a smile.

I can't respond right away because I think she might have a point.

"But what if you don't know if you can trust the things in your heart anymore?" I question. "What if you *thought* you knew what you believed and what you wanted, and who you loved, but your heart turned out to be wrong?"

My mother just quietly sits and considers her answer carefully before she responds. "Does this have anything to do with a certain *Marco* you mentioned to Edna Pearl?" my mother finally asks.

"Kind of," I say, not wanting to get into specifics about that right now.

"Did you ever think that maybe your heart *was* telling you the truth but you *chose* not to believe it?" she asks in a soft voice.

"Maybe…" I trail off as I ponder that thought for a minute.

"I hold that it was your heart that saved you, Eloise," my mom says as she takes my hand in hers. "It was your heart that kept you grounded—even when things got stormy."

"But Mom—I'm anything but *grounded* right now," I protest. "I feel like I've managed to ruin everything…" I say, thinking of Scott as the tears start to fall.

"This storm—this hurricane, I should say—has rendered many of us homeless and distraught," my mom says thoughtfully. "And sometimes, in life, our emotions can do the same thing. But what we all must do in times like these is take inventory of everything that we still have and start rebuilding using that as our courage."

"But I don't feel like I have *anything*!" I say through my tears.

"Well, that's not true, Love," she says. "You still have me!"

I look up at my mom with her pretty smile and fall into her arms. She's right. I do still have her, and my father, and maybe I even have a little more of *myself* than I realized.

At the end of my first flight since I returned to Miami, I feel humbled. Mr. Bennett has offered to transport people out of Miami to be joined with loved ones in different parts of the country who can help get these people back on their feet again. Many of the people seated throughout the cabin haven't ever been on an airplane before, so the experience is pretty incredible for them. Most of the passengers on this flight started out in some of the poorer areas of Miami and had very little to begin with. So when Florence hit, the storm took out more than just their homes—it washed away their lives.

It's a short flight from Miami to Atlanta, so there isn't much time to serve more than a light snack. But I am struck by how grateful the passengers are for a simple soft drink and a packet of pretzels. One gentleman seated near the mid cabin galley could be overheard talking about how all he has left are the clothes on his back and the shoes on his feet. And yet he was smiling from ear to ear because his young daughter, Ruby, was sitting next to him, and they were going to grandma's house. Ruby sat quietly in her seat and joyfully played with an empty paper cup I gave her during the service.

Ruby and her father remind me about how resilient the human spirit can be when there's something to believe in. Whether it's a belief in the love of others or the love of God—or even a belief in yourself and your ability to stay the course—it's that willingness to fight back with hope that keeps people moving forward. When I saw the people seated throughout the plane, I realized how petty my heart had become and how greatly blessed I am to not only be alive, but also to have so much abundance.

So now, as I climb the steps to my sixth floor hotel room, I try to find some measure of gratefulness to get me through the weeks and months ahead. I do my best to focus on the fact that I have such a great job with a boss who believes so strongly in caring for his employees and the people of his community. I try to remember how fortunate I am to have a clean place to sleep every night—unlike my mom and dad, who've been sleeping in a dirty relief center for nearly a week. I focus on how blessed I am to have plenty of food and a place to take a shower. It's amazing how many things I have to be thankful for, but how easily I slip off track when I start to solely focus on the loss in my life.

After I change out of my uniform and put on a pair of shorts and a T-shirt, I head down to the makeshift communications office to see if Harvey's posted any news on Violet and Sugar Ray. When I arrive, the office is empty, so I sit down in front of the computer and start clicking around the desktop until I finally get a connection to the Internet. I go to the WRI Re-Connect home page and look for any new messages. My heart starts to beat a little faster when I see a posting. So I quickly click on the link. A new message from Harvey, sent about 15 minutes ago, pops up on the screen and I quickly begin reading.

Dear Elle

No luck again today. The Humane Society had no matches either. I'm sorry, but if I have time tomorrow, I'll try again.

Harvey

The words slide through me with a stab, and I can feel myself giving up hope. I can't imagine my life without Sugar Ray. How could this happen? How could Violet disappear with my car and my dog and never even try to get in touch with me?

And that's when the grief finally hits me full force. I know Violet, and if she were alive, she'd find me. The thought slams into me without warning, and before I have time to stop it, my heart gives way, and a flood of raw emotions pours out of me. My dog and my good friend are dead. No wonder we can't find them. The storm probably sucked them up, and no one's even found their dead bodies yet because there's still too much debris everywhere.

I manage to run into the stairwell and up the six flights of stairs before anyone sees me. Then I race down the hallway and into my room. I throw myself on the bed and let everything go. I hold a pillow to my face and scream as the pain of losing so much writhes through me. I feel rage rising up inside of me as I think of Marco and how, because of him, not only am I grieving the loss of my dog, but I also no longer have Scott in my life. Heaves of emotion pour out of me, and I can hardly breath. I feel as though all of this could've been prevented if only I'd been more careful. If

434

only I would've been willing to stay in Miami just like my mother wanted me to. Then I would've never met Marco, and I could move on with my life without the miserable pain I feel in my heart right now.

I thrash around on my bed, trying to shake the final throws of my pain out of my body. I can't imagine how this could hurt more. I push the pillow into my face as hard as I can and let out a final moan. I hate myself for trusting the idea that I actually have a soul mate in this world. How could I be so stupid?

Then, suddenly, I feel something on my foot. It feels wet, and cold, like something is tickling me...or dripping on my ankle.

When I pull the pillow away, I can't believe my eyes. Sugar Ray is wigging around at the foot of my bed! His face is bright and clear, and I have to blink hard to make sure I'm not dreaming. I toss the pillow aside and quickly roll to the floor. I grab for my dog to make sure he's not a ghost and Sugar Ray moves in for a kiss. His boxy face connects with my cheek as tears of joy and disbelief wash down and onto his tongue. I can't control my new emotions—I'm laughing hysterically as my dog shimmies and dances all over me! It's him! It's really my boy!

I pull him into my arms and bury my face in his fur. He smells like wet dog, but I don't care! He's alive and he's back with me! He's not dead in my car along the side of the road. He's really here, in my arms, right now!

"Sugar Ray!" I say as I shake with joy. "How did you find me?"

In that moment, I realize that someone had to bring him to me, so I hop up off the floor and walk toward the door. When I open it, I see Violet Harper, leaning against the wall. She's wearing a torn up T-shirt and a dirty pair of jeans. When she sees me, she just gives me a huge grin.

"Violet!" I say as I grab her and pull her in for a hug. "Thank God you're all right!" I say into her ear.

"Yep...I'm fine," she says as she gives my back a quick tap—which I gather is her signal that she's done with all the affection.

"Come in," I say as I release my arms and guide her into my room. "I was just...crying, actually," I say, feeling embarrassed that Violet likely heard or maybe even saw me during my tantrum.

"Well, it's an emotional time," Violet says flatly as she moves into the room and takes a seat in one of the canvas chairs. "Ole Ray is sure happy to see you," she observes as my dog keeps bumping into my leg, wanting me to pet him.

"Oh Violet, you have no idea how happy I am to see him, too!" I say as I lean down and pull him in for a big hug.

I grab a few tissues from the bathroom and then flop down in the chair next to Violet. My mind is swirling with questions, and I don't even know where to begin. So I just start peppering Violet for details.

"Where did you go? Where have you been? How did you find me? Tell me everything!"

"Well, I tried to call your dad a bunch of times when they started to evacuate the mobile park where I live," Violet begins methodically without changing her tone or her demeanor at all. "But I just couldn't find him. So when we started hearing that the storm was gonna be so massive, a bunch of us packed up our stuff and headed to Orlando to stay at a Goodwill Homeless shelter 'cuz they'd allow dogs."

As Violet talks, Sugar Ray rests his head in my lap, and I can see a sweet contentment in his eyes as I rub my favorite spot just above his nose.

"So anyway, I kept trying to call ya in Italy. I left you a bunch of messages and stuff, but I didn't have a number for you to call me back on," Violet explains as she pulls out a dirty handkerchief from the front pocket of her jeans. I watch as she wipes her nose, and I can't believe how happy I am that she's OK. "So I just waited in Orlando. At least we had power and plenty of food and stuff," she adds as she shoves the cloth back into her pocket.

"No wonder none of the local shelters had you listed," I say as the pieces of the mystery start falling into place.

"Yep," Violet says. "I didn't know what to do so I stayed put, but then Scott showed up and brought me here," Violet says, in a matter of fact tone.

"Scott?" I ask, not sure I heard her correctly.

"Yep," she says as she shakes her head up and down.

"My Scott? Scott LaMotte?" I ask again—just to be perfectly clear.

"Yep," Violet reconfirms as a funny look washes over her face.

"He came to Orlando and got you?" I ask, still feeling unsure about what I'm hearing.

"Yep," she says again.

"So is he *here?* Right now?" I ask as adrenaline starts pumping through my body.

"Yep. He should be. He said he'd wait outside for me," she says casually.

"Oh my God! He's here!" I say as the reality really sinks in. "Scott's here!"

"I didn't know it would surprise ya so much," Violet mumbles in response to my reaction.

"Violet, can you stay here with Sugar Ray for a minute?" I ask as I rush around my room looking for my shoes.

"Sure," she says. "Are you OK, Elle?" Violet asks as she watches me scurrying about, wiping my face off in the mirror and running my fingers through my hair.

"I think I will be in a minute," I say after I kiss Sugar Ray on the top of his head and then make a mad dash for the door.

I see my car parked just outside the lobby doors, and my heart starts beating wildly in my chest. But as I move closer to the doors, I don't see anyone inside. So my eyes start darting around, searching for any signs of Scott near or around my car.

"Are you looking for me?" a familiar voice asks from behind me.

When I slowly turn around, I see Scott sitting on a folding chair against the far wall. He's wearing light blue jeans, a T-shirt and a pair of flip-flops. His tan face and sun-drenched hair make him look even more handsome than I remembered. I pull in a deep breath and try to steady my nerves as I take a few steps toward him. He rises up off the of the folding chair and meets me halfway.

"Did Violet find you?" he asks, his voice soft and light.

"Yes, she did," I say, my voice shakier than I'd like it to be. "How did you...?" I can't finish my question because I don't even know where to begin.

"Know that you were here?" Scott adds, in an attempt to complete my question.

"Yes..." I say, not sure that was my original question, but I decide it's a good place to start.

"Marta told me," he admits. "Rumors were flying around about where you were, and Marta said she didn't want me to worry."

"Oh..." I say, mulling over the flow of events. "And how did you know where to find Violet and Sugar Ray?" I ask as I start to sort everything out more clearly.

"Bruno came and got me a few days ago and said that someone kept leaving messages for you," Scott calmly explains. "Bruno let me listen to the messages, and I found out Violet was in Orlando, but I couldn't call her back to tell you were in Miami, so I went to Miriam for help," he says, his eyebrows slightly raised like he can't believe that *Miriam* was his solution either.

"And so she gave you a ticket home?" I clarify as the final facts fall in line.

"Yes, and I flew into Orlando and found Violet and Sugar Ray at one of the shelters that permitted pets," he adds to complete the story.

"So...you came all the way here just to help me get my dog back?" I ask, trying to fish around for any ulterior motive.

"Is that what you want to believe?" Scott asks after a long pause, his face soft and unconditional.

I take a moment, trying to figure out how I feel and what I should say. "No..." I finally say, doing my best to keep my cool so I don't scare him off.

"What do you want to believe?" Scott asks as he takes a step closer to me.

"I want to believe that you and I are OK," I say, unable to look him in the eye.

"I see," Scott says, almost in a whisper. "What if I were to tell you that I love you?" Scott says after another long, awkward pause.

"What?" I ask, unsure that I heard him correctly.

"I love you, Elle," he says firmly. "*I'm in love with you...*" he adds as he gently lifts my chin with his fingers so he can see my eyes.

"You are?" I ask in disbelief as tears of happiness rim up in my eyes.

"Yes...I am..." he confirms in a soft whisper of a voice.

"When did this happen?" I ask, doing my best to contain a new swell of emotions rising up in my throat.

"Since forever..." Scott says as he turns his eyes down and, then, slowly turns them back up as if to see my reaction.

"Really?" I ask with a humble smile.

"Yes, really!" he says with a light laugh. "And this whole thing with you and Marco has been the most difficult thing in the world for me to endure," he admits with conviction as he shifts his weight a bit and moves both of his hands to rest gently on top of my shoulders.

"Why didn't you ever tell me?" I ask as confusion and a sense of excitement takes over, and I do my best to follow his words.

"Because..." he hesitates, like he needs to choose his words carefully. Then, with a deep breath, he looks me in the eyes and says, "I never wanted to lose you as my friend. I never wanted to risk what we had in case you didn't love me the way I love you."

I can't even think of a response. His words are washing over me so quickly that I can't listen to my own thoughts.

"But you, you were willing to risk our friendship to pursue love, even if it was with the wrong guy," Scott says as he pulls his hands away and tucks them deep into his pockets. "You were willing to do the one thing I couldn't, and it made me angry at myself for never giving you the chance to *try* loving me."

"Oh Scott," I say as the tears spill down my face. "I've missed you so much."

He pulls me into his arms and it feels so good to be connected to my Scott. I breathe him in and realize how right this moment is. I feel safe and understood, and, for the first time in what feels like ages, I know I'm home.

Chapter Thirty-Four

Six Months Later

"Elle Butts?"

"Yes," I say as I look up from my magazine.

"The doctor will see you now," the lovely nurse says as she stands near the door waiting for me to follow her.

"Great!" I say as I gather up my belongings and make my way toward the door.

"So, I see that this is your first visit to our clinic," the nurse remarks as we turn and head down a colorful hallway.

"Yes, it is," I say pleasantly as my steps fall into rhythm with hers.

"Well, we're glad to have you," she says as we make our way over to the pre-exam area.

"Thank you," I say, doing my best to stay relaxed. Even though this clinic is an old house converted into an office, the idea of being at the gynecologist still doesn't rank very high with me.

"Have a seat so we can go over a few things before you meet with the doctor," she says as I slide into a flimsy office chair. "Now, I had the Women's Health Center send over your charts and there is one thing I wanted to ask you about briefly before we get started," the nurse says, not wasting any time.

"Ah, yes," I say as I let out a sigh. "My virginity…"

"Well, yes, actually," the nurse says with a nervous laugh. "It's just such a rare thing," she adds as she turns her attention from my file to my face.

"Indeed it is," I add with a smile.

"Dr. Crosby's notes are quite thorough, too. She has several entries regarding how healthy you are and what a very special patient you've become to her," she remarks as she returns her attention to my file. "I think you've made quite an impression on her!" the nurse adds as she looks up with a huge grin.

"Dr. Crosby is really great, but I decided a teaching clinic isn't the best place for me," I say doing my best to answer the obvious question she's embedded into this strange conversation.

"I completely understand," she says graciously. "Now, I see here that you aren't actually due for your annual for another few months...but we can do a complete exam if that's what you want," the nurse offers as she searches my face for an explanation.

"Well, actually, I'm here today to talk to the doctor about birth control," I say, a little embarrassed for some reason.

"Oh," the nurse says with a touch of surprise.

"You see, I'm getting married in two months!" I interject as a huge grin stretches across my face.

"Congratulations!" the nurse says as her face beams with complete sincerity. "That's *absolutely* wonderful!"

Two Months Later

A lot has happened since I returned from Italy and started rebuilding my life here in Miami. And when I say rebuilding, *I mean rebuilding.*

After four months of living and working out of the temporary housing complex, Mr. Bennett was forced to restructure WRI and his airline. It was a major overhaul, which cost some people, including Oscar DeSoto and Michelle Maddox, their jobs. As a result, Mr. Bennett created new positions and wanted to hire new blood to invigorate his vacation empire. But being an incredibly loyal businessman, Mr. Bennett appointed Scott LaMotte as his Executive Vice President of Resort Development and yours truly to Executive Director of Flight Attendant Training.

The promotion came with a huge raise and loads of benefits— including executive perks, travel, and a three-bedroom suite in the new and improved

Wiley. But until construction is completed, the executive staff is housed in one of Mr. Bennett's five star hotels along Miami Beach that oddly enough only suffered minor hurricane damage. Most of the Miami based crew that went to Italy ended up staying abroad and continued servicing that emerging market. Miriam stayed on to manage the base, and I'm happy to report, she and her baggage handler (named Marcello) are happily married. Miriam actually recommended me as her replacement here in Miami, and the two of us have grown quite close in recent months.

As for Gabby and Marco, I learned that they married shortly after I left. Bobbi Henry was the one that shared the news. But she also told me that Marco has a girlfriend on the side—some girl named *Christina*. There was a time when I think my ego would have enjoyed news like this, but right now, I feel sad for Gabby. And I feel thankful beyond words that Hurricane Florence destroyed my life so that I could find it again among the wreckage.

Marta DeSoto's divorce was finalized not too long ago, and she and Lorenzo are engaged. Marta has taken up the art of winemaking, and spends all of her days at *Marbello*. She seems content and has even written to me about her longing to have a baby. As for her former husband, after Oscar and Michelle were let go, their relationship started to implode. I've heard that Michelle has refused to marry Oscar and plans to keep the baby and raise it by herself.

As for my parents, my father has decided he's had enough of hurricanes. So when the insurance money came in for the house, he and my mother decided to move to North Carolina. They bought a rambling old house with lots of rooms and an amazing garden, and they are in the process of restoring the house and making it into a bed and breakfast. My mom has never seemed happier! My dad still sees patients on the side and continues to write for several medical journals on the topic of post-traumatic-stress syndrome. I miss having them nearby, but it means more to me to know that they are so happy.

"Elle, do you want me to go get your veil?" Nora asks as I primp in front of the mirror.

"That would be great," I say as I smile at her. "By the way, you look stunning," I mention as she passes by me wearing her bridesmaid dress. I chose something nice and simple—it's a lavender strapless tea length dress with tiny pearl detailing along the top.

"I've got it, Love," Edna Pearl says from doorway as she enters with my stunning lacey white veil in her hands. "But perhaps you could leave me alone with the bride-to-be for a moment?" she asks Nora.

"Absolutely," Nora says as she gives Edna Pearl a peck on the cheek on her way out the door.

"How are you doing there, Love?" Edna Pearl asks in a cheery voice as she makes her way toward my dressing table.

"I'm giddy!" I say as I start to laugh.

"Oh Darling! I'm so happy for you!" my grandmother gushes as she takes me in. She looks so lovely and proud as I gaze at our reflection in the mirror—she's standing over my shoulder like a guardian angel in my life.

"You know..." I begin, working hard to find the right words. "There's something I've been wanting to tell you for some time now—"

My words are cut short as Edna Pearl interrupts me by reaching her hand around and placing her finger on my lips.

"Not another word, Lovely," she says with a stern, yet somehow soft look. "I know where you're headed, and it just simply isn't worth it."

"It's not?" I ask as I feel touched that Edna Pearl doesn't need to hear my words of apology to forgive me for my awful behavior in Essex.

"No dear—because I've given you a mulligan!" she says with a smile.

"A mulligan?" I question, not sure what a golfing freebie has to do with me.

"Sometimes, we just need to know that the people who love us the most are always willing to give a do-over when we need it the most," she says as she starts setting my veil. "I always knew that you'd figure things out, Love," she says softly as she reaches for a pin to secure the crown of the veil to my hair.

"How come you were so sure?" I have to ask.

"Because, Dear, you have integrity," she says as she stops pinning and catches my eye in the mirror. "You are a woman of your word, and I've always seen that in you—since you were a baby even," she says with a huge smile. "It's your foundation, Love, and no matter what storms or circumstances rock you, I always know that you are grounded in integrity."

All I can do is smile at my grandmother. She always seems to say things so well. She finishes pinning the veil in place, and the stark white lace lightly drapes over my shoulder. As I take another look at myself in the mirror, I feel so happy. Today, I'm marrying my best friend. He's already seen me through the best and worst times in my life, and there's no doubt that I've found my soul mate.

"You look perfect, Eloise," my grandmother says as I stand up and turn to face her. "You are a vision in white!"

My wedding was amazing! It was small and elegant and everywhere I looked, I saw the faces of people I love. Sugar Ray was even there, and so was Violet. They both wore tuxedos and Sugar Ray looked especially dashing! My father proudly gave me away, and my mother quietly wiped her tears of joy as she watched me pledge my life to Scott Jacob LaMotte.

The time simply flew by, and I felt torn when it was time to leave. There were still so many people I wanted to talk to, but the one person I wanted to talk to the most was ready to go. So we slid into the back of a white limousine—compliments of Wiley Bennett, of course—and headed for the airport. We were on our way to Fiji for one whole month! Who could ask for a better honeymoon?

There are no words to express the joy I felt that night, sitting next to my new husband, who happens to also be my oldest friend. And there are no words to explain how perfectly things worked themselves out. To say that the past year has taught me some lessons would qualify as a massive understatement. But the most important thing I've learned is to hold out for what I believe in. No matter how counter-culture my beliefs are, if they are worth believing in the first place, then they're worth holding out for.

I'm sure you'd like all the details on my amazing wedding night—but you're not gonna get any. All I can say is that something this beautiful was *definitely* worth the wait!

Acknowledgements

It would take more than thirty pages to properly thank everyone who has supported me during the creation of Hurricane Season, but I'll try to be brief!

First and foremost, I'd like to thank the love of my life, Lou Zant, who is my perfect match in every way. Thank you for giving me this opportunity to live out my passion and for loving me so completely!

Deepest thanks to Joan Correa and Harriett Hritz, who are brilliant designers, incredible inspirations and fantastic friends!

To my amazing sister, Brenda Skeel, for encouraging me in so many ways, and for sharing your insights and laughter! You make me proud, and I'm blessed to have you as my sister.

To Vanessa Glickman – who is my heart's delight! You make my world lovelier in every way!

And to Madeline Grace, Charlotte and Amelia (Millie Moo) – my hopes for you and the lives you have ahead of you are woven into the story of Eloise Butts.

To all the people who've helped me along the way: Hanni Crissey, Anne Marshall, Sheila Weiss, Cathy Wilson, Kristen Johnson, Julie Seward, Jolynne Wilson, Dana Westmark, Meg Brockett, Andy Proctor, Paul Bentley (Dad!), Amy Parker, Matt from Sir Speedy and Bach McComb. Thank you for all of your excitement and your belief in me!

And finally, to my late dog, Max. You always kept me centered and grounded and you are dearly missed. Thank you for providing Sugar Ray with a soul!